FEVER

ALSO BY MARY BETH KEANE

The Walking People

FEVER

MARY BETH KEANE

**SIMON &
SCHUSTER**

London · New York · Sydney · Toronto · New Delhi

A CBS COMPANY

First published in Great Britain by Simon & Schuster UK Ltd, 2013
Paperback edition published by Simon & Schuster UK Ltd, 2013
A CBS COMPANY

1 3 5 7 9 10 8 6 4 2

Simon & Schuster UK Ltd
1st Floor
222 Gray's Inn Road
London
WC1X 8HB

www.simonandschuster.co.uk
www.simonandschuster.com.au

Simon & Schuster Australia, Sydney
Simon & Schuster India, New Delhi

A CIP catalogue record for this book
is available from the British Library

ISBN Paperback 978-1-47111-298-0
ISBN E-book 978-1-47111-299-7

Designed by Carla Jayne Jones
Printed and bound by CPI Group (UK) Ltd, Croydon, CR0 4YY

TO MARTY

"Jesus Mercy"

—Mary Mallon's headstone
St. Raymond's Cemetery
Bronx, New York

PROLOGUE

1899

The day began with sour milk and got worse. You were too quick, Mary scolded herself when the milk was returned to the kitchen in its porcelain jug with a message from Mr. Kirkenbauer to take better care. He was tired, Mary knew, from the child crying all night, and moaning, and asking to be rocked. And he was worried. They'd tried to spare him—Mary, Mrs. Kirkenbauer, and the nanny had taken shifts with the boy, but the boy's room was just across the hall from his parents', and the boards of the new house creaked and whined, and the women sometimes forgot to keep their voices lowered, and finally Mr. Kirkenbauer had emerged from the master bedroom in his nightshirt to ask what could be done. "Give him to me," he'd said to Mary at the start of her shift, just as the bleary-eyed nanny hurried back to her small room at the rear of the house.

At two o'clock in the morning none of them cared about being seen in their nightclothes. She'd handed the boy to his father, a baby really, still a baby; they called him a boy because he'd started calling himself a boy, but it wasn't true just yet, in six more months, perhaps, yes, but not yet, not with those fat legs and cheeks, that unsteady, tottering step, the fact that he still loved a lap more than any chair. Mr. Kirkenbauer had observed in a whisper, "He's very warm." He put his pursed lips against the boy's forehead. Then he handed the child back to Mary and sat on the chair in the corner as she rocked the boy and told him all the wonderful things the morning would bring. Did he want to see a sailboat? Mary asked. Did he want to throw rocks in the river? Did he want a warm bun straight from the oven? But the child only stared, and cried, and wrapped his hot arms around Mary's neck, tight, like they were at sea, and she his buoy, and he was terrified of losing his grip.

Mary tried not to make too much of the milk being sent back, of the expression on the butler's face that was meant to mime Mr. Kirkenbauer's, and she reminded herself that Mr. Kirkenbauer was exhausted when he complained about the milk, they all were, and who knew what tone he'd really used when he gave the message to the butler, who had struck Mary from her first day as a nervous type. Mrs. Kirkenbauer was still upstairs, sleeping or trying to, and the nanny was giving the boy a cool bath, his third in as many hours. A light rash had bloomed across his chest, and in the very early hours of the morning Mrs. Kirkenbauer had suggested a plaster of bread and milk, or running to a neighbor for linseed oil, but Mary had said no, she'd seen the rash before, there was nothing for it but rest and trying to get the boy to eat something. The Kirkenbauers weren't the richest family Mary had ever worked for. Their kitchen was not as modern as most where Mary had cooked. But they were kind people, they paid her good wages, and other than a few specific requests from Mrs. Kirkenbauer, Mary had leave to do the shopping and serve whatever she liked.

Sometimes, after supper, Mrs. Kirkenbauer pitched in with the scrubbing, which Mary was baffled to discover she didn't mind. A mistress who hung around the kitchen with her hands in pots and pans and pantry would normally be intolerable, and if Mary had been told this was the way it was going to be she never would have taken the job in the first place, but now that she was there, and had gotten to know them, she was surprised to find that she didn't mind a bit. Mrs. Kirkenbauer had three sisters in Philadelphia and said she missed female company more than anything. Mary continually tried to take the temperature of her mistress's ease, so that perhaps, one day, she'd work up the nerve to ask her a question. Had she always been a person of means, or only when she married Mr. Kirkenbauer? The Kirkenbauers didn't know many people in Dobbs Ferry yet, which meant they seldom entertained, which meant Mary rarely had to cook for more than the three in the family and the staff and herself. The house looked at the Hudson, and on Sundays when the weather was fine they had picnics on the riverbank and always invited any among the servants who had not traveled home to their own families for the day.

Mary took the jug of milk the butler extended toward her. "Is it really gone?" she asked as she lifted it to her nose. "It's gone," she confirmed, clenching her teeth against the urge to vomit. She walked quickly to the narrow back door to throw it out. There was a faint sucking sound as the milk pulled away from the jug, and Mary watched it fly through the air as a solid thing until it landed, about six feet away, a white lump in the wet grass. In a few seconds the foul smell filled up the space between the lump and the doorway where Mary was still standing. She fetched the kettle, just boiled, and hurried outside to stand over the wet lump with her head swiveled away as she poured the steaming water over it. She turned back just in time to watch it disappear in curdled rivers, get caught up in the green blades, soak into the ground.

"Is that the end of it?" The butler asked, worried, casting his eyes toward the long hall that led back to the dining room.

"There's more. There's plenty," Mary said. "That was only what I was saving for bread, but I forgot, last night, when I made the bread I used the buttermilk. I was too quick. The ice is low. I broke off big pieces to put in the child's bath, and what's left of the block needs more sawdust. They need a right icebox here is what they need. They need one of those zinc-lined jobs. I put the good milk in the back of the box, but this morning—" Mary thought she heard a footstep in the hall. She raised a finger to the butler to wait.

"This morning?" he said. They were alone. The recently cut timbers of the house creaked under the weight of the night's lashing rain, and now, even with every single window open and every door propped wide, the air was thick and hot. It settled on everything and all morning the collar of Mary's dress had felt like a noose.

"Nothing." It was no use explaining. Mr. Kirkenbauer was waiting in the dining room with his bowl of dry blueberries and his coffee still black. "Here," Mary said, putting a fresh jug onto the butler's salver. She'd have to make new bread for lunch to make up for the mistake, even though there was nearly a full loaf on the counter from yesterday, even though that loaf would be fine with a little toasting, a pat of butter spread on top.

"How's the child this morning?" the butler asked. His room was on the third floor, and thanks to that distance he had gotten a full night's sleep.

"No better, no worse. Poor thing."

The butler nodded. "About the milk, Mary. It's only to be expected in this heat. That's probably why the child feels feverish. I feel feverish myself."

Not all butlers were so kind, but it seemed to work from one extreme to another in every house she had cooked for. Either the staff was a team that signaled one another with silences or a clandestine nod, or they were competitors, each one trying to smudge out the others' good work.

Mary had been with the Kirkenbauers for only a month when the boy got sick, and later, when she looked back, she struggled to remember exactly what circumstances had brought her there, all the way up to Dobbs Ferry, when there were plenty of open positions in Manhattan. Alfred was still finding good work in 1899. He was still getting a clean shave every other day, earning Friday wages he handed over to Mary to pay a portion of their rent, their food. The agency had often wanted to send her to New Jersey, or Connecticut, or over to the western side of the Hudson where the trains didn't reach, but she always refused unless they were short-term jobs that paid too much to decline, and ultimately those families usually went with a lesser cook, someone who couldn't get a job with a Manhattan family. But Mary could get a job with a Manhattan family, so why had she agreed to go up there to Dobbs Ferry to a woman who was not a proper mistress but half-servant herself, the way she leaned in to the pot to be scrubbed, the way she cast her eye around the kitchen for grease. Maybe it was because when she met Mrs. Kirkenbauer at the agency there was something about the woman she liked. She didn't ask Mary if she was a Christian. She didn't ask if she was married or planning on getting married. She asked only about her cooking, and when the woman talked about food, about the responsibility of getting meals together every day of the week, she seemed to be speaking from experience.

"Have you ever made sauerkraut, or do you always purchase it?" Mrs. Kirkenbauer had asked during their first meeting, and Mary admitted that she'd never done either, without adding that no employer she'd ever worked for had wanted sour cabbage and its sharp aroma anywhere near the floral patterns of their halls, the intricate moldings of their ceilings. If Alfred had an evening yearning for it he went out to the streets in search of the roaming sauerkraut man and the steel drum he wore around the city.

"Would you be willing to learn if I showed you once? Are you a quick learner?" How far removed is this woman from her native Philadelphia's version of the Lower East Side, Mary wondered, but simply answered "Yes."

Was that all it took to get Mary to agree to leave the city that summer? Had the wages been better than she remembered? No. Years later, when she had all the time in the world to think about it, every hour of the day if she chose, every single minute, nothing seemed to add up, least of all seeing a younger version of herself step off a train to await pickup by Mr. Kirkenbauer himself because they had no full-time chauffeur. Alfred had begged her to decline the job. He'd wanted her to find something closer to home, promising a Fourth of July fireworks show she'd never forget. He'd already begun stockpiling the rockets and sparklers, and planned to invite everyone in their building to watch. But the Fourth of July fell on a Tuesday that year, and Mary didn't want to organize her summer around one single day, so she left Alfred alone on Thirty-Third Street to fend for himself. Maybe that was the spring when he told her once and for all that he'd never marry her. Not because he didn't love her, but because he didn't believe in it. In the old country, fine, some customs could not be shaken, but what was the point of America if two people couldn't do as they pleased?

Funny how she grew so used to Alfred and the way they were that it was hard to believe there was ever a time when she wanted him to marry her, a time when she thought that he would, eventually, when his mind came around to it, when he admitted to himself and to her it was only the right thing to do. It was even harder to believe that she'd ever considered their not being married their biggest problem. Maybe the summer of 1899 was when she finally admitted the possibility that the things he said were really the things he believed. There was no secret code to crack, no door she could knock upon to make him come around. She was not a woman who should have to convince a man to marry her. There were plenty who would trip over themselves for the chance. That was it, she remembered, a lifetime later, when she went over the details of that summer once again. That must have been it. Her pride was injured. She wanted to teach him a lesson. She wanted space from him to think, maybe to work up the courage to leave him, to try for a different kind of life. So she went away that summer, and wished him the best for his fireworks show, and told him she'd be home on Sundays or she wouldn't, depending on her mood.

"And there's a child, isn't there?" the woman at the office had said during that first meeting, glancing at her notes. Mary noticed that Mrs. Kirkenbauer's clothes were exquisite, every stitch in its place, the fabric somehow skimming her slim figure and hiding it at the same time. She was younger than Mary, with a beautiful German face.

"Yes, one, a boy. Is that a problem?"

"Of course not," the agent had said. "Mary loves children. Don't you, Mary?"

"I do," Mary said in a flat voice.

Mary did not love all children, but she did love that boy. Within forty-eight hours of her arrival in Dobbs Ferry she saw that there would be no way to keep baby Tobias out of her kitchen, so she told his nanny to leave him, set him up on the floor with a toy and let him watch. The clever boy played happily until his nanny was out of sight, and then he reached his hands up to Mary to be lifted so he could see for himself what she had on the stove. "Spoon," he said, when he wanted a taste. "Hot!" he warned when he saw steam coming up from a pot. She gave him a new word every day and he stored it, trotting it out a few days later like he was born knowing it. It got so it was lonely in the kitchen without him. When he was there with her she talked to him all afternoon. "You are a good boy," Mary would say, and he'd beat his chest and say "good boy." When she dressed in the mornings, long before anyone else in the house was up, she looked forward to the tug of his chubby hand on her skirt, his fat little legs sticking out beneath his short pants. She listened for him coming down the hall before breakfast, running as fast as he could manage toward her kitchen, to see her, to press his soft cheek against hers and say her name.

And then came the morning when he didn't run to her, the morning when he walked, slowly, and when he got to the kitchen just sat in a corner and watched in silence, his plump cheeks rosy and hot when she touched them. When she lifted him his body was slack, like he was already asleep, and when she carried him he rested his head in the nook of her shoulder and abandoned himself to her, legs splayed across her hips, arms hanging at his sides. "Bread with jam?" she said to him, a test, the treat he loved most in the world. But he just looked at her, glassy-eyed, like he'd gotten older and wiser overnight and had moved beyond the excitement of bread and jam. As if the boy who loved bread and jam was another boy entirely, and this was a new boy, a more serious boy, a boy who knew as much as any adult. For a few minutes, as she swayed with him in the kitchen and listed all the things he loved to eat, she pretended to herself that she didn't know.

"Tobias isn't feeling well," Mary told the nanny, and the nanny told Mrs. Kirkenbauer. The three women convened in the parlor, where Tobias had fallen asleep on a pillow.

"Too much sun yesterday," his mother said, as she put her hand to his face. "And he had all that pie after dinner last night."

"Should I ask the doctor to come?"

"No," Mrs. Kirkenbauer said. "Sleep will cure him. He'll be better by supper. Leave him where he is."

But he did not get better; he got worse, and after four days of the doctor coming by to tell them that there was nothing to be done except draw the cool bath and try to get him to eat, and on the same day as Mary served Mr. Kirkenbauer milk that had gone thick and sour overnight, Mrs. Kirkenbauer began to feel low, and then the nanny, and then the butler, and then the gardener, who came only twice a week, always taking lunch with them when he was there. After Tobias they all seemed to get sick at the same time, in the same hour, and God forgive her but she ignored the others until she got that baby into the tub. "Tub," he said, a whisper, when she put him in the water, keeping a hand under his arm so he wouldn't slip. She floated chunks of ice she'd hammered from the block and told him they were icebergs, and he a sea captain, and it was his job to make sure the ship didn't run aground. He didn't object to the cold. He didn't demand a toy. He didn't ask for his mother. He didn't cry. After the bath, after his fingers had gone to raisins and she was afraid to leave him in there any longer, she wrapped him in a clean sheet and told him stories while he curled up in a ball like he was still a newborn, his knees tucked up to his chest. He looked more like a baby in the sheet, his curls damp, his cheeks so pink that a portrait of him at that moment might have made him look like a healthy child, the healthiest, like he'd just spent an hour running outside on a chilly winter's day.

And then, on the seventh night of his illness, after a few hours of rocking, while the others called for her from distant rooms, his little body went limp, felt heavier in her arms. His head against her shoulder was a ton weight, his legs like anchors across her thighs. The hot flutter of his breath that had tickled her neck for the past several hours had disappeared. Mary rocked him faster, telling herself he'd be better after he'd had a good sleep for himself. He hadn't had a proper rest in a week and now he was just having a sleep. Just sleep. A good, sound sleep.

After a while, she laid him in his crib and went to tell Mr. Kirkenbauer, the only other member of the household who was not sick. "He's gone, sir," she said, and put her hand on his shoulder before she realized what she'd done. The doctor said Mrs. Kirkenbauer should not be told if she was to have any chance of recovery, and so Mary tried to keep the news from her face when she went in to nurse her. But, one week later, Mrs. Kirkenbauer died as silently as her son, and the butler the day after that. The nanny and the gardener recovered.

Two weeks after the boy's death, after seeing to his little funeral suit, Mary packed her things and walked to the train station, leaving Mr. Kirkenbauer alone to decide what to do about all those dresses, that big, infected house, all those toy boats, the wooden horses, the collection of little shoes and caps. Maybe it was the timber, people said. Where had it been shipped from? Maybe it was the slope of the land and the way the water ran off down to the river. Maybe it was the pipe leading from the indoor privy. Maybe it was all the pickled herring and pigs' knuckles Mrs. Kirkenbauer asked her cook to buy in town. Maybe the mistress didn't know how to run a house, being the daughter of a Philadelphia grocer and the granddaughter of a cabbage-shaver. How lucky for her, the neighbors said, to have caught the eye of Alexander Kirkenbauer. How unlucky for him.

People said the old country was full of death, Mary's old country and everyone else's. The American papers would have a person believe Europe was one large sick ward, the people dying in ditches, blown over by every stiff wind. Alfred's Germany was like her Ireland, from the sound of it: people fighting every minute to stay on the side of the living, killing one another over a bowl of rabbit stew, and praying every day that the roofs of their shelters would stay where they were. When babies were born everyone willed them to live, but there was no surprise when they died, eventually, almost all of them, including the two Mary had cared for herself, bringing them eight, nine, ten times a day to the teat of a neighbor's goat so they could suckle what Mary's sister couldn't offer, having died bringing them to life, and what Mary couldn't offer, being only fourteen at the time, and having no babies of her own. The goat let them suck, but they died anyway, first the boy, and then the girl, and that's when Mary's nana told her it was time for her to leave Ireland, to leave while she was able. In America, Nana said, people didn't die so easily. It was the air, she supposed. The meat.

But people died in America, too, Mary learned quickly. It was just a sneakier death, a crueler death, in a way, because it always seemed to come by surprise. She didn't notice at first, but then she began to see it all around her. A meal pushed away for lack of appetite. A nap in the afternoon. A tired feeling that turned into a head cold, a rash into a ring of fire, a head cold into a fever that ravaged the person, left him beyond the reach of help. If they didn't die of illness, they died in fires, they were run over by streetcars, drowned in the river, suffocated after slipping into a coal hill and unable to scramble back to the surface. Neighbors, strangers on the street, peddlers at the market, children, priests, landlords, ladies. They all died, and every death was brutal. So what's a body to do? Mary thought as she stared out the train window at the Hudson and counted the minutes until she'd see Alfred again.

But that warm, clever little boy this time. The more she instructed herself to think about other things, the more she thought of him, like lifting a black tarp to glimpse something horrible below. Glimpses were all she could manage. His face. That peculiar, angled light in the Kirkenbauer kitchen. The dead weight of him.

Recently, when she and Alfred were talking about marriage and managing to not raise their voices, he'd asked whether she wanted a child. If she wanted to have a child, then that was different. Then they'd have to be married for the child's sake. "But I thought you didn't want that," Alfred pointed out, and she realized it was probably something she'd said. Not because she didn't think she'd love a child, or because she didn't think she'd be a good mother. She knew she'd love their child fiercely, entirely. She'd think about him or her every minute of her life, and that was the danger. They were so fragile, and it was so long until they grew strong. She thought of her sister's babies curled against each other in their cradle, and then the girl alone, how at only eight days old she seemed to be searching for her brother, her newborn fists closed so tight Mary believed for a day she might live. She thought of Mr. Kirkenbauer, the day he picked her up from the train, how he had no idea what was coming.

I'm sorry I left, she'd say to Alfred, who would be surprised to see her home so soon. But she wouldn't tell him what had happened, because how could she possibly explain to anyone about that boy, that baby? How could she begin? Thinking about him for a single second—the strong grip of his small hand, his belly, the happy swing of his leg on the chair when he bit into a piece of orange—any thought of him at all brought a roaring into her ears like she'd been plunged into the ocean with a weight tied around her foot.

No, she decided. No. She'd go home and try to forget and do as she'd always done, which was work hard and be thankful every day for her good health, her life.

HABEAS CORPUS

NEW-YORK DAILY COURANT

March 24, 1907

Cook Accused of Giving Typhoid to New York's Prominent Families

---

So Say Authorities Holding Her Prisoner

Sanitary Engineer Alleges She Communicates the Disease to Others Although Immune Herself

(Staff) New York—The cook for a prominent Upper East Side family has been forcibly removed from her employment and quarantined in Willard Parker Hospital after sanitary engineer and medical investigator George A. Soper alleged that she has been passing Typhoid Fever through her cooking, though she manifests no signs of the disease herself. At the time of her capture she was cooking for one of the wealthiest families on Park Avenue. Dr. Soper further alleges that the daughter of the family was battling Typhoid Fever at the time the cook was apprehended, and has since succumbed to the disease.

Dr. Soper, the medical sleuth at the center of this

case, put the pieces of this groundbreaking puzzle
together after being called upon to investigate a
Typhoid outbreak that occurred in Oyster Bay last
summer. He identified the cook as an "asymptomatic
carrier" of Typhoid Fever, which, in layman's terms,
is a healthy-seeming person who passes a disease
along without suffering any symptoms of said disease,
and most likely without any knowledge of doing so.
Dr. Soper has spent several months making his case
to the Department of Health, and one source reports
that there are many within that organization who are
skeptical about the notion of a healthy carrier, despite
the evidence.

It is Dr. Soper's belief that the woman poses a
life-threatening risk to all of those who eat the food
she cooks, and has been the cause of Typhoid outbreaks in almost every prominent family she's worked
for going back at least five years, likely longer. The
case of this human culture tube, as some would
describe her, is attended to with more secrecy than
any other this reporter has encountered in his career.
It can only be assumed that authorities do not want
to further embarrass those families who hired her
and welcomed her into their homes. In response to a
question on how rare this woman is to science, one
doctor who asked to remain anonymous answered:
"We just don't know."

The woman is rumored to be of fair complexion
with a buxom figure and rosy cheeks. Whether she un-
derstands the charges piled against her is a matter of

concern for the DOH. "We're talking about brand-new science," a senior health inspector explained. "If what Dr. Soper posits is true, then she is the first healthy carrier of Typhoid Fever discovered in North America."

The butler of the family who was the cook's most recent employer, and who gave his name only as "Francis," claims that the daughter's illness and death is nothing more than a tragic coincidence. He tells us that his own wife died of the illness several years back, and so have others he's known who never had any contact with the accused cook. He claims further that the cook was healthy and showed absolutely no sign of illness. "They took her like they would a common criminal," he said, showing visible signs of distress. "And for what? I don't believe what they've said about her." A female eyewitness to the cook's capture stated that "she fought with the strength of ten men, but they overpowered her."

This incredulity, authorities say, is a matter of education, and further denials from the woman may lead to her permanent quarantine. A nurse at Willard Parker, who asked that her name be withheld, says the accused woman at the center of this case is the picture of fury. She refuses meals, declines company, and walks back and forth like a caged animal. When asked if she believes what's been alleged about the woman, the nurse replied, "I myself don't understand it, but I think the woman should try to listen to them. She's not helping herself the way she is now."

Several leading doctors believe Typhoid bacilli

are manufactured in the gallbladder, and a represen-
tative from the Department of Health states that if the
accused woman does not submit to surgical removal
of her gallbladder within the month, she will be transferred to North Brother Island in the East River, where
she will remain segregated from society for an indef-
inite length of time.

When asked for his opinion of the case, Mr. Robert Abbott, a criminal attorney who practices in New
York City, says that her situation strikes him as somewhat similar to that of Niall E. Joseph, whom Boston
authorities have isolated upon suspicion of being a
leper.

ONE

Mary wasn't arrested right away. There were warnings. Requests. It all started with an air of courtesy, as if Dr. Soper believed that if he simply notified her of the danger lurking inside her body she would excuse herself from society. And after, when he and his colleagues resorted to far-less-polite means, they said it was her fault for raising a knife instead of listening, for not doing as she was told.

On a cold morning in March 1907, the Department of Health coordinated with the New York City Police Department and decided that Mary Mallon must be brought in. Dr. Soper suggested she might surrender more easily to a woman and sent a doctor named Josephine Baker to ring the bell of the Bowen residence, where Mary was employed, with four police officers standing behind her. They had not considered that even in the face of such authority her friends would lie for her, help hide her, insist that she could not be the person they were seeking. When they finally found her, she would not come peacefully, so each officer gripped her by a limb and carried her across the snow-covered yard while the rest of the domestic staff looked on. Once the police got her into their truck she started swinging and kicking, until finally they wedged her between their stout bodies and held her as well as they could, and Dr. Baker sat on her lap. "Please, Miss Mallon," Dr. Baker said, over and over, and after a while, "Please, Mary."

Mary assumed they were bringing her to the police station on East Sixty-Seventh, so when the truck continued downtown in a southeasterly direction along the same route she took from the Bowens' to the rooms she shared with Alfred on East Thirty-Third, she thought for a hopeful moment that they might be dropping her at home. They had come to teach her a lesson, she prayed, and now they would set her free. She glimpsed street signs through the small barred window as the driver turned east at Forty-Second Street. They traveled south along Third Avenue until Sixteenth Street, and then east again with such urgency that she could feel the rhythm of the horses' sleek heads pumping. The truck stopped just before the river, at the main entrance of a building Mary didn't recognize, at the very end of a block so desolate that she felt the first stirring of panic that no one she knew would ever find her there.

Dr. Soper was waiting at the entrance to the Willard Parker Hospital, but instead of speaking to her, he just nodded to the pair of policemen who had her braced by her elbows. Up on the sixth floor, they hurried her along the corridor to the Typhoid Wing, where more doctors were waiting in a room with a gleaming mahogany table. One of her guards indicated where she should sit, and before she could properly look around the room, Dr. Soper told her and the rest of the people present that the newest theory of disease had to do with germs and bacteria, and although Mary appeared perfectly healthy, he had good reason to believe that she was, at that very moment, manufacturing Typhoid bacilli inside her body and passing along the disease to innocent victims. He accused her of making twenty-three people sick and being the cause of at least three deaths. "Those are the cases we know of," he said. "Who knows how many more we'll find when we can investigate Miss Mallon's full employment history?" In front of five other men and Dr. Baker, Dr. Soper turned to her, finally, the source of all this trouble, as if waiting for her to say something. Mary felt like her mind had dropped straight out of her head like a stone.

"George," Dr. Baker said, "she hasn't even been here fifteen minutes. Perhaps we could give her time to collect herself."

"Back here in half an hour, then?" one of the other doctors asked.

"In the morning, gentlemen," said Dr. Baker. "There is nothing that can't wait until morning, is there?"

No, Mary thought, this mistake will be corrected by morning and I'll be gone. I'll walk straight home, make a pot of coffee, tell the whole story to Alfred, and never come near the Willard Parker Hospital again.

Dr. Soper tilted his head and considered Mary from across the table. "Tomorrow," he agreed. "Fine."

Mary's bed was at the end of a row, in a large room that held sixteen beds, all occupied except for hers, which waited with the sheets tucked tight and the small, flat pillow placed exactly at the center of the head. Guards stood outside the entrance of the room, positioned so they could see her through the narrow pane of glass on the door. A nurse had left her alone for a moment shortly after showing her to her room, and she'd simply opened the door and walked toward the stairs, but an officer shouted at her to stop, and a passing doctor blocked her way. "I was told I could get word to someone," she said to the officer as he marched her back. "When?" But he only shrugged, rocking back and forth from heel to toe as he eyed her, and she felt a twitch go through her body as she measured the distance to the end of the corridor.

That first night at Willard Parker, when a nurse came in to turn off the lamps, Mary lay on her cot and pressed her hands against her ears. It was a misunderstanding, surely. Everything would be sorted out in a matter of days. Alfred wouldn't expect her home until Saturday and would have no way of knowing what had happened. Even then, he might not worry, believing she'd been asked by the Bowens to stay on through the weekend. She had only the money in her pocket and the clothes on her back. Dr. Baker had said she'd be allowed a telephone call, but who would she call? There was no telephone in the rooms she shared with Alfred. No one in their building had a telephone. She certainly couldn't call the Bowens.

Lying on her side and facing the wall, Mary pressed her palms harder against her ears but could still hear her roommates retching, sobbing, calling for people, relatives, probably, loved ones already dead. She'd seen it all before, but not like this, not so many in a single room, fifteen nightmares twisted together, plus hers, the sixteenth, the strand that didn't look like any of the others. Finally, she gave up on sleep and went over to the window, which looked west along Sixteenth Street. The sidewalk was dark except for the yellow glow of a single streetlamp, and she searched the darkness for another sixth-floor window, and the shape of Alfred standing at it, not even twenty blocks away. If I shout, she thought, how far away will I be heard? She tried to imagine what he was doing at that hour. He never slept well when she was not at home.

The occupant of the bed nearest the window moaned, and Mary looked down to find a girl, no more than thirteen, her long dark hair wet with sweat and stuck in tendrils around her neck. Mary gathered it together and smoothed it away from the girl's face. She turned her pillow to the cool underside. She told her it would all be over soon—and it would, for better or for worse—and fetched her a cup of water. She did the same for the rest of them and one woman clutched Mary's wrist, called her Anna, and begged her not to leave. "We'll be home soon, Anna," the sick woman assured Mary, and Mary agreed that they would.

By dawn there were new guards stationed outside her door and she was back in her own bed observing the practiced approach of the nurses as they advanced on each patient with a bucket of cold water and a stack of clean washcloths pulled behind them on a wheeled cart. Mary forgot her predicament for a few moments as she saw how the abrupt coolness of a damp cloth at the head and neck made each woman still, for a moment, as if listening for something. A cloth under each arm calmed the features of their faces, brought them hope, and at the groin brought relief to their whole bodies, and in some patients, tears.

When the nurse who was tending to Mary's row arrived at her bed, she held up a cloth and looked at her. "You've no fever," she said.

"No."

"I'm supposed to do the compress to everyone. They didn't say yay or nay about you."

"I'll tell them you did it."

"Fine." The nurse continued to observe her. "When did you have it?"

"Never."

"But you're passing it along? People catching it from you?"

"Is that what they said to you?"

"Said it to all the doctors and nursing staff."

"It's a lie."

The nurse tilted her head and looked at Mary's body from her face down to the lump under the sheet that was her feet, back up to her face.

"Well, do you want the cloth anyway? And the water? To wash yourself? I gather you've had an ordeal."

"Yes." Mary sat up in the cot. "Yes, thank you."

The nurses repeated the routine every hour, skipping Mary after that first time. At midmorning, Soper came and perched himself on the arm of a chair that was wedged between Mary's cot and the wall. He told her it was time for her to cooperate, that they had a great deal of work ahead of them. As he spoke his eyes kept glancing over to the nurses as they moved about the room, lifting sheets, moving knees apart. He jumped up and asked to see Mary in the hall.

"How long do you mean to keep me here?" Mary asked, refusing to move until he gave her an answer.

"Come out to the hallway, Miss Mallon," he said.

"No," Mary said, lying back on her pillow and pulling the sheet to her chin.

"I don't want to have to ask for this man's assistance," he said, gesturing toward one of the guards. "One way or another, I must talk to you about your gallbladder."

"One way or another, I must get word to my friends to let them know what's happened to me."

"Later, Miss Mallon. Very soon."

The first time Mary had encountered Dr. Soper was in the Bowens' kitchen, almost one month earlier. She mistook him for a guest who'd arrived too early. It was a bitter-cold day, and there were fires going in every room except for the servants' quarters, where the small stove would stay cold until bedtime. The Bowens had the type of home where it was easy to lose oneself: large in some senses, tall and broad, with great rooms—the distant ceilings covered with paintings of different scenes from foreign places—and windows looking out onto Park Avenue. But the natural light disappeared as one retreated farther into the house, and at the rear of the residence the staff had to work by lamplight all the time.

Mary had looked up from her work—a beautiful pair of ducks whose skin she was pricking with a knife so that the fat would drain out when she roasted them—and saw a tall man clutching his hat to his chest. He had a light step, and she didn't hear him until he was nearly on top of her. He was handsome in that way some men in New York are handsome—neat as a pin, his clothes pressed, his hair and mustache precise. He was not a man who had ever shoveled coal or hauled ice or butchered an animal. He was not a man who owned a pair of work boots. He seemed older, though she later learned that they were the very same age, their birthdays one week apart.

*

Toward the end of her second day at Willard Parker, she answered a few of his questions and hoped that meant he would release her. But just after breakfast on her third morning he summoned her back to the room with the mahogany table and invited five other doctors to ask her questions as well. She recognized three of them from the day of her arrival. Dr. Baker was not present. Led by Dr. Soper, they kept asking if she was absolutely certain that she'd never had Typhoid Fever, if she could recall for them every person she'd known who'd suffered a fever since her arrival in the United States twenty-four years before. "Every person I've known who ever had a fever? Since 1883?" Mary almost laughed. Would they be able to do it, if they were asked the same thing?

"Or in Ireland," one of the doctors said. "Any person who had a fever as far back as you can remember." Their records on her went back to only 1901, and Mary decided they knew enough about her life in those five and a half years. She would not give them more. "I can't remember," she said. Dr. Soper walked over to her chair and asked her to demonstrate how she washed her hands after visiting the lavatory. Feeling so many eyes studying her, and knowing they would just keep asking if she refused, she made a peaceful scene in her mind and walked to the sink at the back of the room with her pulse thumping in her ears. They stood closely behind her to observe, so she went slowly, rubbing the bar of soap on the backs of her hands as well as her palms, between her fingers, taking the kind of time she never did when she had to worry about getting supper on the table at an appointed hour. She dried her hands on the hand towel hanging next to the sink, and they observed this as well.

"What are we missing?" Dr. Soper wondered aloud once

they'd all returned to their seats. Missing from his notes were the details, Mary knew, the small things a woman notices, the expression on a person's face when he turns away and thinks himself unobserved. When Dr. Soper appeared in the Bowens' kitchen that night, she'd reached up to move a length of hair that had fallen out of her bun. She'd lifted her apron to wipe the duck fat from her hands. She'd closed her fist around her pricking knife and asked if she could assist him. He had blue eyes. His face was longish, and white, his cheeks shaved so close that his face looked as smooth as her own, except for the mustache. His lips were parted in excitement. His eyes were glazed over and once they locked on her they didn't move, just drank her in, every inch of her. He looked directly at her face, at her mouth, at her body, like he owned her, like there was no one in the world who knew her body better than he did. The knife was greasy and she couldn't find a sure grip. "Shall I call for Mr. Bowen?" she inquired. "Shall I have someone show you back to the drawing room?" Hadn't there been just a few days earlier an article about a Greek who'd attacked a schoolteacher inside her own home, raped her, left her to die? Bette, the laundress, had disappeared outside to the narrow breezeway at the side of the house.

Missing from Soper's notes was the feeling in her belly when she looked up to find a stranger striding into her kitchen, to hear him demand to know if she was Mary Mallon. How disorienting it was to have a man like him—with his perfectly tailored jacket, his ivory white fingernails, his polished shoes extending from the bottom of his pants, the cuffs immaculate, as if he floated above the mud and shit that made up the streets of New York City, and never walked through it like the rest of them—use her full name and know that he was not lost, that she was the one he was looking for. He'd finally come to a stop between Mary and the stove. She could make out perspiration on his sideburns. He had high, sharp cheekbones and his face was flushed.

A creditor, she decided.

"What's it to you?" Mary asked.

Soper stepped closer. She could smell tobacco on his skin. She tightened her grip on the knife. "My name is George Soper. I'm a sanitary engineer and have been hired by Mr. Thompson to investigate the Typhoid outbreak that occurred at his home in Oyster Bay this past summer. I've reason to believe you are the cause not only of that outbreak but of several outbreaks in and around New York City. You must come with me immediately, Miss Mallon. You must be tested. Can you confirm that you were employed by the Warren family last summer and that you worked for them for six weeks at the home they rented from Mr. Thompson in Oyster Bay?"

Mary couldn't remember her first response, only her wonder at what that had to do with anything.

"Pardon?"

"You're sick, Miss Mallon. You must be tested."

"I'm sick?" Mary forced a laugh. "I've never felt better."

"You are carrying sickness. I believe you are a Typhoid Fever carrier."

She felt dumb and slow, like she'd been turned around and around and then been asked to walk a straight line. She leaned her hips against the counter to steady herself.

"Leave now, please," she said. "I don't know what you're talking about."

"You don't understand, Miss Mallon. It's imperative that you come with me now for testing. I've alerted the lab at Willard

Parker Hospital to be ready for your arrival. You must cease cooking immediately."

He went to take her by the arm, but she held out the knife and the roasting fork together and made a swipe in his general direction. "Get out," she hissed. Mrs. Bowen hadn't been feeling well all day but was upstairs being dressed. Mr. Bowen was hard of hearing. Someone had let Soper into the house, surely. Someone knew he was down in the kitchen, yet no one seemed to be coming. She went for him again with the fork in the lead.

Soper stepped backward into the hall. "You must listen, Miss Mallon."

"I've a mind to stab you with this fork, so you'd better get out of my kitchen."

"It's not your kitchen, Miss Mallon."

Mary made another move for him and he took several steps back. He stumbled for a moment, his knuckles white where he gripped his hat's brim. He looked at her as if he had more to say, but then retreated quickly down the hall.

A few minutes after Soper left the kitchen, Frank, the butler, appeared.

"Where were you?" Mary asked.

"Mr. Bowen was giving me instructions. Who was that? He's just standing on the sidewalk looking at the house. I think he has a mind to come back in."

"He had some cock-and-bull story he'll tell them," Mary said, laying down the knife and fork. She began to pace. They heard the sound of the doorbell.

"Leave it to me," Frank said after a moment. Mary crouched in the hall as Frank opened the door.

"They're not available at the moment," Frank said when

Soper asked for Mr. or Mrs. Bowen. "Would you like to leave a message?"

"I could wait."

"I'm afraid not. A dinner party, you see."

"A message then," Soper grumbled as he searched his breast pocket for a note card and pen. He scribbled as much as he could fit onto the small space. "Make sure you give this to them," Soper said, looking the older man in the eye.

Frank gave an abbreviated bow, took the note from Soper, and wished him a good night. When he had closed the door on the doctor, he walked the message to the fire and threw it in.

"Thank you," Mary said. They watched the paper vanish until Mrs. Bowen's bracelets jangled a warning from the top of the stairs.

Soper's appearance in the Bowen kitchen was Mary's first warning, but it had come coded, and Mary couldn't decipher it. By the time she was sure Soper had left for good, and the ducks were roasted and sliced, she'd decided it was a misunderstanding, and wondered at herself for not saying more. Why had she not told him that she never had the fever, and that she was the one who'd nursed the Warrens back to health? Why had she not told him to check his facts: that the local doctor in Oyster Bay had already concluded that they'd gotten the fever from soft-shell crabs? Mary liked working for the Bowens, but if that man called again and told them his story, or if he sent them a letter by the post, and they believed him and fired her, she'd go back to the office and have them place her somewhere else. If he told that agency, she'd use another agency. If he told all the agencies, she'd go over to New Jersey, where they didn't like to pay fees.

After a week at Willard Parker, Dr. Baker finally came to check on her. "Where were you?" asked Mary. "You said I could get word to someone."

"And you haven't?"

"I keep telling them, but it's been a week."

"I'm sorry, Mary," Dr. Baker said, and Mary's frustration wavered at hearing her first name. The other doctors called her Miss Mallon. "I work at a lab uptown and can't get down here as often as I'd like." She removed a few lined pieces of paper from the thin stack on her clipboard.

"You can . . . ?"

"Yes," Mary said, too grateful to be insulted. "Yes, of course." Dr. Baker also handed over an envelope. "There should be a pen at the nurses' station. I'll tell them you're permitted to use it. When you finish give it back to them and they'll post the letter for you."

"Thank you," Mary said, and placed paper and envelope on her bedside table. Now that she had a means of getting in touch with Alfred, Mary wanted to consider what she'd say, how exactly to describe what had happened. They'd argued the last time they'd seen each other, but none of that mattered now. And there were practical concerns, too. Her friend Fran had asked her to make a birthday cake for her daughter and it was starting to seem like Mary would not be freed in time. She had planned to shape the cake like a daisy, with yellow and white buttercream frostings. The child would be disappointed.

"Will you walk with me?" Dr. Baker asked.

They strolled along the corridor with the guard trailing just behind. "Mary," Dr. Baker said finally, "they've asked me to talk to you about surgery. About removing your gallbladder. I know Dr. Soper has already explained it, but perhaps there are questions he hasn't answered."

In the week since Mary had last seen Dr. Baker, there were several doctors in addition to Dr. Soper who tried to convince her to let them remove her gallbladder. Just that morning, Mary had been called to a meeting with three doctors at once. "We'll get the best man to do the cutting," said a doctor named Wilson, and Mary asked the three men present if they'd agree to be sliced open as well, since there was nothing in the world wrong with them either. What would New York come to if surgeons went around cutting open all the healthy people just to take a look at what was inside? They explained it to her over and over, as if she didn't know what it was to cut a body from neck to navel, but she was a cook, for God's sake; she once butchered a Jersey heifer with only one other person to help and when she was finished, even after draining the cow well before cutting, she was bloodied to her shoulders, and all those wet and glistening parts that made up the cow, when they were laid out on her table, would never have fit back inside that animal the way God made her had Mary decided to change her mind, put her back together, stitch her up like new. All the worse that they planned to slice her alive.

"I won't let them open me. I've told them already. You can tell them, too."

Dr. Baker regarded her in silence for a moment, and then nodded. "They'll send you to North Brother Island. They'll put you in quarantine."

"They can't. I'm not sick. I didn't do anything wrong." Mary thought of the paper and envelope waiting for her by her bed. No matter how Alfred was feeling, no matter what kind of week he was having, he'd hear the beating heart at the center of her message and he'd leave whatever he was doing to find her and help her figure a way out of this trouble. Once, about five years earlier, when she was miserable at a job in Riverdale, he'd shown up in her employer's kitchen one morning to see for himself how low she was, and when she told him everything that she'd promised herself she would not tell him—that the missus had slapped a tutor and threatened to slap Mary, that the man of the house found reasons to brush up against her—Alfred did not make a scene, did not raise his voice; he only listened. And when she was finished he told her the decision was entirely up to her; he'd only come to see her face, but if he had half her talent for cooking, he'd walk out of that horrible house and find something else. "Come home with me right now," he said, and even as she protested that she'd already mixed the batter for muffins, had already sunk a turkey breast in a bucket of brine, she felt a shiver of recklessness and knew she wanted to do exactly that. Alfred put his hands on her waist and made her look at him. "Leave it," he said. So she left the batter to harden on the counter and walked with him to the train station. Along the way, he sang a German folk song and danced along the sidewalk to make her laugh. Miraculously, the family never told the agency, or else the message got lost, because the same agency placed her in a new situation the very next week.

She imagined Alfred storming through the main entrance of Willard Parker. If they block him at the front door, she thought, he'll come through the back. If they lock the back door, he'll build a tunnel, he'll scale the walls, he'll drop in from the sky to fend them off so that I can get home. Alfred, she thought, willing him to hear her. It was something she used to do when she began getting more jobs that took her out of town and away from him. She'd take her break on a quiet back porch and think hard on his name. She'd crawl into bed at night and extinguish every other thing in her mind except for him. Later, when she was back home, she'd tell him what she'd done, and he'd sit up taller and ask which days, exactly, what times, because there was one afternoon when he was walking through the park and had a feeling she was there, trying to tell him something.

"They can, Mary. And once you're on North Brother it will be more difficult to . . ."

"To what?"

"To get back."

"Miss Mallon," a nurse called from behind them. "It's time to give another sample."

"I'll be back in a few days," Dr. Baker said, placing her hand lightly on Mary's arm.

"Wait," Mary said, and heard the panic in her own voice. "Don't forget to tell the nurses. About the pen. About posting my letter."

"I won't forget."

When Mary got back to her room, the paper and envelope were gone. She opened the small drawer next to her bed. She dropped to her knees and searched the floor. She checked under the pillow, inside the pillowcase, under the top sheet, down by the steel casters in case they'd been carried in a draft.

"Did anyone take the paper and envelope that were left here

for me?" she asked, looking from cot to cot to decide which among them was healthiest, which among them would have the nerve. "They were mine and I'd like them back immediately." Her voice was the loudest sound the women had heard since arriving at the hospital, and some of them who had not stirred in days turned to look at her.

"One of the doctors," the girl by the window said. "He came in and put them on his clipboard when he saw you weren't here."

"Which?"

"Him," the girl said, pointing.

"Miss Mallon," Dr. Soper's voice came from behind her, and when she turned he was backlit by the lamps of the corridor. "Did Dr. Baker speak to you about surgery?"

"Can I have my paper back?"

"Not until we've talked about surgery."

My God, she thought, pressing her fingertips to her temples. Didn't these people know when a subject was closed? Had she not made her position clear? Or did they mean to drive her insane with the same questions over and over and over? Everything in the room seemed to slide to the left. She walked quickly to the window and pushed it up. She had a birthday cake to make. She had a man who had no idea where she was. She had to find a new job. There was a quartet playing at Our Lady of the Scapular in two weeks' time and her friend Joan had offered to make her a dress. The cold pushing in through the open window was a salve on her hot skin and she could hear someone whistle for a taxi. The music of a banjo floated through the air from some point north of the hospital. Passing under the light cast by the single streetlamp were a few feathery flakes of snow.

"Dr. Baker said—"

"Dr. Baker isn't in charge here. She shouldn't have made promises."

Mary felt his words like a fist to her gut. She leaned out the window as far as she could. "Hello!" she cried at the street below. She waved her arms so someone might see her. She shouted again but her voice was choked, and Dr. Soper had his arm around her waist. "Help me," she said to the other women as Soper and the guard dragged her across the room, into the hall, and then pushed her ahead of them to a private room farther down the corridor, where Dr. Soper continued to brace her from behind, and a nurse struggled to open a small vial and pass it under Mary's nose.

"I don't know why you always insist on making a scene, Miss Mallon," Soper muttered in her ear as they struggled. She could feel his breath on her neck, the sharp point of his chin where it pushed into her scalp.

"Relax," the nurse whispered. "Just relax."

TWO

Just as Dr. Baker had warned, after two weeks of testing at the Willard Parker Hospital, Dr. Soper told Mary that since she would not agree to have her gallbladder removed, the Department of Health had no choice but to transfer her to North Brother Island. There were facilities on the island where researchers could continue testing, "in a calmer, more focused atmosphere." She could notify her friends and family when she arrived on the island, but not before. Soper watched her every chance he got, and when he turned away Mary felt space to breathe for a moment, until he turned back. She would not beg—they had enough power over her already. Soper had forbidden anyone at Willard Parker to give her a means to contact her friends—no more promises to post messages—and Mary clung to her composure by reminding herself that Alfred must have seen the newspaper articles. A night nurse had shown Mary the article that was in the *Sun*, and said there were others; her capture was mentioned in almost every major paper. The papers didn't have her real name—they referred to her only as the Germ Woman—but Alfred would figure it out. It was possible, she thought, that he'd already tried to come to her. That he'd shown up at the hospital demanding to see her, but had been turned away.

"Isn't that a Consumption island?" Mary asked.

"Riverside is a Tuberculosis hospital, yes. But they've seen Typhoid, too. Diptheria. Measles. Everything."

Mary shivered. "How long?" she asked.

"A few weeks," Dr. Soper said. Mary told herself that she could put up with anything for a few weeks. She'd let them test her and when they got whatever it was they needed from her, the ordeal would be over, and she'd never have to see Soper again.

From the first hour of her arrival, North Brother Island seemed to Mary too flimsy for the roiling East River. It was as if a jagged corner of Manhattan had broken off and floated away before getting caught in the prehistoric rock that lurked just below the surface of the water. North Brother was a little skip of land, an oversized raft made of dirt and grass where the dying went to wait their turn. It was located just above Hell Gate, that point in the East River where half a dozen minor streams met head-on before rushing out to sea, and only a fool would dip her toe in the water there. The entirety of North Brother would barely be big enough for a respectable estate if it were anywhere but New York, but in New York, or at least in Manhattan, where even the very rich live within arm's length of their neighbors, it was a rarity: a stretch of space that was quiet, and private, and where everyone there was meant to be there, adult men and women whose names appeared on the roster of approved persons the ferryman kept under the bench seat of his small vessel, protected from the spray.

There were no automobiles on North Brother, only a single horse, and that one old and mangy, retired from pulling a sanitation cart and donated to science. During the day, there were always a few bicycles leaning against the western gable of the hospital, the side closest to the ferry that carried the nurses and doctors back and forth from 138th Street in the Bronx, but no one ever used those bicycles to pedal around the island, and seeing them there, leaning haphazardly against the redbrick wall or lying on their sides on the grass, Mary needed no further proof that she'd been removed from the city. If she were in the city, in the real city, and not this in-between place, those bicycles would be gone inside an hour, liberated from their spots and cycled away by Lower East Side teenagers. There were few urban sounds on North Brother. No store shutters creaking open in the morning, clanging closed at night. No bells, no rumble of the El overhead, no peddlers hawking their wares, no children hopping balls, no old women shouting from upper-story windows. In their place were the sounds of tree frogs, birds, the gardener's clippers slicing the hedges into neat squares, and everywhere, always, the sound of water lapping the shore. Everything, everyone, stayed put, at least until evening came, when the doctors hustled out to the pier to make the awkward step down into the ferry, and the night shift leaned into the slight incline of the walking path and through the hospital's wide front door. The evening croak of a heron on the island's eastern shore sounded to Mary like a taunt, and chilled her.

Sixteen buildings anchored North Brother, ranging in size from the main building of Riverside Hospital to the gardener's toolshed. There was also the morgue, the chapel, the physical plant, the coal house, the doctors' cottages, the nurses' residences, the X-ray building, the greenhouse, and so on. The circumference of the entire island could be walked in less than three-quarters of an hour, and from any point on North Brother, unless there was a building or a tree blocking the view, one could look back and see upper Manhattan, and north of that, the invisible seam where Manhattan met the Bronx. When it rained, the current that charged over the pebbles and jagged stones of shore reminded Mary of a pack of galloping horses steaming toward the sea.

There were no Typhoid patients at Riverside on the day she arrived, so they assigned her a bed in the main Tuberculosis ward. A nurse provided her with paper and envelopes, a pen with a reservoir of ink. She wrote to Alfred what, by then, surely, he already knew, but unlike the letter she'd drafted in her mind when she was still at Willard Parker, the first letter from North Brother was matter-of-fact. No patient at Riverside Hospital was permitted to have visitors, so she counseled patience, told him it might help to pretend she'd gotten a situation too far away for her to visit—Maine, perhaps, or Massachusetts—and before he knew it she'd be home. She was angry, but had learned that anger wouldn't get her far. "So I may not see you until Memorial Day," she wrote. Worst-case scenario, she thought. Two whole months should be plenty of time. He'd had a difficult stretch over the winter, not working, spending far too much time at Nation's Pub, but she decided not to mention any of that. "Remember the rent if you haven't already."

After listening to the hollow coughs from her fellow patients for a few days, Mary learned to predict the end: when a rattle in the chest sounded like a penny thrown into a very deep well that had gone dry. She observed that the consumptives looked like relatives: the same pall, the same dark rings under the eyes. They would stare at Mary and wonder what she was doing there. At night, she slept with the sheet over her face in case she might breathe in their disease, but after a week she stopped worrying. During the day, she couldn't stop herself from flaunting her health, walking back and forth by the windows, asking the nurses if she could be of assistance. On sunny afternoons she took a book from the hospital library and read in the courtyard. On less temperate days she jotted down ideas for recipes so as not to lose her sense of purpose. She made sure to get outside every day, even if it was just for a few minutes, and when she got back to her cot and nodded to her neighbors, she felt the pink glow in her cheeks, the rise and fall of her chest, the power in her lungs. The confusion on their faces confirmed what she already knew: a mistake. A terrible error had been made, but would soon be corrected.

She submitted to their tests without protest and hoped that the sooner they collected all the information they needed, the faster they would let her go. She had not seen Dr. Soper since the first day she arrived on North Brother, and when she asked about it, Dr. Albertson told her that she likely wouldn't be seeing much of Dr. Soper anymore. He might check in on her now and again, and of course her test results would be shared with him, but his part in her case was likely over. This tiny piece of good news lifted her spirits for a day.

The doctors on North Brother seemed even more greedy than those at Willard Parker to look at her body. They wanted her hands, her belly, her breasts, her hips; they wanted every wet thing that came out of her, top to bottom—but when they came to her face their eyes flicked away. Some of her interrogators weren't doctors who had patients but different types of medical men, like Soper, who called himself an engineer but seemed to know diseases. Some of them only studied things and took notes. The questions had changed since Willard Parker. There, they wanted to know about every fever she'd ever had. Had she ever had a rash on her bosom? Now they demanded to know when she knew. You're an intelligent woman, they said. Several of your employers said you read novels when you had time off. You must have known. How can you ask us to believe you didn't know?

Mary tried to think of images that would block out the questions—any memory at all that would take her away from North Brother. But more often than not, thinking of Alfred and her friends made her less patient with their questions, more frantic to get home. She paced. She counted to one hundred, and when she was finished, she counted again. She closed her eyes, held her hands to her ears, and still, each question was a dripping tap, a loose shingle in the wind, a fly buzzing by her ear that she could never slap away.

One morning, at the end of her second week on North Brother, she looked out from a fourth-floor window to see if she might spot the mail sack being transferred from the ferry and noticed a trio of men framing a small wood structure a short distance away. As soon as she saw it she knew it had something to do with her, and wanted to disown it immediately. Why go to the trouble of building something for a person who will be let go in a few weeks? No, it must be for some other purpose.

"Pardon me," she said to a passing nurse, and pointed out the window. "Do you know what they're building?"

"It's your cottage," the nurse looked confused. "Didn't they tell you?"

"Tell me what?"

"You'll be transferred there once it's complete. You won't have to be here with the TB patients anymore." She smiled gently at Mary as if this might be received as good news. Mary felt as if she'd waded into a lake of cold water and just felt the bottom drop away.

"Why? If they're going to let me go soon?"

"Did they say that? That they're going to let you go?"

"Yes, they did," Mary said quietly as she felt her throat constrict and her body begin to tremble. She stumbled back to her cot and sat at the edge. She calculated back to the day they took her from the Bowen residence—nearly a month. How much more testing did they need to do? She got out a sheet of paper and again wrote to Alfred.

Dear Alfred,

In case you sent a letter in response to my last I wanted to let you know that I haven't received it. I don't trust anyone here and maybe you sent it but they didn't give it to me. They are building a room for me separate from the hospital—just a hundred yards or so away. I don't know why they would go to that trouble if they're going to let me go soon. Will you ask around and see if anyone knows of a lawyer who might help? I hope you are getting on fine. I keep thinking that the last time I saw your face we were arguing and it doesn't sit right that I haven't heard from you since then. Try again to send a letter, Alfred. It will put my mind at ease.

> *Love,*
> *Mary*

She asked a nurse to post the letter immediately, and one week later, she got a response.

Dear Mary,

I was just sending a response to your first letter when I got your second. I saw the article in the paper and knew the Germ Woman was you since you were supposed to return for the weekend that Saturday night and never did. And also because of them mentioning Oyster Bay. I went up to the Bowens and Frank told me everything. I went straight to Willard Parker but a nurse there told me you'd already been moved to North Brother.

Tell me what I can do. I know things were not so good when we last saw each other but I'm feeling better now, no late nights, and I met a Polish man who has a connection in the water tunnels. We have to think about how to get you off that island. Billy Costello has a rowboat but said the waters around North Brother are too rough and no sane person would risk it. I didn't believe him at first and went over to the East Side fishery but the fishmongers there all said the same thing. What do they want with you? If they really think you have Typhoid couldn't they treat you at Willard Parker? Or St. Luke's?

I'm going to ask around to see who knows a lawyer. Don't worry.

> *Alfred*

Mary read the letter three times before folding it and placing it carefully on her bedside table. It was the longest letter she'd ever gotten from him in the nearly twenty-two years that she'd known him, and thinking of him sitting down to write it made her more eager to be back home. The room they were building for her had four walls now, a roof, a door, and needed only shingles and a window. Dr. Anderson said she'd be moved in a matter of days. Alfred hadn't mentioned anything about how he was getting by without her, whether he paid the rent for April, but he knew where she kept the spare cash in their rooms, and maybe that water-tunnel job would be a real lead, maybe he'd love it, maybe he'd find someone who knew exactly how to help her and she'd be back home by summer.

Sometimes they called it a cabin. Sometimes a cottage. A bungalow. A hut. A room. A shack. Whatever it was, they moved her there in April 1907. It was a simple ten-by-twelve-foot structure with a two-burner gas range, a kettle, a sink with running water. They gave her a small box of tea, a bowl of sugar, two teacups. She was not allowed to cook, but prepared food would be delivered from the hospital cafeteria three times a day. To pass the time between visits from medical personnel, Mary was told that she could sew for the hospital, or if she had a knack for crochet, they would provide needles and yarn. She could read. She could explore the island. Mary took all of this information blankly, and as she looked around her new home for the first time, she felt disoriented.

"And linens!" A petite nurse bustled around the small space, showing Mary a wicker basket that held fresh sheets, a towel, a washcloth. "Leave them outside your door when they need to be laundered."

"How long?" Mary asked. How many times can a person ask the same question?

"In the main building we wash them once a week, so I'd say the same for you."

"That's not what I . . ." Mary sighed, and sat on the edge of the cot. "Will you leave me, please?"

"Almost done." The nurse lined up a dozen glass canisters on the counter.

When she finally left, and Mary was alone for the first time since they'd captured her, she felt as if she'd left a crowded room and now approached that same room from a different door. She saw herself from a distance: the walls of her hut, the river just beyond, the chuffing of trains and trolleys crisscrossing Manhattan and the Bronx, so close she could hear the whistles. They are not letting me go. She made herself say it aloud. She'd been watching for the mail sack every day, hoping for a letter from Alfred to tell her that he'd found a lawyer, that help was coming, but maybe he already knew that they'd never let her go. Maybe that's why he hadn't written again: because he hadn't known what to say. Unlike other times in her life, when she moved from laundress to cook, or when she moved in with Alfred without a single promise, North Brother felt like a place that was off the map entirely, no footprints left behind for her friends to follow and figure out where she'd gone. Sure, some knew. Those who were there for the arrest, those who helped hide her for all those hours only to be rewarded with a scene they'd talk about for the rest of their lives: a grown woman kicking, cursing, punching, dragged bodily into a police wagon. And there were the articles in the papers, but none of those said how she felt, what she thought. She was certain that word of her arrest had spread among the other cooks and laundresses and gardeners of Manhattan, but like the fast-moving currents that run deep in the ocean without disturbing the surface of the water, Mary was also certain that there were plenty who did not know. It was possible that after her arrest, after their humiliation, the Bowens had never spoken of Mary to anyone but each other. The agency wouldn't utter a peep for fear of being dropped by other fine homes. The papers would follow her story for a while, but then they would move on, and Mary would still be in her hut, wondering how to get home.

The next morning, after fitful sleep in her new cot, Mary woke to the sound of an envelope sliding under her door. She recognized Alfred's writing from across the room. She tore it open and stood beside the window to read it.

Dear Mary,

Are you doing all right? Have they said anything more about when you'll be allowed home? I went up there to see if I could talk the ferryman into bringing me over for a visit but he has his instructions and they are very strict. I offered him money but he wouldn't take it. I looked across the water to see what it's like for you out there but it's hard to tell.

The water tunnels were not for me. Maybe you predicted as much. I've been shaping for scaffolding work.

I've asked around about lawyers and went to see one who advertised in the paper but he didn't seem to understand what I was talking about when I explained. Then I went back and brought the newspaper articles but he wasn't interested. I will keep trying.

I wish I knew what to do to help. Is there anyone there you trust who can give you advice?

Alfred

"Alfred," she said, and felt bile rising in her throat as her stomach turned. She walked out of her hut to the water's edge. Which day was he standing over there, trying to find her? Maybe they could coordinate; in her next letter she could suggest a date and time. But as soon as she had the idea she felt sick again. To do what? To wave? To blow kisses at each other from opposite sides of Hell Gate? Pressing her fists to her mouth, she closed her eyes and tried to think of what to do.

THREE

They tried to get her to accept the schedule, to stop making so much of the twice-weekly testing of her blood, urine, and stool, the handing over of samples, the visits to the lab, the monthly physicals, the dipping of her hands in chemicals and the scrutiny of her fingernails. They needed to track her patterns, one doctor explained when she asked why twice a week was necessary. The nurses chatted with her as if this had all grown to mean nothing to her, but when they saw that she couldn't get past it, that it was a humiliation she would never get over, no matter how long it went on, they disliked her for it. They came in pairs, and eventually stopped bothering with her, chatting only with each other. Every week, when Monday rolled around again, after coaching herself all weekend to be better, to try, to show that she was a good sport, to prove that she was trustworthy enough to be set free, they appeared at her door with their cheery faces and their glass canisters and made her livid all over again. "But what are the results?" Mary asked. "I keep submitting to these tests but I never get results."

"Positive, I imagine," a nurse said. "Or else why would they keep you here?"

When she posed the same question to Dr. Albertson or Dr. Goode, they said only that individual tests didn't matter. Single weeks didn't matter. They would share results with her as soon as they had enough data to draw firm conclusions. Patience, they counseled. Everything took time.

The only person she didn't mind talking with was the gardener, John Cane, who had nothing to do with the testing and often left a bundle of flowers at her door. Even when her fury spread so wide it swept up everything in her path, including him, he seemed to barely take notice. He just talked and talked and talked. And when she talked, he listened. She searched the newspapers he brought for advertisements for law offices, and wrote letters asking for help. She wrote to the chief of police. She wrote to the head of the agency that had placed her at the Bowens. When the doctors and nurses continually refused to share the test results with her, she contacted an independent lab to ask if they would do private testing for her if she sent samples, and requested additional canisters from the nurses. In her next letter to Alfred she told him to go into the pantry at home, move aside the flour and the sugar, and there he'd find her bankbook. She instructed him to bring the book down to the bank on Twenty-Third Street where she had an account and arrange payment for the Ferguson Lab. "And then take the rest of it for yourself and close the account," she instructed. "Show them this letter if they don't believe you." There wouldn't be much left over, but it was something. She didn't need money on North Brother, and she was worried about him.

*

Some days passed quickly and easily, and some days felt so long and empty that she couldn't even muster the energy to find something to do. Six months went by. Ten. She wrote to Alfred every other week and tried to fill those letters with hope. She reminded him that North Brother was temporary and one day soon she'd be home and life would go on as it had before. It was important that she believe it, she knew, and just as important that he believe it. She found the determined tone of her letters echoed in his, at first, but then as the months slid by, his responses were spaced further apart. When a letter from him did arrive, the messages were so compact that she couldn't find him in the words. After a long silence, he sent a letter in February 1908 that was barely a letter at all:

Dear Mary,

Missing you. Any news? Things are fine here.

Alfred

As always, she'd held the envelope for a moment before tearing it open. She'd studied the way he wrote her name. And then to finally give in to that pleasure, to unfold the paper after looking forward to it for so long, only to find that it was nothing, was almost worse than getting no letter. She vowed she would not write back to him, but then a few days went by and she gave in.

Dear Alfred,

I got your note. Please write more next time. You don't know how lonely it is here and how I wonder all the time how you're getting by. Maybe you imagine there are people around me all the time, but remember that most people on

53

this island are very ill, and as for the doctors and nurses it's not as if we're friendly with one another. I've been knitting and trying crochet. The gardener lets me help him when there's work, and that's a distraction, but the ground has been frozen since December and the first tulips won't push through until April. I've read every book in the hospital library. It's only when I don't hear from you for a long time that I worry I'll be here forever. When I do hear from you I remember that North Brother Island is not my whole world. They don't know what to do with me here. They can't treat me like a sick person because I'm perfectly healthy but if they admit I'm healthy they'd have to let me go. When I ask questions I can see they look upon me as a nuisance. I don't know what's taking so long to figure out. Next month will be a year!

I wake up every day determined to get back home, back to our routine, and I think when I do get back home I won't take any situation that takes me away overnight. Not for a long time, anyway.

How are you doing? Two letters ago you said you were getting regular work. Is that still the case? Any news from anyone in the building? Do they ask for me? Remember to take care of yourself. And please, Alfred, try to be better about writing.

Mary

She wanted to ask him if he was drinking, if his clothes were clean, how he was paying the rent when all of her spare money must be long gone, if he had enough money for the gas meter, but didn't want to remind him of their fights.

On the day that marked the first anniversary of her arrival—a milestone only Mary seemed to notice—she counted his letters and stacked them on top of one another on the small table of her hut. There were nine in all. She calculated back over the year and figured she'd written to him at least twenty-five times. She noted the date stamped on each envelope: two months between the eighth and ninth letters. One month since she'd last written to him—the longest she'd gone without writing since her arrival on North Brother. That she wanted to hear from him, that she needed to see the blank space she'd left behind, was something she shouldn't have to explain, not after how long they'd been together, how well they knew each other. She felt raw, heartbroken, frustrated. If she could see him in person for a few minutes she'd know what he was thinking, but there was no use wishing for that. She returned each letter to its envelope and placed the stack on the ledge over the sink.

She hoped he'd use her silence to think about what she needed from him and send a letter so full that the envelope would be too fat to slide under her door. Still, the weeks passed, and she heard nothing. She continued to hold out. She'd been on North Brother for almost fifteen months, and hadn't heard from Alfred in four months. Her resentment turned to worry. Maybe he'd gotten injured on a job. Maybe he'd been evicted. He was not a violent drinker, but he'd had fights before. Maybe he'd gone to that rough beer hall he liked on Pearl Street and got pulled into a brawl. She wrote to her friend Fran to ask if she'd seen him, if he was getting on all right. Fran couldn't read or write, so the response came back in her husband's shaky hand, taped to a box of cookies from a bakery on Thirty-Ninth Street. The cookies were stale after the three days it took them to get to North Brother, but she ate one as she read.

Mary,

> *Things are the same here. We don't see much of Alfred but he seems all right when we do. He's not up for much conversation, but that's Alfred. He misses you, I'm sure. When will you be home? There hasn't been anything in the paper for a long time.*

Fran

Inside, Fran had folded a cartoon from the *Daily* that she knew Mary liked, and even though she'd already seen it, tears pricked her eyes. So Alfred was in one piece, still making his way up and down the stairs to and from their rooms, and still no word.

"You know what your trouble is?" John Cane asked one morning when he came upon her sitting on the grass outside her hut, watching the ferry dock. "You're not looking on the bright side." It was October, she'd been on North Brother for eighteen months, and she'd still heard nothing from Alfred since that February letter. Her arms were brown from helping John all spring and summer, and now he asked if she wanted to help him prune back the overgrown rhododendron.

"Is that the problem?" Mary asked as she followed him along the walking path. She struggled to find the right words to ask how a person could be so completely and utterly out of tune with the unfairness he was witness to, how he could be so indifferent, and as she was forming the words he pulled off his gloves and handed them to her. He rummaged through his bag for spare gardening shears.

"I think so. You're entirely at your leisure. You have your meals delivered."

Mary sighed. It was useless. He was just trying to cheer her up.

"You hear from any of them lawyers you wrote to?"

"No. Not yet."

He accepted this with a nod as he studied the bush. "Well, in the meantime," he said, and started clipping.

A few days later, just when she'd stopped expecting it, nearly eight months since she'd heard from him last, a letter from Alfred was waiting on the floor of her hut when she returned from her walk. As always, she weighed it in the flat of her hand for a moment. She placed it on the table and looked at it while she waited for the teakettle to boil. When she finally opened it, a dozen seeds slid along the seam and she caught them in her palm.

Dear Mary,

Fran stopped me outside the building a few weeks back saying she'd had a letter from you worrying about me. I'd been telling myself it hasn't been that long, but then I counted back. I'm sorry. I have no good reason for why I can't seem to write as often as you'd like so I won't try to give you an excuse. It's not that I'm not thinking of you. You, at least, know the outlines of my day. You can picture what I do, where I go. But when I try to imagine you out there I don't know what to picture. You tell me you've started knitting and gardening and that kind of thing, but it bothers me to hear you doing things you didn't used to do before. It makes it seem like you are even farther away. I tried to get you interested in gardening, remember the window box I made for growing herbs? The seeds I'm folding

*into this letter are for tomato plants. I thought if they won't let
you cook then at least you can grow something you can eat and
not have to get everything from the hospital kitchen.*

*I'm sorry I can't be better. I miss you every day. I know
all of this has been hard on you—hardest on you. But it's been
hard on me, too.*

Alfred

When Mary opened her palm to look at the seeds, she realized
Alfred expected her to be on North Brother for a very long time.

And then, out of the clear blue, in November 1908, she received a
thick envelope from the Ferguson Lab. They had been testing the
samples she'd been sending for almost nine months, and could
now share with her the good news that her samples came back
negative for Typhoid bacilli 100 percent of the time. They needed
such a long sample period to make sure the bacilli didn't flare
with the change of seasons, or for any other reason. She read the
paragraph again, and flipped quickly through the dozen pages of
results they'd sent. She almost shouted her joy. Shaking, she went
inside her hut to smooth back her hair and compose herself, and
then, clutching the envelope, she walked quickly up the path to
the hospital. The halls were oddly silent. Mary came upon one of
the secretaries. "Where are they?" she asked, almost breathless.

"A meeting. They'll be finished soon."

"Hello, Miss Mallon," came a voice from behind her, and
when she turned she found Dr. Soper sitting in a waiting room
chair, a book open on his lap. She swallowed, clutched the envelope to her breast. She turned her back to him.

"I'm waiting too. How are you feeling? You're looking well."

"Don't you speak to me," Mary said, and walked out to the hall to wait for another doctor to come by. She hadn't seen Dr. Soper in months, and seeing him now flustered her. She read the letter from the Ferguson Lab once more.

She wasn't in the hall for a minute when Dr. Albertson emerged from the conference room and asked if he could help her. He strolled into the office suite where Soper was waiting and she followed, not glancing toward the seating area.

"George!" he said, shaking Dr. Soper's hand. "I'll be right with you. Miss Mallon wants to see me."

Dr. Albertson told her to have a seat in his office, and Mary passed to him the lab results from Ferguson.

"May I close the door?" she asked.

"Well, yes," Dr. Albertson said, surprised.

He listened to her from beginning to end. She knew, she told him. She was no fool. She knew they were keeping her prisoner to study her for reasons they kept only to themselves, and couldn't possibly admit to the public. Dr. Albertson just listened until she was finished.

"Mary," he said kindly. "There is a good reason the Ferguson results came back negative. I'm going to call in Dr. Soper and he'll help explain."

"No!" Mary said. "*He* started all this. It's made him famous, hasn't it? What he said about me?" But it was too late. Dr. Albertson was already waving him inside.

"What's this?" Dr. Soper asked as he entered the office and took the envelope Dr. Albertson passed to him.

"Ah," he said simply when he was finished. "I see."

"The samples must be tested immediately, Mary," Dr.

Albertson explained. "Or else the bacteria die. You've just told me that you often can't get the sample out in the mail for a day, and then it might take three days to get to Ferguson. It's no good. It's not possible to test that way. And what's more, they would know that if they really are scientists, as they claim. Have you already paid them? The results are meaningless."

"You're just saying that because you want to keep me here. What are your results, then? Why has no one told me the results from the lab here?"

"I can tell you, Mary, that so far, your blood and urine come back negative, but your stool comes back with a positive result roughly sixty-five percent of the time."

"That's not true."

"Mary." Dr. Albertson held up one of his hands, and Mary remembered that he'd always been kind to her. "I'm on your side, believe it or not. Don't misunderstand—you do manufacture and carry Typhoid bacilli in your body, but I don't think you should be held for that reason. You are not wrong when you talk about how valuable you are to our work. However, at this point we know that there are many healthy carriers out there, and it's unfair that you should be here while the rest of them are conducting their lives."

Dr. Soper bristled. "Or they should all be held. Or they should be taken case by case. In any event, Dr. Albertson explained it clearly, I think. These results are worthless."

Mary looked at him and was so furious that she spat when she spoke. "You're a liar," she said to Dr. Soper.

Dr. Soper continued as if she hadn't responded. "What I find interesting is that you dismiss our test results completely, give them no credence whatsoever, and yet you wholly believe these private results. So which is it, Miss Mallon? Do you believe in the science or don't you?"

"You are a vile person." Mary's whole body shook as she said it.

"Mary," Dr. Albertson offered, taking the envelope from Dr. Soper and returning it to Mary's hands. "Why don't you take these and think about it for a day and then come back when you have more questions? We can talk about all of this at length." He gave her a look that said he was sorry to have called in Dr. Soper. He hadn't understood. "I know it's disappointing."

"I want to see all the doctors. I want to see them right now."

"I'm sorry. We have several new Diphtheria patients as of this morning. And Dr. Soper has come to give a lecture. Come back tomorrow morning. I'll organize a group of doctors and we'll all talk about this."

"Oh, I'll be back tomorrow. You can count on it."

But she didn't go back the next day, because she imagined them in wait for her, ready to punish her for taking investigative steps on her own. She was not a carrier. She had not made anyone sick. And yet, from time to time she felt a fissure in her certainty, like a reminder string wrapped around her pinkie that she'd forgotten about entirely until, at the end of a long day, she glanced down and noticed it there where she'd left it.

Though she had not yet replied to Alfred's last letter, she decided it was time to break the silence.

> Dear Alfred,
> Thank you for the seeds. I have been thinking about how to respond, but right now I need your help with something

important. I need you to go to the Ferguson Lab on W. 72nd Street and ask someone there to send more details on the testing they did for me. I'm going to write to them as well, but I think they need to see a person standing in front of them. Tell them that the doctors at Riverside won't accept the results. Please, Alfred. Try to remember everything they say. Then write to me right away.

Mary

She didn't know if the letter had reached him, if he'd been sober enough to read it, if he cared about her at all anymore, until two weeks later when the small rectangle came through the mail with Alfred's writing on the front, saying that he'd been to the lab, not only once but twice, but no one there would talk to him about her. "What's happening?" he wrote.

Alfred,

Thank you for trying. I had an idea that these private results would force the doctors here to set me free, but they're ignoring them entirely. I don't want to believe them, but there is one doctor here who seems to be on my side and he's the one who told me the results are worthless. I feel sick thinking of all the money I gave them to do the testing. I had relaxed for a while but now I'm going to work harder to find a way out of this place. You think I'll be here forever, but I won't be, Alfred. I'm going to be home soon.

Mary

For a week or so she went back to old habits, waiting by the pier to watch the mailbag be carried into the hospital. And then, when she realized Alfred had resumed his silence, she armored herself against the hurt by writing more letters to lawyers, doctors, anyone who might help. Time was slipping by quickly, much more quickly than when she first arrived. Another new year arrived. Another winter turned into spring. The mailman rarely made his way down the path to her hut.

Then in June 1909, as Mary was making her way from the water's edge in bare feet, John Cane came rushing across from the hospital with a letter in his hand. "For you," he panted. "I told them I'd deliver it." He watched her study the return address: O'Neill & Associates. "What is it? They said you'd want to see it right away."

"You are so nosey," Mary said as she slid her finger under the flap. They were right. It was a letter from a lawyer named Francis O'Neill. He'd been working on a case in Texas for the past two years, but now he was back in New York City and a letter she'd written to a colleague had been passed on to him. He wanted to meet with her. "I've read all the press," he wrote, "and I'd like to hear your side. The case I was involved with in Texas was also a medical-legal issue. If your situation is as I understand it, and you have not yet secured other representation, then I am confident I can win your freedom." He understood that she was not allowed visitors, but if she told the hospital that he was her lawyer they would have to make an exception.

Still in her bare feet and clutching the letter in her fist, she ran up to the hospital, gave the head secretary the name Francis O'Neill, and wrote back to him within a half hour asking him to come, please come.

FOUR

Mary sent her response to Mr. O'Neill on a Tuesday, and on Friday she watched an unfamiliar young man step off the ferry and steady himself for a moment before continuing up the path to the hospital. He clutched his briefcase with both hands. "Mr. O'Neill?" she asked. She was waiting in the shadow of the hospital's western wall.

"You must be Mary," he said, shaking her hand. She had so much to say and so many questions that she didn't know where to begin.

"Why don't I check in?" he said after a moment, nodding at the hospital doors. "They'll want me to sign something."

"I'll wait down there," she said, pointing to her hut.

Twenty minutes later, after a brief conversation about what was what on the island—Mr. O'Neill seemed interested in the X-ray building—she showed him inside and watched as his gaze skittered across the counter to the pile of rubbage she'd collected for John Cane. She offered him tea, but he declined. He pressed his handkerchief to his nose, and then opened his briefcase and removed a pile of papers. He had with him a copy of every newspaper article about her, plus her records from Willard Parker. She noticed he had notes attached to each item. He opened a notebook to a blank page.

"Let's start with your arrest," he said as he uncapped his pen.

"You mean my abduction," she corrected him, and bit her lip. She didn't want him to think she was unreasonable.

"Well, yes," he agreed. "That's probably more accurate."

They spoke for two hours, and when he left, they had a plan. As Mr. O'Neill explained, the Department of Health may have been within their rights if they'd tested her first, and then put her in quarantine in Willard Parker following a positive result, but not the other way around. They were completely out of line to arrest her without a warrant and to test her once she was in their custody. First, he told her, she would apply for a writ of habeas corpus. There would be a hearing. He warned her that this meant her real name would be released, and asked if she needed to think about that. "No," Mary said. "I've done nothing wrong."

"The papers have been sympathetic to your side," Mr. O'Neill said as he gathered his things. "That will help, too. Don't be surprised if reporters come out here looking for you."

"Will they be allowed to see me?"

"I'll arrange it. I don't see how the hospital can get around it."

"And what about other visitors, could you get them to allow that, too?"

Mr. O'Neill touched her shoulder. "Try to be patient. I know it's been a long time since you've seen your friends. But we have to proceed carefully, and remember, you'll be home soon."

"Wait," she said as he began to leave. She had to address it now or else it would hang over her until they saw each other again. "I haven't worked in over two years. I had a little money saved, but—"

Mr. O'Neill held up his hand. "There's no fee." She narrowed her eyes. He seemed decent, but no one was that decent. She decided to worry about that later, once she was free. As soon as he left, she got out a sheet of paper.

Dear Alfred,

Finally! I have news. I've just met with a lawyer named O'Neill and he seems certain he can get these people to let me go. There will be a hearing, I'm not sure when. Soon. I'll send the details when it's scheduled. I know it's been a very long time and we have much to talk about but I miss you, Alfred. And I'm worried about you. I can't wait to see you again. Let's just forget these horrid two years and celebrate when we see each other soon. I am the same, I hope. Are you?

Mary

As Mr. O'Neill had predicted, within days of their habeas corpus application there was another newspaper article about her in the *New York American,* a long one, and for the first time, they used her real name. Her appeal was popular news in the city, and reporters began to request face-to-face interviews. The hospital allowed no more than one reporter per day.

"Write down about the closeness of this place," she reminded each one who made the trip. "And the cot. Do you see how it cups in the middle?" The numbers used to condemn her were inconsistent: one had twenty-two sick, one dead; another had thirty sick, two dead; the third had twenty-eight sick, six dead. But none believed that was the whole story. She'd been cooking since she arrived in America in 1883, but the records that led to her discovery and capture went only as far back as 1901. "You can tell me," each reporter said in a different way, and each made a show of putting down his paper and pencil like Mary was some kind of imbecile who didn't know how the world worked. "When did you know?" The young man from the *Herald* had a vein that jumped at his temple.

"When did I know what?" she would reply, willing herself to stay calm. She offered each reporter one of the blackcurrant scones the hospital cook had sent down with John Cane. "I've never been sick a day in my life, and that's all I have to say on the matter."

Each reporter shrank away from the plate. "No?" she said, holding the plate aloft a few moments longer, as if the person sitting across from her might change his mind.

Ever since arriving in America, she kept her head down and she worked. She'd found Alfred, but that was no crime. They couldn't lock her up for not being married, for demanding a good wage and getting it, for not attending any brand of church services and loving instead to spend Sundays roaming Washington Market, and then going to hear the fiddler who played on the corner of Fulton and Church Streets. She was thirty-nine years old and healthy. Did any of them realize the strength it took to lift a pot of boiling water? To knead bread for thirty minutes? To pound one of the tougher cuts of beef until it was tender and ready for her skillet? At the end of a workweek she was exhausted in her bones, in the muscles of her shoulders and her back, but still, she often walked all the way from the Bowens' brownstone on the Upper East Side to her place farther downtown because she liked using her own steam, didn't feel like squeezing herself into a streetcar.

"Miss Mallon," the reporter from the *Herald* asked, "do you yourself believe you carry Typhoid Fever and pass it to those for whom you cook?"

She made sure to look him directly in the eyes. "No, I do not."

"Then why has the Department of Health gone to the trouble and expense of keeping you here?"

"That's exactly what I would like to know."

And when it came time for each reporter to leave, she walked with him down to the dock and spoke of other things. The weather. That Frenchman's attempts to cross the English channel in an aeroplane. The hurricane in Texas. "Where do you live?" she asked each one, coming around to it just before arriving at the dock. One was from Brooklyn. Another from Fort Lee. But the writer for the *Herald* lived on Twenty-Eighth Street and Third Avenue; upon hearing it Mary held her breath. Surely, living so close, he'd passed Alfred in the street, brushed up against him at the grocer, sat beside him at Nation's Pub, maybe struck up conversation. The thought came to her that she should give this man a message to bring to Alfred, have him climb the stairs of their building and knock on the door to their rooms. But the reporter was backing away already, thanking her for her time, stepping down into the boat, and Mary felt the chance slip past her like a life ring thrown into the water and swallowed by the waves.

On the morning of the hearing, Mary wondered once again who was paying Mr. O'Neill's legal fees. John Cane said it was possible some of the *New York American*'s readers had pitched in to pay for her defense since the writer took such a forgiving view. He also pointed out that sometimes Mr. Hearst got involved in cases that interested his readers. "Who named John Cane an authority on these matters?" Mary asked him. He'd been getting a little too comfortable with himself lately, standing on the single step outside the door to her cottage as he told her the hospital gossip, having a say-so on matters that didn't concern him in the least. He brought the papers down to Mary to read out the most important passages. That he couldn't read the sentences himself didn't matter when it came to forming opinions on everything from the garbage strike to city taxes to Mary's case.

"And what do you mean a forgiving view? They told the story accurately."

"And sided with you, it seemed to me," John said, crossing his arms and leaning against the rail as if he were born and raised on that very spot.

"Who else would they side with?" Mary demanded.

"I'm only saying," John Cane said. "I'm only making a point."

Mary felt nervous enough about the day ahead, and didn't see how John Cane gave himself leave to make points when he was no more literate than a flea. All she knew was once she stepped onto the ferry later that morning, she might never return to North Brother again.

Her last letter to Alfred was brief. On a small piece of lined paper she'd written only the address of the courthouse, the date, the time, then folded it inside a copy of the article that had appeared in the *New York American*. Surely, when he unfolded the article and read her note, he would remember the last time they'd been down on Centre Street together—how many years ago? Eighteen? Twenty? It was late fall, the weather brisk. They were deciding what to do with the rest of their day when a page ran down the courthouse steps shouting "Verdict is in!" and then tripped, tumbling head over heels until he landed at their feet. "Well?" Alfred asked as he offered his hand and the boy let himself be pulled up. "Guilty," the boy said as he staggered and blinked, uninjured. Mary and Alfred had walked on, laughing with heads bent so the boy wouldn't see them, until all of a sudden Alfred pulled her into an alley, deep into a shadow, where he pressed her against a wall and put his rough hands on either side of her face and told her he loved her, that no one would ever love her as much, and she, feeling a tug in her belly like a hand clenched into a fist, could not say it back, not yet, but felt it there, inside her, waiting to be pried open.

In the beginning, Mary would meet Alfred for regular Wednesday and Saturday evenings out. One Wednesday, he told her that he wanted to live with her, and also told her that he knew she wanted to live with him. So when Saturday came, he called on her earlier than usual and said that he'd found a flat on Thirty-Third Street. Would she come see it? To decide? He'd promised the landlord they'd let him know by the end of the day. Mary went with him and they walked along Third Avenue with Alfred making his case the whole time. He'd known her so well that he'd gone up earlier that morning to place in that gray and narrow kitchen a single hothouse orchid in a red clay pot so that the first thing she would see when she pushed open the door was something beautiful that needed tending. Needed *her* tending. And she'd said, in halfhearted protest, because she felt herself giving in, felt that she'd given in already, "But we aren't married," and he'd looked at her for a long time before asking, "What has that to do with anything?"

The special ferry that would transport her over to 138th Street was due at eight o'clock in the morning. That would give her time to get across the East River and all the way downtown to the courthouse by ten o'clock. She'd been preparing for two days, scrubbing each of her three blouses and hanging them outside in the sun, brushing each of her skirts. In twenty-seven months the two white blouses had gone a bit yellow, the ruffles fallen flat. Two of the wool skirts had gone shiny at the seat and to her shame, when she had them out in the sun and could look at them more closely, she thought she could make out a separation in the worn area of each, two moons next to each other and a narrow space in between. The nurses offered her clothing from the hospital, told her to help herself before they were sent to the mainland and donated, but she didn't want those tubercular blouses and dresses, didn't want dead women's hand-me-downs. Besides, she had difficulty finding blouses that weren't tight across the bust, and how dare they, anyway, assume she'd wear any old thing they offered, no matter what state it was in, how crooked the seams, how flimsy the lining, no matter who'd worn it before her and what kind of tailoring that person had paid for, and what quality of cloth. How dare they? She was no beggar. She was a cook and had earned good wages and she wouldn't touch any of it.

"There's many who'd be grateful, ma'am," one nurse commented when Mary told her to take it all away, and she realized too late that they were only trying to be kind. They retreated from Mary's cottage like it was on fire, and a moment later she watched their work-whites fade into the shadow cast by the main building of the hospital. She told herself to shout after them that she was sorry, that they must try to understand.

The afternoon before the hearing, when she picked out the best of her blouses and the best of her skirts, she asked John Cane to fetch an iron and board from the hospital laundry. "Just give them here and I'll tell them to do it," he said, and held open his arms for the clothes.

"I don't want them to do it," Mary said slowly. "I want you to fetch me an iron and board so I can do it myself."

"You don't even trust them to iron a shirt?"

"Please, John," Mary said before she closed the door. After an hour, she went out and looked at the small side door of the hospital where he usually came and went. She waited two more hours. She spotted him coming around six o'clock, but it was only to bring her dinner, and he promised to come back again. At ten o'clock that night, long after he would have taken the boat back to the mainland, Mary went outside one last time in her bare feet to see if anyone was making his or her way along the footpath, but all was silent except for the distant bell of a trolley across the river. At midnight, she boiled a small amount of water in a saucepan and did what she could with the smooth cast-iron bottom, pushing it along the sleeves of her best blouse. When she was finished, the blouse hung neatly over a chair, the skirt flat on the table like a tablecloth, she climbed into her cot. She tried to imagine something peaceful that would put her to sleep, but instead, her left eye began to twitch. She squeezed both eyes shut, but she could feel it still, the muscle fluttering against her palm where she pressed it as hard as she could. The last thought she had was of Alfred, and how she'd have to explain to him why she had to keep one hand over her left eye.

When she woke, and dressed, and made herself a cup of black tea, she opened the front door of her cottage to find John Cane placing the twelve-pound iron on her front step. "And what should I do with it now? It'll take an hour to warm up."

He held up his hands as if to say it wasn't his fault. Nothing was his fault.

She wasn't going to argue with him that day. She'd save any arguing for the judge downtown.

"You look nice anyhow," John said, and Mary's hand went to her throat. She wished she had a brooch. "Good luck today."

"I mightn't be seeing you again, John. If I don't see you, I wish you all the best." She clasped her hands together and nodded at him. "You were kind to me."

"But surely they won't let you go today, will they? They'd need to see you a few times more?"

"Mr. O'Neill said maybe today." He also said the judge had probably made up his mind long before he stepped into the courtroom. Judges were supposed to be as cold and accurate as scales with the weight of proof added equally to each side, but Mr. O'Neill said they often stepped into the courtroom with the scales already tipped.

"Oh, I'll see you later, Mary. I'm not worried."

"You're supposed to hope you won't see me later."

"Well, now."

"What do you mean? It's like wishing me bad luck. Do you wish me bad luck?"

"Not a bit! And I'll bring a bit extra for your dinner tonight. You'll be starved after all that traveling."

Mary felt the twitch start up again and pressed her hand to her eye before it became too strong to stop.

For the short journey from North Brother Island to the mainland, she folded two small squares of paper over the sharp points of her collar so they wouldn't be soiled in transit. She kept her tie—blue, flecked with black—folded in her pocket until she arrived down-town. She'd known that the journey across the East River would be choppy, and that the ferry would create its own breeze by its speed, so she'd waited to pin her hair until she was escorted onto the pier at 138th Street. "Excuse me," she'd said to her guard, a young man, eighteen, perhaps, twenty at most, and before he could answer she strode off toward the small one-room depot and the door marked Ladies. He'd performed his duty well enough, stepping down into the boat ahead of her like any gentleman in case she should stumble, and up onto the dock when they reached the city. But he didn't offer his arm, and during the crossing— the nose of the boat rising to meet each roll of gun gray water before falling, rising, falling, the two passengers and one crewman jostling side to side on the long bench seat—he'd kept his face turned away from hers and clutched the railing that rimmed the edge of the boat so that he wouldn't brush against her during the passage. When she tried to speak to him, placing her face close to his so he could hear her over the sound of the slapping waves and the roar of the boat's engine, he'd grimaced.

Once inside the narrow lavatory she took two long hairpins from her handbag and held them in her mouth as she twisted and tucked her strawberry blond hair into an arrangement at the back of her neck. The mirror she was accustomed to looking at every day since 1907 was merciless; it was placed near the single window in her cottage and faced north. This lavatory mirror was shadowed and freckled, and Mary examined her face carefully in the forgiving light. Some of the newspapers had included images of her with sharpened features. Others had drawn her fat and aged, cracking human skulls in a skillet like they were eggs, with a bosom that should have tipped her over. To herself, the morning of the hearing, she looked like she always had—pretty, but not unusually so. Clean. Efficient. Ready for work. In different clothes, and a different accent, and with hands that had not spent the better part of twenty years in scalding water, she might have been mistaken for a lady. She'd often been told she was haughty enough.

In the days leading up to the hearing, she kept telling herself there were three possibilities: Alfred would be off the wagon, too drunk to keep track of dates and time and would not come, or Alfred would sober up and get himself there. The third possibility was the worst, and it wasn't until that moment, staring at her reflection in the lavatory mirror, that she faced it head-on: he might not want to see her. Perhaps, in twenty-seven months, he'd worked up the courage to speak to that bright thing who made up the beds at the hotel on Thirty-Fourth Street and who sometimes waited outside Nation's Pub for her brother. "She reminds me a bit of you, at that age," he'd told Mary once, a passing comment, an answer to her question of how his day had been. She liked when he painted a full picture of his day for her and instead of drawing himself slumped on a stool, his head filled with goosedown feathers until halfway into that first tumbler, he told her about the world outside on the street, the call of the chestnut man, the rough comments about President Roosevelt's oldest daughter, the man dressed in a suit of newspaper.

"Ma'am?" a woman's voice called from the other side of the door. "The man says you're to hurry."

Mary swung the door open. It was the woman from the ticket window; her fingertips were black with ink, her forehead smudged where she'd rubbed it. "What man?" Mary asked loud enough for her guard to hear. "That?" She laughed. How easy it would be to get away, to leap onto the streetcar and disappear, or even to pick up her skirt and run. There was no running from North Brother, but here in the city she could simply turn a corner, and another, board a trolley, and be gone. John Cane had delivered two five-dollar bills with her breakfast that morning, money sent from Mr. O'Neill for anything unexpected she might encounter on her way down to the courthouse, and Mary had folded them tightly and slipped them inside her shoe. She observed her guard. The boy was so afraid of her it might be enough to just go near him. Just by walking toward him she could back him up into the river.

The plan was that Mr. O'Neill would get his medical men to answer their medical men and after the hearing, if the judge agreed that she shouldn't have been taken bodily from her place of employment without a chance to defend herself, then she'd be going home to Alfred that evening. Unless Alfred had offered her side of the bed to someone else.

When they finally arrived at the courthouse, Mary searched for Alfred as she followed Mr. O'Neill down the marble-floored hallway. He'd stay in the shadows, she knew, until the last moment. It was possible she'd passed him as she rushed up the steps outside. Mr. O'Neill led her to a small private room just down the hall from the courtroom, where they had a few moments of peace before they went in to present their case. When he told her it was time, she removed the two squares of paper from her collar. Mr. O'Neill had been doing a sidelong inspection of her appearance since greeting her, and now that they were alone he gave her a quick look up and down.

"Well?" she asked after a moment.

"Well nothing," he said. "Good."

FIVE

Mr. O'Neill warned her that the other lawyers would have rounded up as many of her old employers as they could, other house staff she'd worked with, anyone who might tell a story about her that would keep her on North Brother. Her most recent employers, Mr. and Mrs. Bowen, were unlikely to be in attendance. They would not want their name further tarnished by association, and besides, their daughter had died, it was a fact, and there was nothing they could say that would weigh more than that.

One of the last times she'd conversed with Mrs. Bowen, before Soper came looking for her, before the girl got sick, Mary had been wearing her new hat. Remembering that hat nagged her, and after more than two years of circling 'round and 'round why and how she'd gone from working and living in New York City, making a good wage, buying what she liked, to being trapped on an island, her thoughts kept returning to that hat. Where was it now? From the moment she was forced into the police wagon and taken to Willard Parker, she felt like she'd been flipping through a book to find a single sentence, running her finger along a page to find a single word, but when her mind lighted on that hat, she stopped. Her stomach sank. Sometimes one thing leads to another even if the line isn't direct.

Some of the doctors had intimated that she was not right in her mind, that her mental state was part of the reason she could not be trusted, along with her being a woman, and being an immigrant, and being the kind of woman who lived with a man without being married. But she knew the hat had something to do with her capture in 1907, and she knew it now that her case was finally being examined, twenty-seven months later.

It was a lovely hat, cobalt blue with silk flowers and berries cascading around the brim, piled higher on one side of the crown than the other. It wasn't one of those frothy confections meant to appear suspended over the head by magic, one of those ridiculous dollops of cream that required a morning's worth of framing and supporting the hair that it sat upon. It was an everyday hat. A walking hat. The kind of hat where a woman could twist her hair as usual and then just place it on top, a pin here, a pin there, nothing more. The flowers weren't simply cut out from the fabric, but labored over, each one a tiny piece of craftsmanship Mary examined in the shop before pushing her money across the counter. The shop was called Matilda's, and she'd passed it dozens of times before the day she finally went inside. Nothing in the window had ever cried out to her until that hat, so she went in. She was extending her fingers to feel the brim when at the very same moment she remembered that her hands smelled of onions, and the shop's mistress asked if she could be of any assistance. Mary wasn't used to shops being so quiet, the mistress being so solicitous. She could feel the woman's eyes on her from the moment she put her hand on the door's handle. That first day, Mary said, "I'm in a terrible rush. I'll have to return another time." She let a few days go by, and then she scrubbed her hands well, rubbed her fingertips with lemon, and tried again. This time she picked the hat from its peg and held it to the light.

"It's new," the shop's mistress said. "It was made in Paris."

Mary asked how much and kept her face very still for the answer. It was an astonishing number, but she had it. She had the whole price of that hat in an envelope hidden in the frame of her bed at the Bowen residence. She was going to do it. As she walked away from the store she knew she was going to do it. Why not? She had no one to answer to but herself, and what was money for if not to be spent on a beautiful hat? On her next visit, Mary told the woman that if she discovered the craftsmanship to be less than it appeared, she would take the hat straight back and demand her money returned. The woman suggested a plain gray toque with a narrow brim and showed Mary the neat stitching as if to tell her that gray and plain might be more appropriate to a head like Mary's than a cobalt jewel that would draw every glance. Mary ran her thumb along one of the silk petals and bought it on the spot.

When she returned to her room at the Bowen residence, she studied it in the box for the better part of an hour, those flowers, each one centered with a small piece of glass that drew the light, the blue of the petals slightly paler than the rest of the hat, the blue of the berries slightly darker. It was a beautiful thing and she loved it. It lived in its box on top of her dresser for two whole weeks before she put it on her head and wore it outside. She paired it with the chestnut dress coat she'd purchased second-hand, and she worried for it when she stepped into the weather and found the day not as fair as it had seemed from her room. She didn't want it to get wet, or be stolen from her head by a thief. Or worse, it occurred to her as she remembered the week before, when a gentleman's handkerchief was carried away in the wind. Mary had joined the chase for a few steps, until she predicted where it was headed, and when he caught up with it, he found it had landed on the belly of a horse that had died in the street and been left there to rot and draw flies. Mary had laughed when, out of habit, the gentleman reached for his hanky, to cover his face, but of course it was the hanky he'd been chasing in the first place.

She wore it. She stood in the small private room Mrs. Bowen had assigned to her as cook and slid one pin behind her left ear, and one behind her right. She felt its beauty like a living thing as she crossed the street, as she gathered her skirt and stepped as well as she could over the horse shit that had been pushed to the curb and left in a heap at the corner of Sixtieth Street. She felt it like a light shining over her as she made her way east to the streetcar on Third Avenue, still shining as she transferred to the IRT at Forty-Second Street. Mrs. Bowen was to have a dinner party that evening and wanted something unusual to serve to her guests—lobster, perhaps, or sweetbreads. No fowl, she instructed. No oysters. No pork. Nothing her guests might be served by their own cooks, in their own homes. Milton's on Second Avenue had a good selection most days, and high turnover, but Mrs. Bowen didn't trust them, and sent Mary instead all the way down to Washington Market, where she instructed Mary to witness with her own eyes the fish being pulled off the ice. It meant a morning's journey and more work, just so Mrs. Bowen's guests would go home and say to one another, That Lillian Bowen, she'd never serve anything as plain as a roast.

As she descended the staircase to the IRT on Forty-Second Street, she looked down for her next step with her eyes instead of bending her neck and risking the hat. She'd been on the IRT fewer than a dozen times since it had opened with great fanfare, and still found it jarring to see a train shoot out of the darkness so far underground, knowing as she stepped aboard that it would plow into the darkness on the other side. But the hat made her brave. On the train, she fixed her gaze on the doors as the rest of the world pushed in around her.

Because Mrs. Bowen had left the choice of dinner to her, she had to look at everything the market offered: twenty-five butcher stalls, all the vegetables, all the fruit, the cheese, the nine fish stalls, the smoked meat, the tripe. She sampled the coffee cake, the coffee, the dark bread, the light, the butter from Connecticut, the cheese from Virginia. She bought a nickel slice of Westphalian ham and ate it as she walked. She raised a hand to protect her hat against the flying feathers of the poultrymen, from the rough knuckle-cracking work of the butchers and the bits that flew in the air, the cartilage and marrow that made a slick circle around their stalls and forced women to walk on tiptoe until they were safely past.

She kept the hat on her head well enough, adjusting it now and again when it started to tip, and she made her way all the way back to Park and Sixtieth loaded down with packages. The other Irish at market had their hair covered in scarves. The European women from other parts wore tight braids coiled at the back of the neck, or old hats of their husbands' pulled down over their ears. Heads had turned seeing Mary coming in that hat. Seas had parted. When she bargained and told them exactly how she wanted her packages wrapped, they knew she was a domestic, and yet that hat.

As Mary turned the last corner before the Bowen home, she caught sight of her reflection in a neighbor's bay window and decided she was as pretty that day as she'd ever been. The coat hugged her figure—slim, back then—and her hair was shiny and clean. Her eyes were bright from the chill in the air, and her cheeks rosy from the effort of hauling her purchases. She was thirty-seven years old.

She turned onto Park to walk the half block uptown and who did she encounter in front of the residence but Mrs. Bowen herself. And what was Mrs. Bowen wearing on top of her curls? The identical twin to Mary's beloved hat.

"Mary," she said, her eyes fixed on Mary's head. "I expected you ages ago."

"I'm very sorry, madam," Mary replied, even though Mrs. Bowen had no reason to expect her any sooner. She made a point not to look at Mrs. Bowen's head, even though Mrs. Bowen had yet to take her eyes from Mary's.

"You haven't forgotten that the guests will arrive at six." She narrowed her eyes as if deciding whether it really could be the same hat. A copy, perhaps? A poor imitation?

"No, I wouldn't forget that." Mrs. Bowen had called the office that had placed Mary to hire two additional cooks just for the afternoon, and Mary had stripped and scrubbed everything the day before. When Mary arrived at the Bowen residence three weeks earlier, the pots and pans were thick with baked-on carbon, and she spent her first week chipping it away, scrubbing them back to their original luster. While she was at it she tied a rag to the end of a broom and pulled the cobwebs from the tin ceilings. She went through a gallon of ammonia scrubbing the floor. No one knows where to find the pockets of grease in a kitchen like a cook knows, and when the other cooks arrived that afternoon, Mary saw them looking. And she saw them not finding.

Mrs. Bowen seemed satisfied, and though she still wore a curious expression, like she didn't quite understand what she was looking at, she finally managed to tear her eyes away from the top of Mary's head. She put her hand to her own hat for a moment, then turned to enter the house through the main entrance. Mary watched the other woman walk away, and as she felt the weight of the packages in her arms, the ache in her wrists and elbows from struggling with them for so long, on the IRT, on the streetcar, up and down stairs, across puddles and stubborn patches of ice left over in the shade of trees, the scald of the cold against her knuckles, she felt the words slipping from between her lips before she had a chance to stop them.

"I see we have the same taste," she said to Mrs. Bowen's back. It was a foolish thing to say, and as soon as the words were out she remembered her aunt observing once, years ago, that Mary had a twist in her that sometimes made her do and say things that she shouldn't.

Mrs. Bowen turned. "I beg your pardon?"

"Your hat," Mary said, nodding at the other woman's head as if she might not know where to find her hat. "It's identical to mine."

"Oh," Mrs. Bowen said, her hand reaching somewhere in the region of her ear, not touching the hat. "Similar, Mary, not identical. But I see what you mean."

"Not the same?"

"No. Similar. Not the same."

Mary knew that if she snuck into Mrs. Bowen's quarters that

night and switched their hats she would never in a thousand years of scrutiny have been able to tell the difference.

"My mistake."

The servants' entrance was just a few short steps down from the sidewalk but Mary barely made it inside before she started laughing. Bette and Frank were in the kitchen making preparations and could tell by Mary's face she had a story to tell, so she told it, and they all had a laugh over Mrs. Bowen's expression, which Mary did for them again and again as they unfolded the counters from their compartments and laid out the knives and waited for the additional cooks.

They laughed and laughed, and the work went quickly.

A week later, the daughter of the family declined all of her meals and told her governess that she felt poorly, and would have to do her lessons another time. By evening, her fever was so high she had to spend the whole night in the tub. One month later, Mary was taken away.

"Nonsense," said John Cane, when Mary told him the whole story of the hat not long after she was moved to her private hut on North Brother. John had asked if she wanted to keep him company while he transferred to the ground some of the plants he'd started from seed over the winter. She was quiet, at first, content to watch him work, and then he'd asked how it was that they'd captured her, taken her to North Brother.

"It isn't nonsense," Mary said, raising her voice. "They chased me down like a dog. They harassed me at the Bowens' first, then in my own rooms, then they got me one day when the Bowens were out. They had to carry me! They each took an arm or a leg and they carried me. They didn't even give me a chance to get my things."

"What things?" John asked. "You'll send for them. Tell the matron." But Mary didn't know the matron, didn't know what brand of woman she was. Perhaps the matron would like to get her hands on Mary's hidden envelope, her three good blouses, her beautiful cobalt hat.

How to explain that if it wasn't the hat specifically, it was the fact that Mary had purchased the hat, had worn it, had admired herself in it. That she was the type of woman who counted out her earnings—a full month's worth of earnings!—and slid it in a neat stack across a counter to purchase for herself something as impractical as a beautiful hat. If she'd been the type of woman who saved her money, or gave it to someone who needed it more, a neighbor with children, perhaps, or the church, if she'd been a married woman who handed every dollar over to her husband, or better yet a married woman who didn't have any earnings because she was taken up with the care of her own home, she'd never be in the situation she was in. She couldn't prove it, but it was the truth nonetheless.

She'd broached the idea with Mr. O'Neill two years later when he came to see her on North Brother, but it was like trying to explain to a cook in training how to tell when a duck is done even when the juices lie, how to predict whether a soufflé will fall just by feeling the air in the room. "A hat?" Mr. O'Neill said. Then he changed the subject and she could see him dismiss it entirely.

SIX

Mary followed Mr. O'Neill by several paces as they entered the courtroom. The time was two minutes past ten o'clock.

Almost every chair was occupied when she walked down the narrow center aisle. She'd pictured benches, polished wood, the judge elevated above them on a kind of throne, but instead the cramped and musty room was filled with straight-backed chairs in uneven lines. Some reporters had turned their chairs to make a cluster with others they knew. Some people who had no involvement in the case but had been following it in the papers nudged their chairs out of line bit by bit with impatient shifting. She wanted to know if Alfred was there, but she kept her eyes fixed on the neat seams of Mr. O'Neill's suit jacket. There was a momentary hush when those closest to the door spotted her, and a collective creak as several dozen spectators turned to see her for themselves.

Some were on her side, Mary hoped as she crossed the room and kept her focus above the heads of the witnesses. She'd seen

the editorials in the paper, the people who believed she'd commit-
ted no crime and should be set free to live and work in society like
everyone else. Then there were the papers that refused to use her
real name even after it had become public knowledge. The Germ
Woman, their headlines still read. Readers had written in to ask
if breathing near Mary Mallon put a person at risk. What about
touching what she touched? What about entering a room shortly
after she'd left? She hoped the sympathetic were in attendance at
the hearing, but all she felt as she made her way to the front of
the room was the scrutiny of fifty people looking at her so closely
in the muggy air that she felt handled, groped, every bit as dirty
as she was accused of being.

Mr. O'Neill placed his briefcase on a scratched and dented
wood table at the front of the room. The men from the Department
of Health were already seated at a similar table across the aisle, and
Mary made the mistake of looking at them, one by one, until her
glance jumped to the row behind them, where Dr. Soper's dark
head was bent over his notes. A man in a blue uniform stepped forward and announced the arrival of Judges Erlinger and Giegerich.
Mary hadn't expected two judges, but she was relieved to see that
she'd be able to keep them apart in her thoughts: Erlinger was a
big man and Giegerich was no larger than a girl.

"All stand," the court officer called out, and the clap of chairs
being pushed back was thunderous. Mary looked toward the
three large windows on the western side of the room and noted
that the day had darkened, the metallic smell of rain had seeped
indoors. When the people returned to their seats, there was stirred
up in the room the odor of vegetables, of horse, of blood. Judge
Erlinger pressed a handkerchief to his forehead and then briefly
to his nose.

Mr. O'Neill cleared his throat. He began the way they'd discussed, with an account of her arrest in March of 1907. "Without a warrant," he said, "without due process, the liberty of a perfectly healthy individual . . ."

Mary could see that he was nervous. He was five years younger than she, only thirty-four, but he never seemed as young to her as he did when he touched his fingertips to the edge of the battered table and stood.

"Mary Mallon has been quarantined for twenty-seven months with no one to keep her company but a gardener who delivers her meals three times a day. She has submitted to testing—urine, blood, and stool—twice a week for thāt entire period. The nurses who collect her samples are certainly no company, and she dreads their visits because of the anguish they cause. Her friends are not permitted to visit, despite the fact that every doctor associated with her case admits she is contagious only through cooking."

Mr. O'Neill continued, sticking only to what was relevant, and as he spoke Mary found her thoughts drifting. For twenty-seven months she'd craved the streets of Manhattan, the chaos, the noise, haggling over the price of an orange, debating the accuracy of the butcher's scale. She missed her work, rising before the rest of the house, removing the first shining pot from its hook, lighting the fire under it, dropping in a spoon of butter and watching it skid across the warmed bottom. She missed earning money, walking to Dicer's on First Avenue, picking out a basket full of groceries, paying for it with clean, new bills.

She missed Alfred most of all and every morning when she woke she wondered whether he was also awake. She often caught herself thinking of him the same way she once thought of the people from home when she first got to America, all the way across the ocean, twenty-one days at sea. And then when she remembered that the East River was not the ocean, was not even as broad as the mighty Hudson, everything felt more urgent and these were the moments that made her wild, as the doctors called it. Combative. Difficult. Stubborn. Obstinant. Ignorant. Female. There were almost five million souls rushing through their days over there. She could see their chimneys and hear the sharp whistle of trains. Somewhere over there walked Alfred, and unlike those she missed from Ireland who were so far away that she'd quickly drawn a curtain across the possibility of ever seeing them again, the idea of being so close to him and not seeing him made everything worse.

If she had more courage she might have tried swimming across like the young men from the House of Refuge on Rikers tried from time to time, but then she reminded herself that most times, if the papers told the truth, those men turned back, often stopping at North Brother for a rest before doing so, or drowned. John Cane once told her that the East River was the fastest, roughest river he ever knew, especially around North Brother. At the time, she'd been on the island only a month and thought he'd been rubbing it in, reminding her that there were no options for her. But after watching those same waters for twenty-seven months, she knew he'd just been stating the truth.

Ten o'clock in the morning was not Alfred's best hour. She thought of his long, white legs, splayed out on the starker white of their bedsheets. She thought of him standing by the window in his shorts. She thought of all the eggshells and orange peels that had probably collected in the sink for twenty-seven months, all the bottles that would need scouring. She thought of him in work clothes, making his way up the building's stairs to their flat on the sixth floor. Who talked to him in the course of a day? Where did he take his meals? She thought of him running his hand along the curve of her back to her backside and pulling her toward him.

She missed seeing human beings other than herself and John Cane, who had a strange fascination with watching her eat what he brought for her from the hospital kitchen. The night before the hearing, when he should have been worrying about getting her that iron in time, he'd brought her two slices of beef threaded with gristle, a limp salad, a roll. "The people cooking for this hospital should be lined up before a wall and shot," she said as she inspected the meat. John was the tiniest little sparrow's fart of a man, but he laughed with the strength of someone full-size. She'd been asking John to bring her flour, yeast, butter, a few vanilla beans, nothing to make a proper meal, but ingredients for bread, something she could work with in the mornings when it was too early to step outside, but he just held up his hands and ignored her. She wondered what they'd told him about her, why asking for simple ingredients always prompted him to say good-bye and hurry across the green space like he was being chased.

Mary observed two flies float in through the window and then out again. The clop of horses, a large team from the sound of it, passed on the street outside and Mr. O'Neill paused for a moment; Mary heard the door at the back of the courtroom open. She heard a man's low voice asking pardon as he tripped across knees to an empty seat. She heard the voice again, louder, and the sound of it was like a wire pulled up her spine. She felt the small hairs at the back of her neck. The stirring she heard behind her seemed to be moving closer. She felt bodies shifting. Chairs creaked. People exhaled the hot breath of annoyance.

"Sir," Judge Giegerich said, looking at the source of the disruption while holding a hand up to Mr. O'Neill. "Is this entirely necessary? There are two seats on the aisle right in front of you."

"I want to sit near Mary," the man said, and Mary turned to find herself no more than three feet from Alfred, who was dressed in a gray sack suit with the jacket over his arm, and wearing polished shoes. Borrowed, Mary thought. The shirt, too. She hoped he'd give it all back in the same condition. "Hello, Mary," Alfred said. He looked healthy, fuller in the face than he'd been when she last saw him. Eating, she hoped. Sleeping at night. Mary drew a breath, wanting to speak to him, but felt everyone in the room looking at her, the reporters poised with their pencils to paper, the others with their arms folded or their eyebrows raised. She turned back in her seat and faced the judges. Mr. O'Neill concluded his point.

"Mary," Alfred whispered. He'd gotten the seat behind her.

Mr. O'Neill cast a sidelong glance at her, a warning not to turn around.

"You look nice."

Mr. O'Neill turned abruptly and gave Alfred a stern look as one of the lawyers for the Department of Health launched into all the various reasons Mary Mallon must remain in quarantine.

Mary dropped her hand to her side and made a little wave beside the seat of her chair. He would see it if he knew to look for it. The flies flew in through the window again, and this time circled the room. Two more followed. A child's voice below the window called out the names of the newspapers he was selling. There was the sound of someone running. A cart being pushed down the hall on the other side of the courtroom doors.

"How are you?" she whispered over her shoulder. Beside her Mr. O'Neill dropped his pencil and pushed his pad of paper away.

"Oh, I don't know," Alfred whispered back.

"You look well."

"I'm better, Mary. Much better. Than before."

"Good. That's good."

They stared at each other. Mary twisted in her seat, Alfred leaned forward on his elbows. She felt hot, reckless, and wondered what would happen if she got up out of her seat and walked out of the courtroom on Alfred's arm. She noticed that he didn't look nearly as uncomfortable as everyone else in the room. His hand was cool when he reached out and covered hers.

"Will there be a break?" he asked, no longer bothering to whisper.

"Mary, please," Mr. O'Neill said.

Across the aisle, Dr. Soper coughed, and when Mary looked over at him he was looking right back at her, as if daring her to do exactly what she was tempted to do. His hair was combed back off his face and he was one of the few men in the gallery still wearing his suit jacket.

"I don't know," Mary said to Alfred. "I really don't know."

"Well, then I'll see you after. Won't I?"

Judge Erlinger interrupted the man from the Department of Health. "Miss Mallon, do you need to excuse yourself?"

Mr. O'Neill gave her a look that meant it was her last warning. If you leave this room, the look said, this is the last you'll see of me. Mary felt Alfred's hope float up behind her, wrap itself around her shoulders, and pull her toward the door. They would send guards with her, she knew. Without looking at the judges or at Soper, Mary turned and faced the front of the room.

"No, sir," Mary said. "He's an old friend."

A titter went up in the gallery and Mary put her hand to her left eye.

"Go on," the judge said to the lawyer who'd been speaking.

On the other side of the room, in the very back row, a reporter for the *Examiner* noted that the Germ Woman seemed upset. Was she crying? Was she scratching her face like a cat? He leaned forward in his seat, tried to get a better angle. Crying would go over. Crying made sense. He watched her bring her fingertips to her eye and then back to the table and felt his body flinch. He opened his notebook. "Germ woman tearful through proceedings, careless with bodily fluids even in court of law."

SEVEN

Once the hearing date was set, Mr. O'Neill came to North Brother once more. They went over their strategy, and he told Mary that he wanted her to swear before the judges that she'd never cook for hire again. "It's your best chance," he said. They believed she was sick, that she was passing Typhoid Fever from her hands to the food she served. That she'd never been sick a day in her life was of no relevance.

"How can it be of no relevance?" Mary asked. The last ferry going back to the city was due to depart shortly, and she wanted to be clear with Mr. O'Neill on her position before she said good-bye. "How can I spread an illness that I've never had myself?"

"I only mean that it's of no relevance to *them*. But it's entirely relevant to our argument. It's a new theory of disease, Mary," Mr. O'Neill explained. "Dr. Soper—"

"Don't talk to me about Soper," Mary warned him. "What kind of a doctor is he anyway? I've been asking for two years and no one has explained it properly."

"He's a sanitary engineer. He—"

"A what?"

"Part of his job is to track diseases to their source. The garbage, for instance. He's done a lot of work for the Department of Sanitation. And he's been a consultant for the IRT since it opened. Remember when everyone was worried about breathing microscopic steel shavings? They called him. He was already making a name for himself, but finding you has made his reputation."

"That's why I'm here, isn't it? So he can make his name?"

"Mary," Mr. O'Neill sighed. "Things could be worse for you. You have a private cottage. You have the freedom to move about the island."

"An island the size of a park. Where everyone I meet shrinks away from me."

"It could be worse."

"Well, yes, Mr. O'Neill. You're absolutely correct. I could be dead, I suppose."

Of the many witnesses called the morning of the hearing, a few surprised Mary. Most were people who worked for the Department of Health, or who worked at labs scattered across the city, and who canceled out one another with their opposing views of her case. Half thought that since Mary was a healthy person and had never shown any symptom of the disease she was accused of passing on to so many, the city had no right to imprison her. Others felt just as strongly that it was precisely because Mary showed no symptoms that she must be kept in quarantine for life. "Think of the innocent," urged a doctor named Stamp whom Mary had never seen before. "No one will think to avoid her in the streets, no one will hesitate from inviting her into his home. Seeing her good health and her experience, what would stop her from being hired to cook in a good house? The Bowen child was only nine years old when she died of Typhoid Fever."

Mary had hoped that Elizabeth Bowen's death was one more thing Dr. Soper had made up, wanting to make her situation worse. It had seemed too convenient to their cause. But Mr. O'Neill confirmed it was true, and Mary supposed he had no reason to lie. And now there was an unfamiliar doctor on the stand confirming that truth. Mary remembered the quiet girl who read books and listened to her governess and preferred her bedroom and the parlor to the fresh air outside. Sometimes she came downstairs to see what Mary was making in the kitchen, and a few times Mary had let her dip her finger in a sauce, or take a stewed apple out of a pot with a spoon. One time, Elizabeth asked Mary why she wasn't married and when Mary told her it was because she didn't feel like it, Elizabeth said she'd marry Mary in an instant if she'd been a boy.

Then she said, "Is it really because you don't feel like it? Or is it because you haven't anyone to marry?"

"Aren't you bold!" Mary said. "How would you like to pick up someone else's socks all day long?"

Elizabeth made a face.

"Isn't it better to earn wages?"

"Yes," Elizabeth said, entirely convinced.

"And don't forget," Mary told her, "if I were a married woman, I probably wouldn't be here making your supper."

The first sign that Elizabeth was sick came when she wandered into the kitchen and announced that she was tired. Mary had looked carefully at the girl and thought of Tobias Kirkenbauer.

On the day Mary was taken, the girl had been upstairs, sleeping, her governess watching over her. She'd had the fever, yes, Mary remembered that well. She'd wanted to tell them the best way to help her, the best times to put her in the tub, the coolest cottons to wear next to her skin. She'd sent up a bowl of beef broth to give the girl energy, but they didn't want to listen to her, and sent the broth back down with Frank. She wanted to see the girl for herself, but once the family called the doctor they closed the girl's door to all of the staff except for the governess, and when the governess became ill they had the doctor tend to her as well.

One of the reporters had gotten Bette to talk, and Bette told him that Mr. and Mrs. Bowen loved throwing dinner parties more than anything else in the world, and now they were afraid that no one would ever want to come to their home again. According to Bette, Mrs. Bowen vowed that every domestic she hired from now on would be a Swede or a German, because they were more impeccable than every other race. When the reporter asked what Bette thought of Mrs. Bowen's opinion of Germans and Swedes, Bette agreed that it was probably true. She was fired within an hour of the paper landing on Mr. Bowen's desk.

Since the Bowens didn't want to talk, didn't want to even admit in court that they'd welcomed such a woman into their home, that they'd eaten her filthy food and become sick because of it, Dr. Soper interviewed their friends and neighbors instead, and once one of the reporters caught wind that Soper had been talking to the Bowens' neighbors, so did that reporter. It was printed in the *Evening Sun* that the Germ Woman had too many ideas about herself, and because Mrs. Bowen didn't tolerate her attitude, the Germ Woman infected her on purpose. The stories claimed that Mary was resistant to some of the ways of good Christian households, and purposely defied them by meeting strange men on corners.

Mr. O'Neill made a point of addressing the main rumors that were printed in the 1907 papers, because those would be the details the judges would recall. How can I be resistant to Christianity when I'm a Catholic? Mary demanded of Mr. O'Neill. Tell me that, please. And the man I met once on the corner was a stranger only to them, not to me.

Mary shared with Mr. O'Neill the observation she'd made ages ago, that all the great houses of New York City are the same. They are headed by women who should have been male, and should have been ministers, women who go down to the employment agency in their white gloves to look around like they are in a brothel, discussing terms with the madam while each whore to be hired looks on. Then when the terms are agreed upon, instead of directing the cook to the kitchen or the laundress to the laundry, every lady gives a speech about joining a Christian home.

"The first thing they ask is whether I'm churchgoing. You'd think it would be something to do with cooking, but no, they want to know whether I get myself to a church on Sundays. Do you think the right answer is 'Yes'?" Mary asked Mr. O'Neill, who listened and waited without showing any indication of what he thought. "Well, it isn't. Experience taught me that the better answer is 'No.' This gives the lady a chance to instruct a new hire on the beneficence of Our Lord. They all say they want a good cook, but what they want even more is a worthy project."

"What has this to do with anything?" Mr. O'Neill asked. "We

were talking about rumors we'll need to address one by one when we're in front of the judges."

"What does it—? It has everything to do with everything we've been talking about! Don't you see? They—"

"Yes?"

Mary thought to tell him again about the hat, but remembered she'd long since given up on making that point. "Look, if you don't see, you don't see. I wasn't a project for them. I refused to be. I was there to cook as well as I could—and I was damn good at it—but at thirty-seven I was past the project stage." She went along with it in previous employments, but that time, with Mrs. Bowen, a mood took her. The first time Mrs. Bowen brought up Our Lord, Mary laughed, and said He hadn't made it downtown in years.

"Oh, Mary," Mrs. Bowen had said.

There was also the imbroglio about the food cooperatives just a few days after confronting Mrs. Bowen with the twin to her own hat. Mrs. Bowen found Mary in the kitchen to tell her that she and a few of the other ladies had decided to organize their cooks into groups on a trial basis. Together, the cooks would learn the new French methods and more exotic cuisines that she and the other ladies would decide on.

"The idea is to be together," Mrs. Bowen said, "and learn from one another, and it would be a help to you, wouldn't it, having other cooks to work alongside instead of just being here by yourself?"

Mary went to the church hall on Sixty-Fourth Street to meet the other cooks, and saw that there were only two others. They had the whole place to themselves and their conversation echoed in the vastness of the empty, wood-paneled room; it bounced off the many droplets of glass hanging from the chandelier. The back room of this hall featured a state-of-the-art kitchen that sat empty most nights of the week except for Saturdays, when the church held socials for its parishioners. The kitchen had ceramic double-pot sinks, a zinc-lined icebox, plenty of work space. The three cooks were charged with making a meal for six families. It was to be like that just on Mondays and Tuesdays, for a start. One of the cooks, Clare, seemed to know more than the other two and informed Mary that when they finished up Mary was supposed to deliver a meal to the Compton family on Sixty-First Street on her way back to the Bowens'. They were to follow Clare's direction because she had more training in the French method than the other two.

"So I'm now cook for the Bowens and the Comptons?"

"I don't think we're meant to see it that way," said Ida, the third cook. "I think we're to see it as the three of us cooking enough of a meal to do for six families. Not you have these two, or you your two, and so on. You see?"

"And where are the cooks for the other families?" Mary didn't see. She usually considered herself the brightest in any group, but the Bowen girl had been feeling poorly and she was distracted by it. Again and again she'd tried to get up to the girl's room, and again and again she was barred. No one had yet mentioned the word *Typhoid*.

"The other cooks were scaled back," said Clare. "Told they are needed only Wednesday on."

"So," Mary said, like she was waking up from a dream, "we cook here as a group and deliver the food to all these families. That way six families get fed for the price of three cooks instead of six cooks."

The three looked at one another.

"For the purpose of saving money?" Mary said. It didn't seem like the right answer, but there couldn't be any other.

"There's something like this happening on the West Side," Ida said. "I have a friend. Her employer calls it a cooks' cooperative. It's cheaper for them, and she says that the idea is that after a while we won't work for one particular family anymore. We'll be asked to leave our rooms. Then we'll have to get rooms elsewhere and commute to the place we are to cook just like any other day cook or common laborer."

"We won't do this," Mary said to the other cooks. And that night, for the first and last time in her life, Mary intentionally ruined good food, and talked the other two into doing the same. They overcooked the tenderloins. They boiled the asparagus until it was stringy mush. They withheld salt from the potatoes and put it on the cobblers instead.

"I hope it turned out well," Mary said to Mr. and Mrs. Bowen when she served them later. "I'm not used to having to transport my dishes. It's best, you see, straight from the oven to the table."

"Could you not choose a dish, Mary, that would support being transported?" Mr. Bowen asked, as he probed the meat with the tine of his fork.

"Of course," Mary said, bowing her head. "We could limit ourselves to just a few dishes that we know would work."

"Limit?" Mrs. Bowen asked, and pushed her plate away.

Once Elizabeth got sick, and they realized it was Typhoid Fever, there was no more mention of cooking in the church hall, or of cooking at all for that matter. Mary made bread and a thin soup that would keep, and spent most of her hours

hauling ice up the stairs and the empty bucket back down—
the only helpful thing they would allow her to do. They kept
the block in the kitchen sink and Mary put Frank to work
charging at it with a butcher knife until it came to pieces,
little ones to suck, larger ones to serve as floes in the tubs
upstairs where the family bathed, and the single tub downstairs where the servants took turns. There was an ice short-
age in 1907, and ice was very dear, but Mary ordered blocks
on credit and hoped they wouldn't ask for a settlement of
their books before the girl recovered.

In their first interview, Mr. O'Neill asked Mary why death
didn't bother her, why she didn't notice it following her everywhere she went. Mary didn't even know where to look for a
starting point. After so many months on North Brother, so
many years since setting foot in Dobbs Ferry, Mary could still
feel the silk of Tobias Kirkenbauer's curls when he passed
under her hand, and the way he settled himself on her hip, his
arm slung around her neck, as if he had no fear in the world
as long as she was holding him. How could anyone think she
didn't notice, or that it didn't bother her? No one in any court
of law, no man in any room, knows the desperation of squinting through dim light and seeing a baby's cheeks inflamed,
feeling the hot hands, the eyes gone flat with fever. A twist
came in Mary's belly that was the beginning of a prayer. Back
in 1899, when little Tobias Kirkenbauer wouldn't open his
mouth to eat, who pressed the creamy water from the boiled
oats and spooned it into his mouth? I did, Mary reminded
herself. And he held on longer than he would have if Mary

hadn't been there. But they didn't know about 1899. To them, 1899 was not on the record books.

And if it was really true that Elizabeth Bowen died, then of course that bothered her. Of course. The girl was only a child, and deserved no badness.

EIGHT

When Mary was a child, her grandmother told her that as long as she kept the piss pot clean and her apron white, there would be no mistress who would turn up her nose at her. It was over her grandmother's turf fire that Mary learned how to make griddle cakes and brown bread, where she first browned bacon and boiled beef, made salmon with butter and cream, eel and trout. It was her grandmother who taught her the best way to tuck the turnips and potatoes around the meat, and it was her grandmother who saved enough to buy Mary a one-way passage to America when Mary was fourteen. There would be food in America that Mary had never seen, but the rules were the same: cook it right, draw out what's good, don't be afraid of putting things together. Her grandmother's sister, Kate Brown, would give Mary a place to live, help her find work in New York. "Send her," Kate's letter back to Mary's grandmother had read. "I'd love to have her."

Mary's first impression of America when she arrived in Castle Garden in 1883 was that it wasn't a kind place. Soon after she had steadied herself, her bag secure in her hand, she was hustled into one grim line after another, like one mangy cow in a herd. Other ships had also arrived that day and she waited and watched as the kaleidoscope of colors kept shifting: green aprons, yellow head scarves, red tassels brushing the ground, dotted ribbon pulled through belt loops to hold up short pants. The American men were the ones with the broad faces, and derby hats pulled low. She imagined a welcoming party, but instead one ugly man shoved a card in her face and another, even uglier, braced Mary's head with his large hand and told her to hold still while he used a buttonhook to lift her left eyelid and then her right. "Trachoma," he said. "Highly contagious." Mary didn't understand the first word and barely heard the others, locked as she was in a posture of fear. When he finished and announced her eyes clean, she noticed that the man wiped the hook on a towel draped over the railing before moving on to his next victim.

Paddy Brown, Aunt Kate's husband, met Mary when she'd completed all the lines and gotten all her stamps. "Mary Mallon?" he said when she approached the only man left in the waiting area that fit his description. "Follow me." She followed him down a flight of stairs to the sunshine outside. They passed through the gates of what seemed like fortress walls, and then she was on the outside, on the streets of New York City. They climbed aboard a trolley drawn by a pair of glum-looking horses. When they came to the end of the track, they got out and made their way on foot. Mary struggled to keep up with the old man, who with his hunched shoulders and his badger's head kept disappearing into the crowd. "Where is this?" she asked, hoping conversation would slow his pace. "Where are we now?" He raised a callused finger and pointed roughly at a street sign that read "Thirty-Seventh

Street." Finally, as the crowds thinned, and she followed him onto Tenth Avenue, Paddy Brown loosened his stride.

"Wait here a minute," he said just before ducking into a store with a tuft of wheat carved on the sign outside.

"How much farther?" Mary asked.

"Just two doors down."

Mary dropped her bag to the sidewalk and tried to get a feel for what waited for her, but two doors down looked the same as every door they'd passed for the last several blocks: dark and plain. Rusted staircases stuck to the faces of every building, and from their railings hung a variety of sheets and blankets. Where home had been full of greens and blues in summer, oranges and reds in winter, New York was the same color wherever she looked: the muddy avenues, the muck-splattered carriages, the gray shingles, the faded red brick, the coal smoke that hung in the air and blurred the outlines of everything. The buildings were tall—five, six stories. When Paddy came out of the shop with a loaf of bread, she pointed at the bedding hanging above their heads and asked him why. "Too heavy for the lines," he said.

"I see," she said, though she didn't see. She looked forward to Aunt Kate, and tried to comprehend that somewhere inside one of these buildings that showed their shame to the world lived her nana's sister. She searched herself for the tug of home.

"How was the journey, anyhow?" Paddy asked then, looking at her for the first time since meeting her.

The girl in the berth below Mary's had died when they were ten days at sea. In twenty-one days, Mary watched seven bodies slide into the sea, all wrapped in sailcloth and sewn tight. The girl was dropped on the same day as another person, a man by the size of him, and when she fell through the air between the deck and the water, her body bent at the hips, Mary wondered if they'd double-checked, if they were absolutely beyond-a-doubt sure. Someone in the crowd remarked that it was only the Grace of God that would keep the rest of them out of the water, and someone else said Amen, and Mary wondered why God would grant any of them that Grace and not those who'd already been thrown away. It wasn't the first time Mary noticed that God had a haphazard approach to things.

"Was it very rough?" Paddy asked.

"No, it was grand," Mary said and looked back at the garbage lining the street, the haggard people rushing about on the sidewalks.

Mary's aunt had more welcome for her, and scolded her husband thoroughly for not carrying Mary's bag. She'd prepared a rich lamb stew with carrots and potatoes that went cold before them because every time Mary went to put a spoonful in her mouth, Aunt Kate asked another question about a person from home. Paddy and Aunt Kate had no children and were too old to remedy that fact.

"Well, now," Aunt Kate said when Mary had finished giving her the news and they'd taken five minutes to eat what was on their plates. "First thing is to find you good work. Then we'll see. What can you do?"

"I can cook," Mary told her.

"Cook what? Spuds? A bit of ham? What else can you do?"

"I want to cook."

"Mary, love, they have stoves in America you've never seen the likes of."

"I can practice on yours."

"This!" Aunt Kate laughed. "This is nothing. This is a stone's

throw from the turf and the open fire. There are kitchens in
some of these houses that have stoves wider than—" Aunt Kate
stretched her arms as wide as she could to either side. "They have
stoves with four burners, two ovens."

"I can learn, can't I?"

"That's true, I suppose." Kate regarded Mary with a smile.
"Patience, love. It's very good to see you."

After giving Mary a few weeks to settle in, to get accustomed
to the pace of the streets and the chaos of the pedestrians, the
horses, the freight train that plowed along Eleventh Avenue and
didn't stop for anything; after showing her the spider's web of
clotheslines hidden behind the tenements, and the tub for washing; after letting Mary get used to her cot next to the kitchen
table and showing her how to put coal in the stove, and empty
the ashes; after taking Mary to meet yet another neighbor who
wanted to know her business; and after learning that no one
understood her when she spoke except for other Irish and teach-
ing her how to enunciate, speak slowly, try to talk more like an
American, Kate finally announced it was time to go to the agency
and see what kind of job Mary could get for herself. Mary had
just turned fifteen. Kate told her everything she should say, and
made her practice at the table after Paddy had gone to bed. She
had Mary sit across from her with her hands folded, and then
she asked questions about the jobs she'd had in New Jersey and
Connecticut. Mary was to describe how she was an accomplished
cook and had cooked for families in Ireland before leaving. "You
are twenty years old. Same birthday, just subtract five years from
the year."

"But what if they ask where? What if they ask me to describe New Jersey or Connecticut?"

"They won't. But if they do, you go ahead and describe whatever you imagine. Be confident. They've probably never been there themselves."

Mary tried to speak slowly and sound older than she was, but the woman at the agency just told her in a blank tone that they'd place her as a laundress. "Are you a worker?" the woman had asked. "A real worker?"

"I'm a worker," Mary assured her.

"Report with clean clothes. Spotless. And keep your person clean at all times. Be respectful to the family and their guests, and for God's sake don't try to engage them if they don't engage you. If one of the family enters a room that you are in, simply exit as quickly as possible. You have no opinion of politics whatsoever and in fact do not follow politics of any kind. You don't read the newspapers. Do you understand, Miss Mallon?"

"Yes."

The agent handed her a folded pamphlet that repeated everything she'd just said.

"Are you religious, by the way? Catholic, I imagine."

"Catholic."

"The family has probably already assumed you're Catholic, or will when they meet you, but don't mention it yourself."

Mary didn't know what it meant to be a laundress and hoped she could prove herself and one day be allowed to cook, but she discovered in that first situation that cook and laundress are two different tracks, and a laundress never becomes a cook any more than a cook becomes a Lady. At home, they'd washed their clothes in the river and draped them on rocks to dry. Aunt Kate washed her clothes in a basin, twisted them roughly when she pulled them out, and hung them on the clothesline that stretched across the tops of the outdoor privies to the back wall of another tenement. The night before Mary began, Aunt Kate showed her the little square ounce of Reckitt's Blue she kept in the pantry, and explained to her about using it for the final rinse to take out any hint of yellow. Fine clothes needed more careful treatment and she warned Mary that if she encountered anything with a lace collar or cloth-covered buttons, to go over them with the sponge instead of sinking them in the tub with the rest.

The family was called Cameron, and Mary slept on a bunk in a room off the kitchen. She took her meals with the other staff. Room and board would be deducted from her wage. The woman at the agency had gone over the deductions so quickly that Mary didn't have time to calculate until she got back to Aunt Kate's, and together they realized there would be hardly anything left over. "But it's good experience," Aunt Kate said. "There's value in that as well." Paddy Brown made a low sound and shifted in front of the stove.

As the woman at the office predicted, the footman, Nathaniel, who'd been charged with greeting Mary and giving her a tour of the home, told her that she would be required to join in the evening prayers nightly. The mistress did not take her faith lightly and required her staff to approach Our Lord with the same seriousness.

"What if someone refuses?"

Nathaniel studied her face. "Try it," he suggested.

The Camerons had help that cooked, help that cleaned the house, did the laundry, watched the children, taught the children, tended to the grass and pots of flowers outside. When Mary had

a free moment she was supposed to help Martha, who was forever running an oiled cloth over the furniture, up and down the
stairs, beginning every day where she'd ended the last and doing
everything over again so that no speck of dust ever had a chance
to land. The expression she wore on her face was one of com-
bat. She was engaged in a battle that offered no respite, and even
while eating lunch at the small kitchen table with the rest of the
staff, she was squinting over their heads, peering into corners,
and tilting her chin to see in a different light what lurked there.
It was the cleanest place Mary had ever been. The newspapers
Mr. Cameron left open on the table in the sitting room talked of
poor ventilation and crowding in the cities, toxic odors that came
from standing water and horse manure, but the Cameron home
was so protected from anything like that, so unlike Aunt Kate's or
the rooms of any of the families Mary had visited on Aunt Kate's
block where there was no place to keep the garbage except piled
on the curb outside where it would stink until the Department
of Street Cleaning came by with their carts, where every person
who walked through the door of their building tracked the mud
or ash or excrement from the street up the stairs, through the
halls, into their own rooms, that Mary started to feel that she was
also waging a war, they all were, and Mary's particular front was
at the collars of shirts and blouses, the hems of skirts and trousers.
According to the papers, the source of every disease suffered by
every New Yorker could be found in a garbage pile on the Lower
East Side. Mary heard the word *miasma* and the next time she
went home she asked Aunt Kate what it meant. Ever since then
she imagined the city streets seeded with invisible landmines, and
the landmines were these toxic clouds, miasmas, that floated up
from every dirty thing left to fester at the city's curbs. She tried

not to inhale when she made her way to and from the streetcar, or on the many occasions when the sanitation wagon skipped Aunt Kate's block. She felt safer at the Camerons, where all day long, six days a week, she and the others led a coordinated campaign against dirt and disorder, and where the sanitation drivers never clicked their tongues at their horses to speed them past the door.

Every member of the staff had one day's leave per week to go home, and perhaps they weren't as careful when they were back on their own territory. One Monday morning, the Camerons' long-time cook returned to work with the telltale bull's neck but pretended nothing was wrong. She just slammed pots and pans and began the ritual of the water with her chin tilted toward heaven, gasping for air. Mary and the others hid her as well as they could, but Mrs. Cameron liked to come down to the kitchen once in a while to discuss the evening meal and she chose that Monday to tell the cook, in person, that the family was bored of beef roasts, and chops, too, for that matter. Could the cook come up with a trout or a flounder on a Monday?

"Oh," Mrs. Cameron said when she saw the cook's neck, and retreated to the hall. She put a hand up to her own throat. "You're ill."

The cook couldn't speak, so her assistant—the girl who rinsed and chopped vegetables like they were criminals and her knife a weapon—spoke for her. "She's just after telling me they have standing water in the air shaft where she lives and on Saturday when we parted she expected the water to be stinking. This morning she told me, yes, it was fierce stinking and no one in her building can keep a window to the air shaft open with the smell of it. It'll go on until a dry stretch. So she thinks she breathed up that odor in spite of the closed windows."

Just that morning, on her way from Tenth Avenue, Mary had to hold her breath as the trolley rolled by a horse stable, where on Sunday nights the men who cleaned the stalls pushed out all the horse shit and old hay. Next to the stable was Weiss's bakery, and before dawn on Monday mornings the Weisses splashed out all the old milk that hadn't sold the week before. They threw it over the shit pushed out by the neighboring stable. As the sun rose, the milk soured and infected the air. Often, they tossed old eggs, too, and the carcasses of chickens, and crates, boxes, papers, packaging, overflowing ash cans. The eggs bothered Mary most of all, and every time she passed on a Monday, she wondered why they didn't put them in a cake. Or give them to someone who needed them. The waste of it made her never want to buy anything there.

"Why can't she speak for herself?"

"Oh, she can," the assistant said meekly, but the cook sat down on a stool and put her head in her hands.

"You're dismissed," Mrs. Cameron said, taking another step backward. "Please go home and tend to yourself. Be in touch with the agency when you're better."

The cook showed no signs of moving as the assistant fetched her shawl and wrapped it around her shoulders. "You have money?" the girl asked, then looked around. "Could we pitch in for a fare?" Along with Mary, there were two others of the house staff present. Mary slid her hand into her apron pocket and closed her fist around the dime and five pennies resting there. Mr. Cameron always left a tip when she starched his shirts, and it was a game to find it. Sometimes he left it in one of his shoes, twisted into a hanky and tied off with a string. Sometimes in the pocket of one of the shirts. Sometimes he came upon Mary while she was working, sneaked up behind, and dropped it into her apron pocket. Mary would jump at the sudden tug of the money and he'd be there behind her, smiling. It was something, Mary understood, she wasn't to tell the others.

Everyone put coins on the counter. Mary's quick fingers separated out three pennies and she added hers to the lot.

"Well," the assistant said when she came back. Mary could tell she'd already elevated herself to head cook. "I'll need to go to the fish market. One of you will need to start—"

"Pardon me," Nathaniel said, breathless from running down the stairs. "Missus says you're to go, too. And that if any of the rest of you feel ill, you should do the right thing and excuse yourself."

"Me?" the assistant asked. "But I feel fine!"

Nathaniel shrugged. "And the rest of us are to take fifteen minutes to scrub the kitchen again."

After the scouring, Mr. Cameron appeared in the kitchen and asked who could cook a meal until the office sent over another woman.

"I can," Mary said, taking a silent survey of the fruit and vegetables on the counter, the cheese and milk she'd seen in the icebox. Mr. Cameron ignored her.

Martha could not change positions and was off limits. "Jane?" he asked the children's tutor, but she said she'd never cooked a thing in her life.

"I can cook," Mary said again.

Mr. Cameron frowned. "Mary, then."

And so Mary took off her laundering whites and put on the cook's apron instead. After that first meal—baked whitefish with leeks and tomatoes, and a vanilla cake for dessert—Mr. Cameron teased that they would cancel their request to the agency for a replacement cook and instead ask for a replacement laundress.

He took on the habit of having his morning coffee in the kitchen before heading out to work, and then, after one morning when Mrs. Cameron came looking for him and demanded to know what exactly he thought he was doing, he stopped. And Mary was left alone. A week later, the new cook arrived, and Mary was sent back to the pile of muslins and linens that had been waiting for her. I will leave this position, she decided. I will go to a new agency and tell them a history as cook, and they will believe me. And if they don't believe me, I'll go to another agency. She took out her small brush, her square of starch. She rubbed the dry patches on her hands.

NINE

There were times, over on North Brother, with John Cane staring at the way she spread jam over a piece of toast and bit off the corner, when Mary felt like none of it was real. Even two years on, the doctors still spoke to her like she was a child, and she tried to find new ways of reminding them that she'd served food to people who once dined with the President of the United States of America. And after tasting what she'd prepared, they looked up from their plates to study her more closely, knowing she was not entirely what she seemed. Beneath the plain attire and the cook's hands, behind the thick Irish accent and the working-class posture of exhaustion, they saw something else: a level of taste, an understanding of what those seated at the table were really after—a challenge to the palate, a meal to be enjoyed and not just consumed.

Mary wanted Mr. O'Neill to know that there were some doctors who had an unhealthy obsession with her bathroom habits, far beyond the scope of the case. "They'd watch me go, if I let them," she told him. Two years earlier she wouldn't even have been able to say that much, wouldn't have even been able to make a glancing reference to "going." They could make all the insinuations and comments they wanted about Alfred, and the rooms they shared, why they weren't married, what kind of woman this made her. None of it bothered her as much as the discussion of her bathroom habits. Shortly before Mary met Mr. O'Neill, one of the nurses who came to collect her samples joked that she envied Mary. "You've got your cottage on the water, free rein of the island, no balance to be paid to the grocer, no child hanging off you, no husband to face at night, no younger brothers to put through school. There's more than a few who'd trade with you." The nurse said this as Mary placed on the floor the usual glass canister that contained her sample, mixed in a solution that looked like water. The nurse handed her a second canister for her urine. Mary usually tried to shroud the contents of the canisters with paper or a napkin, wrapping them separately at first and then together, like a package that needed a bow, and doing so allowed her to pretend for a moment that what was happening was not really happening. But that day, because of the nurse's comment, Mary shoved the jars in the other woman's direction without wrapping them, pushed them into her hands so roughly that the nurse fumbled, almost dropped them. The contents sloshed inside.

"Careful, Miss," the woman said.

"I'd say the same to you," Mary answered.

The doctors admitted that more than a third of the time Mary's samples came back showing no Typhoid bacilli whatsoever. And her urine came back negative 100 percent of the time. When Mr. O'Neill asked about past pressure they'd put on

Mary to submit to gallbladder surgery, they conceded that they no longer believed her gallbladder was to blame. Her intestines, perhaps. Her stomach. They weren't sure.

"Good thing you were stubborn about surgery," Mr. O'Neill said to Mary later. "It would have been for nothing." Mary had occasionally wondered why no one had mentioned her gallbladder in a long time, and now she wanted to go up to the hospital and demand an apology. They were animals. They would have risked her life for sport.

"Let it go," Mr. O'Neill said. "We'll address all of it at the right time."

He said that it was essential that they humanize her at the hearing. "Make me into a human?" Mary asked, confused.

"Well, yes. What I mean is, we have to paint your story so that anyone, no matter what their station, will sympathize. And better yet, make them afraid that they could end up like you."

"So in acting for me they're really acting for themselves."

"Exactly. So. What were your feelings when you were told you were being brought to North Brother? Were you aware of the Tuberculosis hospital here?"

"My feelings?"

"Were you afraid? Did you even know of North Brother? Where exactly it was, for example?"

"Of course," Mary said, looking at him steadily. "Of course I knew where it was. Doesn't every person in this city know?"

Mr. O'Neill seemed about to say something but changed his mind.

"You think I don't follow a newspaper, Mr. O'Neill? Even the illiterate in this city know exactly where North Brother is. There's more to getting news than reading it in the paper. There's talking, too, isn't there? Or did you assume we don't talk about the same topics you talk about? Wasn't the *General Slocum* disaster only five years ago?"

She did not admit to Mr. O'Neill that she'd never heard of North Brother before June 1904, when the *General Slocum* burned. But forever after, she thought of those people whenever an errand brought her near *Kleindeutschland*, little Germany, where most of the people on the *General Slocum* that day were from. More than one thousand people had burned to death or drowned, and Mary thought of that number when she looked out over the East River now—men, women, children all bobbing in the rough water, pushed back and forth and under. A story went around in the weeks after the tragedy that the manufacturer of the life preservers had slipped in iron bars to make the weight minimums, that the captain and crew had abandoned the ship and its passengers and taken a tug from North Brother back to Manhattan, refusing to look at those in the water who cried out for their help. Inmates from the House of Refuge on Rikers swam into the water to help people, and then swam back to their prison that night.

Mary often went down to the spot where survivors had stumbled ashore, sometimes imagining that she'd been on board, that she'd been one of the women who jumped into the river and made it to North Brother, and when she wasn't looking—occupied, perhaps, by the sound of her own breathing, distracted by her gratitude for her life, her back turned, her ears closed—she'd been left behind and forgotten.

The hearing would not be a quick one; that much was clear within an hour. As the sun rose higher and heated the odors of the room,

Mary felt weaker. She watched sweat run down the sides of Mr. O'Neill's face. Judge Erlinger's eyes had begun to close. One doctor, instead of answering anything specific about her case, lectured exclusively on the bleeding of horses, and how it was no longer necessary to bleed a horse to death in order to obtain the maximum amount of serum to make vaccines. "Take Diphtheria, for example," he went on. "There have been several cases where the horse's reaction is so strong that death came too quickly, and the glass cannulae used to collect the blood were broken in the horse's fall and destroyed."

A murmur went up among the other doctors. Mary leaned over and asked Mr. O'Neill why they were talking about horses.

"The best thing," the man went on, "is to always bleed from the carotid vein, and not the jugular. The jugular will weaken the horse too quickly, and in most cases results in less blood collected. But even more important, the use of supports must"—he banged his fist on the chair for emphasis—"become standard practice across the labs. A large male horse can be suspended with two stout ropes, one passing behind the forelegs and one in front of the hind legs. Once the support is in place, the cannula should be inserted into the artery. By this method it's possible to obtain five usable gallons from a single horse."

"And where do you stand on the Mallon case?" the DOH lawyer urged the doctor.

"In terms of Typhoid, I think the answer lies in widespread milk pasteurization, cleaner water, better education on personal hygiene. Typhoid is entirely preventable."

"Should she be let back into society or not?"

"I—" the doctor faltered, looked over at Mary. "It's my opinion . . . that she should not."

One Department of Health official asked the judges to consider what exactly motivated Mary to take the job uptown at the Bowen residence in the first place. Did she harbor a resentment of some sort against the upper classes? Did she resent the Bowens in particular? Perhaps because of the food cooperative Mrs. Bowen had attempted to organize? Without waiting for answers, the official then sat back as if he'd just put the final piece in the puzzle.

"I worked for the Bowens because of what they paid me," Mary whispered urgently to Mr. O'Neill, who bellowed an objection. It was illogical, Mr. O'Neill pointed out. A woman can't be accused of lacking the ability to comprehend her affliction at one moment, and then accused of wielding it like a weapon the next.

"And why did her employment with the Warrens end in Oyster Bay? Why did she not continue to work for them once they returned to the city?"

"Because it was a temporary job," Mary whispered to Mr. O'Neill, but he shushed her. He'd asked her the same question during their preparation meeting and already knew the answer. The Warren job was never meant to be permanent. Their regular cook was to resume her position in Manhattan once they returned from Oyster Bay.

Mary studied the judges' faces and saw doubt.

She got home from Oyster Bay on a Friday in September 1906. It was a beautiful day, and better still because she had a pocket full of money that had been pushed into her hand from a grateful Mr. Warren. Little Margaret Warren would play again, would beg ice cream off another cook, would grow up and marry and do all the things a girl should do. Her sister, her mother, the two maids, and the gardener would also live. All the family except for Mr. Warren had already returned to Manhattan, and Mary had left two of the maids drinking cold watermelon soup on the back patio. They'd hugged her good-bye together, squeezing her between them and saying again what a shock each of them got when she pushed them into an icy bath, clothes and all. They blessed her, thanked her, said they knew they wouldn't have their lives if it hadn't been for her.

She'd gotten to the station in plenty of time to catch an earlier train, but she'd written her plans to Alfred the previous week, and wanted to stay with the schedule she'd sent in case he planned on meeting her. So she sat on a bench in breezy Oyster Bay and watched a train pull in and then pull away. When she got to Grand Central Station she waited on a bench again with her bag on her lap to give Alfred a chance to find her.

After thirty minutes she pushed through the grand doors onto Forty-Second Street and began walking home. Something had come up, she decided. He didn't have time to send word. He probably had a perfectly good reason for not showing up. Because it was a Friday, every rusted fire escape in their neighborhood would be weighted down with damp cottons and thin wools in every muted shade of white, gray, brown, from Patricia Wright's careful calico to the yellowed squares of muslin Mr. Hallenan used to strain his coffee. Where twenty years earlier this had shamed her, now she took comfort in the sight and knew she was closer to home. A few tenants had gotten hold of the new round-about lines that could be extended out a window into the sky without needing to be anchored on another building or another fire escape.

The rooms Mary shared with Alfred were on the sixth floor, at the very top of the stairs. Unlike the narrow tenements of the Lower East Side, 302 East Thirty-Third was a broad building that held within the yellow brick of its exterior walls thirty-six flats. There was a central staircase wide enough for three bodies to climb the stairs side by side, and from this central stair branched two halls that reached north and south, three flats per hall, six per floor. The sixth floor saw the highest turnover, and some of the rooms stayed empty for weeks at a time. Anyone with rooms on the top floor aimed to get lower as soon as possible, but Mary liked the sixth floor. Their rooms always seemed to get better light than those on lower floors and Mary liked standing at the sink and looking out over lower rooftops. When lying in their bed she could turn her head toward the window and see nothing but blue sky.

When Mary arrived home that Friday in September, she opened the door to their rooms and was hit by the odor of linen that needed washing, rotting banana peels on the counter, the single window shut tight. The letter she'd sent to tell Alfred what time her train was due was open on the table, and she could see that he'd made an effort to flatten the folds. He might have gotten work. It happened that way sometimes: no prospects on the horizon and next thing someone comes looking for him with a tip about a company looking for a driver, or need for a man who could shovel coal.

Mary set about stripping their bed and washing the linens, but when she had everything soaking in the tub, she couldn't find any soap. She decided to run down to the grocer. Not wanting to break one of the new paper bills Mr. Warren had given her, she went to the jam jar of coins they kept by the stove for the gas meter. But there was no jam jar, no coins, and after seven weeks of missing him, of hoping he was getting on, Mary was as furious as she'd been the day she left. Sometimes—and staring at the empty space where the jam jar used to live was one of these times—Mary felt she'd tripped into a space beyond fury, a place where all of this was so astonishing that perhaps she was the one who was wrong. She took a deep breath and went over the facts: I told him to not dare touch the gas money. Do not dare, I said to him. And he looked at me like he wouldn't dream of it. His look said: the nerve of you to say that to me. I told him I'd send word when I was due home and if he could have the rooms straightened a bit. After a seven-week job I don't want to walk into a pigsty. He was insulted. And now Mary stood in the middle of the kitchen and contemplated the naked bed in the next room, the dirty plates and mugs on the sideboard. She could walk out the door with the same bag she'd just hauled from Oyster Bay, and leave him to manage the sopping bedsheets. She smiled. That would be a surprise to him.

But if he's working, Mary reminded herself, he might have needed those coins to make himself presentable. Peeling one bill from the thick fold in her pocket and leaving the rest hidden in the closet, she went down to the street to buy a cake of soap. She hoped that by the time she came back, washed the sheets, and hung them on the fire escape, Alfred would be home.

But the dinner hour came and went, and still, Alfred did not return. She went down to visit with Fran.

"And how's Alfred?" Fran asked. "Glad to have you back?"

"Oh sure," Mary had said, avoiding her friend's eye. "Of course he is." Mary knew for a fact that Fran's Robert came home for lunch on any day when he could take the full hour.

When five o'clock arrived, Mary wrapped her shawl around her shoulders and went out to look for him.

For several blocks around their building, quitting time found the streets thick with men: men rushing for streetcars, men leaning against buildings and in door frames. As Mary crossed over Thirty-Third Street she observed that even the horses were wild at quitting time. Several water wagons were heading in a line toward the stables on First, and each horse that passed bent its long muscular neck and turned a vein-threaded eye toward Mary.

Once she crossed Thirty-Fourth Street, she could see the blue door of Nation's Pub on the next block, the flag above, the pair of potted plants that welcomed patrons inside. She walked by the wide door without slowing her pace, granting herself only a small sideward glance as if the place meant nothing to her, no more than any other business that lined the avenue. The late-summer afternoon brought a cool breeze, and Mary pulled the sleeves of her sweater over her hands. Her knuckles felt like two rows of rough stones.

When Mary passed Nation's again, she took a better look. The window next to the door was clouded, but yes, she thought she saw him, slumped at the end of the bar. Yes, that was the posture he would have after so long sitting. She had no plan except to pass by and confirm that he was there, that he was safe, that he wasn't in any trouble. Once she found him, she planned on going back to their rooms to wait. Or to pack her things and leave. Or to go about her business and sleep, pretending there was no Alfred, and that she was obligated to no one but herself.

But on her third pass, the bright blue door swung open, and a man stepped out. Mary looked past the open door at the man she thought was Alfred—a blond man, she saw now, heavyset, his nose a bit like Alfred's, yes, but nothing else. Then the door slammed shut. He's told them about me, Mary supposed. Our arrangement. Might have said how much it suits him. Might have had a laugh about it. He was cruel when he drank, but then when he drank more he was kind again. It all depended on the dose, and sometimes Mary hoped that if he had to drink at all that he would drink past cruelty and into the Alfred she loved, the one who loved her and told her that he would never have lived so long without her, and my God, she was beautiful. Did she know? Why didn't he tell her all the time? Just one or two drinks past kind Alfred was helpless Alfred, and this was the Alfred she feared she'd meet later on that night. There was no arguing with helpless Alfred, no high horse to ride out into the city streets and away from him. Helpless Alfred would get home around three or four in the morning and would call for her from the bottom of the stairs. One by one, doors would open from the first floor to the sixth. He'd sit on the very first step, head in his hands, and shout for her without pause, and when every person who had a door onto the stairs woke up from his shouting, they'd shout for her, too.

"Where were you?" he'd ask when she finally ran down the six flights. She used to bother with tying her robe, but not anymore. "Why didn't you hear me?"

"I was all the way upstairs," she'd say in a whisper, hoping to shush him. "I was asleep. I didn't hear you."

"Jesus Christ, Mary," Mr. Hallenan on the first floor would say. "Where the hell were you? Why didn't you hear him?" Mr. Hallenan didn't care who in the world saw the graying hair on his belly.

Then Alfred would put an arm around her shoulder, his other

hand on the railing, and she'd haul him up the six flights. In their rooms, she'd take off his shoes, his stinking socks, his pants and shorts. Sometimes he'd realize he was naked and he'd cry: long ugly sobs full of phlegm that shocked and embarrassed her every time. Sometimes, when she was lucky, he just sank into their bed and went to sleep. The worst nights, even worse than when they fought or when she had to strip him, were the nights when she finally got him upstairs and he sat by the window for an hour or so, looking at the quiet below, before staggering to his feet and going out again. More than any other kind of night, those were the ones that drove her to the agency to ask for another situation, one that would keep her away full-time, somewhere far away, where the train back to their rooms would be too long, too expensive for a day's journey. It was a night when he came back home only to go out again that had driven her to Oyster Bay.

Standing outside Nation's Pub, she tried to think of what else she could do to pass the time and stop herself from wanting to see him, but it was no good. She needed to know what he'd made of his weeks away from her. And she needed to know how he was faring. A body could not hold up long against such an assault, and all summer long, before leaving for Oyster Bay, she'd observed him becoming weaker, his pants drooping around his hips, his broad chest narrowing inside his shirt. His face had taken on a gray-green tinge, and the skin at his neck had loosened, become slack.

"Sometimes I think about when we met," she'd said to him on that early-August morning when they last fought. Even in a weakened state he was no fool and knew the ultimate point she was driving at. Once upon a time, not so long ago, he'd worked, he'd been strong, he'd been handsome. Years ago, she had an employer who held back two weeks' wages because he thought she was in league with a tutor who'd stolen jewelry from his wife, and Alfred had gone directly over to that grand, glossy black door on West Eighteenth Street, the entrance the family and their guests used, and put the man straight. When Alfred came back and handed over her wages, Mary was so relieved that she sobbed into her hands like the kind of woman she considered her opposite.

"What could you have said to him that I didn't already say?" she'd asked, looking at the bills fanned out on the table.

"Nothing," Alfred had said, and then grinned. "I guess I had a different way of putting it."

She'd been over the story before, hoping to shame him into seeing the difference between now and then, hoping to light the fire that would drive him back to the way he was. On that morning in August, the day she left for Oyster Bay, Alfred wouldn't even humor her.

"Leave then, why don't you, if you're so disgusted. Go on."

Mary knew women were supposed to be the softer sex, a species so warm and nurturing that God granted them the gift of bearing children, caring for them, looking after a home, nursing the sick to health. But sometimes Alfred made her so angry that all the warmth went out of her body and instead her thoughts became murderous, if she managed to have thoughts at all.

Mary pushed open the door to Nation's and took one step inside. One man glanced up and then nudged the man next to him, who nudged the next man, and so on. There was a plate of crackers, cheese squares, and a few slices of bread on a table near the back, and Mary's quick eye told her they'd been out since morning; the cheese had gone hard at the edges. The man behind the bar tucked his apron into his belt and came around. "I'm sorry, but—"

"I'm looking for Alfred Briehof. Have you seen him? He hasn't been home."

"Jesus," one of the men at the bar muttered. "Briehof has a home?"

"Are you . . . ?"

"I'm his—"

"You're Mary."

"I am."

"He left a while ago. Did you check with the chestnut man on Thirtieth Street?"

"Was he . . ." Mary hoped he wouldn't make her say it. "All right?"

The bartender shrugged. "He was all right, I guess."

Mary tried to decide what to do.

"I think you should go home," the bartender said as if hearing her thoughts. "He had that mopey look that means he's homeward bound."

What do you know about his looks, Mary wanted to ask. I'll kill him, she vowed. I'll stand behind the door and get him before he even enters the room. Fran had killed a man in Jersey City a few years back. Robert was on nights at the time and the man had broken into their rooms, was standing at the foot of her bed, and she'd grabbed her husband's spare gun from under the pillow—the one he'd left for her for exactly that sort of crisis—and shot him dead.

"Thank you," Mary said to the bartender, and left.

What Alfred did when Mary was away was never clear to her. She wanted to ask Jimmy Tiernan, who lived on the third floor and went to Nation's himself sometimes, but whenever she thought she had her chance, Patricia Tiernan appeared over his shoulder and gave her the daggers. Fran didn't have a door on the stairs and claimed to never hear Alfred on the nights he howled. Joan had a mind the size of a thimble, and all that thimble contained were thoughts of future babies she'd have with her husband. Once, when Joan mentioned that they'd been married going on six years and hoping all that time, Mary had snapped, "My God, Joan, do you need the formula written down for you? Do you know what goes in to making a baby?" But as she watched Joan close her eyes against her question, keeping one long, delicate finger on the lid of the coffeepot, Mary realized Joan would never have a baby. "I've heard it takes a long time for some women," she offered by way of apology. Joan must have forgiven her because she continued to wave Mary inside whenever she caught her passing.

It was useless to ask Alfred himself, because according to him he never drank more than he could handle, and when Mary was gone he never drank at all; he only worked or tried to get work. The longest she'd been gone without returning home was three months, but even on the jobs where she was close enough to get home for the odd Sunday, one day was not enough to see what was happening. Who helped him up the stairs when he called and called but never got any answer? Not Mr. Hallenan, who hated both Alfred and Mary. Not Jimmy Tiernan, who wouldn't be allowed out. Maybe he got up the stairs himself. Or maybe he slept wherever he landed. Or maybe he told the truth, that when Mary was gone he didn't drink at all. Maybe that behavior was something he saved for her, a punishment, perhaps, for always leaving.

*

In some of the homes where Mary had worked, the families had pots and pans by the dozen, sinks with two chambers, iceboxes that could keep a hock of ham frozen for a whole summer. In the rooms she and Alfred shared, they had one skillet, one tall stockpot for boiling, and one small saucepan. But those three vessels were enough for two, enough for the sort of meals Alfred liked most.

That evening, in case he would return, Mary walked downtown from Nation's door and then east, to the butcher on Second Avenue that stayed open until six. When she finally got there and smelled the raw meat combined with the sawdust on the floor and the fresh herbs on the counter for those who liked to take home their cuts already seasoned, she knew that he would come home.

Back in her own silent kitchen, she cleared off the cluttered table and used it to prep. She filled the pot with water. She rubbed the small pork tenderloin she'd purchased half-price with plenty of salt and pepper, a bit of nutmeg she grated, a pinch of cinnamon, a dash of sugar, a teaspoon's worth of onion powder she measured with her cupped hand.

After a while, she heard noise on the stairs, steps on the fifth-floor landing. She opened the door and waited.

"Mary," he said, and stopped climbing two steps from the top. He clutched the railing.

"Are you all right?" she asked. Not seeing him for a long time and then seeing him again was a famine and a feast her body knew the rhythms of better than her mind. The light was dim, and Alfred, with his dark hair and eyes, his dark clothes, threatened to fade into the paneling, the deep wines and forest greens of the cheap wallpaper the building's owner had pasted up so many years ago. Mary couldn't stop herself from walking over to him. She couldn't stop herself from holding out her hand. He was every bit as handsome as he'd been when she was seventeen and he twenty-two. He was every bit as strong.

"I'm all right," he said, taking her hand between his and drawing it closer for a kiss.

"I made supper," she said to him, tugging him gently up the last two steps until he was standing in front of her.

He put his hands on either side of her head and then cupped her face. He clutched her shoulders and pulled her to his chest.

"Thank you, Mary. I'm very glad."

Things stayed good between them for two weeks, and then like a balloon with the tiniest puncture, they started to sink. He came home later. He wouldn't touch what she cooked. Instead of talking with her in the mornings, he rolled over and stared at the wall until she left to spend the day cooking down at a firehouse social, or a church hall, or a company picnic, or one of the other day jobs she'd arranged by grasping at connections, following up on every rumor, showing up at doors with her knives folded neatly in her bag to say that she heard there was need of a cook.

September, October, November: they moved around their rooms keeping furniture between them. Once, just before Christmas, they'd been about to pass each other on the stairs when Mr. Hallenan stepped out on the landing and said the missus had kicked him out. Alfred and Mary had looked immediately to each other and laughed, she facing up the stairs, he facing down. They'd laughed together at Mr. Hallenan's expense, and for one instant they stepped outside of that particular moment in time.

Sometimes, very late at night, he told her he knew that all the cruel things she said to him were the truth, and it was easy to talk to him then, to pile on more and more because in those moods he would just accept it, tell her she was right, absolutely right. But during the day, whenever she caught him sober, and worked up the courage and energy to face this thing that was eating away at them, she'd take a breath to speak and before she uttered one single syllable he'd already be cringing, closing his eyes, looking away, bracing himself for the volley that would follow, and it was that cringe, before she'd even said a word, like she wasn't even allowed to speak, like she wasn't even allowed to raise the slightest objection to the way he was living his life, the way he winced before she'd even fully turned from the counter, that had driven her to the office to find a situation that would keep her away from him. She told Mr. Haskell, who ran the agency, that a regular day off to come home didn't matter to her. She was willing to go as far as Connecticut. She'd go up to Tuxedo if they paid her enough, and gave her a private room.

"There is one family that just got in touch yesterday," Mr. Haskell said as he went through her file. "Bowen is their name." He looked up to gauge whether the name rang a bell. "There are cooks in front of you, but you have Priority in Placement." Priority in Placement was a phrase she'd seen on her employment file and scribbled on the envelope where her employers gave the agency honest reviews of her work, her person, how she fit with the family, how open she was to suggestion, how she got on with the other staff. That she had this designation made her lucky, Mr. Haskell wanted her to understand, but she still had to be careful. The Warrens might take that same house in Oyster Bay next summer, and the summer after. Did Mary know how many cooks in New York City would love to spend the summer in Oyster Bay? Did Mary know that President Roosevelt had a home there?

How could Mary not know it? Every head in town was swiveled toward the ugly brown mansion. Mary gathered that not all of the Warrens' guests had voted for the man, but by God were they happy to be eating and sleeping and swimming so near.

"There was sickness in the Warren family over the summer," Mr. Haskell said after reading the letter Mary had carried for him all the way from Oyster Bay. "Typhoid. You didn't get it?"

"No."

"Ever had it?"

"No."

"And you stayed on to help nurse those who got it." He glanced at the letter again as if to double-check what was written there.

"What else could I do? I've been near it before and never got it. I helped nurse the Draytons. Remember the Draytons?"

Mr. Haskell frowned, and Mary felt a clutch of panic. Had she gotten the Drayton job through the agency? She couldn't remember.

"I'm sure the Warrens appreciated it very much." Mr. Haskell leaned back in his chair. "Did they give you a bonus?"

"They kept paying me the wage we'd agreed on for August, so I got three additional weeks."

"And no more?"

"No more."

135

The more was given in cash and had been deposited in her bank account weeks earlier.

Mr. Haskell regarded her for a moment. "Report to the Bowen residence by noon on Monday," he said.

TEN

Someone had propped open the doors and the ceiling fans were humming, but none of it made a bit of difference in the sweltering courtroom. Mary heard the creak of Alfred's chair behind her, and was about to turn when Mr. O'Neill scribbled a word onto his pad and pushed it toward her: "Soper." She looked up to find the guard crossing the room toward him, and one of the other lawyers announcing his full name. "Do not react," Mr. O'Neill had warned her during their preparations. "Show that you are paying attention, but be respectful." Soper stood from his chair as neatly and silently as a paper removed from an envelope and unfolded along the seams.

How had he figured it out? Everyone wanted to know. And, oh, how he loved to tell the story. Mary imagined him perfecting that calm remove in front of a mirror at home. How? It was simple. One merely had to be brilliant and determined. She wanted to point out that the story had been in all the newspapers—surely everyone sitting in the room already knew it—but no, they would give the doctor a platform, and they'd all have to sit through it again. She felt her stomach clench as he sat back in the chair and crossed one leg over the other. Mary closed her eyes, counted to ten.

"Dr. Soper," the other lawyer said after listing Soper's credentials, "please explain to us the events leading up to your investigation in Oyster Bay, and your conclusion that Mary Mallon was at the root of the outbreak that struck the Warren family in the summer of 1906."

Soper relaxed further, placed his hands neatly atop his knees. He was so well rehearsed that Mary wondered if he even had to pay attention to what he was saying.

"I was busy with the subway sanitation problems, but there was something about this case that pushed me on the train to Oyster Bay to have a look. I got there in the second week of January 1907, and I'll admit that I was no more clever than the other investigators Mr. Thompson hired, at first. Like them, I initially thought the family might have gotten Typhoid after eating soft-shell crabs, and then I thought perhaps it was the water. I dropped blue dye in the commode and then waited to see if the drinking water ran blue. It didn't. I swabbed the tank but found no typhus bacilli. I stayed for three days and interviewed shopkeepers in town, a police officer, the postman who delivered mail to the Warrens the previous summer. Except for a governess and a music teacher the Warrens had brought with them from Manhattan, they'd hired all local staff, and I went to their homes and asked them to recall everything they could from the week the illness broke out, who among the household had gotten sick and when. Finally, the stable hand, a man named Jack, mentioned in passing at the conclusion of our interview that he didn't think any of the sick would have made it if it hadn't been for Mary. I double-checked the notes the other inspectors had forwarded to me, but none mentioned a servant named Mary. The only cook on my list was a woman named Bernadette Doyle. When I pressed Jack, he said that Mrs. Doyle left at the end of July. Her daughter was expecting a baby that came early. So the Warrens sent for another cook. Mary got there on the third day of August.

"I was calm as I made a note, and then checked it against the first sign of fever: August eighteenth. You can imagine how exciting this was."

The lawyer nodded that he could imagine, and glanced toward the judges.

"I wanted to make absolutely certain," Soper continued. "'Are you sure about the date?' I asked Jack.

"'Sure I'm sure,' Jack said. 'The day she came was my birthday. She made the best peach ice cream I've ever had, and she was nice to look at.' These were Jack's words, you understand. He told me that this cook named Mary stayed on to look after everyone who had come down with the fever. Not until they had all recovered did Mary return home. At that point it was mid-September.

"After that," Soper said, "it was so simple, a child could have figured it out." He described returning to Manhattan and contacting the agency the Warrens had used to find Mary. He had them send a list of all the other families Mary cooked for through the agency, in addition to the residence where she was currently employed.

"One by one the families got back to me reporting Typhoid outbreaks within a few weeks of Mary's arrival. I assembled the data, and one afternoon in late February, I went over to the Bowen residence and rang the bell. I was willing at that point to believe it wasn't her fault—as you know, there are still many doctors who cannot accept the theory of a healthy carrier—and I was prepared to explain it to her. I had not expected to be spoken to so rudely and threatened with a knife. I left a note for Mr. Bowen, but when I passed again several days later, I was shocked to see Mary's head disappear into the servants' entrance."

"And what have you since learned about that note?"

"That the Bowens never received it."

Mary could still see the flick of Frank's wrist as he threw the note into the flames. The Bowens had fired him several weeks after Mary's capture, and she hadn't heard anything about him since. Fired for helping her, she considered once again and felt the guilt of that press up against her. Fired for knowing her. For being her friend.

"When did you next attempt to speak to Miss Mallon?" the lawyer asked.

"A week or so later, at the building where she lives on Thirty-Third Street." Mary noticed that the courtroom seemed to darken around the edges of her vision, and she felt herself pull away. She felt all over again the shock of arriving home after a week's work, just getting settled, hearing the knock on the door, and seeing Alfred open it to find Dr. Soper. "It's very important that I speak with you," he'd said, ignoring Alfred entirely and taking a slight step forward as if he'd been invited inside.

She sipped from the glass of water Mr. O'Neill nudged toward her.

"And?" the lawyer pushed.

Dr. Soper glanced in her direction so quickly that Mary wondered if she had imagined it. He smoothed the lapel of his jacket.

"And I was unsuccessful. Neither she nor her companion

would listen. It's possible that the first time I met Miss Mallon I was too abrupt, too scientific about the problem. I'll grant that. I had a sense of urgency when I went to see her at the Bowen residence, and perhaps I didn't consider her feelings. When I visited her at her own rooms, I tried a different tack. When she saw it was me at her door, she shouted, 'What do you want with me?' So I asked her very calmly, 'Haven't you noticed that disease and death follow you wherever you go?'"

He was telling the truth about what he'd said, but Mary remembered his tone, and it wasn't calm. It was an accusation. Still standing at the door, Alfred had looked back and forth between them, and then stepped away. She remembered shouting, but not what she'd said. She remembered that he seemed to grow more calm as she got more upset.

"And what was her response?"

"Anger, as far as I could tell. Once again, she came after me with a knife."

A knife with a blade so dull it could barely cut butter, Mary thought. She'd wanted to argue with him that day, but she couldn't make sense of what he was saying, couldn't get past the jolt of seeing him again. Disease and death didn't follow her any more than they followed anyone else. People had been dying her whole life. First her father, in a fire. Then her mother, of a cough. Then, a few years later, her brother, then her other brother, then her sister in childbirth, then her sister's two babies, and then her beloved nana while Mary was en route to America. Had they had fevers? She supposed they had, but she couldn't remember, and anyway, those sicknesses that kill a person always come with fever, and in Ireland they didn't name their fevers. People became sick. They died. She never heard the word *Typhoid* until she came to America.

"Was this the first time you learned that she had a companion?" The attorney checked his notes. "Mr. Alfred Briehof?"

"Yes."

"And what can you tell us about that?"

"When I first arrived at the address the agency had provided to me, I saw Mary outside on the stoop, presumably having just arrived home. I was about to announce myself, but a man approached and embraced her. On the street. I assumed she was engaged to be married, but I've since discovered that she is not. It was Mr. Briehof who answered my knock when I tried to speak to her at the door to their rooms not ten minutes later."

"Can you describe their rooms from what little you saw?"

"Mr. Briehof appeared disheveled. I noted dirty dishes on the press, and there was an odor of overripe fruit."

The attorney continued. "Please describe to us what you did after failing for a second time to convince Miss Mallon that she must come in for testing."

"I leaned more heavily on the Department of Health and the NYPD to take action because I knew I would need their help. After finally persuading them, we came up with a plan. We enlisted a female doctor to help, hoping Mary would be more willing to cooperate with a female, but that was not the case."

"And that doctor was Josephine Baker, correct?"

"Yes."

Mary scanned the people on the other side of the room, but didn't see Dr. Baker among them.

Judge Erlinger called for a lunch recess at noon. Mr. O'Neill suggested they eat together, but Mary wanted to spend the three-quarters of an hour with Alfred. Mr. O'Neill started to protest that they had items to go over, but then he relented. "I have to send a guard," he said. Mary found Alfred leaning against the back wall of the courtroom, watching her approach. She felt the damp wrinkles in her clothes as she moved closer to him, a rumpled sack of laundry that should be pushed into a basin and wrung out to dry. Her hair had collapsed; she could feel it bobbing at the back of her neck. She was nervous.

Alfred took her hand and squeezed it once before leading her into the hall and down the steps outside to the corner, where a man with a pushcart was selling ham sandwiches. The guard stayed a few paces behind. What was it that was different about him? He pulled off his collar and unbuttoned his shirt. He pulled off the shirt's cuffs, rolled up the sleeves, and threw the collar and cuffs in the bushes. Without them, Mary saw that the shirt was worn so thin it was little more than gauze, the outline of his undershirt obvious in the sun. He moved his hand to her waist. She had decided that she wouldn't let him kiss her until she'd said her piece, but now that the moment had arrived, she decided she could spend the rest of her life saying her piece. She hadn't seen him in so long, and here he was, looking and smelling and moving like Alfred. She waited, but he only touched her cheek.

"I have only half an hour myself," Alfred said.

"Work?" She doubted it—what job would allow him to show up after noon?—but it was a day for letting things go, for keeping peace. She wanted him to look forward to her release, not dread it.

Alfred nodded. "It started as a day-to-day thing, but they've not said anything about stopping, so I keep showing up and they keep paying me. It's going on six months now."

"What is it?"

"The ice trucks. Or rather, the ice company stable. They let me drive the truck last week when a man was out, but that was just for the week."

"Do you like it?"

Alfred laughed. "You know you're the only person who's asked that?"

"I know if you don't like it you won't keep going."

Alfred pointed to a step where they could sit. "For now, I like it. The boss says the horses like me. There's not much to it, really, except brushing them and feeding them and making sure the stalls are clean. I run the ones who don't get assigned a truck on a given day, and there are a few injured ones, but there's not much to do for them until they heal. If they heal. I had to put one down. That was the only really bad day, and it was hard going back after that. He was hit by another truck on the corner of Madison and Fiftieth and his leg broke at the ankle. I had to go up there and shoot him."

Alfred put his hand on her hair and traced his finger along her hairline, around her ear, down her neck. He stopped at the collar of her blouse. "But why are we talking about me? How about you? You look well, Mary. God, it's good to see you."

Mary brought his broad hand to her lips and kissed it. She studied his face. "You said I was the only one who asked whether you like it. Who else would ask? I mean, who else have you told?"

Alfred shrugged. "What do you mean? I tell whoever asks me what I do."

"You seemed surprised that no one else has asked if you like it. Who would ask that, except for me?"

"What are you getting at?"

"Nothing."

"All right."

"I'm only saying that it's a funny thing to say. That I'm the only person who asked that. To say it when you wouldn't expect anyone else to ask that. Would you?"

"Mary."

"Are you seeing someone?"

He pulled his hand away. "Why would you ask that? Are you?"

"Am I? Are you serious?"

"There's people out there. You're not alone. That gardener."

"You'd know the lunacy of that question if you'd really read my letters. If you'd written more often—"

"Look. No point discussing it now, Mary, is there? With you coming home?"

"But I told you in the letters how lonely I was, how worried I was about you. If it was you out there I would have written every week. You know I would."

"Well, you're a better person than I am, Mary. Isn't that it? I'm a beast with no regard for anyone but myself, and you're a paragon of virtue."

It wasn't supposed to go like this, arguing over a past neither of them could change, criticizing each other's choices just like they'd been doing before she was taken. She was hurt. She was very hurt. But she had to make her mind change the subject if they were going to be together again once she got home. She'd resolved to not start up on him the first time she saw him after so long, that she'd be pleasant and forgiving and that they'd start from scratch if he was willing, but as usual she found it impossible to stop. Just as her mind was warning her not to say something, her lips were already saying it. Alfred shifted on the step. He wore

145

that expression of disdain that had made her so wild before she left, like every word she spoke was something to recoil from.

"And you hardly ever wrote back. I didn't know if my letters were sinking to the bottom of the river."

"I wrote back."

"A handful of times."

"More than that, Mary." Alfred sighed. "What could I have done? It's been hard for me, too, you know."

"Look. The last thing I want to do is argue with you. Not now. I'll be home soon and that's all that matters."

"About that. Might as well tell you now."

"Tell me what?"

"Home. It isn't on Thirty-Third Street anymore. I moved. Had to. Couldn't afford that place without you. And a few of the women in the building got involved in the Temperance League and were driving me crazy, waiting for me at the bottom of the stairs, sliding pamphlets under the door. A few of them followed me one afternoon saying Bible verses, and when I got to Nation's the men chewed me out for leading them there."

"Alfred! Why didn't you tell me?" They'd lived in those rooms together for thirteen years. She loved the place. She imagined she'd always live there. In her letters to him she'd asked about the place, about the people in the building. Brief as they were, he'd never said anything in his letters about having trouble with the rent, so she'd assumed—hoped—he hadn't gotten too far behind. She tried to shake off her disappointment. Home was wherever Alfred was. "So where have my letters been going?"

"Held at the building. Driscoll keeps them for me. I collect them when I'm over that direction." Mary didn't know Mr. Driscoll very well, but remembered he was one of the few in the building Alfred liked talking with when they crossed paths. He'd been a florist, Mary remembered Alfred telling her, until his joints got so painful he couldn't work anymore.

"And where have you been staying?"

"Orchard Street."

"Oh, Christ."

"It's not bad. I rent my bed from a family and meals are included. There's a son. Samuel."

"What's their name?"

"Meaney."

Mary wondered where her things were now—her pots and pans. Her clothes. The silver teapot that had been Aunt Kate's. Let it go, she breathed. Let it go. She reached for every piece of information he gave her and tried to make the parts fit into a whole. Alfred coming and going on Orchard Street, sitting down for meals with a family she'd never seen, careful of himself around Samuel, heading out to the Crystal Springs stables and working a full day. She wanted to ask him about drinking, if Mrs. Meaney waited up for him, if they helped him to his bed at night and took off his socks and shoes and reminded him to wash his sheets once a week.

"So where will I go? Later today?" Mary asked.

"Come to the stable. I'll be there late anyway. My room on Orchard isn't big. And with the boy there I doubt they'll allow you to stay. Or—"

"Or?"

"Or you could stay with someone until we get a place of our own again. Someone in the old building?"

Mary heard her name called from the end of the alley. The break was almost up, and Mr. O'Neill wanted to go over what would happen next before they reconvened. Her guard had fallen asleep with his hat pulled down low over his eyes. She wouldn't be foolish enough to try to escape today anyway. Not when she'd be free in a matter of hours.

"I have to go," Alfred said. "I'm late as it is." They brushed the crumbs off their laps, and then he took her into his arms and hugged her, lifting her off the ground for a moment before setting her back down. "I'm sorry, Mary. I'm sorry I didn't tell you. We'll figure it out later. When we see each other. We'll figure it all out. I promise." He told her the address of the stable.

"Yes. Okay. Later."

"A lot has changed, Mary. You'll see."

She'd been a child when she met Alfred, only seventeen, more than twenty years of her life tied to this person, no way to untangle that knot now. They'd moved into the rooms on Thirty-Third Street in the summer of 1894, when Mary was twenty-five. Aunt Kate had died of pneumonia over the winter, and Paddy Brown had gone from saying very little to saying nothing at all.

"Kate loved Alfred," Mary said gently to the old man on the day she told him that she'd be moving out, that she and Alfred had found a place together.

"Kate thought he would marry you," Paddy Brown said as he felt along the mantel for his tin of tobacco. Mary found it for him, pried it open, removed a plug, and offered it on her palm. When he got the pipe started she sat by him, and he put his hand on top of her head. "Take the things she wanted you to have," he said after a while. It was the longest conversation they'd had in six months.

For weeks after moving in together, after arranging the few things she'd brought from Kate's, after going to the market and buying new bed linens to fit their new double bed, and a bright yellow tablecloth for their new kitchen table, she thought she'd never rest again. What woman could rest with him so near, and even when he fell asleep she'd lie awake, contemplating the weight of his arm where it lay across her ribs, the gentle tug she felt when the stubble of his jaw got caught on her hair. When she worked, all she could think about was getting home to him, and he said it was the same for him. They talked late at night over coffee, when they went to bed, when they woke up, and when they weren't together they stored up all the things the other would be interested in and carried those items home. Even when winter came, and the gas-meter jar was often empty, they simply crawled into bed together and piled every blanket on top and then shivered with their hands cupped over their mouths. He'd take her frozen feet and pull off the layers of stockings until they were bare and then he'd lift up his sweaters and press her feet to his warm chest. When Mary thought of those days now, she could still feel that astonished joy, that belief that no one else in the world could possibly be happier than they were.

Alfred hugged her again, and released her again, and there was something in the hug and the release that told Mary something was not right.

Again, Mr. O'Neill shouted her name. The guard came over and stood beside her.

It was the time, probably. Twenty-seven months could make any two people a little awkward together, even two as close as Mary and Alfred. Also the guilt, Mary remembered. Alfred was always like a hangdog when he was guilty, and she shouldn't have ridden him for not writing more often. Not when they were about to be happy and together again, Alfred working, eating three square meals, home at nights. Maybe leaving Thirty-Third Street was a good thing. Now they could get a new place together and truly start over.

"I love you, Mary. I really do."

"All right, Alfred," Mary said. "We'll talk about that later."

"We will," he agreed.

Together, they walked down the alley toward Mr. O'Neill, who was pointing to his watch and frowning.

Everyone came back from lunch recess more overheated and red faced than when they left. A few of the reporters did not return at all, and Mary wondered if that was because they'd felt certain of the outcome, and if so, what their predictions had been. She noticed Dr. Baker sitting in the second row. The men seated beside her had their backs to her, talking to other men.

The scientists talked about new discoveries in the world of contagious diseases, new vaccines that were in development, how it was likely that more people like Mary would be discovered, people who carried disease but never succumbed to it themselves. They used the words *bacilli, serum, agglutinins*: words that made Mary feel like her mouth was stuffed full of cotton that she couldn't manage to spit away.

Eventually, they began discussing her capture—specifically, why Dr. Soper and the Department of Health decided to take her by force. It would be one thing if this woman were an educated person, the Department of Health officials argued one by one, but Mary Mallon had no formal education, and lived with a man of low moral character, to whom she was not married. Several employers had reported that they didn't like to cross Mary, didn't like to demand veal when she'd planned on poultry, and that wasn't natural, was it? What kind of cook inspires that kind of caution in an employer? Mrs. Proctor of East Seventieth Street recalled a time when she'd asked Mary to make Irish stew, assuming it would be one of her specialties, and Mary refused!

When Bette answered the door of the Bowen residence on that cold March morning in 1907, the police officers pushed past her and spread throughout the house. "She's not here!" Bette shouted, and the note of urgency in her voice reached Mary, who was up on the third floor. She pulled back the curtain of the nearest window to see the police truck. She heard someone running up the back stairs, and discovered that she couldn't move. "The police are here," Frank said the instant he appeared at the door. "I have an idea."

Mary saw the solution before he said it out loud. "The Alisons," she said. The Alison family, who lived next door to the Bowens, had recently had a piece of their fence cut open behind the homes so that their servants could travel back and forth. Mrs. Alison and the children had left for Europe a week earlier, and Mr. Alison would be at his office all day. Frank held up his hand as they listened to the brisk footsteps of the officers walking through the rooms of the floor below them. "You listen for your chance," he said. Mary nodded and felt suddenly very cold. Her whole body was covered in a thin layer of sweat, and she began to shiver. Her coat was downstairs in the servants' closet and there would be no time to get it. It was snowing outside.

Only seconds later, Mary heard Frank shout from the first floor and then the rush of hard-soled shoes to the stairs. Mrs. Bowen was out shopping. Mr. Bowen was at his office downtown. It was supposed to be an ordinary Friday, a better-than-ordinary Friday, since Mary would have to cook only for the staff, and for them it would be easy: no serving, dinner together around the table in the kitchen. Clutching the doorknob for help, Mary peeked into the empty hall. She stepped out and stayed close to the wall until she got to the narrow back stairs. Down she went, silent as a cat, until she reached the back door of the house. Outside, the snow was falling faster. Feeling nothing but her own heart beating in her chest, she ran along the footpath that led over to the fence and unlatched the door that led from the Bowens' yard to the Alisons'. When she looked back to see if anyone was watching her, she noticed her footprints in the snow. She hurried back to cover her tracks, and then, walking backward, leaned over to brush away the footprints with her hands.

The door to the Alison kitchen was locked—the servants mostly having been let go while the family was in Europe. At the edge of the yard was a supply shed. It was a small structure, little more than a low closet with a roof, but the door was unlatched, and when she stepped inside there was just enough room among the pruning sheers, the bags of sand, and the drums of kerosene for one person to crouch and wait.

She didn't feel the cold at first, and considered herself well protected in the little room. But after a while she could feel the wind where it slipped in between the spaces in the planks, and her knees ached from crouching. She shifted a few bulky canisters of oil and made room to sit on the packed dirt ground. She wished she could hear what was happening on the Bowen side of the fence. Would Frank or Bette remember to get her once the police officers gave up and moved on? There was nothing to do but wait.

*

Later, Mr. O'Neill would ask her what she made of Dr. Soper's pursuit, why she wasn't more surprised to be hounded the way she was. "I was surprised!" Mary said. "I was shocked!"

"But you didn't behave like a person who was surprised and shocked," he insisted. "You behaved like a person who expected to be pursued. Do you understand the difference? You reacted too quickly. How did you know when you looked out the window and saw the police that it was you they'd come for? That's the problem they have with you. That's part of the reason they don't believe you when you claim to have had no idea you were spreading disease."

"I'm not spreading disease."

"You see? Even there. You sound like a person who's been defending herself for years, long before anyone accused you."

"Meaning?"

"Meaning, there must have been a moment when it crossed your mind that all of this was true. The question they have is whether it occurred to you after their accusations, or before."

"I don't understand."

"You do understand. Think."

Alone in the silent supply shed, Mary tried to think about only nice things, normal things, what she needed from the grocer's, what she'd cook for Alfred next time she went home, but instead she kept thinking of the officers searching for her. She thought of the people who'd been sick in Oyster Bay, and how she'd known they would make it if she worked to keep the fever down. It was a fast-moving fever, that one. Doctors talked about fevers as if they were all the same, but there were fevers and there were fevers, and Mary could distinguish one from another with the touch of her

153

hand. One day everyone was playing tennis, riding horses, and the next they complained of being dizzy. They stopped eating. The gardener vomited very near the water cistern. Mrs. Warren fainted on the porch. Mary had seen it enough times to know that Mrs. Warren and the other adults who caught it would survive. They were in pain, yes, and called out nonsense, and tossed and turned and sweated through all their sheets and vomited bile. Still, Mary had seen Typhoid Fever at its worst, she'd seen death come a few times, and in each of those times the fight was mismatched from the beginning. The Warren girl was the only real worry, the poor child, only eight years old. She didn't have the fight in her that the others had. That was the dangerous moment, when the patients didn't have the fight, when they just slept and stared and preferred to keep their eyes closed. When the moaning stopped. When the nonsense stopped. And that girl was so quiet to start with.

Mary threw her whole body into beating death away from the girl. She filled the tub to the brim and reached her own hand in the water to show her what it was like to splash inside the house, over the wood of the floor, a thing that would never be allowed if everyone were healthy, and the girl seemed interested in that. Mary told her about her passage to America, and what Ireland was like. The girl would never go to Ireland. England, maybe, Mary informed her. Paris. But not Ireland. Not many went to Ireland, they just went away from it. But it was her home just like New York City was the girl's home, and what was it the poet said? Every savage loves his native shore. And that's when she knew the girl would survive. She leveled her eyes on Mary, and there was life behind them. "Are you a savage, Mary?"

"I am. Like we all are."

And the girl considered it. "I'm not," she said.

"No?"

"Absolutely not."

So the Warren girl survived, and everyone else in the Warren house survived and they still wanted her.

That's part of what was so worrying about the Bowen girl, that they wouldn't let her anywhere near. If she could only just see her, but even now, with the police searching the house for her, Mary was sure the girl's nurse had not so much as stepped out into the hall to see what was going on. When they knocked on the door to pass in ice and fresh linens, the nurse blocked their view of the girl's bed with her body, accepted what was given, and shut the door again.

Then she thought of the boy, the Kirkenbauer baby, only two years old. Just two. Barely two. Crouched in the Alisons' storage shed, her hands stinging with the cold, she tried everything to keep him out. She hummed songs. She recited poetry. After returning home from the Kirkenbauers' back in 1899, she didn't even look for another situation for a whole month. She made sandwiches and sold them to the men who worked at the lumberyard on Twenty-First Street. When they handed over their coins and she handed over the sandwiches, they were perfect strangers to her, and she decided that was what she wanted: to cook for people but not to know them at all. She didn't want to see people when they woke up in the morning. She didn't want their children hugging her legs and learning her name.

Mary waited in the shed for what felt like hours. She was hungry. She was stiff and cold and worried about getting sick. Who would cook for the Bowens if she got sick? She unwound a long piece of burlap from around the garden equipment stored on a shelf behind her and wrapped it around her shoulders. She hugged her knees to her chest and exhaled hot breath on her fingers. At one point she thought she heard Bette calling her, so she opened the door and saw a policeman's hat moving along the other side of the fence. She tried not to think about time, and whether she'd be there all night, whether she should risk running alongside the Alisons' house and out to the sidewalk and away downtown. In one moment she felt sure they'd give up, go home, and never come for her again, and in another moment she knew they'd be waiting for her on Thirty-Third Street. They'd be waiting for her everywhere she went.

After what felt like several hours of almost perfect stillness, she heard the creak of the fence door swinging open, the crunch of footsteps in the snow. Frank, she prayed. Come to tell her the coast was clear. She heard footsteps pass her little shed, the shadow of a man darkening the slim spaces of sky between the wood slats. A person was standing at the shed, facing it. Mary could feel the stranger sizing up the little structure, the perfect hiding place. "Mary Mallon," a man called out. The world was thin, brittle, frozen solid, and the man's voice threatened to crack everything open, smash all the lovely icicles hanging from branches. She pressed her lips together and closed her eyes. More steps approached to join the person already at the shed. A woman's voice, efficient, fed up, stood out from the others.

"She's in there," the woman said, as if it should have been obvious to everyone, and in one last surge of hope Mary imagined her pointing her finger away from the storage shed to the trees, to the clouds.

"Mary Mallon," a man said again, and it was the tone in his voice that told Mary it was over. He really did know she was in there, and he'd give her a moment to decide to come out before he went in and got her.

Someone pulled the lever that opened the door, and four men and one woman leaned in to look at her. Mary's hips and knees felt like kitchen scissors gone to rust.

"I'm not going anywhere," Mary said as she worked to ignore the searing pain in her joints. "Leave me alone."

"Mary Mallon," one officer said. "You are under arrest. You have—"

She shoved him. She put her head down and threw out her arms and shoved him. When another officer approached, she kicked, and next thing she knew one was trying to pin her arms, while another had gotten her around her waist. She felt one at her ankles. She reached out and grabbed a handful of the woman's hair. The snow in the Alisons' backyard was churned up, and Mary felt the wet of her skirt through her thick wool stockings. One of the men caught her left arm, and when he did he twisted it around behind her back. When she turned to knee him, another officer grabbed her right arm. They lifted her, carried her across the Alisons' small yard to the narrow path that ran beside the Bowens' house. She tried to kick, to buck, to twist in their arms, raising her knees in the air and then letting fly with every bit of strength she had left, but she was stiff from sitting in the cold for so many hours, and her movements felt clumsy, poorly aimed. One of the officers was telling her to be quiet, relax, that she was only making everything worse for herself, and next to all of this buzzed Dr. Baker, who rushed up to the door of the truck and pulled it open so that the men could shove Mary inside.

Dr. Baker walked to the front of the courtroom. It was the pattern of the day; one description of Mary in a given moment was not good enough. They had to get two, three, four people up there to say the same thing. One of the police officers had already had his turn and had told them all about it, said Mary was an animal, worse than an animal because even the wildest animal can be coaxed, usually. There was no coaxing Mary that day. No reasoning with her. She was like no other person he'd arrested in his life. He had scratch marks on his arms and neck for days after.

As Mary observed the plain-looking woman turn to the judge before taking her seat, she knew it would look worse that she'd attacked a woman, and Dr. Baker was a smaller woman than Mary, and a woman of the class that allows women to become doctors.

But Dr. Baker surprised her. She admitted that she'd had to sit on Mary during the ride to the Willard Parker Hospital, but other than that she said simply that Mary had seemed frightened, and that the others had covered for her. "As anyone would expect them to," she added, "being Miss Mallon's friends." No one else had said anything about her having friends.

"Dr. Baker, did you find her to be unreasonable?"

Dr. Baker hesitated. "We didn't try to reason with her. When she went missing we focused on finding her, and when we found her we simply forced her into the truck. So I couldn't comment on that. Other than two brief conversations we had when she was still being held at Willard Parker, I've never spoken to Mary Mallon at any length."

"Wouldn't you agree that a woman who hides in a shed for so many hours to avoid arrest has a guilty conscience?"

Again, Dr. Baker hesitated. "I would say that a person doesn't want to be arrested, guilty or not guilty. And I would say that none of us here would like to be arrested." Dr. Baker stared out across the heads of all the witnesses in the gallery, her hands folded neatly in her lap. The attorney asking the questions searched through several sheets of paper and then pushed them aside and turned to Dr. Baker without notes.

"Dr. Baker, as a resident of New York City and as a medical doctor, would you feel comfortable letting Mary reenter society? Allowing her to leave North Brother Island and return to her former life?"

Dr. Baker frowned. She remained silent for a long time, and in the gallery the spectators wondered if she'd heard the question. Finally, she spoke. "It's my opinion that Mary Mallon does not understand the medical threat she is to those around her. However, neither do many of the medical personnel who've become acquainted with her case in these past two and a half years. I can say only that I don't think Miss Mallon should be allowed to cook. All the medical doctors in this room have admitted that she is a healthy person. What happens when more healthy carriers are discovered? Do we send them all to North Brother?"

Mr. O'Neill smiled in his seat. The other attorney frowned. "Dr. Baker," the other attorney asked, "is it possible that you have particular sympathy for Miss Mallon because she is a female?"

Dr. Baker tilted her head and considered. "Perhaps."

ELEVEN

In the end it took several more days for the judges to decide what to do with her. Instead of sending her all the way back to North Brother for the night, they put her in a hotel with guards posted outside her room, and on the morning of the second day, ten minutes were wasted in arguing over who would foot the bill for such a luxury. The City of New York? Which department? One of the DOH representatives shouted, "That woman is expensive enough as it is."

She spent three nights in the hotel all told, and except for the fact that her bed was made every afternoon when she came back from the hearing, it wasn't that different from North Brother. The hotel laundry wouldn't lend her an iron, so she gave in and sent her skirt and blouse downstairs for them to clean, which they did, in plenty of time for each morning's proceedings. The mousy girl who brought up her clothes on the morning of the fourth day said, "Good luck to you, Missus. We hope they let you go," and Mary imagined a whole staff of women standing behind her, rooting for her, waiting to hear what would happen.

And then, back in the oppressive courtroom, at ten o'clock in the morning of July 31, 1909, Judge Erlinger stared out across the heads of every man and woman in the room and announced that Mary Mallon's release would be a hazard to every New Yorker and could not be justified. She would be returned to North Brother Island immediately.

Mary heard the words as a kick to the gut and gripped the table to steady herself. "What does it mean?" she demanded of Mr. O'Neill. Everyone in the room seemed to have woken up. Some of the reporters jumped from their seats to shout questions at the judge, at the collection of experts, at Mr. O'Neill, at Mary.

"It's just for now," Mr. O'Neill said. "We'll keep working. Look, their own experts said there are others like you, that—"

"Others like me? Do you believe I'm giving out the fever?"

"I think it's irrelevant, Mary. I've tried not to think about it too much, but yes, the lab work is sound in my view, and two-thirds of the time it comes back positive."

"Their labs! Run by their people! I'm telling you, it's Soper. He's—"

"Mary, calm down. Please. It doesn't matter. What matters is that you are perfectly safe to be around as long as you are not cooking, and they can't go locking up healthy people whenever they feel like it. There has to be a better solution."

Mary absorbed Mr. O'Neill's calm response and remembered that for him, and for everyone else in the courtroom, the hearing was no more than a handful of days, a set of hours, an errand, an item on a list. For Mary, it was her entire life. After this, Mary made herself understand, all of them can go home to their families, meet someone for a picnic, take a trip to the ocean if they want. Each person here has complete freedom, except for me.

When she thought about going back, the long automobile journey uptown, the ferry crossing to North Brother, it all seemed inevitable, and all the other possibilities she'd imagined—being with Alfred, getting new rooms together, finding work—were just dreams behind locked doors.

"The judges said you can have visitors now," Mr. O'Neill offered by way of consolation. "You can write to your friends and let them know."

Mary stood on her tiptoes so that she was almost his height and felt tempted to spit at him, to walk up to the judges and spit at them as well. As for Soper, she felt her hands turn to fists. Their experts had worried that she had a violent streak—what proper woman would raise a knife to a man of status?—and perhaps they were right. Who among her friends, after not seeing her for more than two years, would put aside their work to spend half a day traveling all that way uptown, all the way across Hell Gate, to sip a cup of tea in her cramped kitchen for thirty minutes?

And how would Alfred react to this news? She was glad he was absent.

John Cane was there to meet her ferry and tell her all the news since she left. The she-cat who skulked in the vegetable garden had birthed a litter of kittens, and all the babies had been taken home by nurses except for one. Did Mary want it? For company? The hydrangeas by the south wall were fully bloomed in the heat, even though he didn't expect that for several more weeks since last year they hadn't blossomed until August. Did Mary remember? Did she remember planting the rusted nails with him? Well it worked, that trick, and now they've flowered a deep periwinkle blue. He went on and on, as if she'd been gone for a year and not just a handful of days. The moment she opened the door to her cottage it was as if she'd gone out only for a walk, and everything—the courtroom, the judges, Dr. Soper, the hotel—seemed like a hallucination, like she'd never left, like she'd never seen Alfred at all. He'd tried to see her at the hotel the first evening, but they told him to see her over at the courthouse. He never did. Working, she supposed. He could have left a note with the clerk at the courthouse or one of the guards at the hotel. Even if they had to read it before handing it over, she'd like to have had a note from him. But there was no note, no visit, and now she was back on North Brother with John Cane buzzing in her ear.

She went over to her desk and removed a sheet of paper. She sat for a while, not sure of what to say. After a few minutes, she picked up the pen.

Alfred,

You've heard by now that I was taken back to North Brother. Mr. O'Neill said he is going to keep trying. I'm not sure what to think—I'm just so tired. I barely saw you at all.

I'm allowed to have visitors now. I would love for you to visit me here, Alfred. It's not ideal, but at least it's something. I'll wait to hear from you.

Mary

She addressed the letter to the stable instead of Thirty-Third Street, and left it poking out from under her doormat on the step where the mailman would notice it. Then she closed the door of her cottage and curled up on her cot. Her body smelled ripe. Her best blouse would be ruined for good. It was so very hot. The walls so close. Late at night, when she was sure no one would see her, she carried the heavy chamber pot outside, emptied it in the river, and returned immediately to bed. In the early mornings she heard the foghorn of the lighthouse behind the hospital. She listened to the rhythmic tap and scrape of the bricklayer's instruments as he pointed the brick of the new walkway that connected the hospital to the outbuildings. She heard John and his gardening shears slicing through the green, and she heard someone leave meals on her step three times a day. After a few days she decided that was the way it would be from now on. She'd stay in her hut and if they needed her, let them break the door down. If they wanted her samples or wanted to draw blood, by God they'd have to drug her and get ten men to hold her. No more. After several days—her head felt light from lack of food, her teeth thick and soft, and under her arms itched for a scalding washcloth rubbed with strong soap—John pounded on her door and warned her that he'd brought a nurse and they were going to enter without an invitation if she refused to come outside. Finally, as threatened, he opened the door, and the smell of fresh-cut grass turned her stomach.

"My God," he said, turning his face toward the fresh air of outdoors and drawing a deep breath. "Are you suffocating yourself?"

"Get out."

"I've brought Nancy," he informed her, as if she knew who in the world Nancy was. As if she cared. "Tell her," John urged the girl. The nurses got younger every season.

Nancy looked at him and then at Mary.

"Tell her," he said again, nodding toward her hand. Mary noticed the girl was holding a newspaper.

"There's a dairyman," Nancy said. "In Camden. Upstate."

Mary waited. The girl whispered something to John, but he couldn't hear her. Mary promised that she'd kill them both with a single shot if they didn't get out.

"They say she gets mad if . . ."

"If what?" John asked.

"Yes, if what?" Mary asked.

The girl took a step backward. "If anyone says anything about her having the fever."

Mary sat up in her cot.

"Don't worry about that," John assured Nancy. "Just keep going."

"There's a dairyman in Camden who's passing the fever through the milk."

Mary sat up straighter. "What do you mean?"

John took over. "She's just after reading it to me. He's a dairyman. Had the fever forty years ago and hasn't been sick a day since. There were outbreaks of Typhoid wherever his milk was sent, at groceries and markets all over New York City, and now they've traced it to him. Got lots of people sick with it. They're saying maybe hundreds. More than—"

"More than what?"

"More than they claim you made sick. A lot more."

"Where are they sending him? Not here, I guess. Camden is all the way up near Syracuse, isn't it?"

"That's just it. They're not sending him anywhere."

"What do you mean?"

"Because he's the head of his household and has a family, they've decided it would be too much of a hardship to put him in quarantine, so he can stay exactly where he is, as long as he promises to never have anything to do with milk production. So he has his sons running it and he's bossing them."

"You mean they're isolating him somewhere in Camden. Somewhere he can be near his family."

"No, Mary. I mean they're letting him stay in his own damn house. You understand? With his wife. With his dogs and his sons and his grandchildren. Not a thing has happened to this man except being told not to go near the milk that's distributed for sale. As for the family's milk he can do as he pleases. None of them have ever had Typhoid, so your Dr. Soper believes they must be immune."

"Soper? Soper went up there?" Mary tried to make sense of what she'd just been told. "Hundreds, you said? Hundreds? They say I infected twenty-three." It was one of the rare times she'd said it out loud.

Nancy piped up. "I think, if I may, that you're considered, more of a . . . well, a special case? There's a bit on you at the end here." She held out the folded newspaper for Mary to take. "This man knew he had Typhoid forty years ago. He remembers it well. You claim to have never had it at all. So."

"I claim?" Mary said. She advanced toward the girl with her arm stretched out for the paper, which the girl handed over before backing away. "You can go now, please, and tell the other nurses not to bother coming down here with any more glass canisters for collecting or they won't like what I do with those canisters when they get here. I'm finished with all that. You understand?"

"I understand."

When the girl had left, John announced that he was going to sit on the step outside where the air flowed a little easier. "She was trying to help, Mary," he remarked over his shoulder. "She didn't have to tell me about that article, but she did. She said she thought you should know."

"Everybody is trying to help. And look where all their help has landed me." She scrutinized the back of John's head for a moment, his sunburned neck, and then, sighing, went over to sit beside him.

"If you hadn't bit Nancy's head off, she would have also told you that the article says there are likely many, many more like you and this man up in Camden. It says the Department of Health already has leads on several of them from tracing local outbreaks."

"And none of them are in quarantine."

"Nope."

Mary tried to ignore the reek of her body and looked over at the moon, just an impression yet, the sky still blue around it. Her muscles felt weak from lying in a prone position for so long. She leaned over to the tray John brought with him and broke off a piece of the bread.

"But I was the first so I get the prize."

"I guess so."

John plucked a blade of grass and stuck it in his mouth. He leaned back on his elbows and closed his eyes. "I like it out here, days like this. Feels like the country, and this island gets a good breeze compared to over there." He lifted his chin to indicate the water, the tall buildings on the other, larger island to their west. He sat up. "Oh, before I forget, I cleared a path down on the other side, you know, by that heron's nest you found that time? It goes all the way down to the beach and you can't see the hospital from there if you walk down a bit and get the trees between you and it."

Mary imagined him doing all of this, making progress through the weeds and brambles, overgrowth that had not been touched in years, maybe ever. His arms were berry brown from being out-doors. She wondered sometimes if he was strong enough for all the work he did. Perhaps it was the work that kept him strong. He must be well into his fifties, maybe more, but then Mary remembered that she was almost forty. Forty years old. Her own mother had died at thirty, her nana at fifty-eight. When had he cleared that path, with everything else he was supposed to be doing? He said the board of the hospital wanted primroses along the eastern gable, mums added to the garden. They wanted the lawns cut, the hedges kept trim, everything about the island as neat and orderly as the corridors of the hospital. Riverside was a showpiece hospital, an example to all other hospitals built to house and study contagious diseases. But John had his own way of doing things, just as Mary had her own ways of operat-ing around a mistress who believed she knew her kitchen better than Mary did. If he was wanted for anything, a messenger could always follow the smell of his pipe, which he took out of his shirt pocket now and stuffed with tobacco. So he'd been sure, all along, that she would be back. Or maybe, it occurred to her now, he'd just been hopeful.

"Thank you, John."

John nodded as he touched his match to the tobacco and drew it alive with short, careful puffs. "Did you see your man over there? At the hearing?"

"I did."

"Good," John said. "That's good."

She spent August and September prowling the edges of the island. Every morning started cooler than the last, and soon she had to bring her shawl for warmth. She walked without stockings on the packed sand and held her shoes in her hands as she stepped from smooth stone to smooth stone that led, if she chose to follow, out into treacherous waters. She rested on the southernmost point of the island and found South Brother, the smaller sibling of North Brother. From her point of view the other island looked green and thick and far happier without the insult of quarantine hospitals and daily death. Sometimes, if she was very still, a snowy egret came to stand by her and inspect her, its plumage so pure and beautiful that Mary wondered how it could be an inhabitant of the same place as the other living things, all of which struck Mary as filthy and tired, just as Mary was. Sometimes, with the sun behind the bird and with its plumage on display, the delicate creature glowed and felt to Mary like a sign that good things were possible.

No one ever looked for her anymore. In the beginning, if she didn't answer the door of her cottage, and couldn't be found in one of the flower beds close by, they'd send out a search party. "I thought I was free to roam as I please," Mary would say, furious at yet another promise broken, and doubly angry because they always responded, "You are, of course you are," even as they led her back by the elbow, the glass canisters clinking in their skirt pockets.

Never in her life had she had so much time. She tried to remember being a child, but even those years seemed full of responsibilities: fetching and boiling water, cleaning, baking, gardening, raking, doing her lessons by the lamp while her nana used her quick knife to separate potatoes from their jackets and pile them high on the table. The nurses never came near her now, and she wondered if that had been part of the judges' order, the fine print she hadn't stayed around to read, that although she had to stay within the ordered boundaries, no one was to bother her with tests and analyses, no one was to rap on her cottage door twice a week.

Several weeks after the hearing, the middle of September 1909, Mary got a letter from Alfred. When she saw the mail carrier headed toward her cottage she figured it was just another update from Mr. O'Neill, and didn't bother hurrying to intercept him. When she saw the handwriting on the envelope, her hands went sweaty. She studied it for a moment, and then she tore it open.

Dear Mary,

I hope they told you I tried to see you at the hotel where they kept you. I don't know why they wouldn't let me. I don't remember if I told you that I thought you looked very beautiful the day that I saw you, and I'd almost forgotten, truth be told, how beautiful you are.

I'm writing now because I'd like to go up there to see you. I had hoped that you'd be free and there wouldn't be any need but now I worry it will be even longer. Maybe another two years even. Maybe more.

I've inquired about the ferry and since it doesn't go on Sundays except for the hospital people I will plan on seeing you there a week from Saturday. Maybe you can let the correct people know that I'm coming so that they don't give me any trouble when I get there. We can take a walk or do whatever it is you do to pass time. I just want to see you.

Until then,
Alfred Briehof

There were several details about this letter Mary didn't like. For a start, there was, "I'd almost forgotten." Nor did she like "two years . . . Maybe more." Most of all, she did not like the formality of his signature, "Alfred Briehof."

TWELVE

Alfred had a pushcart once. He'd had many jobs, but the pushcart months stood out. He said he was sick of hauling coal baskets, and even more sick of emptying ash cans, and above everything sick of answering to a boss. He had had just about every type of physical employment a man could have, and his body needed a break. By his own description he was a genial person and liked to look his fellow man in the face. So he went out and rented a pushcart for twenty-five cents a day. "It's standing, Mary," he said. "Standing and talking. And making a living besides." Alfred preferred to sit while talking, and preferred most of all to sit with a glass of strong liquor nearby, but Mary didn't point out any of this. It was possible, she supposed, for him to know himself a little better than she knew him, so she swallowed her concerns and said it was a great idea. She knew the butchers of the East Side better than he did, knew which of them kept their thumbs on the scales, which stored their meat on cellar floors where the rain seeped in and sewer pipes might burst, so she helped him find a supplier. There were already three poultrymen on the street where he planned to set up, so he started out selling cuts of beef, pork, and lamb. For a quick lunch to make his cart known he offered slabs of corned beef with a side of beans, a boiled potato for an extra five cents. Mary showed him how to keep it hot, how much to put on the plate.

By the end of the very first month he learned that meat was not the thing. Fat black flies pestered him all day long, laying their eggs while doing so, and made themselves so at home on his cart that he was forced to switch to fruit. The Jewish and Italians had the advantage with the fruit suppliers, taking all the semi-rot for themselves and leaving to the rest of the peddlers only the best fruit, for which the suppliers had to charge full price. Between the cost of the good fruit and the cart and the tipping of police officers and the paying off of the grocer from whom he rented sidewalk space, plus the nod to the collector and the man-of-influence, who was no more than a saloon keeper up the block, Alfred was deep in the red after only two or three more months. On top of that, since he was set up next to one of the poultry-men, the flies came anyway, and hopped from the putrid carcasses the other peddler had cast behind his cart over to Alfred's lovely apples and pears, where they perched and laid more eggs.

Once he gave up on fruit, he switched to hot corn, and that went all right for a while, maybe three or four months. But he got bored with corn and switched to something that no one else for ten blocks thought to sell—children's toys. Small toy boats. Wooden horses. Dolls for girls. Noisemakers. Funny hats. Toys were the best yet: Alfred opened his cart for business around nine in the morning, and closed before supper, by four. There was no worry about rot. No worry about his goods baking in the sun.

Even the children left him alone except to buy what he offered. When the fruit carts got pelted with their own goods, and the fish cart got overwhelmed, overturned, and rolled down Forsyth Street, Alfred was left alone to sell for five cents what he'd purchased for three.

When Mary looked back on the best days with Alfred, leaving out the early days, when they were both so young and had nothing in the world to do but spend their days off taking walks or sipping coffee, the time that Alfred spent as a toy vendor was the happiest in their entire history. Mary remembered visiting him on his corner, the way he was with the children who approached him, drawing them in with his promise of shining train cars and paper birds. Even the ones who showed up with only a penny could buy a sweet. It was a good time, and it lasted longer than Mary expected. One whole year: October 1904 to October 1905. And then, about the time the weather turned cold, he began arriving home in a quiet mood. He pushed his food around his plate. Where once he would say that it was a great life, he took to saying it was a good enough life, for the time being.

"Maybe you want your own store?" Mary suggested. It was not impossible. With a few more years of saving, the right rent, and the right location, maybe it could happen. 1905 had been a very good year for Mary. She'd worked continuously, and on her days off she'd taken side jobs cooking for Ladies' Luncheons.

But Alfred was shocked at the suggestion. "My own store? What I want is fewer toys in my life, Mary, not more. These kids"—he put his head in his hands—"you wouldn't believe the noise they make. I caught one putting a handful of sweets in his pocket without paying, and when I made him turn his pockets inside out he said he had paid when I know very well he hadn't. I would've thrashed the kid if his father hadn't been standing right there, grinning, probably telling the boy what to do. They're worse than the flies."

He began sleeping late, opening his cart at noon, leaving at two. On the same short block as Alfred's cart were twenty-four others, all packed in tightly against one another. Most were food peddlers, and Alfred claimed that under their carts was a year's worth of garbage. Mary didn't see why this was so upsetting to him all of a sudden, when it had been like that all along. Unlike other neighborhoods, where the garbage piles were removed regularly by the Department of Sanitation, the rubbish on the Lower East Side was packed four or five inches deep all along the block, and there was no skirting it. Each day's new garbage got trampled underfoot by the crowds, and when the city sweepers came with their wispy brooms on Tuesday mornings it was like using a teaspoon to empty beaches of sand.

"But it's getting to winter now. Winter always smells better than summer."

Alfred could not be convinced.

When the first snowfall came he didn't bother going to his cart at all, and instead checked with the Department of Street Cleaning to see if they needed an extra man on their snow-removal crew. The DSC took him on, gave him a crisp white uniform with matching hat, and out he went to pick up his cart, broom, and shovel with all the other white wings. Colonel Waring, New York City's latest street-cleaning commissioner, referred to the white wings as his army, and Mary supposed it was an army of sorts, an army fighting against the enemy garbage, which was as powerful and intimidating as any foreign invader. But in February 1906, after a record-breaking snowfall, and after the DSC had to go upstate to Otisville to draft seventy-five additional men from the sanatorium to help clear the snow, they told Alfred to turn in his uniform.

"What did you do?" Mary asked when she found out. It was a habit she couldn't seem to shake, asking questions she'd never get answers to. "They're desperate for men. They're advertising everywhere. And in the middle of that they let you go?"

When she could see he wasn't going to answer, she followed him down the stairs to the street, stuck to him as he rounded corner after corner, trying to shake her. Finally, he turned around.

"Will you let it go, Mary?"

"No. I don't understand. You have to tell me."

"It's—I don't know. It's not a real goddamn army, but they seem to think it is. It's freezing outside. Every man's gloves are soaked through by lunch. So I had to keep warm."

And Mary knew exactly what had happened. He'd gone to work with his flask, kept it in his pocket or his boot, and had sipped himself to warmth while he was working. And one day, he'd sipped too much.

After that he stopped trying to get work altogether and instead went out early in the morning to sit in Nation's Pub all day long. Mary let it go for a few weeks, reminding herself that men were like cats that needed to lick their wounds for a good long time before going to battle again. And then she stopped letting it go. When he got up and dressed she asked him a dozen times where he was headed and when he finally told her what she already knew, she couldn't stop herself from flying down the stairs of the building after him, telling him that he'd better wake up, pay attention, life was not something to be frittered away on a barstool, and if he wanted a woman who would mollycoddle such a man he'd better look elsewhere. Alfred had always been a drinker. Since the very first day. But he'd been a drinker like all men were drinkers, a constant slow-paced drinker who walked the ledge easily, and in fact got through the day with more work behind him with the help of a little nip now and again. There was a time when no one could shovel coal like Alfred. No one could lead a pack of horses. No one could lift a piano. And what harm if during a job the men passed a flask and had a laugh and kept going, shoulder to the wheel? But what Alfred had done was work his way to the limit of the ledge to peek at what was below. He edged and edged and finally, inevitably, he tumbled forward.

The moments he came out of it were brief, and slipped by Mary like a breeze on a humid afternoon. One day, he was sound enough to fix the plaster by their window, and even repainted the whole wall. Another time, after Mary mentioned only once that they needed a new mattress, he went out and got one and carried it up six flights on his back. He put it on the bed, made up the sheets, and carried the old mattress down to the curb before Mary came home. "Surprise!" he said, after encouraging her to go lie down and rest after such a long day. She didn't check her emergency envelope in the closet. She didn't care. He'd heard her, and acted, and she would not ask a single question and ruin it. Another time, after not coming home for twenty-four hours, he arrived sober, and shaven, and told Mary he was going to take her out for a steak dinner. They'd go to Dolan's, and after, they'd walk down to Germantown and go to a beer hall. Instead of asking him where he'd been, she suggested they skip Dolan's and bring their dinner with them to the beer hall so he'd have more time there, more time for him to speak German with his countrymen, and more time for Mary to listen to that choked language coming out of him. He never spoke German at home. He'd never taught her a single word, and sometimes she wondered if that was the key, if that was the thing that hung between them, and if she were only able to understand him in his first language, she'd be able to understand him completely, and they'd be happy, and everything would make sense.

And then he disappeared again for a few days. Twice, Mary spotted him rounding corners in their neighborhood, and worse, heard him mentioned by the neighbors. "When I talked to Alfred yesterday," one or another of them would say—and Mary would not be able to hear the rest over the blood that rushed to her head. "I can't live like this," she said when he came home next, but he just smiled, and hugged her, and told her he missed her, and pulled her toward him until they were hip to hip, and how did he smell so clean when he'd been on a bender? Where did he go wash himself before coming home? More and more she found herself unable to get past that wall of questions. She couldn't kick sand over that inferno of fury that had started inside her with just one piece of kindling, and then grown with another, then another. When he pulled her toward their bed, she could no longer force her mind to think only of the warm cave of his body, even though she knew things were always better when she did put everything else aside and let him lift her and move her, let him be the Alfred she loved most.

The Fourth of July 1906 saw good Alfred, sober Alfred. He enlisted two other men on the block to go up to East Harlem with him, and together they bought two crates of fireworks, and told as many as they ran into that they would be setting them off at midnight, in the middle of Third Avenue. He referred to it as the annual tradition, though Mary could think of only one other time when he'd ever organized a fireworks show. Down on the street, when midnight came, he'd yelled at everyone to stay the hell back so that no one would get killed. Just as he was about to light the first match he remembered the Borriellos, and their three young boys, and how they wouldn't want to miss it. "Run up, will you, Mary? See if they're awake." He was standing in the middle of the street with a match. Mary and everyone else knew the Borriellos would be awake because who in the city could sleep on such a night? It was the kind of summer night when even the thinnest cotton sheet felt as heavy and stifling as a rough wool blanket. People had taken their pillows to the roofs, to the fire escapes. It was the first unbearable night in a stretch that would last until August, and most of the men had come down in their undershirts. They were all sweating and panting and waiting for the sky to be illuminated.

Mary ran up and pounded on the Borriellos' door. "The boys," she said to Mrs. Borriello, who answered by cracking the door half an inch. "Do they want to come down to the street to see? It'll just be a few minutes. I'll keep an eye on them." There was a pause, and Mary thought the door would be shut, but instead it opened wider and two boys stumbled out and raced past Mary in their bare feet. The baby, the three-year-old, struggled to keep up with his brothers. "They worry I'll change my mind," said Mrs. Borriello, smiling.

"And you? And Mr. Borriello?" Mary said. "Will you come down?"

"I'll watch from the window. My husband is on nights."

"Make sure you watch," Mary said as she turned and rushed after the boys. "I'll bring them right up after."

More people had gathered by the time Mary returned to

the street. A ring of children formed an inside circle, closest to Alfred, and behind the children was a larger ring of adults. Mary recognized people she'd seen come and go at the Second Avenue grocer. She recognized a boy and his father from Twenty-Eighth Street. Alfred hollered at all of them to move back, farther, farther, and finally, when he felt everyone was far enough away, he crouched over the box of cylindrical packages, little circles and rockets with their fuses hanging out like tails, and made a selection. Before Mary could tell him to be careful he'd struck the match against a stone and staggered backward, holding up his arms as if the people who waited were a pack of animals who might stampede.

"What happened?" the older Borriello boy said as the crowd watched the small flame travel up the fuse of the first rocket and then fizzle out.

"A dud," another boy shouted. "Try another!"

Alfred selected another, but the same thing happened. A few of the men stepped forward to confer, and the crowd started getting restless, moving in different directions.

"All right," Alfred called after a moment. "Problem solved." Again, he told everyone to move back, again he told everyone to beware, and on the third try, when he touched the match to the fuse, the little ball of fire ate the thin rope in an instant, and the rocket flew with a wild shriek into the sky, above the tenements of Third Avenue, arcing west for a moment before exploding red, white, and blue high over their heads, seeming to cover the whole island of Manhattan. The audience was transfixed, their faces lit, the kids openmouthed, and for the next half hour, until the very last sparkler had died, Mary was proud of him, that he'd done this for all of them, and she remembered why she loved him.

He was good for three weeks after that. He wasn't working, but he stayed away from the bars, and sometimes made supper, and bought the newspaper for Mary, and went for long walks. When the message came that she had to go to Oyster Bay sooner than planned because the regular cook's grandchild had come early, he acted as if she were lying, as if she had made it up to get away from him. So he disappeared, and when he finally came home just in time to say good-bye, she slipped past him and down to the street. She didn't want to look at him. She didn't want to hear herself say all the things she knew she'd have to say.

The remainder of his toy stock—a set of two play cups and saucers for girls, a china cat with one blue eye and one brown, marbles, a checker set, nearly a dozen toy soldiers without the faces painted on—all of it had been sitting in a box in the corner of their bedroom for the past six months. Before leaving for Oyster Bay, Mary left the whole crate outside the door of the Borriello family.

Looking back from the quiet of North Brother, her bare feet covered in wet sand and with an egret for company, the water lapping at the fallen hem of her skirt, it all seemed like a very long time ago, far longer than just a couple of years. Fighting with Alfred, that hot spring and summer of 1906, up and down the stairs of their building with sweat running in streams between her breasts, it all seemed like a fever that had now broken, and like so many of the patients she'd nursed, now she was on the other side, amazed that her skin was cool to the touch, bewildered by the stark blankness of everything without that heat to color it, without those swings from joy to rage. At the center of everything, like a selection of notes played at a lower register while the rest of the song sways and dives around it, was the fact that she loved him. She'd loved him since she was seventeen, and even when she wanted to take her skillet and swing it at him, even that time when she did take her skillet and swing it at him, she loved him. Everything would be easier if she didn't.

On the evening before Alfred's visit, Mary dragged the tub from a cobwebbed corner of her hut and out to the middle of the room. She ran a damp cloth along the inside to pick up any dust, and then she poured in kettle after kettle of boiling water until it was halfway full. She usually went up to the hospital when she wanted a bath—they had tubs there with running hot and cold water—but she didn't want to be seen or questioned or rushed. She readied her soap, her tooth powder, her washcloth, her shampoo, and when she stepped in and lowered herself, the water rushed for the edges and sloshed over the brim. It ran in streams toward the door.

Mary washed. She pinched her nose and dipped her head under the surface and then rubbed the shampoo into her scalp with her fingertips. She dunked again to rinse. She soaped her neck, her long arms, her legs by lifting one out above the water in a straight line and then the other. She stood up, quickly, and soaped her breasts, her belly, her hips, between her legs, and plunged back into the exquisite warmth of the water and wondered why she didn't perform the same ritual more often.

She soaked, and thought about what attitude she should take when she greeted him. It was unforgiveable, how little he'd been in touch. If it were Alfred who'd been locked up, she would have sent him the things he missed the most. She would have tried to see him even if they told her there were no visitors allowed. But it wasn't Alfred who'd been taken away, and what was the point of saying how she would have been, and how he should have been, and marching out the long list of grievances when he was coming, finally, tomorrow? Maybe he was turning over a new leaf. Aunt Kate, before she died, said he was a rogue, but the charmingest, handsomest rogue she'd ever seen in her life, and Mary knew she liked him, because whenever he stopped up for her, Aunt Kate made him sit in to a plate of stew, and if they had it, a dram of whiskey. Later, Aunt Kate would go around her rooms pointing out pieces Mary could have when she married. Her mantel clock. Her lace-fringed pillows. "And if I'm gone," she said, "I've written it all down for Paddy. 'On Mary's wedding day,' I wrote, and a list of things to be yours."

Mary pulled a clean dressing gown over her head, removed a mason jar from the shelf, and emptied the tub jar by jar until it was light enough to push to the door, where she tipped it. She listened to the water rush down the single stair, onto the grass, into John Cane's pansies and snapdragons. He would not have to water in the morning.

She went about brushing and separating her hair. She had no curlers, so she twisted each section around her finger and then pinned it against her scalp. She had only a dozen pins, and her hair was thick and long, so twice she'd run out and had to start over again with a better sense of proportion. He would probably notice right away the pains she'd taken. He knew her well enough now to know she didn't wake up with curls. Or maybe he'd never noticed.

She counted the years since they met: almost twenty-five.

Two years fewer than she'd been in America. She was employed by the Mott family the first time she saw him, and even though she was washwoman she also worked a little in the scullery as assistant to the cook. It was the agreement they'd come to at the office. If she was ever to be hired as head cook, she had to have experience. She'd left her work trimming beans when she heard the bell ring. Where was the maid? She wiped her hands, and as she came down the hall she could make out the outline of a man's arm and hip in the thin strip of glass inlaid in the thick oak. Other than the bell, the house was completely silent. There were no guests expected that day.

"I've brought the coal," the man said when she opened the door. His barrel sat on the step beside him, and his clothes were covered in coal dust. He had a smudge on his forehead that blended with his coal black hair.

"This is the front door," she said to him in a fierce whisper, quickly stepping outside and shutting the door behind her. "Do you deliver through the front door at other homes?" She glanced back to peer through the strip of glass to see if anyone was coming.

"I usually deliver to businesses," he said. "I'm covering." He didn't seem to notice Mary's response and made no move to lift his barrel and move along. He crossed his arms and leaned against the iron banister that led up the three wide steps to the door.

"So what are you then? Nanny?"

"No," Mary said. He had high cheekbones that reminded her of a wolf. He also had a masculine jaw, a throat flecked with black stubble. On the first floor of Aunt Kate's building lived a sixteen-year-old boy who always seemed to be hopping a ball on the street when Mary entered or exited the building, and once in a while he came up to knock on their door. Mary had no more interest in him than she did in any other boy in Hell's Kitchen. He was someone to talk to when there was nothing to do, but when he tried to kiss her inside the first-floor vestibule, Mary had dodged him and then laughed. Now he hopped his ball outside another building.

"Washwoman?"

Mary nodded, and clutched her hands behind her back. He seemed to Mary to be at least twenty-five, and as they each waited for the other to speak she noticed the gentle flutter at his neck.

"Alfred," he said, extending his hand. Mary shook it quickly and then looked at the black dust he'd left behind on it. "And you're Mary."

"How did you know?"

"All the Irish girls are named Mary. Every single one. Swear to God."

"Ah," Mary said, her glance falling again on the flutter at his neck. She wanted to put her thumb there, feel the beating of his blood. The horse he'd left on the street seemed an angry animal. He was pitching forward and back, stamping with impatience, and the hill of coal in the cart was sliding, a few hard lumps hitting the road. Perhaps the horse knew its master had knocked on the wrong door. It was March, late in the winter for a delivery of coal, but the family had almost run out and feared the cold nights that late March and even April might bring.

"Aren't you gonna tell me not to swear to God?"

"What?" Mary said and felt as if she had to shake herself awake. "What are you?" She thought she detected an accent in certain words, but she couldn't pin it down.

"All American," he said, and opened his arms wide. Every time he moved, a fine layer of black dust drifted down to the step where they were standing. He lowered his arms. "German. But I've been here since I was six."

"And how old are you now?"

"You ask a lot of questions." He seemed amused. "Twenty-two. You?"

"Seventeen."

He looked at Mary that day, bright green eyes rimmed with lashes as black as the coal in his bin, and for a few seconds Mary no longer cared if someone came up the hall and spotted them through the glass. His work shirt was unbuttoned at the very top, and underneath, the neck of his undershirt had gone black with soot. When he took off his clothes at the end of the day, there would be parts of him that could not be scrubbed clean, and other parts that were pure white.

"Which door is it, then?"

Mary pointed to the servants' entrance, which also served for house deliveries, especially deliveries of dirty things, like coal, or things that might drip, or have an odor, or in general any type of thing that the family would prefer not to know about. Just inside the servants' door was the chute where any coal man would know to send the black stones down to the cellar.

"They like to know their beds are warm, their underwear clean, but they don't like to know how it gets that way."

Alfred raised an eyebrow. "That's cheeky."

Mary didn't know why she'd said it out loud, but now that she had she couldn't disown it. She hadn't expected a reprimand, especially not from a man who'd left a trail of coal that someone else would have to sweep away. Not even sweep, Mary corrected herself, remembering how coal dust smeared and spread further when wiped. She'd probably have to fill a bucket and drag it out there to splash the dust away. The work that would be, and in this cold. Mary was tired of having wet, cold hands in wet, cold weather.

"It was cheeky of you to ring this bell," Mary said. "Use your head. Does any family take a coal delivery through the front door?"

Alfred shrugged, but Mary noticed the skin around his collar become mottled. "I told you I'm covering."

Mary leaned over the rail and again pointed out the lower door, almost around the side of the house but not quite. As she leaned, he also leaned, to see what she was seeing, and Mary felt the rough cloth of his work shirt against the thin cotton at her back. She sensed the body within, solid and strong. "There," she said, and when she looked back at him over her shoulder he wasn't looking toward the door at all. Mary worried about the lamb's blood she'd wiped on her apron, about Mr. Mott's twelve dress shirts that had to be soaked, rinsed, dried, pressed, and hung, and about him, this grown man, who even on a cold, wet day seemed to give off warmth like a flagstone in summer, long after the sun goes down.

Still with that half smile, he took both handles of the coal bin, heaved it up with a forward thrust of the hips, and made his way to the far door.

"I'll see ya, Miss," he said. Inside, with the doors closed tight, Mary listened to hard knots of anthracite slide along the metal throat of the chute, the crunch of his large tin scoop driven into the pile again and again.

Saturday morning was overcast, and the skies threatened to storm. When she woke and smelled rain in the air she told herself not to be disappointed if he didn't come. The ferries wouldn't run if the waters were too rough, and it wouldn't be his fault. But when she

MARY BETH KEANE

went outside to see if she could spot the dock through the fog, everything seemed to be running as usual. John Cane stepped out of the mist and onto the path just before Mary, with a covered plate in his hand.

"Everything all right?" he inquired, peering at her unusual hairstyle.

"Fine." She took the plate, peeked under the lid, and sighed. After two and a half years she was getting to the point where she would mug someone for a good plate of eggs and rashers. "Are the ferries operating on time?"

"They are," John said, putting one foot. "Why? Expecting someone? That lawyer?"

"You are the nosiest person I ever knew in my life."

"Your man?"

"I don't put it that way, but yes."

"What kind of name is Alfred anyway? What's his surname?"

"Briehof. It's German."

"What part of Germany?"

"John, do you have any work to do today? Are you paid to work, or just to visit?"

"I just like to know things is all."

"Doesn't everyone? But not everyone thinks it's right to ask."

"Not everyone. That's true. Take you for example. You've hardly asked me a single thing."

"Okay, tell me something about yourself."

But John just shrugged and walked back up to the hospital.

Mary saw him before the ferry docked. She saw his dark head swaying with the rhythm of the water. She watched him leap from the boat to the pier without the assistance of the handrail. She watched him say something to the ferry's captain, and then both men wheeled around to face Mary's bungalow. She lifted her arm and waved.

They walked toward each other. He leaned in to kiss her when they met on the path, but she told him to wait, not yet, she'd say when. He looked so good, and so young, and so healthy. His teeth were clean and white. His neck was shaved close without a single nick. He was tall. He moved with the ease of a man who was well fed, and well washed, and had full use of his lungs and got physical exercise every day. So this is how she appeared to the patients of the hospital. This was the light they were looking at when they sat, wrapped in blankets and propped up on hospital benches and stared at her, struggling to recall what being fully alive was like. Mary and Alfred, they weren't as young as they once were, but they weren't so bad, not so bad at all. She pointed out the hospital building, the chapel, the coal house, the male dormitory, the morgue, the nurses' quarters, the physicians' quarters, the lighthouse, the female dormitory, the stable, the sheds, and her own little shack, which she promised to show him later. She led him down the path that John Cane had cleared for her, down to the beach and her snowy egret. They found a damp log to sit on, and she pointed out the Bronx to their left, and to their right South Brother and Rikers. To their far right was Astoria, and behind them, of course, was Manhattan. She asked him if North Brother was as he had pictured it.

"No," he said. "There's more here than I thought. It's like its own little village. And yet . . ."

"What?"

"It's still empty. Where is everyone?"

"They're patients. Most of them will die here. Or they work here, and they go home at night."

Mary waited for him to kiss her again, but the moment seemed to have passed. He seemed darker now, caught up in thoughts of his own, and she worried that he regretted coming, that he'd come up with an excuse to leave.

"How are things at the ice company?"

He didn't seem to hear her. "What's to stop you from getting on the ferry one day and going over? Disappearing? Couldn't you work under another name?"

"The guards, for a start. The ferry captain. It's always the same man, and he knows me."

"You could hide. You could wait for a moment when he's not looking and then hide on the boat, under the bench, and then sneak off on the other end when he's occupied with something."

"You saw the size of the boat. And they run it only if there's people to take it. Do you think it would work?"

Alfred was silent, brooding over something.

"Besides, I don't want to work under another name. I haven't done a thing wrong. I should be allowed to work under my own name. Mr. O'Neill says he's making progress, and . . ."

"Mary—"

". . . there are men who've done the same as I'm accused of and they're walking free—"

"I have to tell you something."

Alfred walked to the water's edge, picked up a stone, and threw it.

So this was it, Mary thought, this, whatever this was, this was the thing that had driven him uptown and across Hell Gate to see her. He kept his back to her, and she remained silent. She would not make it easier by drawing it out of him.

"I wanted to tell you when you were kept at that hotel, but then they wouldn't let me see you, and I didn't want to tell you during the hearing because I was afraid you'd make a scene and hurt your case, so this is better, really, this way, alone here. I think it's best anyway."

"Why would I make a scene?" Whatever it was, she would not make a scene in this spot, the only peaceful place she'd discovered on the entire island.

"You've been gone for more than two years now . . ."

Mary put her hands to her head and her chin to her knees. She knew it. She damned well knew it. She knew it, and she didn't know she knew it.

". . . and most of the papers say they're never letting you off this island."

Mary stood up from the log, brushed off the back of her skirt, and headed up the path. He took a few quick steps after her and caught her arm.

"Like I told you, I couldn't afford the Thirty-Third Street rooms, so I took a bed at the Meaneys'."

"Oh, yes! The happy Meaneys and their son Samuel, for whom you like to set a good example."

"For whom Mrs. Meaney forced me to set a good example. After a week there she said I could stay on only if I stopped drinking."

"And yet you're still there."

"I did the Oppenheimer Treatment. I'm still doing it. Her husband did it and it worked for him and she thought it might work for me."

"It's bogus. Everyone knows it's bogus. They take your money and you drink the quinine until you're so sick you can't take a sip of anything, and then the cure is telling you not to drink. Then the day you stop the quinine it doesn't work anymore. The husband is still not drinking?"

"The husband is dead."

Mary squatted on the path, touched her fingertips to the ground to steady herself. That was it. She almost smiled. She'd felt it between them when she saw him in New York, but she couldn't put a name on it. Now she could. Alfred remained standing.

"How long dead?"

"About five years now."

Mary felt her stomach lurch. "You said the Meaneys might let me stay with you there until we found our own place. You said you'd ask. When you spoke of them you said 'They' and implied a mister and a missus."

"I did."

"Why?"

"I"—Alfred leaned against a tree—"I just thought I'd explain it all later, away from all those people. Or I thought maybe I'd leave the Meaneys that afternoon once you got free and we'd get our own place again. I hadn't decided. I was still deciding. Liza is not as strong as you are. I'd have to be very careful about it."

"And now you've decided."

"I wasn't given a choice! Those judges decided! What am I to do, Mary? Live like a monk for the rest of my life? You know I love you. And as God is my witness, to this day I've never met anyone like you, but I thought there were things we understood about each other. And there's the boy. He's a good boy, a smart boy. He—"

Mary held up her hand. "I don't care one fiddle about that boy, or about delicate Liza." She itched to slap him, but it would hurt him more if she didn't care. She felt her lungs heaving, her blood moving just under the surface of her skin, but instead of taking a stick and beating him, instead of unleashing the long string of words that had lined up, she simply walked away. At the top of the path, at the point where John had to get on his knees with his scythe and clear the brambles and thorns, she turned around.

"I have only one question, and I want you to tell me the truth." She would not cry. She would not let her voice waver. "I begged you to stop drinking. I hauled you up all those stairs. I gave you money when you couldn't work. I shaved you. I cut your hair. Do you know how good things would have been if you hadn't been drinking? Remember how good those stretches were when you didn't drink? Do you remember?"

"I remember. Of course I remember." He stepped toward her, and she stepped back.

"So why, when Liza Meaney asked, did you march yourself straight to the doctor's office for the Oppenheimer cure?" Mary felt the pin curls loosen from the bun where she'd gathered them. She felt how lank and pathetic each tendril was that hung about her face.

"I don't know. I do know that I love you, Mary. As much as always. And I could never love her like I love you."

"You can love her as much as you like, Alfred."

"Wait." Alfred grabbed her elbow, and she spun, turned on him ready to fight if he came any closer. "There's one more thing."

"What's that?

"And just know before I tell you that it's because of the boy. He's still young, and it's only—"

Mary laughed. She tipped back her head and laughed. She laughed at the birds, at the tops of the trees, at the waves, at the furious, roiling Hell Gate, at the sound of the foghorn in the distance, at the thought of John Cane hurrying with her plate, at the doctors, at the nurses, at their needles, their test tubes, their glass collection canisters. She laughed at her own stupidity, and at the stupidity of all the fools working and living and breathing over in Manhattan. She laughed at herself, for ever having been sorry to have left it.

"You've asked her to marry you."

"And she's said yes."

After he left, after she watched the ferry pull away from the dock and churn west, Mary went back to her spot by the water. Her snowy egret had not shown itself while Alfred was there, and stayed hidden now. She hugged her knees, feeling the hollow place that laugh had bubbled forth from earlier. If there was something funny in what he'd told her, she could no longer see it.

After a while, she realized it was getting dark, and it had started to rain again. The loose sand that met with the tree line was pressed down by the drops, and then it was pouring, the drops hitting the river so hard that the surface of the water jumped and frothed, and she hoped if his ferry had not reached the other side yet that it would fill up with this angry weather and sink. And then she hoped it wouldn't.

Late, long after the supper hour, long after the island had gone dark, she saw electric torches approaching from the small wooded divide that separated her from the hospital. She heard voices on John's path.

Two nurses approached her and put their umbrellas together to cover her as they walked her back. "What are you thinking, Mary?" the one asked. "What are you doing?"

The other said, "You'll make yourself sick."

THIRTEEN

"How are you doing, Mary?" Mr. O'Neill asked.

It was the fourth day of February 1910, their second face-to-face meeting since the disappointment of the hearing the previous summer. It was unseasonably warm, and instead of meeting in Mary's bungalow, or in one of the meeting rooms of the hospital, Mr. O'Neill suggested they sit at one of the new picnic tables at the Tuberculosis Pavilion and take in the fresh air. So far, Mary had not seen anyone else use the new tables, and said so to Mr. O'Neill. "Even better," he said. "We'll be first." He wanted her to be outside when he told her the news. He wanted her to be able to whoop and shout and dance. He wanted her to be able to celebrate in full view of all those hospital windows looking down on them from above, all those eyes behind the windows, observing, trying to guess what was going on. Hers was the longest case he'd ever worked on, and at home, over the weekend, his wife had already invited their friends to open bottles of champagne and toast him.

Of all the women he'd ever encountered in his life, Francis O'Neill decided that Mary Mallon was the hardest to read. Last time he'd come to see her, just before Christmas, he told her that there was hope for her case, more hope than ever before. A new health commissioner was to be installed early in 1910, and he'd already gone on record with his sympathy for Mary's plight. "It's likely he'll release you once he takes office," Mr. O'Neill told Mary. He imagined this would be a Christmas gift to her, a baton of hope that she could carry through the holidays, but the news didn't seem to register at all. A few of the doctors at the hospital mentioned that she seemed to have mellowed since the summer. Where she'd always seemed to take great pains to appear neat and presentable, to tell Mr. O'Neill her opinion on all matters, related to her case or not, she now seemed subdued, worn down. Her hair was unclean and falling out of her bun. Her collar drooped. Her lips were so chapped that he could see where they'd cracked, and bled, and dried, and broken open again.

"I guess we'll see," was all Mary said then, and instead seemed more interested in the food he'd brought for her, all wrapped in parcel packages like Christmas presents. Smoked ham, cheese, candied walnuts, chocolate-covered cherries, Christmas cookies. She opened the walnuts for them to share during that meeting, but he didn't want to put his fingers in the box where her fingers had been, so he told her that walnuts didn't agree with his stomach. "Shall I open the cherries?" But he said no, he'd eaten just before leaving the city, and she'd leveled a look at him as if to say she'd heard that one before.

Back then, he'd attributed her mood to the general lowness some people feel around Christmas, and reminded himself that it was hard enough to be alone at the holidays, and even harder for her. But now, on a fine February day with every promise of spring in the air, he'd come to see her with more news, and she didn't seem any more interested than before.

"Health Commissioner Lederle has been installed," he said once they were seated.

"Who?"

"The new commissioner I mentioned when we last met."

"Yes. Yes, of course."

"And one of the things we've been talking about—not just he and I but many medical people—is how many carriers there are, Mary. It's become clear now that there must be hundreds of them. Thousands. Your case is not so special after all, and that's a good thing."

Mary frowned and picked at a splinter of wood in the tabletop.

"Mary"—he waited until she looked at him—"he's decided to release you. The paperwork has already gone through. You will be off this island and back home by the end of the week."

He brought her a present to go with the news. It was his wife's idea, and when he agreed, she'd gone straight out to get for Mary, whom she'd never met, something colorful and beautiful, something any woman would be proud to wear. "Men don't understand about having nice things to wear," she said, and he told her to go to the same shops she visited, spend the same as she would spend on herself. He took it out now, and pushed it across the table toward her. She laid the package on her lap, but only played with the string.

"What do you mean about my case being not so special? That means they still believe I gave the fever to all those people."

"Well . . . yes."

They'd been on this case together long enough to be frank.

She was every bit as intelligent as she insisted she was. "It is true, you know," he said. "You are a carrier. It's difficult to accept, but you must have had time to think about it over these three years. The point is that it's not your fault."

"But I cooked for so many people who never got sick. I cooked for hundreds of people over the years. And only twenty-three, I don't—"

"That's part of it, too. The way it comes and goes. And some people are immune. That's one of the reasons they've kept you here, to study your patterns, but it's not your responsibility to provide them with the data they need, and Lederle agrees. They can't lock up everyone who carries the fever. The best alternative right now is to let you go on the condition that you will never cook for hire again. You are no harm to anyone unless you are cooking."

Mary sighed. Of course. It was what he'd been urging her to volunteer since the very beginning, to quit cooking, to give up one life and sign on for another.

"The commissioner has objected to your confinement since day one, and through his own contacts he's already gotten you work at a laundry. It's on Washington Place, right by the park."

Mary did a few quick calculations in her head. She'd have to stay in a boardinghouse at first, and then she'd have to get a room to share. A laundry. A laundress. Time was moving backward.

"And you'll have to check in with the Department of Health every three months, so they can keep track of you, take your samples and all that. You're not the only one. They're doing that with all the carriers they know about so they can more easily locate the source of an outbreak if one occurs."

"For how long? The checking in, I mean?"

"For the rest of your life," Mr. O'Neill said. "Or until they find a cure. Or until vaccination becomes routine."

"For the rest of my life," Mary repeated. "What if I move?"

"You'll have to let the DOH know, and then you'll register wherever you end up. Are you thinking of leaving New York?"

"No." She wasn't, and didn't even know why she'd asked. "What about Soper? Will I have to see him again?"

"No," Mr. O'Neill said. He leaned closer to Mary as if they were old friends catching up. "I hear he's trying to peddle a memoir and is having no luck."

Mr. O'Neill's smile disappeared when he saw Mary's face. Mary hated that man more than she hated any person she'd ever known in her life.

"Just open the present, Mary." He tapped the box.

She untied the ribbon, folded back the tissue paper, and discovered the most beautiful emerald green shawl she'd ever seen. Along the edges were birds stitched in royal blue. She wrapped it around her shoulders and pictured how it must look against the red in her hair. She remembered her beloved blue hat with the silk flowers. Where had it ended up? She imagined it hanging in George Soper's office, a memento of his life's work.

Mr. O'Neill waited for her to speak, and she knew he wanted her to say more, to jump up and down and be happy, but she couldn't speak because she didn't trust her tongue to contain its acid, and it was not his fault if he didn't understand the difference between a cook and a laundress. She'd make a third of what she was making before, probably less. Her knuckles would itch and crack and bleed and cramp and when she became an old woman her hands wouldn't work at all anymore, and she'd have to get neighbors to come upstairs and open jars, twist doorknobs. It would be like Mr. O'Neill having to leave his position as attorney and go to work instead as the bicycle messenger who brought paperwork back and forth between the law offices and the court-house all day.

But she closed her eyes and took a breath and decided to sweep away every disappointment, to look instead at what he was offering. She remembered how scared she'd been in Queenstown, waiting for that ship to lower its gangway, and again in Castle Garden, where no one understood her brogue and a stranger had hooked her by the eyelid and peered at her like he would an inter-esting fish. She'd been scared when she met Alfred, and again when Aunt Kate died. She'd been scared before, she'd be scared again. She'd be fine.

"Thank you," she said. "It's really lovely. Tell your wife thank you, too."

"I will."

The next morning, she opened the door of her hut to find her newspaper had been opened and refolded so that an article from the city section was on top. "Typhoid Mary to Be Released by Week's End" the headline read.

"Typhoid Mary," she whispered as she reached for the paper. Unlike the other names they'd given her—most often the Germ Woman, a title that seemed and felt anonymous, something she could easily disown—Typhoid Mary had a ring to it, and as she studied the boldface type of the paper in her hand she felt it settle on her. She felt it stick.

Word spread quickly around the island. The nurses came in pairs and groups of three to say good-bye. Maybe they had more sympathy than she'd credited, Mary considered as they bade her best wishes and good luck. Maybe she'd been kinder than she thought. Even Dr. Albertson made his way down the path one afternoon. "Good luck to you, Mary," he said, and continued on his way for a walk.

John Cane avoided her. One morning, when it snowed, he cleared her step while she was in the hospital signing forms, and she could see by the footprints he left that he was avoiding the path. "John!" she called to him another morning. She was walking from the lighthouse and he was over by the nurses' dormitory, shaking salt on the narrow road. But he didn't hear her, or wouldn't listen, and by the time she arrived at the place where he'd been standing, he was nowhere in sight.

Finally, on Thursday afternoon, she caught him walking near her door. "John!" she called out from her step. She waved him over. He seemed to hesitate, but then turned onto the path that led to her hut.

"Are you avoiding me?" she asked, smiling, hoping to disarm him. She didn't want to leave him angry with her, and she didn't want to leave without him accepting that he had no reason to be angry.

"Nope."

"Do you know I'm leaving tomorrow?"

"I heard something about that."

"Well, aren't you going to say good-bye?"

"I was going to wait." He stamped his boots and left treads of snow outside her door. "You still have another day. Don't get ahead of yourself."

"John—"

"Besides, it's like you said, those people are tricky and they might change their minds at the last minute, and then won't we all feel a bit silly for having said good-bye?"

"They won't change their minds. It's all signed and sealed. I have a job waiting for me."

"Well, good. That's good."

Mary understood what was eating him, but there was no possible way to say it. After he'd pinned her for not asking him any personal questions, she'd made sure to pose a few, now and again, in light conversation, and over the months she'd learned that he had no wife, no children, and lived on East Ninety-Eighth Street with his younger brother, who was bigger and stronger than John, but who was not right in his mind, and could not hold a job because he was prone to fits so violent that he'd once bitten clear through his own tongue. This brother tried to care for John like a wife, doing the cleaning, the shopping, the cooking, but he was not a wife, not nearly a wife, and Mary also understood without ever needing to ask the question that what John wanted his whole life long was a real wife, and he had not given up.

"I want to tell you something," John said, and Mary cursed herself for letting it come to this. "I want to tell you that I don't think things are so bad here on North Brother. I think it's a pretty spot and your bungalow is sound, if a little on the damp side, but show me a building that isn't. And I think you have to admit you've had pretty good company when you've sought it. You've had someone to talk to, is what I mean. Would you agree?"

"I agree completely."

"But you still want to leave."

"Yes."

"Well, then I want to tell you something else. That Alfred who came here that time. Your man. Yes, I know you said he's not your man anymore, and yes I know you didn't put it like that, but I can put two and two together, and what I want to say is that Alfred is not a good character. I don't mean because of what the papers said about the way you lived, or any of that. I just mean man to man, I can tell a good one from a bad one, and I don't trust that one to stay away from you once you're over there again. Remember I said that, and remember that he didn't have the patience to wait for you while you were here, like any other man would. Like a few other men I can think of would have done without a doubt. And now look where his impatience got him. Don't forget that, Mary, once he comes around."

"I won't forget," Mary promised, and all the humor she'd felt a moment earlier, all the warmth toward her friend, disappeared, and instead she felt her stomach tighten, her head fill up with electric sparks.

"Well, I had to say it," John said, and now, his burden lifted, he seemed like the old John, at home with himself and with the door frame of Mary's bungalow. "And maybe we can visit sometime, over there, and I can tell you the news of North Brother. We can go for a walk or something."

"John." She stepped forward and hugged him, and felt where the top of his head met with her ear. She couldn't help it, she felt it was like hugging a child, a solid, muscular child, but still a child, a child's narrow shoulders, a child's way of clinging to her when he wants comfort, and she couldn't muster up a single morsel of attraction toward him. "Let's do that."

FOURTEEN

When Mary was seventeen but passing herself off as twenty-five or twenty-six, turning from the sidewalk and pushing the heavy wrought-iron gate that led to the front door of a house like the Warrens had rented in Oyster Bay, or the Bowens had on Park Avenue, would have made her body a hard knot of dread. It was worse when the woman of the house was young, newly married, maybe only eighteen or twenty herself. Girls of twenty know by instinct who is at least their own age and who is younger, and Mary would compensate by marching into the kitchen with authority, maybe even a little disdain. She'd thicken her accent like a gravy on the stove and hope that would explain to them why she seemed so young. A cultural difference, Mary could see the young mistress thinking. This is the way Irish are, I suppose. Once, when she arrived to cook for the Hill family on Riverside Drive, the mistress had taken one look at her and told her outright that she didn't believe Mary's age or experience. Mary had just turned eighteen, and had slowly been getting jobs the agency didn't know about. Aunt Kate would hear about something from a friend, or Mary would answer an ad in the newspaper. In addition to a home so large that it could have housed a dozen families, the Hills had three carriages, six horses, and a pair of Shetland ponies for the children, who were not yet old enough to ride them. Mrs. Hill told Mary to be on her way.

"I only look young," Mary insisted, feeling as she said it exactly what she was: a skinny child who hadn't eaten a proper meal since her last employment. "You'll get no one else out here today. I might as well make dinner before I go."

Mrs. Hill hesitated. "I am hungry," she admitted, and patted her considerable belly. "Only porridge this morning."

After showing Mary to the kitchen, Mrs. Hill left her alone to create something wonderful out of the bland bits and pieces that had been left behind by the previous cook and the pale chicken carcass the porter had been sent out to fetch that morning. Mary found flour, butter, eggs, raisins, rosemary, three old apples she knocked on and then tested for juice with her front teeth. An hour later she brought Mr. and Mrs. Hill, along with their two children, plates of walnut and raisin chicken salad, with fresh bread and baked apples on the side. She stayed at the Hills' until her true age was exposed by a porter who'd overlapped with her at a job in Brooklyn Heights. For the next few months Mary had to go back to washing and ironing, giving her the feeling that life was just one long, narrow road, with no turns, no peaks or valleys.

"I can't take it," she used to say to Aunt Kate when she'd go home.

"You'll take it," Aunt Kate assured her. "You'll take it like everyone else."

She'd been repeating the words to herself since stepping onto the ferry: You are no longer a cook. You are a laundress. You signed the papers. Better to be a laundress in New York City than a cook trapped in a bungalow on an island of death.

The boardinghouse where she'd slept since Friday night served decent-enough food, to Mary's surprise, but she didn't like the company. Men slept on a different floor than the women, but they all took their meals together, and there was too much eyeing and gawking for Mary to be able to enjoy her plate. To the one wall-eyed man who kept breathing in her direction, and then whispered that he liked the look of her, she'd stated plainly that she'd make him sorry if he ever came near her. He'd laughed, the food he'd just eaten a pulp on his exposed tongue, but she'd stared at him without changing her expression. He snapped his mouth closed and turned back to his beef and barley.

When Mary walked into the laundry on that Monday morning in February 1910, she felt flat, tired, and hungry, as if all those years between hurrying after Paddy Brown in Castle Garden and that moment, pushing open the door to a Chinese laundry, were no more than a matter of weeks, and she was no older now than she'd been then. The laundry was on Washington Place and Greene Street, directly next to the taller Asch Building, and on Mary's first day the entrance was blocked by a lake of icy slush so deep she had to hitch up her skirt to stride through it. It was a busy street, full of students from New York University and women working at the factories up and down the block.

The laundry was open to customers every day except for Sundays, and the washers, too, had the day off. But those who ironed and hung had to show up for at least four or five hours on Sundays in order to press and fold or hang what had been washed the day before. It was a small operation—a front room to welcome customers; a middle room where Chu, the owner, slept; and a back room where all the washing and pressing took place alongside a little kitchen and sitting area that they were allowed to use for thirty minutes out of every day. Chu did not speak to Mary, but directed all his instructions to another Chinese man named Li, and Li translated all Chu's instructions for Mary. Here is where you stand, he told her. Here is how you wring. Here is how you shake out, how you hang, how you feel for dampness. In certain fabrics it was preferable to iron before completely dry; in others the garment must absolutely be bone-dry before touching with a hot iron or else the iron would stick, and the garment would burn, and Mary would be out of a day's wages. The irons must be kept hot, but not so hot that they would scorch, and they must be kept clean. Mary would find, Li warned, that by the end of the day the irons would feel heavier, and Mary would be slower to move them, and so she should be on guard for this always. Everyone was to take turns up front if Chu was not available, or if he couldn't make himself understood, or if the customer did not want to speak to a Chinese.

Li gave her the main instructions for handling the customers: no one, under any circumstances, could pick up laundry without a ticket unless Chu gave his explicit permission. Mary should not be surprised if people came in asking for clothes that had never existed, and then demanding compensation for those imaginary clothes. She must never concede. If she thought she was being swindled, she should stop and get help. Keep the cash drawer locked. And finally, because Mary spoke English, she'd be asked to serve as interpreter from time to time.

"But you speak English," she said, interrupting him.

"You are white. They won't try so many tricks with you. My father was born here, and me as well, but I still have a Chinese face."

"But not as Chinese as Chu," Mary said, before she'd stopped to think that maybe it wasn't a good idea to have him know she'd been studying his unusual face.

Li regarded her with an expression she couldn't read. "My mother was white. And my father's mother. There are only two dozen Chinese women in all of New York City. Three dozen at the absolute most." His face was very grave, and Mary knew that whether it was true or not, he believed it. Then when she thought about it, she realized she couldn't remember ever seeing a Chinese woman. Not in the markets. Not on the streets. Not in the tenements. Nowhere.

"You are Irish, we know, and we hope that doesn't cause trouble for us. The Irish cause trouble for the Chinese more than any other. You being here is a favor because Commissioner Lederle vouched for you."

Mary didn't know what to say to that, so she didn't say anything.

"How do you know him, by the way? Did you work for his family?"

"No, I don't know him," Mary said quickly.

"Yes. Well," Li said, and then told her to get to work. "He brings his shirts here from time to time."

The work was as tedious as Mary remembered, with none of

the magic that came with cooking. Where she needed only her knife and a pan of hot butter to turn a few ordinary, ugly spuds into something wonderful, the laundry offered no real transformations. The two Lithuanian women remained hunchbacked over their tubs of water all day long, their bodies angled to get strength in their arms where there wasn't any left. They had red faces, and Mary supposed it was the physical effort of their work, and from keeping their noses so close to the hot water and its broth of chemicals made to strip the clothes of odor, of any evidence of the bodies that had worn them. After twenty minutes of instruction on the box, Mary was made the mangle woman. Li stood at the head of the contraption, a flat box about three feet long and ten inches high, and showed her how to wrap bed linens or tablecloths around the pins below, and then how to push the wheel on top to make the box roll over these large, flat items that didn't need detailing or shape. Later, when she was done with the items that needed mangling, she could be boss of the irons, sanding and polishing the ones that had cooled. Amid all of this labor, this orchestra of pushing and pulling and wrestling with waterlogged fabrics, walked Chu, who gave Mary stern looks and clicked his tongue.

On Mary's second day, she arrived at the laundry at the appointed time, but an hour into her work realized she'd been expecting something different that day, some slight deviation from the day before. By the third and fourth days she realized that there would never be any deviation. She arrived. Hung her coat. Pushed up her sleeves. Began to work. At precisely the noon hour she stopped to eat an apple and a wedge of cheese, while the Lithuanians sat across the table from her and made a picnic of black bread and dumplings stuffed with some kind of minced meat that Mary wanted to take apart with her fork and examine. They spoke in their own language and didn't bother with Mary at all. At half noon she was back mangling, rolling the large, flat board over florals and plaids, linens and thin cottons. In the afternoons she marked time by the sudden surge of girls that spilled onto the sidewalk as the shift changed at the shirtwaist factory next door. The ones arriving called out greetings to one another as they hurried to the entrance. The ones leaving for the day stood in groups of three and four on the sidewalk outside the laundry and talked of their plans. Once in a while one of them would hold out her hand for the others to admire a new engagement ring. Listening to them, Mary felt apart from everything around her, as if someone had gotten hold of her and was warning her to stay quiet as she watched the hours and days of her life unfold, someone else playing the lead.

You'll take it, she heard her aunt Kate say. You'll take it like everyone else.

In the evenings, even though it was late and dark, and even though she didn't like walking to the boardinghouse at night because the block was almost abandoned, Mary roamed the city and tried to look forward to summer, when there would still be a little light left in the day once her work was over. She drew a large square in her mind and avoided every point between Twenty-Fifth and Thirty-Eighth Streets, and between Second Avenue and Park, in case she would run into someone she knew. Not that it mattered, she reminded herself, with Alfred all the way downtown. After so many years together, even avoiding the place where they'd lived, reminders of him stood on other corners, other blocks. Between the two of them, they'd worked or walked every neighborhood.

At night, in her narrow single room, the light from the lamp not strong enough to read by, Mary lay on her back and remembered she was still young. She was working. She was luckier than most. She was not a woman who felt loneliness. She was not a woman who got weepy or complained. She was not, had never been, and wouldn't become one now. And then, as sometimes happened when the hour got late, and there wasn't enough to occupy her, and she couldn't sleep, and her whole body felt full up with a question in need of an answer though she couldn't think of exactly what the question might be, she thought of him, the other him, that baby, that boy, dead now for eleven years. She imagined Mr. Kirkenbauer remarried, with other children, another wife, another new house. Did anyone ever visit that boy? He'd been thriving when she met him. He'd been growing, and running, and learning his words, and accepting everything he was taught with joy. And then Mary had arrived for a job and he was dead within five weeks. That one, that baby, more than any of the ones on Dr. Soper's list, more than even her sister's twins who'd seemed like little more than empty vessels from the very start, more than any of the ones they accused her of harming, Tobias Kirkenbauer bothered her most.

If it was her fault, like they said it was. If she was to blame. If she was a walking, breathing germ, a death sentence. If it was her arrival that had killed him. Her letting him eat off her spoon. Her kissing him and squeezing him. If he really did die because of her, then she asked Jesus for Mercy. She didn't mean to, she told God. She didn't know. Late at night, long after the other boarders were most likely asleep in their beds, she wondered about all those lab tests that came back positive, and all those lectures they gave to her about Typhoid bacilli and hot soup versus cold salad, and what heating at high temperatures does to food, and where germs like to grow and thrive, and how, in all likelihood, it was her ice creams and puddings that were to blame. She thought back to the ship that brought her to America, and all those bodies that had been dropped into the gray ocean, a trail of heavy, sewn-up sacks she could follow back home, if she ever chose to leave America one day.

Anyway, it didn't matter anymore, Mary told herself in the morning as she rushed to rub a washcloth over her face. It didn't matter, she repeated as she struggled to pull on thick tights under her skirt, and watched her own breath hover around her face as she grew more agitated. She knew, once again, that she hadn't killed that boy any more than she had killed any of the other people in that great, wide, filthy, throbbing city. It would be laughable, really, if it weren't already criminal for them to have locked her up, one woman, a cook, when every corner of America hid a pestilence just waiting to be stirred up, set free.

After six weeks at the laundry she'd made enough to rent a bed from a widow on the west side. She'd seen the ad in the paper, and instead of mailing her inquiry across town she'd walked it over and pushed it through the mail slot of the building. Although the building was not grand, Mary acknowledged when she was back on the sidewalk looking at it that it was a perfectly decent one. And with just two women in the rooms it wouldn't be much to keep it clean and everything in its place. The widow wrote to Mary with the date that she should come and the price of the bed. It will be like living with Aunt Kate, Mary decided as she gathered her few things from the boardinghouse. It'll be something to get used to at first but after a while it will become routine, and she'll look forward to seeing me, and who knew? Mary might be there for the rest of the woman's life. She'd heard plenty of cases where a boarder becomes like one of the family, and she didn't see why it wasn't possible in her case as well. How difficult it must be, she thought as she crossed the avenues and bent her head against the spring wind, to be an old woman in this city, to have to worry about gathering wood or coal, putting food on the table.

She walked and walked, and finally turned on Eighth Avenue for the final stretch.

"Yes?" a woman answered Mary's knock, but a young woman, younger than Mary, with Mary's same style of hair and a nicer blouse.

"I'm here about the bed. I wrote last week and Mrs. Post wrote back to say I should come today."

The woman sighed, throwing up her hands. "Come in." She moved aside with a theatrical half curtsy, and Mary stepped past her into the small kitchen. She admired the window over the sink, and the little square of stained glass that someone had hung to catch the light. Then she turned slightly and noticed a cot. That would be fine. She'd slept in plenty of kitchens. Abutting the foot of that cot, she noticed another. Then, on the other side of the kitchen, another.

"Oh, there's more," the woman promised, pointing to the next room. Mary peeked into a darkened bedroom and took in the larger bed pushed up against the wall, the buffer of cots all around. There was nowhere to walk. The person or people who slept in the larger bed must have to crawl over the cots to get to the door.

"But the ad," Mary said, wanting to argue the situation into the one she'd imagined, and not the one that was.

"Look, you want to stay? Great. I'm out of here next week. You on a regular shift or a night shift?"

"Regular. Day."

"Well, that's working for you. The night shifts—we have two nurses here—are the real losers in this. They can't get a wink all day with the racket she makes. She needs us here but she hates us here. You already left the other rooms you were in?"

Both women looked down at Mary's small bag, and the other woman laughed.

Mary's was one of the cots in the bedroom. She thought she'd gotten lucky when she saw that hers was closest to the door, but then she learned she'd been right when she imagined that the others would have to crawl across the other beds in order to get out of the room. In the middle of the night she was woken by a knee near her face, a foot flicked across her belly, the general rocking and creaking her cot made with the weight of another body trying to pass. There was a flushing indoor lavatory down the hall from their rooms, but long before Mary's arrival, someone had made the decision that the hallway privy encouraged too much movement in the middle of the night, and so a chamber pot was set up in the corner of the bedroom farthest from the door. If she wasn't woken by someone traveling on top of her, she woke to the sound of someone letting go a stream of urine into a ceramic pot, followed by the sound of four other women tossing violently in their sleep to shut out the noise.

She had to find something else. She thought about her old building, about Fran and Joan. Fran's place was full up with her own family, and Joan? They would make room for her, she knew. They would sympathize. But it was their sympathy that stopped her. They had each warned her about Alfred in their different ways—Joan quietly, and Fran less so, but she had not listened. And now here she was, just a few years later, living in a boardinghouse while Alfred made a new family with a new woman. No, she wouldn't be able to stomach it, the inevitable human need they'd have to point out that they'd been right, and she was wrong. Instead, she asked Li if he knew of anyone looking for a boarder. She told him she'd even live with a Chinese. She tried to ask the Lithuanians, but they didn't understand her. She stopped in at all the churches, Catholic or not, between the laundry and Mrs. Post's, to read the bulletin boards. She scoured the ads in the papers. She quietly suggested to two of the other women at Mrs. Post's that they strike out together and find a place to themselves, but neither of them was interested, or else they didn't believe it would be possible for three women to rent rooms together without a man to sign for them.

Then, very early one Tuesday morning, she heard her name being called.

"Mary!" a woman's voice chased her from across the street. "Mary Mallon!"

She turned and saw Joan Graves hold out her hand to stop traffic as she rushed across the street to Mary's side.

"I can't believe it!" Joan said, and threw her arms around Mary.

"Joan," Mary said simply, and let herself be hugged. She was happy to see Joan, silly Joan, talented Joan, who could sew more surely than anyone Mary had ever known.

"I heard there was a hearing, but I thought they'd taken you back to the island."

"Oh, you heard all about it, I'm sure."

"Well, it was in the papers. We followed it, Fran and I did. But you're here. And look at you! I thought you were sick. Have you been sick? What are you doing now? Where are you living? Why didn't you come see us right away?"

"I was planning to, but—"

"And what about Alfred, have you seen him? He told Fran's Robert that he did the Oppenheimer cure."

Mary didn't remember Joan being so aggressive. She didn't remember her as a piler of questions, and she was absolutely certain that the old Joan would never have brought up the cure, which was a roundabout way of bringing up the problem, and the drink, and the late nights, and Mr. Hallenan's shouts up the stairs. The Joan Mary knew might have brought it up privately, with such subtlety that Mary wouldn't know what she was talking about right away. Not out on the street. Not first thing after seeing her after so long.

"Where did you see Alfred?" She might as well ask rather than be distracted by wondering all day long.

"In the building. He does odd jobs for Mr. Driscoll now and again after he finishes up at the stable. You haven't seen him?"

"No."

"I'm sorry, Mary. I heard about . . . his new place. I don't know why I asked that."

Mary wanted to ask several questions at once: Did he seem happy? What did they talk about? But she didn't ask anything. No, she was not interested. She would not beg for information. She would not ask for Joan's husband, and all of their neighbors, just so at the end of that long list she could ask discreetly about Alfred. She wouldn't do it.

"I'm late, Joan. It was great seeing you."

"But you haven't seen me! Mary, you must come by! Will you come for supper one night? On Sunday? When were you released?"

Mary was already sidestepping toward the laundry, which she could see was open and accepting customers. Let them fire her, she thought. Let them try. She'd march straight up to Lederle's office and ask him for the money from his wallet. She'd wait in the street outside Soper's office and mug him as he made his way home.

"I'm not sure I can, Joan. I'll let you know."

"Yes, let me know. If not this Sunday, then next Sunday."

"I'll let you know." Mary had turned now, was walking away.

"Oh, and Mary!" Joan called after her. "Mary! I almost forgot!" Mary steeled herself. She'd met Alfred's Liza. She'd met precious Samuel. Mary wanted to take her scarf and stuff it in Joan's mouth.

"We have a baby girl now. She's eleven months. You have to see her. She's the sweetest thing, and—"

Mary stopped. "You had a baby? You're kidding me."

"I'm not kidding," Joan laughed. "You were right. Sometimes it does take a long time. Will you come by, Mary? To meet her?"

"I can't believe it." Mary looked around as if the baby might be hiding in an alley, peeking out at them.

Joan laughed. "Fran is minding her. She lets me get out by myself for an hour."

It was Mary's turn to laugh. "Fran! I thought she said she was done with babies once she got her last one in school. She once told me she'd push Robert straight out the window if he said he wanted to have another."

"You know Fran. She was the first one cooing into the bassinet when she was born."

"What's her name?"

"Dorothy Alice." Even saying the child's name, Mary saw, cast a glow of joy on Joan's face. All the impatience Mary felt just a few minutes previously was gone, and now she hugged her friend, told her that she was happy for her. Joan would be a good mother, and if the child had half the heart Joan had she'd be a kind person. For the first time since leaving North Brother, Mary forgot why she hadn't seen her friends in so long, and wanted to go straight over to the old building to tease Fran. Joan would make a pot of coffee and the three of them would gab away the morning. Who cared about Alfred? Not her. If she passed him in the hall she wouldn't even turn to look at him.

As the moment began to pass, Joan frowned. "And you're not sick, right, Mary? You don't look sick. What they said about you and those people you cooked for? It's not true, is it? That's why they let you out?"

Mary sighed. "They only ever said it was the people I cooked for who got sick."

"And that wasn't true?"

"Well, a few got sick. A handful really, out of how many I've cooked for. But it was a coincidence. It was a—well, it wasn't fair anyway. There's a dairyman upstate—"

"I knew it. I said to myself, our Mary has no disease, the way you used to work so hard and run up and down those stairs. So you'll come and meet the baby, won't you?"

And as Mary heard herself promise that she would, she knew it was true. She wanted to see Joan's baby. She wanted to see Fran. Even Patricia Tiernan would be a familiar face, and what had she craved those three years on North Brother but a familiar face? What had she wanted most but to talk to someone who knew things about her that had nothing to do with Soper or Typhoid or even cooking? And they were her friends. They would understand that she didn't want to talk about Alfred, that there was nothing to say. Never in all the years they'd known one another did either Joan or Fran say a word about their not being married, only concerns about his health, and how hard she worked, and if, perhaps, she didn't sometimes wish she had a man who took care of her and not the other way around. But there hadn't been judgment, not really. And she had to hope there would be no judgment now, either, after the humiliation of his leaving her, marrying someone else.

FIFTEEN

She worked. After two months at the laundry Li told her that they'd been worried about taking her on as a favor, but that she was as fine a worker as any Chinese, as any person Li had ever known. He told her that Chu was also very pleased. The Lithuanian women acknowledged her more often, nodding and giving her brief smiles before turning back to their stew of cottons and wools.

In the window of the corner grocer she found an ad for a woman boarder. The building was on Thirty-First Street and Second Avenue, and she decided not to care that it was so close to the old building, but when she went over there she saw that it was little better than Mrs. Post's. There were cots everywhere, and a pair of exhausted-looking women sitting at a table without talking to each other while she got the ten-second tour and a rundown of the rules. There had to be something better, but it was impossible to really look, with only half a day off every week, and the long hours of the weekdays. She pursued another ad she'd seen in the newspaper, but when she got there nothing seemed right—the large living area, the high ceilings, the separate kitchen, the man who emerged quietly from one of the three bedrooms and held a hushed discussion in the corner with the widow who'd answered the door at Mary's knock. The man skulked by Mary and ran down the stairs of the building without saying good-bye or good day to anyone, not even the women lounging on the silk sofa like cats stretched out in the sun. Mary realized where she was just as the young widow came over to her and asked her to take down her hair, reaching, as she said it, for Mary's pins. Mary held tight to the banister as she made her way back down to the street.

She searched for a month. Six weeks. Two months. The weather grew warmer, the rooms at Mrs. Post's closer. The nightly foot to the face or the belly was growing familiar, and that worried Mary more. She refused to grow accustomed to living that way. There had to be people who were honest and needed someone like Mary to help. June passed. July. Two of the women at Mrs. Post's left, and with the breathing space those two empty cots offered, Mary decided to wait a few weeks, to spend her Sunday afternoons doing something else for a change, walking in the park, taking herself out for a sandwich. A few weeks turned into the entire summer. Then, at the end of September, as she was walking north along Third Avenue near Thirty-Sixth Street, she ran into Mrs. Borriello and one of her sons at the produce cart that traveled around the neighborhood.

"I remember you," the son said before anyone had said hello. "Mama," he turned. "She used to live in the building. Wasn't she—"

Mrs. Borriello hushed the boy by touching him lightly on

the shoulder. She spoke in Italian. "She says hello, how are you doing?" the boy said. "She said she is glad to see you."

"I'm happy to see you," Mrs. Borriello said in accented English.

Mary smiled at Mrs. Borriello, who had aged since Mary saw her last. "How are you?" she asked the boy. Carmine, she recalled. And the youngest one was Anthony. She calculated the oldest brother to be dead four years now. How well she remembered that afternoon, the hush that fell over the building when the news went up and down that the boy, sent by his mother to gather wood by the bulkhead on Twenty-Eighth Street, had been reaching for a piece of driftwood when he slipped into the river and was swept away. It came out later that Carmine, who'd gone along with his older brother, had run along the riverbank looking for help and came to a group of laborers having a break up on the pier. "Please!" he begged them. "My brother!" But all they did was look where the boy was pointing, and after a minute, as they all watched the boy drift farther away, and as they took their lunches from their pockets, one of the men offered the boy half a sandwich for strength before he went home to tell his mother. Mary wondered now if they ever fished the boy's body from the river.

"How is Anthony?" Mary asked.

"He's doing good." The boy looked at Mary, and then down at his hands, and then back at Mary. She wanted to touch his face. "Hey, ah, did you hear about my father? That he died?"

"No," Mary said. She put her hand on Mrs. Borriello's arm. "I'm sorry to hear about your husband. How? He was a young man."

Mrs. Borriello pulled her scarf tighter around her hair. "A freak thing," the boy said. "He was down framing a new building on Broadway and Broome, and they said he had the harness on to do a little welding job up on the beam, and then a strong wind came and he lost his footing and the harness broke. And he fell. It was the fourth-story floor beam."

How many times had the boy heard the story, Mary wondered, to be able to tell it so matter-of-factly? What could he understand about beams and framing and the building of buildings? He was probably about ten years old now, but he seemed to Mary both older and younger. Older with his swagger and his way of speaking for his mama, but younger when she examined his soft face, his long eyelashes, the way, underneath everything he said, he seemed to look at each of the women and ask, Did I say it right? Is that really what happened to my papa? Just a beam and a broken harness and a gust of wind? And before that my brother? Is it really possible that he was there beside me one moment and swept away the next? That there was nothing tying him more closely to his life? Or my papa to his?

"Your poor mother," Mary said in a whisper as she examined Mrs. Borriello's dark brown scarf that blended with her dark brown hair, her drawn face, her quick hands passing over one grapefruit and then another until she found one she liked.

Mary leaned slightly toward the boy, wanting to hug him. "When?"

"Almost a year."

"One year in October," Mrs. Borriello added, also looking at her son. All three were quiet as the shoppers rushed around them and the produce man kept glancing at them and at their pockets to make sure they hadn't stuffed them without paying.

"Hey," the boy said. "I remember the fireworks that time. Remember?"

"I do," Mary said, taking him by the shoulders and pulling

him toward her. I am lucky, she thought. When I think I am unlucky I must remember that I am lucky. I am blessed. The boy let himself be hugged, and then politely pulled away.

The woman said something in Italian, and the boy tried to signal his mother with his eyes that he didn't want to translate. "She says you have also had sadness," he said finally. "But your sadness is a blessing in disguise, maybe. Maybe not, but maybe. That man was not a good one, and Our Lord works in mysterious ways." The boy added on his own, "He comes in sometimes. He seems different now."

"You might be right," Mary said, placing her hand on the woman's arm again to say good-bye. She began to turn away, to wish them a good day and best of luck, when a thought came to her. "Carmine," she said.

The boy waited.

"Does your mother have a boarder?"

"A boarder?"

"Someone who lives with you and pays a little of the rent."

"No." He looked at his mother, who was scrutinizing Mary. Mary got the feeling that she understood everything. She wanted to ask how they were making ends meet, but she knew that would be intruding too far. How to put it? She turned to Mrs. Borriello and spoke to her directly.

Mrs. Borriello waited, and Mary felt she was already preparing a phrase to turn Mary down. "I have a regular job, six and a half days a week, and I earn decent wages, though not as good as I did before. Before the island. You understand? When I was a cook. This job is in a laundry but the pay is regular. I could live with you, Mrs. Borriello, and help out with the rent and around the rooms. I am neat, and the boys already know me. I would—"

Mrs. Borriello let go a stream of Italian, and the boy protested in Italian for a few sentences, before turning and walking down the block a little, leaving the women alone.

"I've been thinking about something like this," the woman said. "I don't like the idea of a stranger. I don't like to put it in a newspaper."

"But I'm not a stranger. You saw me come and go for many years."

"Yes." She stared at Mary, and Mary recalled the portrait of the Sacred Heart she'd noted that time she stood in the Borriellos' dim kitchen after the older boy's death, Mrs. Borriello not yet able to get out of bed. This was a religious woman, and Mary was sure she'd disapproved of Alfred and their arrangement. What woman would approve? She'd been crazy, and foolish, but what woman would have given up on him, knowing what he was like at his best? He was worth it, she wanted to say to Mrs. Borriello. And she loved him. And Christian doctrine preached forgiveness as much as it preached anything else. Underneath that scarf and those widow's weeds was a young woman, perhaps younger than Mary. You understand, Mary wanted to say to her. I know you understand.

"No guests," Mrs. Borriello said. Mary's face burned. It was no matter, Mary thought. A few weeks of living together and the other woman would see that Mary was not like that. It had just been Alfred she'd made an exception for. Only Alfred. And now Alfred was off and married and raising another man's son.

"Never," Mary agreed. She shook her head emphatically from side to side so the woman would understand. She felt a flush of sweat spring up on her neck. The boy was kicking a dried horse turd along the curb and glancing over at them. "My boys stay in their bedroom. You get the cot in my room or the kitchen."

"Yes. Fine."

Mrs. Borriello named her price. It was more than at Mrs. Post's, and it meant Mary would save nothing. Not a single dime unless she ate less, or washed her hair less often, or walked everywhere she went, or picked up another job for Sunday afternoons. If I offer less, Mary considered, she will take it. She said herself that she doesn't want to advertise.

"Yes," Mary said instead. "I can do that."

Mrs. Borriello seemed surprised for a moment, and then happy. She waved over the boy. Mary shook the other woman's hand, and then the boy's. Each paid for her fruit, and they made their separate ways until the following Sunday, when Mary would move in.

She had not given a single thought to the others in the building when she'd made the suggestion to Mrs. Borriello, but when she walked away, and realized what had just been arranged, it felt again like time was moving backward, and that no matter how hard she tried to keep her eyes pointed to the step ahead, she kept getting knocked off balance, turned around.

She gathered her belongings from Mrs. Post's when most of the others were out. It was only natural to feel that she was going home. Only when she saw the number hanging over the door—the dark entryway, the worn staircase beyond—did she truly understand what she'd done. At the bottom of the stairs was the same faded mural of a man on a horse, children picking fruit from trees. The plaster molding that had long ago been painted to match the wood of the banister had been chipped away further, and sat along the baseboard in small piles of dust. After so many months of avoiding the place, of swinging wide so as not to run into anyone, there she was, the prodigal daughter without a thing to show for herself except for a scorch burn on her wrist, and swollen ankles, and a set of ten raw knuckles. They would laugh at her. She imagined Patricia Tiernan standing smug in her kitchen, saying what she always thought, what she always knew, while her fawning family gazed at her and nodded. She thought of the others who had never liked her, had never liked Alfred, and then how she and Alfred had thumbed their noses at what the others liked and didn't like.

But now she was back, alone, and for the few seconds it took her to cross the landing she thought about returning to Mrs. Post's, or to a boardinghouse, or asking if she could stay at the laundry for a week until she could find better accommodations. Everything about the place was familiar: the sag in the center of each stair, the smell of damp rising from the basement. If she were still cooking, she could have afforded their sixth-floor rooms on her own. Who lived there now? She thought of her old bed, her table, her sink, the spices she kept in the press.

She began to climb the stairs. When she got to Mrs. Borriello's and knocked, the door opened immediately, and Mrs. Borriello took her bag and placed it under the cot, which was set up with pillows against the wall during the day to look like a small sofa. She nodded at Mary to sit. As soon as Mary pulled in her chair Mrs. Borriello served her coffee with sweet condensed milk and fresh bread with salted butter. At the center of the table she placed a bowl of fat, ripe blackberries. Mrs. Borriello sat across from her boarder and the two women ate and sipped and enjoyed the silence. It was the most delicious meal Mary had tasted since before North Brother.

"I want to thank you—" Mary began, but discovered a blockage in her throat that the words couldn't skirt by. There was nothing to cry about, but the pressure behind her eyes was too much, and Mrs. Borriello was beside her, rubbing her back, saying that she must be tired, why not a short nap before the boys come? Mary agreed that she'd like to lie down for a few minutes, not sleep, but just lie down, close her eyes, pray to God that things would get better for her here and not worse. "Oh, first I want to give you this," Mary said. "Yesterday was the first of the month, so it works out nicely." She opened her bag and removed from her wallet the price they'd agreed on, but the other woman just looked at it on the table, at the bills Mary had fanned out, at the coins piled on top.

"Is it okay?" Mary asked. There was nothing else in her wallet if she owed more, if she'd misunderstood. She'd bought new wool tights that week, and twice in ten days, after closing the laundry with Li, she'd gone to the little counter that sold hamburger steaks until midnight. She knew she shouldn't have done that. Once? Fine. But twice? And couldn't the old tights have been mended?

Then Mrs. Borriello dipped her head and covered her face with her hands. "Yes, it's okay," she said after a moment. When she composed herself, she told Mary that she was going to her room to lie down, too.

Mary knew that avoiding her old friends now would make everything worse. It would be better to seek them out immediately, try to explain to them what had happened, let them see her face. Her silence from North Brother would be easier for them to understand

MARY BETH KEANE

than why she hadn't sought them out since her release. Joan was no
obstacle—she'd already forgiven Mary by the time she'd flagged
her down on the sidewalk. Little Dorothy Alice cried in the mornings and over the sound of her wailing came Joan's soothing voice,
singing about doggies, or sleigh rides, or the Kingdom of Heaven.
Later, walking to work, Mary found herself humming along.

There was Patricia Tiernan, who'd never liked Mary. Ever
since Mary came back Patricia seemed shocked to see her making
her way up the stairs. "Oh, hi, Mary," Jimmy Tiernan said to her
as they passed one evening, and just like in the old days Patricia
appeared on the landing above them and looked as if she would
choke him with her mind if she had the power.

As for Fran, the first time Mary saw her after returning to the
building, her old friend was cool. She returned Mary's greeting,
and then continued up the stairs while Mary looked after her,
feeling like she'd been slapped. After a few days, Mary worked up
the courage to knock on her door. "Please, Fran, can't I come in?"
It might have been the "please" that melted the frost. Fran opened
the door and Mary took her usual chair while Fran hunted for
something sweet for them to eat.

"Why didn't you come see us, Mary? I was sick when they
sent you back to North Brother after the hearing. We had no
idea you were released, and then Joan said she ran into you on the
street. You could have stayed here. Why didn't you just ask? You
didn't have to go to a boardinghouse. You didn't have to go up
there and pay Mrs. Borriello for a corner of her kitchen. I don't
even understand what happened."

"I don't know," Mary said, and it was true: now that she was
sitting there, looking at her old friend, she couldn't remember
why she let it go so long. "Why didn't you come to my hearing

if you were following the case? Alfred was there. And I didn't hear from you after, either." She could see on Fran's face that it had never occurred to her, and Mary never expected Fran to give up an entire day sitting in a stuffy courtroom, but it was the only way to get past these small hurts—to answer with another hurt. You've been injured? Well, so have I.

"I didn't know I could have gone to the hearing. I thought it was just lawyers and reporters. And you know I'm not a good writer. Sure, Robert said he'd take down a letter for me, but you know how that goes. You could have written to me more often, too."

"You're right, Fran. I don't know why I said that. I'm sorry. It's just that Alfred—"

Fran leaned forward. "I knew it was Alfred. You didn't want to run into him here." Fran asked her if she'd seen him in the week since she moved back.

"No," Mary said. "Have you? Joan said he does odd jobs for Driscoll."

"I haven't seen him either. Sometimes he's here a lot in a given week, and then not for a few weeks. And I think he tries his best to avoid me and Joan."

Though Mary had instructed herself not to care, to try to forget about him, it was Alfred she had in her mind whenever she pushed out the building's front door and remembered her posture, when she put a protective hand to her hair. She braced herself to see him and then when a few days went by and she didn't see him, she realized she was disappointed.

"So tell me everything," Fran said. "Start from the beginning." As their coffee went cold, Mary described Dr. Soper, what he said about her, the day they captured her, the Willard Parker Hospital,

North Brother, John Cane, the nurses and their collection canisters, Mr. O'Neill, the disappointment of the hearing and then finding out about Liza Meaney, the boy, how disorienting it was to be back in New York City without being a cook, how she feared she'd never get used to it. When she finally stopped talking, Fran was quiet for a minute and then announced that she'd like to punch that Dr. Soper in the face, and Mary laughed. Never before had she thought about Soper and laughed, and it felt, for the first time, like that terrible part of her life was truly behind her. The two women talked until the clock struck midnight and when she left, Mary knew they'd be fine.

LIBERTY

SIXTEEN

Living with Liza seemed perfect, at first. It had been years since Alfred felt what it was like to be sober and sound on his own two feet, his lungs full of air, his spine straight, his body strong. When he came home, Liza didn't seem the least bit surprised that he'd worked all day. She didn't make a fuss over it, like Mary used to, and with Liza he could sense no panic that he would change his mind, that the next day would see him having slipped down to the place of a man who didn't work. He was healthy and capable and Liza didn't watch him like Mary did. She didn't narrow her eyes and know things the way Mary knew them, sometimes before he knew himself. When he brought her his wages, she looked at him like he'd handed her a block of solid gold, and she needed those dollars and cents. The boy ate as much as Alfred and Liza combined, and he was smart. He needed books, scratch pads, decent clothing, shoes.

But after almost ten months of the arrangement, Alfred faced what he knew all along, that Liza Meaney was not Mary Mallon, and never would be. When they made love she was dutiful and kind. She never made up an excuse, or pretended to be asleep, or told him to go fly a kite, and she looked politely away when he removed the night cap from its tin. If she'd ever seen one before she didn't mention it, nor could he tell if she liked or disliked what they were doing. One time, to test her, he stopped abruptly, pulled away, tugged on his trousers, and told her they could do it later since she wasn't feeling up to it, and she said that was fine, as if he'd suggested they walk north along Broadway instead of south. "Oh, well, you don't seem fine. You seem distracted," he said, and she didn't argue. She just pulled her dress back over her shoulders and went about fastening the row of buttons. Another time he kept pushing, and nuzzling, and reaching under her clothes to see when she would stop him but she never stopped him, even though he knew she was tired and wanted nothing more than to sleep. He kept testing and testing and next thing he knew he was inside her with Samuel doing his homework in the next room, and only once, one single instant, when the bed creaked, did she push him away and look to the door in case Samuel might have heard.

This is how most women are, he told himself. This is how women should be, only he'd never known what a woman should be like because he'd mostly ever been with Mary, who was not a normal woman. Even the newspapers noticed it. Back when she was first captured most of the newsmen commented that she had the bearing of an Irish person, but one reporter observed that she in fact had the bearing of a man. Irish or not, he didn't specify. It was true sometimes she stood with her legs planted wide, especially when she felt herself backed into a corner, but nothing about Mary was manly to the eye and so it must have been something else that this man had seen, a way of conducting herself, a way of glancing around a room. Fran Mosely, who saved the papers for him back then, had said she didn't understand that one at all because who in their right mind seeing Mary's thick mane of strawberry blond hair and slim waist would see anything other than a woman. Alfred had said, "I know what he means, I think," and Fran had looked at him like he was the bastard she'd always suspected him to be.

Mary didn't need the money he brought in because she had her own money, more money than he earned. He knew exactly how she felt about everything, because she told him, usually very loudly, often while banging pots and pans for emphasis. When she didn't want him to touch her she told him to get lost, but when she did, she didn't mind reaching for him first, coming around to his side, kissing the back of his neck and asking if he was too tired. Liza Meaney would never do that. Not in a thousand years. At first, he thought how wonderful that was. How ladylike. Liza was like a delicate bird and how much more interesting that made everything when she let him unbutton her, and how fiercely she blushed when he lifted her to sit on top of him, or whispered to her to turn around. She looked disoriented and terrified whenever he moved her to a different position, and after just a few seconds she always dove back down to the covers and to her back where she felt comfortable and safe, and he'd laugh. "Okay, okay," he'd say, and he could see how much he'd have to show her, if she was willing to be shown, but after ten months he could see she didn't want that. Sex for Liza Meaney would always be part of the transaction they'd agreed upon, and although she liked him, and was attracted to him—Alfred felt sure he'd be able to tell if she wasn't—she saw sex with him the same way she saw making his breakfast, washing his clothes, having supper on the table when he got home.

They'd been engaged for six months but still weren't married. She showed her ring to all their neighbors—a simple silver band—and maybe that's all she'd wanted, for the world to know that she was not the kind of woman who lived with a man without a promise. At first, she said she wanted to figure a way to bring her mother from England for the ceremony, and sometimes she said she wanted to wait until the school year was over, so Samuel wouldn't be distracted. Distracted? Alfred wanted to ask. What would be so distracting? Or for that matter, what was there to cross an ocean for? Alfred had imagined himself and Liza walking to City Hall, signing a few papers, and then going to a restaurant for supper. But he didn't say anything, and when the weeks wore on without any letters arriving from England, without any discussion of whether they'd have a small party, he stopped worrying about it. Maybe accepting the engagement without pushing actual marriage was the small way she was asserting herself, that and making him continue with the cure, even though he felt he didn't need it anymore.

The medicine they gave in the beginning made him sick, and he assumed that was part of it: making the patient so sick that he wouldn't be able to hold alcohol or anything else. He was weak for two weeks, curled up in bed and vomiting into the bowl Liza gave him, and still, she came in every four hours with another dose she'd measured out into a teacup, just as the doctor had instructed. "It's for people far worse than I am," he'd told her when he first came back from Bellevue, where he'd gone to see what it was all about. Ads for the cure were posted all around the neighborhood, and published in big block letters in the newspapers. "I saw them.

Jesus, I saw them. I'm not like that. My God, one man, he wasn't much more than a boy, he was sweating a puddle on the floor but kept complaining of cold. I just like to have a nip now and again and if you go out and find a man who never has a nip now and then I'll saw off my right arm."

"You'll go if you want to live here," she told him simply, so he went back, and back, and soon they sent him home with directions on how to dole out the medicine and at what intervals. After a month they said he could stop taking the medicine, but to keep a supply in his old pocket flask. That he'd never had need for that flask proved he never needed the cure in the first place. It was just a matter of deciding, and he'd decided. It was a 100 percent guarantee as long as he followed the doctor's instructions, and the doctor's instructions were, don't drink.

Samuel was preparing for a test that would allow him to skip two grades ahead at school and take a few courses at the community college. If he scored high enough he would go for free, except for the cost of books. They had to be very, very quiet around the flat so as not to interrupt the boy's studies, and for the first time since he'd known her, Liza shushed him one morning when he began to ask if there was any more coffee on the stove. She shushed Alfred and cast a worried look at Samuel, who had his head bent over a mathematics book, and Alfred saw then that she'd never love him, never love any man, as much as she loved that boy.

The ice company stable did not offer overtime, and the evenings were too long between five o'clock, when his shift ended, and ten o'clock, when he went to bed. To get out of their rooms and give the boy some quiet, Alfred had started checking in with Michael Driscoll. The old man needed boards replaced on the floor, a cabinet fixed, his rotted bed carried out to the sidewalk and replaced with a new one, the plaster on the wall behind the sink touched and smoothed. "A little late for this kind of attention," Alfred had teased the first time he went over.

"Never too late," Driscoll had said. "I've my eye on a fine woman."

"You're joking."

"You'll get there. Then you'll know. And someone else will laugh."

Fair enough, Alfred supposed, and went on with the work he was assigned. When he finished a job, he'd let a few weeks go by and then he'd check in on the old man to see what he'd stored up for him. In the stretches when Driscoll had no work for him he hung around the stable after his shift to talk to the man who relieved him, or he walked down to the docks to watch what was being unloaded.

One evening, though he didn't know Alfred would be stopping around, Driscoll answered the door as soon as Alfred knocked. "Well? Did you see her?" The old man asked, and looked over Alfred's shoulder toward the empty stairwell. He coughed into his sleeve, and then rolled it up.

"Who?" Alfred asked.

"Mary. She's out there. I was talking with her not one minute ago."

"Mary Mallon is in this building?"

"She moved in with Mrs. Borriello a week ago. You didn't know?" Alfred felt a tremor travel down his arms and legs, and he thought he heard a woman's step pass in the hall. He looked hard at Driscoll's face to make sure the old man wasn't having him on. He'd sent a letter to her hut on North Brother a few months earlier and when she didn't write back he figured she was still that angry with him, and had a right to be. She'd said the lawyer was optimistic. She'd said it might be only a few more months. But why would he have believed it?

"Are you serious, Driscoll?"

"I swear on my life."

"How? When was she released? Was she looking for me? What did you talk about?"

"She was just passing through the vestibule as I was searching for my key. I said hello and so did she so then I said I was glad to see her back and she thanked me. She might still be climbing the stairs. Go on. Go after her."

Instead, Alfred pushed past him and looked at the weeping faucet that needed to be fixed. As he took inventory of what he'd need, he felt the other man's eyes sizing up the shape of his back, his stance, trying to read what was written there. He needed time to think. He had no idea what he'd say. Every part of his body urged him toward the door. Why was she staying with Mrs. Borriello? What was she doing now? He imagined what he'd say to her, and when he realized he couldn't think of a place to begin, he imagined instead what she'd say to him, and knew that the first thing she'd ask was whether he was married yet to Liza Meaney, and after he said that he wasn't, she'd ask if he was still living with her and her boy, and he'd have to say yes, and then the meeting would be over.

"I can't come around tomorrow," Alfred said gruffly to Driscoll once the faucet was fixed. "I'll do the rest another time."

"You'll have to face her sooner or later," Driscoll said, and Alfred had a wild impulse to shove him, to throttle him, but it passed immediately. It was himself he was angry at. No one else.

"Why do I have to?" he said, though he wanted to do more than face her. He wanted to run upstairs right that second to see her, beg her forgiveness, take her into his arms. How had it happened? How had he missed it? How could he have failed to know she was back in the city?

Alfred stayed away from 302 East Thirty-Third Street as he tried to make sense of Mary's return. In the mornings, when he woke to Liza's blonde curls on the pillow next to him, he thought immediately of Mary, sleeping so close to the rooms they'd shared for so many years, seemingly back in her old life except without him. "Everything all right at the stable?" Liza asked several times, and he snapped at her that it was, and tried to stay out of their rooms even more than usual. Another time she asked him if he carried his medicine with him when he went out, and he realized she thought he'd fallen off the wagon. It was true he'd gone and stood outside Nation's Pub for the first time in months, but he hadn't gone in, and the pull he felt from 302 East Thirty-Third was much stronger. Finally, after two weeks of turning 'round and 'round the news of Mary's return, he finished his work at the stable and made for Driscoll's place, to finish up the work that was there waiting for him, and to decide one way or another if he would ever go near the place again.

As he walked up Third Avenue he felt the possibility of seeing her again like a singing bird lodged in his chest, struggling to free itself. He stopped at the peanut cart on Twenty-Ninth Street to get a bag for himself and Driscoll to share, but even this was a show for her, in case she was watching, in case he should turn around and she should be standing there, half smiling, ready to say, "Well, well, well. Look who it is."

It was the first truly bitter evening of the season, and there was no one on the stoop or in the vestibule when Alfred arrived at the building. He stood at the bottom of the silent stairwell and looked up, counting the railings to the fourth floor. When Driscoll didn't answer his knock Alfred felt along the top of the door frame for the key that was hidden there, and let himself in. "Hello?" he called, and when he got no answer he opened the door to Driscoll's bedroom and found him lying there, twisted up in the sheets. "Not feeling myself," Driscoll said without looking at Alfred, and as Alfred got closer to the bed he could see that the older man was wincing, and trying to find relief from whatever was bothering him by shifting from side to side, clutching at his pillow. He coughed for several minutes. For the first time in two weeks, Alfred pushed thoughts of Mary to the side.

"What is it?" Alfred asked to the back of the man's head, and noticed how thin Driscoll's hair was there, how small and delicate-seeming the back of his skull was, like a smooth, hairless egg.

"Go on," said Driscoll. "Another time." But Alfred stood there like a boy, unsure what to do.

"I'm just feeling poorly. Come around in a few days."

"Can I bring you something? Have you eaten?"

But Driscoll only moved closer to the wall.

"I'll check on you tomorrow," he said, and when Driscoll didn't respond, Alfred left. He stood at the bottom of the stairwell for a minute, tempted to go up to see Mary, but he'd be back the next day and between now and then maybe he'd think of the perfect thing to say.

Alfred arrived home in time for a nearly silent supper with Liza and Samuel. In the morning, he decided he couldn't go another day without seeing Mary, and once he'd decided, he had no patience for being at the stable, alone with the horses. Now that the weather was cold, the demand for ice was way down, as was the supply until the winter harvest. The trucks went out every day, but mostly to businesses, a few blocks here and there to the rich houses that didn't care to keep their milk or butter on the window ledge like Mary had always done, and Liza did now, but preferred to serve ice in glasses to their guests, even in the winter months. Lately Alfred had felt that pinch that told him he would not last there for much longer. He would have to find something else. Ten blocks north was a stable the ice company rented to the Department of Health, and that was more interesting. On quiet afternoons Alfred walked up there with the ready excuse that he was still concerning himself with company property. When he first started at the stable he didn't understand why the Department of Health needed so many horses. Whenever a horse got too old to haul an ice truck, or was too difficult to drive through the city, the men at his stable always said that the Department of Health would take it, and now Alfred said it too, but he didn't know why until one day, a bright autumn afternoon, he walked the ten blocks to distract himself and when he got to the stable he saw that the large side room that used to be a dairy, back when the city had cows, had been turned into a slaughter-house for horses. There were two horses up on slings with gashes in their necks and a glass instrument stuck in each bloody wound. Below the horses' mighty bellies were lined up rows and rows of buckets where blood had been collected, and all around were men in white lab coats.

"Out!" one yelled when he saw Alfred. The man was crouching beside the larger of the two horses, checking the glass tube, and when he scrambled up to shoo away Alfred he slipped on a small spot of blood on the floor, knocking over a full bucket as he tried to right himself. The other men cursed and glared at Alfred. The horses, who were still alive, each turned a wild, terrified eye to Alfred, and seemed to understand that he was the only one in the room who might help them.

"Jesus Christ," Alfred said when he got back out to the glare of the street, the flies in front of the stable door frantic with the smell of blood. He passed through the other door to the stable proper, where there were a dozen horses munching on hay as if they were out at pasture. "What are they doing?" Alfred asked the boy who was sitting on an upturned bucket in the corner, reading an old newspaper.

"Bleeding," the boy said, and simply turned the page.

Later, when he and Samuel were elbow to elbow at the table waiting for Liza to spoon out their supper, it was Samuel who told him what he'd probably seen, that the horses were being bled for their serum, which would be used to make inoculations against disease. "Diphtheria, probably," the boy said. "I read about that. Or Typhoid, maybe. They're working on something."

"Come on. Horse blood?"

"Horse serum. They inject the horse with the disease and wait for the horse to develop the means to fight it and then they take out the blood and whittle it down to the fighting parts and then they put that in an injection and give it to people. Didn't you ever wonder what's in the shots people get?" The boy leaned back in his chair and regarded Alfred.

Alfred was ashamed to say he had not ever wondered what was in an injection. Before seeing Dr. Oppenheimer he'd never gotten an injection in his life, and now he wondered what the doctor was putting in him. There was witchcraft in the old country, but nothing this dark, as far as Alfred could remember. Certain herbs and weeds. A way of mixing. Poultices smeared on chests, aromatic flowers ground down to powders and stirred up into tea. But this horse-blood business seemed like more sinister magic. Liza had turned from the stove to listen to her son, and now, understanding that her boy was finished explaining, she turned back to her saucepan of gravy, her cheeks spotted with pride and pleasure.

Now, the day yawning before him until it was time to sign out and walk over to Thirty-Third Street, he considered going up to the DOH stables to pass the time. Instead, he signed himself out for five o'clock, even though it was only two.

Driscoll was not better. Alfred opened the man's door slowly, and knew immediately by the silence and the cold kitchen that he was still in bed. He found Driscoll in the same position, and when Alfred put his hand on the back of his neck it felt like a furnace, and Driscoll moaned. "Should I get you something?" Alfred asked, feeling like a big, hulking, useless thing that was too stupid to know how to help. He went to the kitchen and ran a dishcloth under cold water. He brought it back to the bed, laid it across the old man's head, and then worried as he saw the sheets darken where the wet touched them. Driscoll shifted away. "You need help, I think," Alfred said, more to himself than to the old man. A doctor. But he'd never called on a doctor before.

He could have knocked on Fran's door, or gone up to confer with Jimmy Tiernan, but he marched on past the second-floor landing, past the third. He needed Mary. The elderly sisters who also lived on the fourth floor had their door cracked for air and Alfred knew he could stop and ask them. He'd seen Driscoll talk to them from time to time, and when one of them injured her knee Driscoll had gone up there with a baked cod on a platter because they couldn't get out. But instead of stopping, Alfred kept going to the Borriellos' door and drew a breath. If Mrs. Borriello answered, he'd have to speak up, speak slowly, and then everyone would hear and his whole reason for going up there would be confused. Because he was really going up there for Driscoll. And if it ended up that he and Mary would start talking again because of it, fine, as long as Driscoll improved.

The younger boy answered, and when he saw who it was his eyes went wide.

"Is Mary here?"

The boy raised a finger to Alfred and then shut the door. Alfred heard movement inside, a chair pushed back along the wood floor.

When the door opened again it was Mrs. Borriello. The boy peeked at him from behind his mother. "Yes?" she said.

"I'm looking for Mary. I understand she's been staying here?"

"Why?"

Alfred felt himself getting annoyed. "Mr. Driscoll isn't well, and I thought Mary would know what to do."

"Sick?" Mrs. Borriello said.

"Yes. Since yesterday. Maybe longer. Is Mary here?"

But Mrs. Borriello was already gathering her scarf. She said something to the boy before slipping past Alfred and down the stairs to Michael Driscoll's door. The boy regarded Alfred from the door frame. "She doesn't get home until later."

"Yeah? Are you in charge of her schedule?"

"No. I'm in charge of the lamp. I bring it back to the kitchen when she gets home from the laundry and we do our figures at the table while she's eating. My brother and me, I mean. Then when she's done I take it back to my room. My mother says it's our lamp, not hers, but we have to let her borrow it to eat by because it's not right to ask a person to eat in the dark when there's a good lamp a room away."

"She works at a laundry? Where?"

"It's almost on Washington Square."

"Which side? What street?"

"Mr. Briehof!" Mrs. Borriello was calling for him from the bottom of the dark stairs.

"Didn't you used to live upstairs?" the boy asked.

Mrs. Borriello shouted again.

"He needs firewood," the boy said. "Better go in and get some of ours. She wants me to go down to her."

The boy ran down the stairs, shouting something to his mama all the way, and Alfred turned and put his hand on the Borriellos' doorknob. He pushed the heavy door and listened as the bottom brushed the floor like all the doors did in 302, leaving little arcs of scratch marks as welcome mats to every room. The wood was stacked by the stove, twigs, parts of branches, bits and pieces they must have collected from around the city. Alfred went over and selected a few of the heftiest pieces. When he turned he noticed the cot, and on the cot two folded blouses. On the windowsill above the cot was a woman's comb, a collection of hairpins, hair powder, a tub of cream. He recognized the comb and the brand of cream. He left the wood on the Borriellos' table and sat on the edge of Mary's bed. He didn't dare touch the blouses—it was bad enough he'd mussed the bed—but he studied the collars for signs of her skin, some detail that might have been caught in the material. He sniffed them, then leaned over, his head between his knees, to peer under the cot, searching for some lost thing she might have given up on and which he could keep, but there was nothing except dust. He thought about leaving her a note, the long-overdue letter she'd wanted so badly when she was on North Brother, the empty tin of tobacco from his pocket that she would know was his, knowing his brand and knowing they would tell her the story later, how he'd come knocking and how he'd spent a few minutes in the flat, alone. He heard the boy's light steps on the stairs, two at a time, so he went to smooth the quilt, but then decided, no, he'd leave it the way it was, let her imagine him sitting there, thinking about her. He gathered the wood, and by the time he had it in his arms, the boy was there with his brother, to tell him that their mother had banned them, had sent them upstairs with instructions to close their door and not to come down again. And if she wasn't home by supper, they were to be good boys and boil themselves an egg and clean up after and go straight to bed. There was something in the building, and she didn't want them around until they figured out what it was.

Driscoll was worse. His fever was high and he complained of pain in his back. When he coughed into his pillow he left behind spots of blood. He couldn't hold the teacup Mrs. Borriello had filled with broth so she sat on the edge of his bed and lifted it to his mouth. "Slow," she said. "Little sips." At moments he seemed to feel better, but then he was again moaning and clutching at the bed as if it were just a matter of getting deeper, of burrowing himself away from his rooms into a cooler place underneath it all, where he might find some relief.

"Should I run out to get medicine? A doctor? He has a little money, you know."

Mrs. Borriello peered at Alfred. She seemed to want to make herself into a wall between the two men.

"I mean for the doctor. I think he could pay a doctor. And I think a doctor has to see a sick person anyway, even if he can't pay."

"I think that's true."

"Because I've never seen something like this. Have you?"

"Yes. The blood on the pillow. The coughing with fever. I saw it one time."

"Okay then. I'll go."

"Where?"

"I don't know. I'll go up and ask Fran. She had the doctor come once. For one of the children." He wanted to ask where Mary was, what time she'd be home.

They heard the scrape of the door being slowly pushed open. "Mama?" came a boy's voice. Mrs. Borriello was across the room in an instant, pushing her youngest son into the hall and trying to shut the door on him. She shouted at him in Italian, but still he tried to insert the toe of his boot in the door. As they struggled, Alfred stepped out into the hall and lifted the boy under the arms.

"Go, go, go," Mrs. Borriello shouted at both of them, and then added something in Italian.

"I'm staying with my mama," the boy cried as Alfred carried him to the stairs.

"You have to go up," Alfred said.

Mrs. Borriello shouted again.

"She says to tell everybody, don't come down here. Bad enough there's the two of us already. Three of us including me. She says she'll kill me later. To you she says stand back from the door when you talk to Miss Fran about the doctor. Want me to do it? She says we could be breathing it now, whatever it is."

As Alfred climbed the steps with one hand bracing the boy by the upper arm, he thought of Liza and how she'd worry but there was nothing he could do and really it would be the wrong idea to go home to her now and carry this thing to her, to Samuel. She'd understand that he had to stay in 302 until he saw this thing through. And if Mary arrived home later and the boys told her everything—how Alfred had searched for her, how he'd stayed on to help their mama, how he'd rushed down the stairs with their wood and kindling to help Mr. Driscoll—and if hearing about all that made her want to see him again, to talk only, and if talking softened her toward him enough so that she didn't object when he touched her, then he couldn't help that, either.

SEVENTEEN

The one doctor Fran knew of had moved uptown, but Mr. Stern from the third floor knew of a good man who made house calls. Jimmy Tiernan was elected to go to West Sixteenth to fetch him, and as he rushed down the stairs and out onto the dark sidewalk, Patricia looked after him, relieved that her man was traveling farther away from whatever poison was dwelling at Mr. Driscoll's. First thing in the morning she was going to bring their children to her sister's in New Jersey and stay there until this thing passed.

Jimmy Tiernan didn't return until nearly eight o'clock in the evening. He shouted through Driscoll's closed door that the doctor would be there shortly. Alfred and Mrs. Borriello took turns sitting with Driscoll. A few times, Alfred tried to raise the subject of Mary. When it was Mrs. Borriello's turn to sit with Driscoll, Alfred sat in the chair in the corner of Driscoll's bedroom. "Your son said Mary works at a laundry now?"

Mrs. Borriello glanced over at him quickly, and simply nodded.

"Does she like it? She was a laundress before, you know. When I met her."

When Mrs. Borriello showed no indication that she'd even heard him speak, he knew that there was no point in trying. When it was his turn to sit with Driscoll he patted the old man's head with the compress and realized he'd never before been around anyone as ill. At nine o'clock came a strong knock on the door and an unfamiliar man's voice announcing himself as Dr. Hoffmann. Relieved, Alfred jumped up to open the door.

Dr. Hoffmann asked about Driscoll's first symptoms, how long he'd been in the state he was in, what his health was before he came down ill. He pulled the older man up to sitting, and Driscoll fell toward the doctor's lap like a sleeping child lifted from his crib by his mama. The doctor listened to Driscoll's chest, took his pulse, and then told Alfred to go straight to the nearest grocer and ask them to call for an ambulance. As Alfred rushed down the hall, he heard a voice behind him.

"How is he?" Mary asked. She was standing two steps above the second-floor landing. She was wearing a dark green dress that buttoned in a double-breasted style up to her throat. She was as familiar to him as his own reflection in the mirror, and he saw clearly how silly he'd been, playacting with another woman, a woman he barely knew, and who barely knew him, when his life was here, standing on the landing above him.

"I'm to get an ambulance."

"Well, go!"

Alfred ran. He pumped his arms and lifted his knees and dodged pedestrians who stepped before him. The faster he ran, the younger he felt, and though his errand was serious he felt buoyant: Mary was back. She would forgive him. They would make up, and he would leave Liza. He and Mary would find new rooms together; he'd get good work. He leaped over a pile of horse manure. He nodded to the wandering sausage man, who watched him pass with amazement on his face. How could he refuse marriage to her now when he had asked Liza Meaney? Maybe Mary wouldn't want to marry him now; maybe she had no interest. It didn't matter. None of it mattered. Not so long as they lived together again and came home to each other every night.

When he returned to Driscoll's rooms, Mary had taken over Mrs. Borriello's spot by the bed and was talking to the doctor. Mrs. Borriello sat at the table with her head in her hands.

"What is it?" Alfred asked from the frame of Driscoll's bedroom door.

"Looks like hasty consumption," Mary said without turning.

"They'll take him to a sanatorium," the doctor said. "Each of you should watch yourself for symptoms and at the first sign you should segregate yourself."

It was nearly midnight when the ambulance took Michael Driscoll, and once the neighbors retreated from their perches on the landings where they'd watched the spectacle, Mary remembered what the nurses used to do at Riverside after tending to a patient, and instructed Alfred and Mrs. Borriello to wash their hands. Mary knew Alfred was looking at her as he leaned against the wall that divided the kitchen from the bedroom. She hardened her belly and kept her eyes from meeting his. She spoke to him as if he were anyone, someone she'd just met, not the man she'd loved since she was seventeen years old. "When you get home you should wash yourself well. Boil your clothes or throw them away."

Now that Driscoll was at the hospital there would be no need for Alfred to come around anymore, and if he stopped coming, then this, an interval of several hours, wouldn't mean anything and she could go back to pretending he didn't exist. She heard him draw his breath as if to speak but then release it again.

Mrs. Borriello took Mary by the hand.

"Hold on," Alfred said, taking two quick steps toward the door as if to block it. "Mary," he said softly. "Can I come up to talk a minute? Or can we take a walk?"

"It's the middle of the night!" said Mrs. Borriello.

"She can speak for herself."

"Why?" Mary asked.

"I have to talk to you, Mary."

"Another time maybe," Mary said, and Mrs. Borriello followed her boarder out the door.

Upstairs, the boys asleep, Mary found Mrs. Borriello's largest pot and filled it with water. She filled the kettle, too. Once the water was boiled, the women took off their dresses, and their underclothes, and shoved them to a corner of the kitchen. Mrs. Borriello stepped into the bath first while Mary dropped their underwhites into Mrs. Borriello's pot and stirred them like she was checking on a stew. Then Mary bathed while Mrs. Borriello stirred, the water at such a rapid boil the pot hopped on the stove. When they were both dressed in fresh clothing, their damp hair loose around their shoulders, their undergarments drying over the sink, Mary made coffee and poured it into two cups. Mrs. Borriello yawned. The kitchen was warm, and comfortable, and Mary's body felt clean and soft under the fresh clothes. Mrs. Borriello stretched her arms over her head and purred.

"What's your first name?" Mary asked.

"Emilia. My family called me Mila."

"Pretty."

"Not many call me Mila now."

"No."

The clock on the mantel ticked its rhythm and Mary remembered Aunt Kate, how they'd sit in the silent kitchen until late, Kate sewing, Mary sipping tea and reading aloud from the newspaper, until it came time to go to sleep.

Mila Borriello began smoothing her fine black hair, first one side, and then the other. She pulled it away from her face and twisted it behind her head. In only her camisole, and with her cheeks still rosy from the steam of the bath and the warmth of the room, Mary could see that she was still a beautiful woman.

"How old are you?"

"I am thirty-four years old." Mila smiled. "You thought older?"

Mary nodded. The two women regarded each other in silence.

"I was married before," Mila said. "Before Salvatore."

"I didn't know that."

"Of course not. How would you know?"

Mary waited.

"His name was Alberto. Is Alberto. He's still alive someplace, I don't know. Last I saw him was in Naples."

Mary felt the room seem to settle down around them. Her hand rested on the table not six inches away from Mila's hand. She'd never invited her, Mary considered now. She'd never asked her up for tea or coffee, or knocked on her door to see if she needed anything from the market. When Mary, Fran, and Joan made a plan to go put their feet in the fountain, or walk in the park, they'd never asked if Mila Borriello felt like joining them. Alfred sometimes wondered why the Borriellos didn't live downtown on one of the Italian streets, but mostly they didn't think of the Borriellos at all.

"This Alberto, he was father to my oldest boy. You remember."

The drowned boy, also Alberto. They called him Albie. Albertos become Albies in America.

"I'm not sure I understand."

"He was not such a good man, Alberto. In some ways, yes, a decent man, he always made good wages, but in most ways, not such a good man. He loved me, and loved his boy in his way, but he was not the way a man should be. He lifted his hand to me every day and I knew he would lift his hand to my boy. Maybe he would wait until my boy got strong, but maybe not. At first I thought I could spend a little less, sit a little less, but then I saw he would do it anyway and I'm not a woman who deserves hitting. So one day he beat me with the leg of a chair and I left him. I took the boy while he was out of the house and stayed with a woman neighbor, and then I came to New York City and called myself a widow. Then I met Salvatore in America and told him all of it. Some men, they would leave a woman who told him a thing like that. Some men would side with the other man even not knowing him, even the man all the way in Naples. Not Salvatore. He believed me and trusted me and then we had our own two boys, Carmine and Anthony. He was kind to me every day of his life."

Mila looked at Mary very seriously. "They don't know this, Carmine and Anthony. They think Alberto was their full brother, their father's son."

"I understand." Mary remembered that horrible afternoon. "I'm so sorry about Salvatore. And about Albie. We never talked about—"

"It's fine," Mila said, and set her mouth in that familiar way she had, a widow's pursed lips, worried brow.

They were quiet for a long time.

"I don't think of that day too much. Sending them out for wood. Much more I think of before we came here, when it was just the two of us, that baby with me on the ship, and how careful I was to give him the cleanest portion of the sheet, and the best of what we had at meals. You've never seen a baby cling the way Alberto clung to me in America when we got here first. Sometimes it's hard to understand that that baby turned into my boy. That that baby disappeared, and turned into a boy, and then that boy disappeared. So he left me twice. Do you understand?"

"Your English is very good."

"I don't mean my English. I mean do you understand about having a baby and worrying sick over him and finally getting him away from a dangerous thing and then having so much good happen and then the baby grows into a handsome boy and then he is gone? One, two, three, gone. I pushed him out of me, and nursed him, and soothed him, and then one day he left here and didn't come back. Like he was nothing and everything I felt for him was nothing and all that time we felt it was good, and strong, and special, it was really no stronger than a strand of hair snipped in two.

"A few months after the accident a man came with a document to sign, and that was it. Salvatore signed it and explained to me that there was nothing else they could do. They never found him in the river. He never washed up anyplace. Salvatore was as sad as I was, but it's different for men. He went to work and came home and seemed the same but I knew better. We had three boys, and then we had two."

A memory of Tobias Kirkenbauer ambled across Mary's

mind: she saw herself tying him into his pram, pushing him down to the water with a picnic of bread and cheese. What did they say to each other? What was that funny way he said her name? She recalled the tiny hairs on the doctor's top lip when he warned her not to tell Mrs. Kirkenbauer that the boy was gone. If Mrs. Kirkenbauer had asked for him, Mary would have lied, and yet she died anyway. Though Mary had seen enough death to know what it looked like when it came, it was always a shock to see that whatever it is that animates a person can slip away so easily, like a drop of water slipped down a drain. Perhaps she found out, Mary considered. Perhaps a mother knows.

"I'm not telling you this for you to say sorry, Mary. Any decent person is sad to hear such a thing so it's useless to say anything in response. I'm telling you this so you can see I know a little about men and about life. A woman who is married twice and has three children and gets herself to America with an infant alongside knows a little about the world and about men. You understand? You can imagine what it was like on that ship without a husband and with a boy to suckle."

Mary waited for what she knew was coming.

"You should stay away from that Alfred."

Mary felt the old defensiveness rise up but swallowed it back down again. "Well, anyway, he's married."

Mila Borriello touched Mary's hand. "How many hours was I with him since he found Mr. Driscoll and came up here to knock on my door? In all those hours, not once does he mention his wife. The only woman he mentioned was you."

Mary felt ashamed at the soaring she felt in her chest upon hearing this, at the familiar lightness in her bones that used to come over her when she'd hear his key in the door. Now that he'd seen her, he'd make excuses to come back, and she had to decide what she'd do when that happened. Liza Meaney will never know him like I do, she thought. Then she remembered that Liza Meaney had cured him, had convinced him to stick with a job, and for Liza Meaney he'd proposed marriage, become a stepfather. She had a vision of herself on North Brother, looking across the water at Manhattan, thinking about what he could possibly be doing that would keep him from writing to her, from trying to see her. No, she decided. No.

EIGHTEEN

On the night Driscoll was taken by ambulance, Alfred slept in the old man's rooms. He heeded Mary's advice and washed himself in the basin. Not wanting to sleep on the bed Driscoll had been coughing into, he found a spare blanket and made a bed on the kitchen floor. In the morning, he walked to the stable with his thoughts full of Mary, and how he could put everything right again.

As he cleaned the stalls and fed the horses, he decided he'd wait until after Samuel's exams to tell Liza what he now knew— that he could not be with her, and certainly could not marry her. He'd wait until after Christmas. After the New Year. But when he got back to their rooms that afternoon and saw them there, mother at the sink and son at the table, and the way she warned him with a look to keep quiet, and winced when he took off his boots by the door, and followed him around, touching everything he touched to straighten it, right it, clean from it whatever invisible grime he might have carried there on his fingertips, he knew he would not be able to stay there one day longer. He returned to his boots and went out the door before she could ask where he was going.

Back on the sidewalk he headed straight into the barrage of sound—children shrieked, their mothers calling after them; the horses clopped, whinnying and snorting at anything that came near them; the carriages squeaked and rattled; the automobiles honked and sputtered as they tore down the streets, the passengers gripping the crossbars.

Alfred sank into the bright busyness of the Lower East Side. He noticed now that many of the windows had Christmas candles waiting until nightfall to be lit, and remembered that Christmas was just ten days away. The day was warm, more like October than December, and he walked in a westerly direction across Allen and Eldridge Streets, through the blocks of all Italian—Mulberry and Mott. He headed south along Lafayette, and then west again until he came to the outdoor market on Chambers, where a twelve-foot Yule tree was standing at the northwest corner, decorated with beads and tinsel. He bought a loaf of bread and a few slices of smoked trout wrapped in a newspaper. With the bread and fish tucked under his arm, he turned east again. After a few blocks, he stopped on a curb and ate his meal while a group of children kicked a ball around him. Licking his fingers, he continued toward the East River, passing the faces of a hundred tenements standing shoulder to shoulder, like a row of tight-lipped and straight-backed soldiers. The zigzagging fire escapes, chipped and rusted, marred each façade, and Alfred knew without looking that the interior hallways were similarly spoiled, the plasters cracked and crumbling, the pastoral scenes painted over and over again until every color was a shade of gray. On one block alone he passed a delicatessen, a butcher, a baker, a milliner, a tailor, and a factory that made women's shoes. He passed a police officer who was trying to coax a dog from the street, and another officer yelling up to a man who had thrown a pile of chicken bones from his fifth-floor window. The man shouted back to the officer in German, and then pulled the curtain across. "Want me to tell you what he said?" Alfred asked the officer.

"Don't bother," the officer replied, and continued on.

Alfred turned and turned and turned again until before him was the Brooklyn Bridge, that shining, massive jewel suspended over the water and held there, it seemed from Alfred's vantage, by magic, by a simple crosshatch of wire and string. He was a German, the man who thought how to do that. Alfred marveled as he stared at how the bridge seemed to take a flying leap across the tidal strait below. He recognized the gothic towers of the old world, except instead of appearing bulky and grim like they did in the Rhine country, here in America they held only promise, and the arched portals carved into them seemed to Alfred to welcome those who crossed like a collection of solemn ancestors, holding the new Americans in the palms of their hands.

He walked across the bridge and then jumped the trolley on the Brooklyn side, held tight to the bar, and after a long time hopped off at Coney Island, where, passing the Loop-the-Loop and packs of young girls pressed into circles, talking behind their hands and laughing, he remembered bringing Mary there when Aunt Kate was still alive and watching her as she danced with other girls. Even then it was a rare thing to see her so joyous, and even more rare as time went on, but it was worth the wait and even severe Mary, even worried Mary, even Mary with a cook's slouch was worth a hundred Liza Meaneys.

It was nearly midnight when Alfred got back to Liza's rooms, and after climbing the narrow stairs he listened at the door for a minute to discover whether she was still awake, waiting for him, or if the boy was still studying at the table. He thought about what he'd say, whether he'd hold her or if that was wrong, whether he'd tell the boy himself or let her do it. He heard nothing, and there was no light under the door.

It will come as a shock to her, Alfred knew. She might not be able to make ends meet without him. She mightn't be able to send the boy to school. But she'll take on another boarder. A woman would be better for her, and the neighbors would like it more. I'll send her a letter, he decided as he turned and made his way back down to the street. It would be kinder to Liza to avoid the shame of having to watch him leave, or the temptation she might have to beg him to stay. It would be more honorable to allow her to face that on her own and then she could tell Samuel whatever she liked. Alfred would simply never return to Orchard Street at all. As for the few articles he'd left behind in her place, she could do what she liked with them.

Then he remembered he had thirty-one dollars saved in a coffee can on the top shelf of the pantry, and that stopped him as he crossed the first-floor landing. He looked up the dark stairwell and listened. After a few seconds, he shook his head and waved his hands in front of him as if he were scattering that paper money in the breeze. He stepped toward the heavy front door, believing he'd made his decision, but he thought of that money again as he placed his hand on the knob. He could see it as a stack, turned on its side and curved against the can. It smelled of coffee. What would Liza do with it? Buy books for the boy?

He climbed the stairs again. He placed the palm of his hand against the door and then turned the knob, slowly, slowly, so that the lock wouldn't pop like a gunshot and wake her up. He pushed it open only far enough to slide his body inside and in three steps he was standing at the pantry, peering toward the top shelf. Empty. He scanned the lower shelves, the counter, the curio in the corner. The floorboard creaked as his thumb grazed the miniature collectable bell she'd gotten from Philadelphia, years and years ago from her husband, the boy's father, dead at twenty-seven. Alfred was rooted in the still silence until he remembered the small hollow in the brick wall between the window and the curio, a little space gouged out long before his arrival and impossible to notice unless a person went looking for it. Liza had pointed it out to Samuel as a good place to keep his earnings, and Alfred went up on tiptoes now, reaching around the curio to find it in the moonlight. There was his coffee can, and next to it, a chipped sugar bowl full of the boy's earnings. Graceful as a ballerina, he leaned down, plucked up both, and barely felt the floor under him as he slipped out the door, back to the hall, down to the street.

For the first time since taking the cure, he reached for the flask that held the medicine, and there on the dark sidewalk he tipped it into his mouth, pretended it was whiskey, and swallowed every drop. When he was finished, he waited to see if the medicine would do the trick, if it would take all that wanting away and turn it into satisfaction, into the calm easiness of sobriety as Dr. Oppenheimer had described it, the peace of needing nothing, of feeling sound in body and mind. Instead, he felt violence in his belly, and as quick as he could lean over, he vomited on himself and all over the step. He stumbled to the curb and vomited over the dog shit there. He dropped down to his hands and knees and vomited again. When he saw in the dim light of the gas lamp a policeman coming up the street with his hand on his club, he moved along as quickly as he could. He stuck close to the buildings and walked north until he came to a church with a small cemetery beyond its gates. He tried to vomit again but nothing came because there was nothing left, so he retched drily behind a headstone, wrapped his coat more tightly around his body, stumbled over to a bench, and slept.

In the morning, cold to the bone and with an aching neck, he made his way to Washington Square Park. The Borriello boy had said the laundry Mary worked at was almost on the park, but he hadn't had a chance to tell him which side, how close "almost" was. Buttoned into the inside pocket of his coat was his thirty-one dollars, plus Samuel's eleven. Eleven dollars was nothing compared to the dinners he'd put on their table, compared to all the pencils and books and scratch pads he'd purchased. The groceries, the new kitchen curtains, all acquired with the money he'd given her. She'd made out well, he told himself, the thick stack of money a lump on the left side of his coat.

He began searching at the park's south end but found no laundry. There was a laundry a block from the park's west side, but when he went in to inquire about Mary, they didn't know who he was talking about. It was the same at the two laundries he found within a few blocks north of the park. Then, on the park's east side, he spotted a sign and knew it must be the place. He watched a Chinese move around the front of the store, and then had a glimpse of her, passing through a back room, carrying a stack of folded clothes. Though the vomit had dried on his pants and shoes, the stench seemed as strong as it had been when fresh, and when he touched his hand to his face he knew that he needed a wash and a shave. He was hungry. He wanted to rinse his teeth. The Chinese came to the door, noticed him, and turned his back.

He needed to make himself presentable. He needed to consider what he'd say. Instead of speaking to her right then, as he'd planned, he walked to the old building and got himself into Driscoll's rooms by the key Driscoll left over the frame of the door. He stripped in Driscoll's kitchen and then went into the old man's closet to find a shirt, pants, fresh socks, hurrying out of the contaminated room as quickly as he could. He found Driscoll's blade and cream. When he was finished, and standing in the kitchen with Driscoll's bedroom door shut tight, he made a mug of strong black coffee and sipped it beside the stove. He felt jumpy, as if being chased, as if those pursuing him were crouched outside in the street, spying on him from the upper floors of the buildings lining the avenue. He placed Driscoll's key on the table and locked the door behind him.

He walked directly over to the laundry—it was near quitting time—but she would not see him. A Chinese looked him up and down with those inscrutable eyes and told him that she could not be disturbed. He told the man he would wait as long as he had to. He raised his voice and sent it toward the back of the shop, where the sounds of cranks and pulleys and the sudden hiss of steam went on as if he weren't there at all. The smell of damp clothing and hot irons filled the small space, and he wondered if she smelled like that now—where before she'd smelled of fruit and fresh bread, now she might smell of starch and laundry powder. She'd heard him. He could feel it. She was listening. He told the Chinaman to call the police if he wanted to. He didn't care. And then, not fifteen minutes later, he was back on the street again, walking into the wind that pricked his face like a hundred thousand needles, turning a shoulder to slice through the throngs hustling about with their packages tied up with string. He circled around the neighborhood for a while, and then went back to the laundry and stood outside the door.

"Mary," he said, when she finally came out, as he knew she would, eventually. Two other women had already left, and the sign on the door said CLOSED. "I need to talk to you."

She stayed several feet away from him on the sidewalk and wrapped her scarf around her head. "No, Alfred, I don't think so. I think the time for talking is past."

"I didn't marry her, you know."

Mary leveled a look at him. "And? What am I supposed to do? Thank you?"

"No! I only—"

"Go away, Alfred. Please. Leave me alone."

He watched her walk away, and he waited for her to stop, look over her shoulder, think of something more to say to him. But she turned onto Greene Street and disappeared.

He needed to change his tack. He needed to find a way to explain himself. In the short term, he realized he shouldn't have locked himself out of Driscoll's flat. He had his stack of money but he didn't want to waste it, so he walked over to Eighth Street, to a delicatessen where an old friend from his coal-hauling days worked slicing meat, and asked to sleep in the pallet in their supply room.

In the morning, he waited outside 302 East Thirty-Third, but he must have arrived too late and missed her. He passed by the laundry a few times to kill the hours until they closed, but didn't catch any glimpses of her. Christmas was now only eight days away. Pale children begged from morning until night, and there was a Santa on every other block. The markets smelled of clove and cinnamon and the men hocking evergreens were asking astonishing prices for trees that by New Year's would be brown and brittle and back on the curb.

What he needed was courage. What he needed was to figure out exactly the right thing to say. He shoved his fists deep into his coat pockets because when he set them free his arms felt out of rhythm with his body. He put up his collar. He walked faster. His flask was empty now, and he kept reminding himself to go to Oppenheimer's office for more of the medicine, but it was like the old prayers of his childhood: his mind said the words but the words were meaningless and he barely heard them. The thought of filling it with something better came to him innocently, the first time, as he passed a pub he used to like. But as soon as the thought entered his mind it gained traction, and wouldn't be pushed away. He tried to think instead of how he and Mary would talk, finally, and how life would go on, but every time he let his guard down there it was, an itch in his chest demanding to be scratched. He walked and walked and bought a comb for his hair and better socks for his feet, but there it was, squatting in the corner of his mind and smirking at him. If I limit myself to a dram, he considered. His groin tingled. He felt his pulse in the soles of his feet and his fingertips. If I tell the barman it's only the one, and to not under any circumstances sell me another. If I drink it up quickly and then go on my way. If I never do it again after this.

He walked back to the pub he'd passed that morning. Quickly, quickly, he caught the barman's eye and held up his first finger. The barman found a bottle, and Alfred nodded. The barman found a glass, set it on the bar, poured from one vessel into the other, all of which Alfred watched closely, as if trying to spot the sleight of hand in a card trick. The barman restored the bottle to the shelf and placed the glass in front of Alfred. Alfred removed his hat, swallowed it down, and returned the empty glass to the bar.

"Jeez, brother," the man said, eyeing him. "We don't run tabs here."

"I have money."

The second time, Alfred looked at the amber liquid for a moment before swallowing it in two long gulps. The polished wood of the bar stretched out to his right and curved into the shadows at the back of the room. The glasses lined up in neat rows behind the barman caught the faint sun coming through the windows. He felt nervous out there in the city, the tendons and sinews of his body mimicking the hectic pace all around him, leaving him exhausted, leaving him unable to relax, his ears always cocked like a hare waiting for the sound of approaching hounds. Here, Alfred noticed, the encroaching city stopped its march at the door, and at the center of his body the heat from those two small drams worked better than any overcoat, worked better than the warmest feather bed. The others seated at the bar were silent except for a pair of gentlemen toward the back discussing something in a whisper. There was no music playing, and the barman had not even bothered to put out the token plate of cheese. Alfred felt a familiar calm traveling outward from his belly. He had lost his mother as a boy but he knew that feeling was what a boy feels when he steps into his mother's arms, that tenderness, that fierce compassion. He shifted in his stool to find the familiar position. He rested his chin to his fist.

He counted the days since he'd shown up for work at the stable, and wondered if he still had a job. If they fired him, maybe it would be for the better. That way when he got his fresh start with Mary he'd find something else. He ordered a beer with his whiskey. He could move furniture, maybe. He could go out and harvest ice instead of waiting in the stables for it. When the quitting hour rolled around he didn't bother going over to the laundry, deciding instead that he'd have better luck catching her outside their old building. He didn't bother with dinner or supper. The other men left and a new group took their places. His stack of cash was getting lighter, and sometime after supper, after the barman had cleaned the glasses and wiped down the top of the bar, he asked Alfred if he had somewhere to go. Alfred straightened up, leapt from the stool, hurried out to the street.

The laundry had been closed for several hours, so Alfred sat inside the vestibule of 302 East Thirty-Third Street for six hours before she appeared. He was leaning with his back against the wall, his legs stretched out in front of him, when he opened his eyes to find her looking down on him with a newspaper under her arm and an umbrella in her hand.

"What are you doing?" she said.

"Waiting for you."

She leaned over to sniff the air, and then like she'd been scalded she jumped, pulled her long skirt to the side, and tried to step past him to the front door.

"Wait," he said, and quick as could be he reached for her ankle. He felt that delicate knob of bone move under his thumb as she tried to wriggle free.

"Let me go," she said with that fierce look she got whenever she was angry. He let go. "What do you want? Why are you here? I wish you'd keep away from me."

"Didn't you hear me say I'm not married? I didn't marry her."

Mary gave one of those quick breathy laughs he knew marked the point when she was about to lose her temper completely. He stood and stepped back until he was against the wall. He'd forgotten what she could be like. He'd forgotten everything. She held her pointing finger one inch from his nose.

"You stay away from me, do you understand? Don't come to the laundry. Don't come to this building. Don't look for me on the street."

"You don't mean it. I know you don't mean it." He thought of her stooping over him in the early mornings. He thought of her pushing his clothes into the tub, and wringing them, and shaking them out in two deft snaps before hanging them by the stove. He thought of the soft swing of her breasts while she worked, and the swell of her bare white hip in the morning, and the way she was careful about her hands, always rubbing the fingertips in lemon to take away the odor, and how he wanted to kiss those hands now and tell her that she could not send him away. Sometimes, not often, but sometimes, she would listen to a story he told her, about the bar, about some person he'd met there, and if the story was funny she'd laugh. She'd drop what she was doing, sink into her side of the bed, and laugh. Sometimes, not often, she would ignore the dawn light that insisted it was time to wake up, and instead she'd roll over toward him, throw her arm over his chest, make a nest in the crook of his arm. Even when she was upstate, or in New Jersey, or across town at a situation that didn't permit journeys home, he never felt alone knowing she would be coming back to him.

She made a small choked sound now, a sound he'd heard out of her only once or twice since she was seventeen. She drew a deep breath, and when she looked at him again she had composed herself.

"Please," she said, and he felt sobered.

"But Mary, I know it would be different now. I haven't—"

Mary moved forward quickly as if she was going to hit him, all that rage simmering just below the features of her face, leaving a mottle of her cheeks, a man's rage, as they'd noted in the newspapers, an animal's rage, an immigrant's rage, something that required four, five, six generations to be properly bred out. But it was only a flicker, and when he blinked she had already drawn herself back, closed her eyes, and then, after a beat, descended the front steps to the sidewalk. "I mean it, Alfred," she said, and next thing she was gone.

He roamed the city to clear his head, pausing only on park benches and barstools. He spent that night stretched on the long seat of a Model T parked under a tree on Fifty-Seventh Street, the owner's blanket pulled up to his chin, and then spent the next day at Nation's Pub. When the car was gone the next evening he found another. He went on this way for a few days, until he remembered the ice company stable, and how warm it would be there with all the animals lined up in their rows, the doors and windows shut tight. Since it was now just a few days until Christmas, there would be no one there except the poor soul who got elected to come by to feed the animals, shake out fresh straw.

The stable was empty. Alfred scrambled through a window that stayed closed all winter but was never locked. Inside, staggering now with exhaustion, he pushed bunches of hay together on the dirt floor, found a spare horse blanket. He'd tell whoever came that he was back on a shift, that he was meant to be there. They would believe him.

He slept for hours, and when he woke it was deep darkness, the horses breathing gently, the one closest to him snorting, as if asking Alfred if he'd awoken, if he was all right now. He sat, pulled his stiff knees to his chest. Mary would come around. She had to. If she didn't, Alfred considered, then there was not a single person in New York City, not a single person in the world, who cared what happened to him.

Alfred stretched, went into the back room in search of food, and instead found half a bottle of John Powers. Solemn in the face of such good luck, he picked it up as carefully as he might a baby, and brought it tenderly back to the spot where he'd slept. He slid to the ground. He pulled a blanket across his knees. Closing his eyes, he uncorked the bottle and drew a long, ravenous mouthful.

Some time later, he wasn't sure how long, he noticed the sky outside was gray and he couldn't decide if that meant day was turning into evening, or night into morning. He placed the empty bottle on the windowsill. He made his way to the back room again, where a simple straight-back chair loomed before him, and behind, the horses made threatening noises with their throats and stamped their feet. It was darker now, and he found a lamp, found a bottle of oil, found a match. Had Christmas come yet? Was it now? He removed the glass and the wick holder and poured in the oil from the plain, unmarked canister in the corner of the room, cursing as some dripped onto the seat of the chair.

He twisted off the blackened top of the wick with his fingertips. He shook out a wooden match and struck once, twice. The match broke. He dropped it on the ground, kicked it, shook out another. This time, he heard that small suck of surrounding air, and when the light was born, Alfred held it for a moment before touching it to the tip of the wick.

Later, looking back at the moment when the flame met the cloth of the wick, he would see it so clearly that he would wonder if he'd been more sober than he realized. He couldn't recall the weather outside, or the state of his clothing, or the color of that horse blanket, or the last meal he had put in his belly, but he could remember that flame, and the white of that wick. It was as if his mind had taken a photograph that he was able to study only later, the position of the can, the direction of the spout, the odor of the oil. He touched the flame to the wick and swore later that he knew just before it happened, an instant before, a heartbeat before, a space of time so small it would have been impossible to measure. He knew as he was doing it, as he watched the orange meet the white, and one hair to the other side and he would have known before; he would have stopped. He touched the flame to the wick and the room exploded.

NINETEEN

And just like that he was gone. I wanted him to leave, Mary reminded herself. I asked him to. All he did was listen. Christmas came and she gave the Borriello boys a set of checkers to share. They had bought her pins for her hair, and as they talked, and ate, and admired the Christmas tree they'd decorated with strings of popcorn, Mary expected him to knock on the door, beg to see her. Why hadn't he married Liza? Did she kick him out when he came home stewed or did he need a drink only when he saw Mary? At the laundry, the Lithuanians gasped when she told Li to tell Chu that she wouldn't be wrangle woman anymore. She'd had enough. She would wash. She would do her turns at the front of the store. But no more ironing on a Sunday half-day either. And on top of that she wanted a raise.

"He won't do it," Li warned. "Irena and Rasa have been here five years. No increase. Not for you, either."

"Well then, Irena and Rasa deserve a raise, too," she said. "What would you do if all of us left you at once? How much business would he lose training three at the same time? More than three, since together we do the work of five. There's striking and organizing going on all over this city. Why not us?" Even outside of the laundry she felt the world back away from her lately, grant her passage in a way it didn't do for others. When she walked into shops and pushed her goods across the counter, people shrank further within their overcoats. She argued prices to the penny. She inspected packages for dents, fruit for bruises, meat for dark spots, clothing for loose threads, and brought everything to the attention of the grocer or the butcher or the shop assistant. She bought a pair of shoes and brought them back two days later to say there was a wobble in the left heel. "There's no wobble," the man said without touching the shoe, without even putting down the polish rag he was holding. Looking at the haughty expression on his face, he a cobbler with black fingertips, his vest hanging open and missing a button, Mary felt as if time slowed down. She took the shoe out of her bag and dropped it to the counter with a clatter. She felt the eyes of every other person in the shop. "There is a wobble, and I want my money back."

"Did you wear them?" the man asked as he inspected the sole, and she said of course she wore them. How in the world would she know about the wobble if she hadn't worn them? The clock ticked. She could hear the soft grunts of a second man stretching leather in the back room, the rhythmic punch of the sewing machine. The man at the counter pointed to a sign: No Returns on Worn Shoes. She nodded at him and then, raising her voice, announced: "This place sells broken shoes and refuses refunds." She went to the shop door, pushed it open, and repeated it to a group of women passing by. A man browsing the selection inside the door slipped by her and hurried down the street. She picked up the sign on the women's side of the display window.

"This says Comfort Shoes. Is that meant to be a joke?"

"What's your story, lady?" the man asked, his hands on his hips.

"I spent my money here thinking I'd gotten something for it. I'll stand here for a month if I have to, telling people about this place, and about the crookery that goes on here." She crossed her arms and looked at the man until finally, releasing a single loud sigh, he opened the cash drawer and returned her money.

One day in January, she saw a cook she recognized leaving from the side door of a restaurant, and the thought of that woman basting and chopping and sautéing in there felt to Mary like a hand closed over her throat. For the first time in all those months of her new life she didn't return to the laundry after her lunch break. Only at home, at Mila Borriello's table, did she feel some peace. She watched the boys do their figures. She took the scrub brush from her friend and helped her wash the floor.

Jimmy Tiernan came upstairs and knocked one evening when his Patricia was out. Mila and the boys were also out. "Come in," Mary said, pointing at an empty chair.

"Nah," Jimmy said, and leaned against the jamb of the door. "I was just wondering if you've seen Alfred."

Mary turned to the counter and made herself busy with the coffeepot, measuring out spoonfuls and cups of water. "No. Why?"

"Well, a little while back I told him about a job starting up—you know, the new skyscraper being built down across from City Hall. He seemed interested, said he was getting bored at the stable, and told me to get him on. Then I don't hear nothing from him. Not a peep. I told the boss I had a guy I wanted to get on but he can't hold it much longer."

Mary turned and leaned against the counter. "I haven't seen him, Jimmy. I don't know."

"Well, where is he?"

"I said I don't know."

"Okay, okay," Jimmy held up his hands. "I just wondered because I tried that address down on Orchard and the lady acted like she didn't know who I was talking about. He hasn't been around there, either."

Mary brought her fingertips to her temples and rubbed. "You know how he is. You tried at Nation's?"

"Yeah, I tried Nation's. They haven't seen him, neither. Tommy says he came in like a king a little before Christmas but they haven't seen him since."

Mary put her hand on the door. Inch by inch she moved it, and inch by inch Jimmy Tiernan retreated back into the hall.

"Well, if you see him, Mary, tell him thanks for nothing because I went out on a limb here, you know?"

Mary shut the door and Jimmy shouted from the other side. "But tell him check in with me anyway, will ya, Mary? When you see him? Tell him I'm not mad! Just wondering is all."

Mary curled up on her cot and closed her eyes.

One Sunday in February 1911, an Irishwoman named Mrs. O'Malley, whom Mary knew a little and who lived in the building across the street, came looking for her to help with a hog her husband had won in a round of cards up on 102nd Street. Drunk and cocky, the husband had shown up at home with the two-hundred-pound beast on a tether, and could not explain to his wife's satisfaction how he'd gotten the animal so far downtown. She told Mary that he presented the hog to her like he was giving her a basket full of money, or a room full of red roses, something beautiful or practical that she should appreciate, but instead it had been up to her to guard the animal where it now lived in the alley behind their tenement, tied to a piece of fence beside the common privy. He'd been there almost a week.

"And now I guess it's time to do something with him," Mary said.

"It is," Mrs. O'Malley said. "And I'm useless."

There was no sense asking if she'd consulted with a butcher, because Mary knew, if the tables were turned, she wouldn't have sought out a butcher, either. He would charge more than the pig was worth, and keep the best parts for himself.

"I've a good mind to turn him out and pretend it never happened, because where in God's name will I store the meat, but every time I go to do it, it nags me that someone else will get him. I'd rather keep some of the meat and give the rest away. My neighbors will pay me something for it." The woman clasped her hands together. "I'd be very grateful to you."

It was not cooking, it was butchering. All the cooking would be done by those lucky ones who got a part. Still, Mary hesitated. She rubbed her eyes. She tried to think about it clearly while also wondering if she was still strong enough to butcher a full-grown hog.

"Show him to me," she said finally, and Mrs. O'Malley clapped once before grabbing Mary's hand and thanking her.

Full of purpose now, Mrs. O'Malley led Mary down the stairs, across the avenue, in through her building's front door, out through the back door, and down four rickety wooden steps. There in the frost-bitten and muddy yard was the hog, rooting at the base of the fence. Mary crouched beside him, put her hand on his back. At least it's winter, she thought. They wouldn't have to worry about flies. She took off a glove and tested the dexterity of her fingers in the cold. The animal grunted and stamped. The fog of his breath rose up to meet Mary's throat and she felt the same suspicion she always did when she was around animals, that they knew their fate, that they were born knowing it, that they were wiser than any human gave them credit for. She felt tenderness for him.

"What floor are you on?"

"Fifth." Mrs. O'Malley turned and pointed up to a distant window.

"We'll do it here," Mary said, without taking her eyes from the hog. "I have good knives at my place, but you find me a long, thin one for sticking him. Get me a saw if you can find one. A hammer. As many clean buckets as you can manage. Twine. I'm going to search out a few bits of wood to raise him up. When we have everything I'll need boiling water. A lot of it, and quickly. When you've gathered everything and put on the water, go around and ask the neighbors who wants some of the meat. Tell a few of them to come down to help us turn him. Then come straight back to me."

By the time Mrs. O'Malley returned, Mary had led the hog to a shaded patch of clean-looking grass in the farthest corner of the yard. Mrs. O'Malley handed over the hammer and the knives Mary had instructed her to bring, and the four buckets she'd scrubbed—three borrowed, one her own—and when she was ready, when both women had removed their coats and gloves and hung them carefully on the fence, Mary told Mrs. O'Malley to get up on the pig's back and brace him for the blow. It had been eight or ten years, at least, but her aim was still perfect, and the animal fell heavily.

"Now," Mary said, grabbing him by his massive head and using every drop of strength in her body to stick him. As she pressed the knife deeper, Mrs. O'Malley held the first bucket against him to catch what she could. Mary's heart pounded and she felt the heat from her body form a barrier against the cold of the day. Both women looked troubled as they watched so much of the sweet blood run into the grass, under the fence, down the gentle dirt slope toward the privy.

"Did you put on water?" Mary asked, and Mrs. O'Malley jumped up, ran into the building and up five flights of stairs. When she came back a few minutes later she was holding a pot full of boiling water, and poured it over the animal from head to hoof. "I've another," she said, breathless, when the pot was empty, and came down a moment later with a second pot. Mary went to work with the blade of her knife, removing the hair.

An hour later, Mary ran her hand gently over the pink skin to feel for an errant hair, and felt something move inside her as she looked at the animal, its blank eyes staring at an old metal bucket. He was a pathetic creature, had probably had a miserable life, and here he was. Mary pushed the knife into the pig's belly, feeling with her fingers that the intestines were still intact. She pulled out the guts and tossed them toward the second bucket. Moving back up toward the head, she felt the hem of her skirt heavy with blood. She twisted and pulled the hog's head free, and dropped it in the third bucket.

"I'll take that for my trouble," Mary said. Smelling the inside of that body was like smelling Ireland again, and she remembered being a girl, bringing the cow's stomach and intestines to the river, and the chill that ran through her to see the eels shoot out from under rocks the very same instant, it seemed, as the first drop of filth hit the water.

By the time Mary arrived at the heart, the neighbors had begun to line up with their pots and bowls. Mila was there, and both boys, each with a vessel to carry a part home.

Late that night, much later than her usual bedtime hour, after deciding that her clothes could not be saved, she scrubbed her body in the tub, pressed her knuckles into her aching arms, cleaned underneath her fingernails, and noted that she felt wide-awake. Mrs. O'Malley had pressed money into her hand, and Mary had taken it, but it wouldn't have mattered to her if she'd gotten nothing. All day long, and even now so many hours after helping Mrs. O'Malley wrap up those bits and pieces she wanted to keep for herself, Mary felt like someone had finally turned on a proper light after living for so long in a dim room. She smiled at the snout peeking up over the rim of Mila's largest pot.

"You haven't seen him yet?" Jimmy Tiernan called from across the street one early morning in March. Mary pretended she didn't hear. He caught her again coming into the building a few days later. "I think it's the strangest thing," he commented, as if he and Mary were a pair of abandoned children, together in their hurt. She tried to let it in one ear and out the other, but once again, she began looking for Alfred when she stepped out of the building in the mornings. Michael Driscoll had not survived and several of them from the building had gone to the funeral Mass, but Alfred did not show. The first anniversary of her release from North Brother came and went without anyone noticing, and by herself she took the IRT uptown, walked over to the river, and stared across. She had never looked up John Cane. They'd never taken their walk together in Central Park.

She'd felt less patience at the laundry ever since butchering the pig. What she'd told herself to accept, what she'd tried to face as permanent, could not continue. She was not a laundress and she never would be. It was no different from being on North Brother, looking out over the churning water at the life she was missing on the other shore.

And then one warm Saturday afternoon in late March, when she was working the cash register and insisting to a gentleman that they'd done their absolute best with the ink stain on his shirt pocket but that it simply could not be removed, she stopped to sniff the air. The gentleman also sniffed, and followed his nose to the door. For the first time in more than a year, the Lithuanians put down their garments, dried their hands, and came to the front of the store. Everyone heard the alarm bell sound next door.

"What is it?" Mary asked. From somewhere over their heads came a sound like thunder that grew louder every second until one of the street doors of the Asch Building swung open and people, mostly young women, began to run out to the street. Leaving the gentleman's shirt on the counter and clutching the key to the register in her fist, Mary left her post, walked out to Washington Place, around the corner to Greene Street, and when she saw the crowds looking up she also looked up, and saw what appeared to be a heap of clothes falling from an upper-floor window. Saving their materials, Mary thought, but she wondered at the moaning from the crowd as another bundle was sent down. A man fainted and the people beside him barely noticed. Mary moved closer to the outer fringe of the crowd. The fire truck's siren could be heard in the distance, moving closer. Coins rained from above along with the bundles of clothing, and Mary wondered that no one was reaching for them. No one was moving except for one woman who was wailing and thrashing and calling out for God, and Mary worked her way closer, excusing herself and pushing forward through the police officers who did nothing, the gentlemen and ladies, the bakers from across the street, the passersby, a pair of children who were looking up with open mouths. Finally, when Mary got through the crowd, she saw that the bundles had legs and arms and faces, many of which had been singed black. She looked up and saw framed in a ninth-floor window a trio of girls holding hands. The girl on the left was swatting her hair, which had caught fire, and all three were shouting something that no one on the sidewalk could understand. They jumped at the same time, and two of the three held hands until they hit the sidewalk. The third, the one with the burning hair, covered her face with her hands and as she fell her body became piked, her head almost touching her knees, like children do sometimes when they are jumping off rocks into water and want to impress one another. It took Mary a second to understand that there was no water, this was no game. These girls were jumping to their deaths, and far above their heads the crowd could glimpse a man's arm as he helped them to the ledge as easily as he might have assisted them up the boarding step of the trolley. Two more followed. Then two more. They jumped from other windows as well, in singles, and pairs, and groups of three. The man who had come into the laundry with the ink-stained shirt shouted at them to wait, please wait, the fire trucks were coming and they would be saved. Wait! he commanded, even after they were already falling.

Finally, a fire truck arrived, and then another. The crowd made way for them. The trucks pulled up close to the building, the firemen unwound their hoses, stretched their ladders up, up, up as high as they would go, and after looking hard at those folded-up ladders, and looking again at the distance to the eighth, ninth, tenth floors, Mary dropped to a crouch and prayed.

"They're not going to reach," a nearby man's voice said. "By God, they're too short by three stories." The collective moan grew louder and louder and swallowed everything. Two more jumped. Then another. Another. When they hit the ground it was as loud as an automobile crashing into a wall. Through the forest of legs at the base of the Asch Building, Mary could make out the back of a woman's head on the sidewalk, the careful braid threaded through her curls.

The laundry was closed for a week as the bodies were lined up in makeshift coffins on the sidewalk, and families tried to identify their loved ones by a watch or locket, by a pattern of stitches on a stocking, a particular ribbon in the hair. The line went on and on, hundreds of bewildered people in their mourning clothes, while the charred and broken bodies waited to be claimed in the crisp, late March sun. In the days after the fire it seemed to Mary that everyone in the city, from the Upper West Side to the quays of Lower Manhattan, moved about in grief. Papers were sold. Cafés were open. But the world went silent. In another week or so the accusations would begin. Why was the exit door locked? Why hadn't the alarm sounded on the upper floors? But in those first few days, when people spoke, it was of one subject only. All those girls. All those beautiful girls.

TWENTY

"How could I go back?" Mary asked her caseworker at the Department of Health. It was a busy place, and among the clicking of heels on the polished wood floor, the scrape of chairs, the racket of a ringing telephone, and the blusterous arguments spilling out from behind half-open office doors, Mary had to raise her voice to be heard. It was the end of May 1911, and Mary had been checking in with them every three months, as required. The first time she'd checked in, the whole office seemed to halt when she announced her name. Every man or woman behind a desk paused to watch her approach. They'd glanced at one another as she took a seat in the waiting area, and when her name was called their eyes followed her across the room. Now, at her fourth visit, a different caseworker each time, they barely noticed her, and most didn't look up from the stacks of paperwork on their desks. The staccato music of struck typewriter keys, the zip and ding of carriages returned, never ceased. The office was sinking under all the paperwork—file drawers left open, envelopes, writing pads, stationery, ribbons of ink loosened from spools and piled on chairs, on windowsills, heaped in corners. She wondered if she could talk them into letting her check in every six months instead of every three. She debated telling them about quitting the laundry, but there was nothing to feel guilty about, and if she was as free as they claimed she was, then there was nothing they could do to her for it.

"I couldn't possibly go back. You don't know what it was like that day."

"Ah," the man said, looking again at the address. "I see." Everyone had an opinion about the Triangle Waist Company tragedy, but relatively few, considering the size of the city, had been there to witness it. "Go home now," Mary had said to a pair of boys who had stopped to watch. They reminded her of the Borriello boys. But they didn't move, only stared up at the burning Asch Building like everyone else, until Mary took the smaller one by the shoulders, turned him around, put her forehead against his, and shouted "Go home! Do you hear me? Go home!" He blinked at her, and then, taking the older boy's hand, they ran away together.

The man riffled through some papers. "How have you been making ends meet since leaving the laundry?"

None of your business, Mary wanted to shout, but instead she counted to ten. "The woman I board with takes in lacework for a milliner. She's been showing me how."

"But no cooking, correct? I see here that that is the agreement you came to when you left custody. You understand that?"

Mary could tell by the change in his face, the sudden light, that he had not realized until that moment who she was. Her file said Mary Mallon, but she could guess what he was thinking: Typhoid Mary.

"It says here that you risk infecting others if you cook for them."

"I know what it says."

He closed the file, pushed back from his desk.

"It will take a while to get you a position at another laundry," the man said. He brought his hands together and regarded her for a moment. "Have you considered factory work?"

"Factory work?" Mary blinked, thought of herself among the throngs of women who waited outside the glassworks or the clocks manufacturer for the starting bell. They had to ask permission to use the lav. They had to punch in and out with time cards. At night, when they left, they had to be patted down in case they'd pocketed the small parts, just like the girls in the Triangle fire had been checked for scraps of silk and velvet.

"Do you realize I've cooked for the Blackhouses? For the Gillespies? I've cooked for Henry and Adelaide Frick and several of their friends." She crossed her arms. "I won't be working in any factory."

"You're not in a position to be haughty, Miss Mallon. We're not an employment agency, so we have to assign someone the job of getting new work for you. I just don't have the time. Truthfully, you might have better luck going through an agency. They might know of vacancies at private homes."

Mary wondered how old he was. If he still went home to his mama for supper.

"I've been finding work since I was born. Put that in your file. I don't need any help from you, and I certainly don't need to be helped into another situation as wrangler."

The man sighed. "Fine. Whenever you get something make sure to stop again and let us know the details."

"I look forward to it." She slammed his office door on her way out.

For the first time since leaving North Brother more than a year earlier, Mary felt unobserved as she made her way down the avenue. The man had forgotten to send her for a sample, and she smiled, quickening her step in case he might remember and run after her. Why had she never considered quitting before, finding something with better terms? She stopped in on the fishmonger on First Avenue and bought a pound of mussels. She stopped again for white wine, parsley, butter, a pair of shallots, a loaf of bread. It would be a treat for Mila, supper ready when she came home, and lately she'd been doing more and more of the cooking, and Mila had agreed that she could take the price of the groceries out of her board. No one had ever said anything about cooking for herself, or cooking for friends without being paid for it, but still, before she cooked for them the first time she reminded Mila of what Dr. Soper had said about her, why she'd spent almost three years on North Brother. She loved cooking, and would like to help, but if Mila didn't want her boys to eat what she made she would understand.

"Did you have the fever?" Mila asked.

"No," Mary said. The truth. More truth: "They say that doesn't matter."

"How could it not matter? And you cooked for Alfred? When you were living here before? And for other people?"

"Yes. Of course. It's how I made my living."

"Well then, you cook. I trust you."

Mary made that first pot of stew with the boys in mind, and hummed as she chopped the carrots and the celery. Only when it came time to ladle it into bowls did she feel something nagging

her, a sharp chill that started behind her neck and traveled down
her back. She hesitated, but they were already lusting after the bits
of tender meat, the steam rising up to their cheeks as the snow
floated down the airshaft. They reached for their bowls and she
handed them over, and after, for several weeks after, even after telling herself it was fine, it was completely fine, they'd gotten into her
head, was all, they'd made her nervous of herself without true cause,
she found herself observing them for signs of illness, and wondered
if this was a sign of her guilt, a sign of admitting that she knew
something that she could not face. But they never did get sick, not
even a head cold, so she kept cooking for them: shepherd's pies and
roasts and coq au vin, quiche with bacon and leeks, and she felt
both happier than she'd felt since 1907, and angry once more that
she'd signed the paper promising to never cook for hire again.

"So what will you get?" Mila asked that evening when they
finished supper, the blue-black shells in a pile at the center of the
table. "You're still not allowed to cook?"

"No." She'd been wondering since leaving the DOH if baking
counted as cooking or if it was a different category altogether. She
thought of the dairyman upstate who was allowed to stay on and
supervise his dairy. There was a bakery looking for help not five
blocks away. "Ah," Mila said. "And they would know, I suppose."

Mary nodded.

"How would they know?"

Mary didn't know how they would ever find out, but she had
signed the paper. They would return her to North Brother if she
lied to them and was caught.

"Do you think baking counts as cooking? Or is it a separate
category?"

Mila considered the question very seriously.

"Baking is a different thing. And anyone who says otherwise doesn't know about either one."

"That's what I think, too," Mary said.

The next morning, she walked to the bakery that had advertised for help. The man who managed the place showed her their equipment, explained how many rolls, buns, cakes, and pies they made and sold daily. There was a front counter where people could come in and order from what was displayed behind the glass, but most of the business was in the large orders that went directly to grocers nearby. He quizzed Mary about her experience, and then, leaving her alone in the kitchen with the other baker, instructed her to make something that showed them what level of skill she had.

"Where's the cocoa?" Mary asked, opening and closing cabinet doors, pulling and pushing drawers. "Do you have a double boiler?" The other baker, an older woman named Evelyn, pointed to a corner of the counter. She stayed silent but watched closely as Mary gathered ingredients. Mary saw her looking from the corner of her eye as she folded and poured and whipped and mixed. When the timer dinged, Evelyn dropped the pretense and turned from her work to watch Mary remove the soufflés from the oven.

"Wait. They might fall still."

"They won't fall," Mary said, and they didn't. The manager took her name without showing any sign of recognition, and told her to report first thing in the morning. Mondays were mostly rolls and buns, Fridays mostly cakes and pies, in between was a free-for-all—from cranberry-nut bread to fried dough to custom cakes decorated with sugar flowers. He sent her home with two-day-old apple strudel, and she held the box flat in her palm all the way, thinking of what the boys would say when she showed them, thinking how they'd rush through their dinners with their eyes on the oil-dotted box.

What will I say? She demanded of herself three months later, the next time she walked up to the DOH office where she'd once again sign next to her name, her residence, her place of work. It was August now, and they were baking with blackberries and apricots. She brushed flour from her sleeves and the front of her dress. She washed her hands thoroughly, and loosened the pins that kept her hair in a severe bun while she was mixing and beating and pouring. She told them at the bakery that she had to bring an ill neighbor to the hospital, and Jacob, the manager, told her to be back in one hour. One day, when she got the courage, she might march Mila and the Borriello boys to the DOH headquarters to say that she'd cooked for them, and they had survived, but then they'd just say what they always said, which was that it didn't matter. Some people were immune. Some people had protection built in to them already. And sometimes she wasn't infectious. Maybe she'd write to Mr. O'Neill about helping her get back to cooking. But not today, not yet, and when the man asked her where she'd found employment since her last visit, she was about to tell him, getting ready her argument that baking and cooking were entirely different occupations, when instead, she heard herself say that she worked in a shop, as an assistant.

"What kind of shop?" the man asked.

Mary brought forth her thickest brogue. "Oh, one of them kinds of shops that sells nice things to rich people. Pretty-looking things."

As he scrutinized her, she tried to look and feel as blank as possible—a middle-aged woman with a thickening waist, poor posture, ugly shoes. She blinked. She scratched behind her ear.

"Trinkets?" he asked. "What sort of pretty things?"

"I dunno. Colorful things. I don't see much of the selling as I work in a room at the back."

It was all true, in a way. All true if you slanted it a bit, made the colors run together.

A girl came in with a stack of files and placed them on his desk. He sighed, pushed the pile to the side, and then scribbled "shop assistant" in Mary's file and handed it to her. "Put the address," he said. She took the pen from him and held it in the air for a moment as her mind raced and she realized she was about to write the real address. She changed the street number by one digit. An honest mistake, she could say later. I wasn't entirely sure. She signed. He signed. Then he summoned the secretary and told her to lead Mary down to the basement to give her sample. Mary knew her own way to the small room, but she was escorted anyway, and once there a nurse made conversation about the weather, about Vinie Wray being shot outside the stage door of the Hippodrome, about the Sanitation Department's new plan to remove garbage at midnight, about a shipping company owned by J. P. Morgan announcing that it was building the world's first unsinkable ship, while Mary squatted over a bright white bucket and prayed to God for something to happen so that she could be on her way.

"Do you want me to get the bulb and syringe?" The nurse asked.

"No, I do not," Mary said. "I want you to leave me alone."

"Can't do that, ma'am." She tapped Mary's file.

From her left Mary heard the traffic of the hallway on the

other side of the locked door, and on her right the sounds of the street floated in the screened window. The nurse closed her eyes and leaned against the wall.

"Stuffy in here," she said. "Feel anything?"

"I'm not doing this," Mary said, pulling up her underthings, straightening her skirt.

The nurse took a step forward. "It hasn't been thirty minutes. Look, why don't we take a break and try again in a while. You don't want to have to come back tomorrow, do you? Can I bring you a glass of water?"

"You can drown yourself in the river if you like," Mary said as she walked across the room and opened the door. "I'm leaving."

Twenty minutes later she was cracking eggs into a ceramic bowl.

She didn't go back the next day, or the next week. She expected them to look for her, but they didn't. Summer ended, and in the autumn she and Evelyn baked with pumpkin, nutmeg, clove. Sometimes, when Jacob said that a customer had requested fresh peaches or sliced strawberries placed on their cake or pie, she thought back to what they told her on North Brother about heating food until all the germs would die away. "Do you know what a germ is?" they'd asked her, like she was a child sitting for an examination. Only later, back in her hut, facedown on her cot, the rush of Hell Gate just twenty-five yards from her gable, would she try to make sense of what they told her about invisible microbes that floated in the air, that traveled up the nose and into the mouth. So many years later, it still sounded like a fairy tale meant for children, a little world too small for the human eye to see, or like religion, in that they were asking her to believe such a thing existed without giving her a chance to look at it, hold it, understand it.

Standing there at her station, so far from North Brother, with the quiet of the kitchen, the familiar shape of Evelyn's bent neck, the light from the window shining over her work, the sound of bells jangling on the door up front and then the different bell of the register drawer opening and closing, the rhythmic beat of her spoon against the bowl as she worked it 'round and 'round and 'round the batter, she felt peaceful. She straightened slices of pear. Using her fingertips, she arranged blueberries into a neat semicircle, and then strawberries alongside. Quick as a blink she swiped her finger into the ice-cream bowl to see if it needed more sugar. She licked quickly from the mixing spoon and then, without thinking, plunged it back into the bowl. She made a sheet cake that would serve forty with fresh whipped cream between the layers. The layers slid a bit while she was anchoring them. She touched them into place. Touched them again. Pushed the cream to the edges with her thumb. At the end of the day, when she washed all the stickiness from her hands, she recalled all those moments of touching but she couldn't see how one small movement, one nudge, one lick, something all cooks do, all bakers, all mothers and grandmothers who had to see if a thing was finished, if it tasted right and good, how something so inconsequential, something she barely noticed herself doing, could mean anything.

She went back to the DOH three months later—November 1911—signed the papers again, skipped the sample, and once again she walked out of the building without being stopped. In the bakery, once December arrived, they crushed bits of peppermint and sprinkled them over icing. Mary stayed in her corner of the kitchen, Evelyn in the other, and they worked in peaceful silence. Sometimes sugar burned, sometimes pots boiled over, but for the most part their movements in the kitchen were harmonious, one pushing a pan into the oven when the other pulled one out. If Mary's timer rang while Evelyn was near the oven, she would open it and check on what was in there, and Mary did the same for her. She worked hard, stayed on her feet for ten hours straight, ate a dinner of burned corners and day-old bread, and every night she went to sleep happy.

Another Christmas, another bitter winter. The Hudson froze and children skated on its shores. Several times Mary thought she spotted Alfred, once entering the bakery, another time loping up the avenue, but it was never Alfred, and she hoped that wherever he was he was warm and dry. Maybe he'd gone to Canada. He'd always said New York was too small for him, too cramped. Maybe he'd gone south. With so many Negroes moving north it was said that there was work down there. Or maybe he was still in New York City, back with Liza Meaney. Maybe they'd married and gone upstate. Maybe Liza had helped him back on the wagon and gone through with the marriage. Maybe they'd had a child together.

When 1912 came Mary remembered that Alfred would have a birthday that year, having only one in every four, and calculated how many birthdays he'd had so far, and how it always seemed to soothe him, seeing February 29 on the newspaper, as if it proved that the date really did exist, and so did he. On the day after Alfred's birthday Mary heard it said that a man had jumped from a moving airplane with the help of an enormous silk cloth that unfurled from a backpack as he floated all the way to the ground, unharmed, and it struck her that Alfred would be interested in that. It's the kind of thing that would have kept him home for an evening, to talk about that with Mary, how man was getting more and more clever every year.

There was no use thinking of Alfred anymore, or expecting him to appear, or feeling as if he was watching her sometimes, or thinking of things she would say to him if she ever saw him again. She'd known him more than twenty years, and late at night, when she was tucked into her cot in the Borriellos' kitchen, the boys snoring in the room beside her, the vent rattling behind the stove, the voices of other tenants traveling up the airshaft so that she could hear their conversations as plainly as if they were sitting at the foot of her bed, she quizzed herself: do you really think Alfred is gone for good? It had been fifteen months since she'd seen or heard from him. "Yes," she whispered to those who might hear her along the airshaft, and pulled the blankets up around her shoulders. But shrouded inside her mind, hidden so well sometimes she feared she'd never find it again, was a single flame that she cupped with her hand, and blew into, and added twig after twig to. He'll be back, she thought, and like every night when she had trouble sleeping, once she admitted what she knew was true, her head sank deeper into the pillow, and she finally fell asleep.

In April, the *Titanic* reached Queenstown, and Mary thought of what a beautiful journey that would have been compared to her own crossing. Only five days later she'd not gotten twenty feet from her building when a newsboy shouted at her, "J. J. Astor is lost on the *Titanic*! As many as eighteen hundred dead!" He waved the *New-York Daily Courant* in her face, and she fished out coins to purchase it. People were huddled around, sharing their copies and reading bits aloud.

"And Mrs. Astor?" a woman called.

"Alive!" The boy shouted. "She's being brought on the *Carpathia*!"

All of New York stayed on the subject for the whole month

of April. Mila said she couldn't sleep for thinking of it, all those drowned people in the icy waters, so far from home. When the *Carpathia* arrived it was swarmed with those who wanted to get a look at the survivors, most of all Mrs. Astor, who stopped to let a holy man bless her pregnant belly. And when the *Mackay-Bennett* got to Halifax with three hundred of the bodies, Mary wondered why the survivors came to New York, but the dead did not, and what a gruesome job for the men at the docks that day.

In May 1912, one whole year after Mary started at the bakery, Jacob pushed open the swinging door that led to the kitchen and told her to come up front, there was a man there who wanted to see her.

"A man?" she asked. "For me?"

Mary's hands shook as she returned the sifter to its spot. Evelyn halted her beating of half a dozen eggs to glance at her. "Did he ask for the baker or ask for me by name?"

"Just come up front," Jacob said, and Mary noticed that it was unusually quiet up front for that hour of the morning. Normally, Mary could hear the chatter of customers at the counter, making their selections, some standing there eating what they purchased straight from the paper bags, but that morning she heard nothing except the sound of waiting, and Jacob holding open the door as she went to the sink, washed her hands, dried them, unpinned her hair, and then pinned it again. If Alfred went to the building first they would have told him where to find her. The Borriello boys met her sometimes, walked home with her, and even Jacob had gotten used to seeing them there. Sometimes she sent day-olds with them at midday so they could eat them before she got home. When there were lots of day-olds she sent enough for Fran and Joan as well, and she knew that sometimes those stale pastries and cookies and slices of pie never made it to Thirty-Third Street. Sometimes those two rascals found a patch of sidewalk, set themselves up on the ground, and ate every last crumb.

She touched her fingertips to the counter and thought of him standing out there. She would know in an instant if he was off the wagon or on. She pictured him married to Liza Meaney and decided it was best to believe that he was when she pushed out the door to face him; that way she wouldn't be disappointed.

But she didn't see anyone until Jacob stepped aside and she saw a man who was not Alfred standing before the window, his hands clasped behind his back.

"Mary Mallon," Dr. Soper said. He didn't step forward. He didn't extend his hand. "I'm just after telling your boss about your history, and he's agreed that you are to be let go."

Mary felt all her blood rush to her throat and a reverberation begin in her ears. She staggered, and placed one hand on the counter. His hair shone, his shoes shone, his cheeks were as smooth and bare as a baby's bottom, and his mustache was trimmed to perfection, every single little hair. He was as she remembered him, a wax figure, a nose that could stick a pig, a pale, ineffectual weakling of a man who preyed on healthy, strong women.

"He's told you lies," Mary said to Jacob, her voice a choked whisper, and then noticed the counter, where the newspaper articles about her case were lined up and labeled.

"I can't risk it, Mary," Jacob said.

"Have you had any complaints?" she demanded. "Has anyone come back to say they were made sick from what they ate here?"

"I've already told him that they haven't, but he said that doesn't matter. If they got the fever they might not realize where they got it. We wouldn't know."

Mary picked up a plate of lemon squares and flung them across the room at Soper. Soper stepped neatly to the side, then reached over and locked the entrance door.

"What did I tell you?" he said to Jacob.

"Please, Mary," Jacob said. "He says we can't sell anything until you're gone and the kitchen scrubbed. I'm losing money every minute. If the DOH puts a notice in my window I'm done for, do you understand?"

"Miss Mallon. Please gather your things and come with me." Soper said. "I'm bringing you directly to Commissioner Lederle's office."

Evelyn slipped through the swinging door and put her hand on Mary's shoulder.

"You're making a mistake," Evelyn said to the men. Mary felt herself sway, and Evelyn braced her harder. She let Evelyn guide her to the back room.

"It'll be fine. You'll get something else," Evelyn assured her as she stuffed the largest box with pastries.

"You don't understand," Mary said as Evelyn dropped loaves of fresh bread into the canvas satchel Mary took back and forth every day. He'd come with news clippings, and yet no police. He'd found her by chance. He carried the clippings around in his pocket. Maybe he'd followed her. Maybe the DOH had let him see her file and he'd gone looking for that address, one digit off, a building that didn't exist. He'd suspected, but wasn't sure, so he sussed out the situation himself. If he'd been sure, he would have brought police. Right now, she figured, he was strongly regretting not thinking out a better plan.

"Go now, this way, so you won't have to face him," Evelyn counseled. "I'll stall him."

Mary had taken one step out the door to the alley when she thought to explain to Evelyn what had happened. How would she put it? With only a few seconds, how to make her understand?

"I used to cook for a family uptown, and they said—"

"Oh, I followed your case," Evelyn said, pushing her out with more force. "I recognized you on the first day."

Mary gaped at the woman, and Evelyn shrugged. "You didn't lie. You told your name. Go on now, Mary. Good luck."

Clutching the box of pastries and with her bag of bread pinned under her arm, Mary ran down the alley and out onto the avenue.

TWENTY-ONE

Mila watched in silence as Mary swept her powders and creams from the sill. In the twenty months that she'd lived there, Mary was careful to keep her things within the space she'd been allotted: under her cot, the windowsill, a shelf in the pantry, one drawer in Mila's dresser. "Where will you go?" Mila asked as Mary shoved her belongings in her old velvet satchel.

"I don't know," Mary said as she looked around for the boys' scratch pads. But when she found them and touched the tip of the pencil to the paper, she realized she didn't know what to say. She drew a picture of a bird, and below it, two stick-figure boys holding hands.

"What will you do?" Mary asked as she picked up her satchel and placed it at the door.

"What will *you* do? You write to tell me where you land," she said, and Mary swore that she would. "And you'll come back, won't you? After everything has settled down?"

"Yes, yes. Of course."

"Why don't you go down and stay with Fran for a while? If they knock I'll tell them I haven't seen you."

Mary imagined Soper showing up with an army of policemen behind him. She imagined them staking out the entrance of the building, kicking down doors, throwing back bedclothes, and peering into closets.

"I'm sorry. I just have to go."

She had been rushing since she left the bakery and felt breathless, faster than everything moving around her. She passed Fran's floor without slowing, passed Joan's door, glanced down the hall toward Driscoll's old rooms, where a young man had been living for a year, and when she burst out onto the sidewalk she bent her head and walked north for no reason except that there were fewer people in that direction, and she'd be able to walk faster. She hopped onto the trolley on Thirty-Sixth Street, and held on as it turned, then came to an abrupt stop to let a dog cross the track, and again a half block later to let people on. She exited at the rear and hoisted her bag over her shoulder.

There had been no trace of Alfred since she left him behind in the vestibule that early winter morning almost a year and a half earlier, and she considered going to Nation's to find out if they'd seen him, but when she got her chance she kept going, past the bright blue door, past his other favorite spots. She arrived at Grand Central Terminal, where she dodged the trolleys approaching from every direction, and entered the building. Once inside, she followed the ramps up and around until she came to the main waiting area, the ceiling so distant it might as well have been the sky, and found an empty space on one of the long benches lined up before the timetable.

Every person who passed her was on his or her way someplace. Those seated looked up at the board once in a while, then at the clock, then back down at their hands to wait a few minutes longer. The announcer made a boarding call for Scarsdale, for Poughkeepsie. From behind her they called for Philadelphia. The best dressed waited in a separate area for the Twentieth Century Limited to Chicago. She scanned the boards for a train to Dobbs Ferry, and then watched closely as the people who wanted that train stood up, checked behind them for forgotten items, hurried off. The announcer made another boarding call. Another. Mary moved her bag from her lap to the floor by her feet and felt her back bend to the curve in the wood. She touched her fingertips to her closed eyelids and felt a tingle in her nose, the sob that had been brewing there all day rise up like a wave lifts itself from the rest of the ocean, rushes forth, spreads itself on shore.

"Madam?" a man tapped her on the shoulder. He wore a uniform: a jacket and matching cap. "Would you like to wait in the women's parlor? Do you know where it is?"

Mary thought he meant the lav, so when he led her to a large oak door and knocked twice, and then told the woman who answered that Mary just needed to rest, and should not be charged the twenty-five-cent fee, she felt afraid that he'd misunderstood something about her, and when they found her out, there would be trouble. But he encouraged her forward, and the woman who opened the door led her first through a small room where women's light spring coats were hung, and then into a larger room, finished in quartered oak, a Persian-style rug covering the floor. She pointed out one of several rocking chairs. "Thank you," she said to the woman, and the woman gave Mary a small curtsy as she backed away. Mary registered the small round vanity mirrors placed here and there, the full-length mirrors by the changing rooms. Though it was set up like a lounge in a private home, every step of a woman's toilet was available for sale, and adjoining the oak-paneled room was a fingernail manicuring room, a shoe polisher, a hairstylist, a seamstress. There was an area where a woman could change from traveling clothes to evening clothes, and women in blue uniforms bustled about to help them. One approached Mary, reached for her bag, but Mary clutched it closer, and the woman went away.

She could have stayed in that warm and gleaming room for a month, but they wouldn't have let her, and so what was the point of staying for even an hour if she knew she'd have to leave again, eventually, and had nowhere to go. She studied a painting on the wall—a river, a field of flowers—and remembered her promise to John Cane that she'd look him up, go walking with him one day. She could go to him, she knew. She could meet the ferry and when he got off she could approach him, tell him what had happened, ask if she could stay with him for a while, and he would let her. She'd have to listen to him, and he might pretend at first that he wouldn't let her, but he would, in the end. She knew he would. Or he might know of someone who needed a boarder. There was a brother, too, she remembered, something wrong with him, but nothing she couldn't handle, she was sure, just until she got on her feet. She would be kind to him.

But when she left the ladies' parlor and made for the uptown IRT, she paused only for a second at the top of the steps before she walked on, walked east, back to the boardinghouse where she'd stayed before finding her cot at Mrs. Post's. If the woman remembered her she made no sign, and as she was led up the back stairs she knew before they stopped at a door that it would be the same room she'd slept in back in 1910. "Breakfast at seven," the woman said, and when Mary shut the door and dropped the latch, she collapsed onto the narrow bed and slept.

Breakfast was two rows of glum faces spooning porridge into their mouths, chewing, swallowing. Mary pushed away her plate. When she stepped out into the sun a dozen pigeons clucked and flew off as one. Along with the loose gray-black spots they left on the sidewalk were feathers, old milk cartons, a box of cracker meal broken open and left now to be blown around in the breeze.

With her bag slung over her shoulder, she walked for an hour. West, mostly, but also south. She stopped to stuff paper into the heel of her shoe. Her shoulder ached. At ten she stopped at a park, took off her shoes, and walked on the grass behind the benches while she ate a pear. When there was not a single bit of flesh left on the fruit, she picked up her bag and continued south, until she came to City Hall, and across from City Hall, the almost-complete skyscraper where Jimmy Tiernan spent his days hanging dozens of stories above the sidewalk, guiding terra cotta panels into place. The pyramid at the top made the whole thing feel like a cathedral, Mary thought, as she tipped her head back and gazed up.

"Jimmy," she called out when she saw him coming almost two hours later, one set of hunched shoulders among so many. There was a ring of yellow sweat at his throat.

"Mary," he said, and stepped away from the pack. His lunch pail was small in his large hand.

"Can I talk to you a second?"

"What's happened?" he said, crossing his arms over his chest. "Did Patricia send you?"

"No," Mary said, and hesitated. The other men were watching them. They were lined up now against a wall, some squatting, some standing, some sitting, spread legged. They pulled sandwiches and thermoses from the depths of their pockets and ate. She turned her back to them, so she could see only Jimmy.

"I wondered, um, if you ever found out where Alfred went."

"What do you mean?"

"Don't you remember looking for him last year? When there was a job here for him?"

"Sure. But did he disappear again?"

Mary blinked up at him. "What do you mean? Did you find him after that?"

"You mean you didn't know?"

"Know what? I haven't seen him."

Jimmy took her by the elbow and led her over to the steps of City Hall.

"There was an accident, Mary. A fire. A lamp exploded in his hands and he got badly burned. He was in Willard Parker for months, and then at a hospital for burned people up in Harlem."

Mary shook her head. "What are you talking about?"

"I found out only because I got so curious I went over to the stable one afternoon to see if they'd seen him. They said it happened right there, at the stable, just before Christmas in 1910."

"Jesus Christ."

"Then when he got out of the burn place he came down here looking for me, looking for work, I guess, but there wasn't nothing to give him. So I says to him, 'Briehof, what you should do is head west to one of the middle states. Good work there. Make yourself a little house.' And I swear to God, Mary, I think he did it. I think he just went and did it, just like that. Crazy as a loon, that guy. You didn't seem to want to talk about him so I told Patricia to tell you. I know you two don't get on so well but I figured she'd told

309

you or told Fran to tell you and you ladies had talked about it and decided what to think about it. And then I figured he'd write to you. He asked about you, you know."

"No. No, Patricia didn't tell me."

Jimmy picked up his sandwich, and offered half to Mary. She took it gratefully.

"Where's the hospital?"

"West 127th, I think. Maybe 128th. Between Broadway and Amsterdam."

"Maybe they know where he went. Maybe they have an address."

"I doubt it, Mary. When he came to see me it was November. Six months ago. And then if he headed west . . ."

How could he have traveled so far away without telling her? How could he have been so badly hurt without her knowing? They sat in silence, looking up at the top of the skyscraper. "Fifty-five stories," Jimmy said. "You believe that?"

Mary could just make out the shape of a man on one of the beams near the top.

"But he was all right? Recovered? How bad was he burned?"

"Pretty bad. But he was better when I saw him."

"Why didn't Patricia tell me? You should have double-checked, Jimmy. You should have known Patricia wouldn't tell me. I have a good mind to go up there and tell her what I think of her."

Jimmy sighed. "Don't take it up the wrong way, Mary, please. We have enough trouble."

The burn hospital was newer than the buildings surrounding it, the stonework not yet blackened. She expected something like Willard

Parker, or like Riverside, but it was a modest building, four stories, no sign of its purpose except for a small placard over the door with simple letters: St. John the Apostle Burn Recovery Hospital of Morningside Heights. There were trees lining the street and a group of young girls clustered around a toy pram. Mary rang the bell, and the door was answered by a nun dressed entirely in white. The nun ushered her into the small, marble-floored reception area. The halls were silent, and Mary glanced quickly up the stairs, at a large, stained-glass window on the landing between the first and second floors. Aside from Central Park, where it was possible to hear birds and crickets in summer, and aside from North Brother, it was the quietest place Mary had ever visited in Manhattan.

"I'm looking for a patient named Alfred Briehof," Mary said to the nun in a whisper. The sound of a bed being rolled on casters echoed from an upper floor. "I know he's been released, but I wondered if you had an address for him."

"Briehof," the nun said. "Excuse me."

Bending her head so that Mary could not see the expression below her habit, the nun turned to a desk and pulled open a lower drawer. She ran her fingers across the names at the top of the files. Forward and back her fingers crawled. She closed the drawer and opened another, ran her fingers again.

"Briehof," she announced, pulling a file out of the drawer. "Released," she said once she'd looked it over. "Let's see here. Yes, back in November. Pardon me. What is your relationship?" She glanced at Mary's bag, which she'd placed on a bench in the waiting area.

Mary cleared her throat. "I'm his sister. Just found out about the accident. I'm visiting New York and this is the last place I have for him."

"I see," the nun turned back to the file and Mary prayed that it didn't note anywhere that he was German. She considered what she'd say if the nun asked Mary to explain how brother and sister could have different accents.

"He signed himself out."

"Is there a new address?"

"No. I'm sorry."

Mary sighed. "Was he very bad?" The nun tipped the file so that it would flap open again.

"Hard to say," she said after a moment of reading. "He was here for several months. That's a long time. On the other hand, he's alive. He left."

"Yes," Mary whispered. It was true. "Does it say anything about him going out west? To find work?"

The nurse shook her head. "No, but if he left the area that would explain why he missed his follow-up appointments. Patients with his injuries usually come in to get new prescriptions once a month." Mary thought of all the states he'd ever mentioned wanting to see. How would she find him now?

A piece of paper slid out of the file and onto the floor.

"Wait," the nun said. She read the sheet that had fallen. "I see. He stopped in just a few weeks ago with a few complaints. You were right. He'd been in Minnesota for a few months, but he returned just a few weeks ago and the doctor gave him new prescriptions. It references that he lives on 125th Street, but it doesn't say East or West or any building number."

The nun turned the paper over to check the back. "I suppose you could try the doctor's office. Explain that you're his sister." The nun took a pencil from her pocket and scribbled the doctor's address on a corner of the paper and then tore the corner off.

"Thank you."

"I assume you already tried his next of kin?"

"Who?"

"His wife. I imagine she knows where he is. Though seeing her address now I wonder why he isn't living with her. Perhaps their situation changed due to his injury."

"His wife?" Mary tried to control her expression. "It's been several years since I've seen my brother."

"Well, he listed a wife when he was admitted," the nun glanced down. "A Mary Mallon of East Thirty-Third Street."

TWENTY-TWO

When Alfred woke, he was on his back, a pillow tucked under his head, another under his arm. A small, square window. A distant ceiling. A closed door. He shifted his leg and gasped at the pain it brought. Part of his body was covered with gauze. There was a lamp on the table beside his bed and he tried to turn toward it. He lifted his right arm and felt a brilliant heat light up inside his body and blossom forward, pushing out from his muscle and bone.

When he opened his eyes again there was a nurse looking at him from behind a clipboard. He opened and closed his eyes several times. Sometimes it was light in the room, sometimes dark. Sometimes a man was watching him, sometimes a woman, usually no one at all. In the background there were sounds: shoes scuffing a linoleum floor, people talking in low voices, the squeaking wheels of a rolling cart. But instead of interrupting the silence, the atmosphere of total stillness, of nothingness, that sensation of floating through an in-between place, the noises only emphasized

the void, drew attention to it, and after every small bump or rattle
the world seemed even quieter than before.

Several times a day, from somewhere so near his body he
knew he could reach out and touch it if he could make his body
work, was the delicate tink of glass, and the unmistakable flick of
a finger, once, twice, and then a pinprick, usually in the crook of
his elbow, sometimes in his forearm, occasionally the back of his
hand. After a moment—one, two, three—he felt a small quiver
at his center, pressure on his chest and head that lasted just long
enough for him to begin feeling panic, and then peace, as if someone had warmed a blanket by the stove and pulled it up over him,
tucked it in at his shoulders and turned out the light. It was a
feeling like being born, a baby tucking chin to chest and pushing
into that dark tunnel, or the lead weight used to plumb a depth,
and the prize was reaching that destination, finding the depth,
and sometimes he felt the sea rocking under his bed. He heard the
sound of the ocean. He heard his mother's voice, took in the smell
of the Alps, German grass under his feet, German air. Then, as if
he'd taken one giant leap across a continent and ocean, he was in
New York, a mountain of coal behind him, Mary on the other side
of a gate, Mary stirring a pot with her back to the room, Mary
unpinning her hair and shaking it loose. He spoke to his father.
He spoke to his brother. He laughed with Mary as they danced in
Coney Island, in Hoboken, in Manhattan. He whisked her across
the gleaming black-and-white floor of his hospital room. He was
seven years old and there were thin slices of pine strapped to his
feet. He was fifteen and strong, dodging a policeman on Mercer.
He was forty and tired, but summoning the strength to get up and
start again.

Eventually, there were things he knew, and so somebody must

have told him, though he couldn't think of who or when. Time stretched and stretched until it snapped: an hour felt like a week, and then a week felt like a day. He knew it was the new year, but then the nurse put a hand on Alfred's cheek and told him it was the Ides of March. March already. Almost spring. He was in a hospital. He'd been badly burned. There was some question about whether he'd use his right arm again: everything below the elbow had been destroyed almost to the muscle. His upper chest on that side was in better shape, but there was still a risk of infection. Had he spoken to them? They asked him questions sometimes, and waited for answers. How do you feel? What exactly happened? Don't you know how lucky you are?

They fed him. They washed his body. Catholic? He'd nodded, yes, he guessed he probably was, but had he ever been baptized? He'd been to Mass a few times, with Mary and her aunt Kate. A priest came to offer the Eucharist one Sunday and he opened his mouth to accept it. After, he had bad dreams about them finding out and putting him on the street, but he continued to accept it, Sunday after Sunday, and eventually he looked forward to the priest's visit, the knobby hand he always placed on Alfred's head before leaving. On Easter Sunday they brought him lamb with mint jelly and fed him in forkfuls small enough for a child. On the Fourth of July they told him to look toward his window, where he could see flashes of blue, pink, bright white sparklers rising up and landing somewhere nearby. He could hear birds, and then, after a few weeks, the birds disappeared. Spring and summer had come and left again.

They told him he was getting better. He had no infection. He'd be able to use his arm one day though it would not be pleasant to look at. His nerves had been badly burned and yes, that was bad news, but on the other hand it meant he wouldn't feel pain there anymore. He was being moved. It would be uncomfortable but they'd give him something for it.

The burn hospital was uptown, they'd told him. It was a charity hospital, run by nuns, all of whom had vowed to live in service to St. John the Apostle. They didn't expect anything in return. A donation, perhaps, whatever he could spare. It was in a quiet neighborhood. Quieter than this? He'd asked, and they laughed. "Something for the journey," the nurse had said, and he closed his eyes to listen for the tink, tink of the little glass vial.

There were trees outside his window at St. John's. Their shadows swayed on his wall when the wind blew. The nuns wanted him to walk more, to do laps around the hallway. They wanted him to practice lifting a teacup, gripping a fork, washing himself. He complained of itching all over his body. He vomited. He didn't like it there. He wanted to go back to Willard Parker. They gave him his medicine by tablet—two round white pills three times a day that he placed on his tongue and tipped back into his throat before the nun could pass him a cup of water. The pills helped, eventually, but not like the needle. The needle sent him floating from the very instant it punctured his skin. Syringes were expensive, a nurse explained, and they were a charity hospital. They had to use what they were given: morphine, opium, codeine, cocaine, heroin. Tablets, tinctures, salts for sniffing. It was all the same, all for managing pain. They wanted to be a bit careful about the morphine, they told him. In the past, they'd noticed several patients had difficulty weaning after they were healed. Several doctors suggested cocaine or heroin instead. They usually brought him a tincture of opium after supper, and he swallowed every bitter drop, but he couldn't sleep in so much silence. The groaning of the trees kept him up all night. It was too cold at St. John's, and when it wasn't too cold it was too warm. He was getting worse.

"You are not getting worse," a nun informed him in a subdued voice. "You have healed wonderfully. It's been more than ten months since the accident." He wanted to take her by the shoulders and shake her. Didn't they realize the extent of his injuries? Even when he finally slept it was not restful, and only when he began howling through the night, waking the other patients, did a harried doctor appear with a needle and syringe. After, he was serene. He slept. They added the nightly injection to his bedtime routine.

He spent afternoons trying to make his way around the corridors and he wondered at his old self, how he always seemed to be on his way somewhere, itching to get free of whatever room he was in. Now, even with so little to do, the days passed quickly and sweetly. He walked. He rested. He considered the shadows on the wall. He closed his eyes and listened. He returned to his room for his medicine and noted that he never had to even look at a clock. His body told him when it was time, and sure enough, usually within a minute of returning to his room, resting at the edge of his bed, someone would appear with a white cup, and he took anything they gave him as he anticipated the after-supper hour when the doctor would appear with the syringe.

In November, they told him he was ready, that he should start planning. Was there a job to get back to? Someone to contact? Crystal Springs had given him a settlement of one hundred dollars, which by some miracle the hospital hadn't taken from him. He left twenty-five dollars to the nuns. On the morning of his discharge they shaved him, cut his hair, gave him a suit of clothes, a hat, shoes, a small container of tablets for the pain. A doctor named Tropp who kept hours at the hospital, and had his own office nearby, would prescribe something else if the tablets didn't do the job. If he ran out of medicine and Dr. Tropp was unavailable, he should go to a pharmacy and ask for something. Any druggist would give him a tincture of opium or a small dose of heroin until the doctor could see him.

When he got outside to the street for the first time in eleven months, he walked immediately to Dr. Tropp's office. He told the doctor that the nuns had given him pills, but that at night he needed something stronger. Just as he'd hoped, Dr. Tropp asked if he was familiar with administering medicine by needle. "Of course," Alfred said. Once Alfred had paid, the doctor handed over a small bag containing a single glass syringe, two needles, several vials of liquid morphine, a prescription for more. Back on the sidewalk, Alfred placed the bag carefully in his jacket pocket. He climbed the long staircase to the El platform and protected his pocket as the train pulled in and the other riders pushed against him. His arm was ugly but worked just fine. He could grasp a fork, turn a knob. Sometimes it ached and felt tired. They had shown him exercises to make the muscle stronger, but he found the medicine was the best to help that feeling of lopsidedness, of tightness on one side and looseness on the other. The medicine was an equalizer and made his whole body the same, his thoughts peaceful and quiet and the days kind. His chest was taut, like the skin there had shrunk, but the medicine helped that, too. With the medicine he felt at ease, and he moved along the paper-strewn streets in an even rhythm, throwing one foot loosely in front of the other, feeling the momentum of his arms swinging by his side. Even his head felt perched perfectly at the top of his neck. At Thirty-Fourth Street he climbed the stairs to the street, walked south one block, and then across, all the way east, until he spotted the old building. He halted, brushed his pocket to make sure nothing had been damaged. He moved a little closer, and then sat down on a stoop.

Was she still at the same laundry? Still staying with Mila? It wasn't long before he saw her, walking up Third Avenue from the opposite direction, a young boy on either side of her. They were talking, competing for her attention, and she was serious with them though Alfred could see that whatever they were saying, she was happy. She was holding a box. She placed her hand on the head of the shorter boy, and he took the box from her. The two boys ran ahead and she shouted something after them. She touched her collar, the back of her hair. She looked young. Nowhere was that put-upon expression she used to wear, that hard look she got when she moved around him in their rooms, running a rag across the counter, closing her mind to the fact that he was there. If he washed a pan he should have scoured it. If he put away the sugar, she found some he'd spilled on the floor. He was useless. He was lazy. He was a drunk. He didn't love her. He didn't know the half of what she did for him.

"Alfred," she used to say, more softly than she ever spoke when he was sober. "You have to stop this."

She quickened her step, and Alfred walked out to the middle of the sidewalk. She was directly across the street now. If she turned her head, she'd see him there. Do it now, he told himself. Now. But he just watched her, and then she was gone, disappeared into the building and up the stairs.

Driscoll was dead, the Lower East Side was off-limits in case he would run into Liza, so Alfred paid the bartender to sleep on a cot in the back room of Nation's for a night. He had no desire to have a drink, and again wondered at his old self. The next morning, he went downtown to talk to Jimmy Tiernan. Jimmy knew someone who knew someone who'd gotten work in Minnesota, clearing land, and who said it was the best work he'd ever had in his life. Hard work, but good work. Clean air. No punch card. No boss breaking balls every minute. Jimmy wanted to go there himself, but Patricia would never agree to it. They could build a log house—three, four, five rooms, however many they wanted. They could clear land and sell the timber. They could keep livestock. Plant crops. But the farthest Patricia would go was Queens. He laughed. "But you," he said to Alfred, "what's stopping you? Go in the spring, when the weather isn't so bad."

It had been raining in New York for two weeks. Steady, gray, wet rain that made the city wilt. In Minnesota, in the winter, Jimmy said it gets too cold to rain. The air would freeze the damp hairs inside a man's nose, but at least the sky was blue and big.

A train left Grand Central Terminal for Chicago twice a week. From Chicago Alfred could switch to a train headed for Minneapolis. From Minneapolis he'd just have to find his way as the days took him. It was difficult imagining there were cities so far away, cities with their own riverfronts and barges and garbage and odors. It was sobering to think of traveling so far, at such speed, and still covering only half of America. New York was not like the rest of America, not even close. Anyone who read a paper knew that. In Minnesota every farm had good water, a creek slicing through, rich earth, plentiful grazing. The people ate only white bread and meat, every day. The trees grew up straight and grazed the sky. There were people who set up their homes and didn't see other families for all of winter, which in Minnesota lasted a full six months. In New York, there was no way to escape other people, acquaintances and strangers—they brushed by him every minute of every day, begging for coins, asking that balances be paid. They bumped him in the street without apologizing. They smelled of their kitchens, their cabbage and beets and smoked meats and spices brought all the way from the old country, sewn into the linings of cuffs and pockets. They grabbed the best of the fruit at the market and grazed his toes with their automobiles or their wagon wheels as he crossed the street. Minnesota wasn't the only option. There were other places: Wisconsin. Wyoming. New Mexico and Arizona were said to be hot year-round, and if a man went walking in the desert he'd be tanned like leather inside an hour. There were Indians in the middle country. New York had places with Indian names but no Indians anymore. They'd all gone west.

He told Jimmy it was a good idea. He didn't need to think about it. He'd go. He'd build a house there, way out in the country, and send for Mary. One way or another, he'd convince her to give him another chance, to join him out west where they could truly start over again. He hated thinking about the last time they'd spoken, that morning in the vestibule of the old building, the sight he must have been after so many days drinking, sleeping here and there. And the look on her face that told him how serious she was, how desperate she was to make him go away. When he spoke to her next he'd have something to show for himself. A plan. She'd see how sorry he was.

"Now?" Jimmy had asked. "Wait until Christmas. Wait until the New Year."

"Now," Alfred said.

He bought an honest ticket to Chicago, and an honest

meal aboard the train, but for the switch between Chicago and Minneapolis he slipped onto the train and into the tiny lav until the train started moving. When he finally opened the door an attendant saw him and was about to shout when Alfred held up his hand and then with the other hand reached deep into his pocket. A dollar would shut him up, and was still less than the price of a ticket. Feeling tired, and beginning to worry that it was a terrible idea to venture so far from New York, Alfred stepped back into the lav and with one foot bracing the door, and the other on the ledge of the commode, he removed a needle from his jacket pocket, wiped it on his shirt, attached it to the delicate syringe, and pushed it into one of the small vials of morphine. He drew the plunger back as the train leaned into a turn. For the rest of the journey the young man ignored him as Alfred slept across two seats at the rear of the car, and when he wasn't sleeping he stared out the window at the trees, which grew taller and stronger the closer he got to Minnesota. He pictured the trees in New York, imagined them gasping for air, fighting for space.

Once in Minneapolis he found the riverfront and got a job loading sacks of flour as big as a man for the Gold Medal Factory. The boardinghouse he found was cleaner than any he'd seen in New York, the people less threatening. They all looked at Alfred with some curiosity and after a few days he realized he was the one they thought of when they locked their doors. The worst of his arm was visible only during the inside hours, when the men worked so hard they started steaming, and Alfred rolled up the cuffs of his shirt. The nuns had given him a bad haircut and he hadn't shaved since Harlem. He needed to clean his clothes. He needed to find a doctor and a druggist. Seeing the bruises on his arm, and on the other arm, the deformed skin, a man on his shift suggested a place on Hennepin Avenue that would help him. A smoking lounge, the man called it, and Alfred went there expecting it to be run by a Chinese, but like everything else in Minneapolis it was run by a white—a lean man, once blond, with a beard and a caftan tied around the middle with a rope. The man had come to Minneapolis from San Francisco and greeted Alfred as though he might be a long-lost brother from the opposite coast. "They're different here," the man informed Alfred. He instructed him on how to hold the pipe, and waved a hand toward the chairs scattered around the eerie silence of the room. Alfred didn't respond, so the man returned to the front room, and no one spoke to Alfred.

He chose a rocking chair by the window, which faced the Mississippi and a little island in the middle of the river. He thought of Mary and her hut. When he closed his eyes he saw her pacing, looking out across the water toward him. He wondered if she'd gone looking for him since the accident. He assumed Jimmy Tiernan had told her what happened, and he knew he should send her a letter. He hadn't had a drink since Christmas 1910. He would tell her that. Or maybe it would be better to wait until he'd been north, seen what it had to offer, seen what kind of life they could make there.

After two weeks he began asking for work up north, clearing land. The men he spoke with told tales of snow that reached the tops of trees, air so cold it would freeze a man's pecker in under three seconds if he went out to take a leak. The fish froze in the rivers. Birds that didn't go south dropped from the trees like stones and woke up again in the spring melt to fly away. He'd have to drag his food out there and back. He'd have to pack enough for four months, at least, maybe five. He'd have to be strict about what he ate so he wouldn't run out. "Cover up that arm when you go looking for work," a man advised him. "No one will want to see that coming."

"It's ugly but it's fine," Alfred said, looking at the skin of his right arm. It reminded him of candle wax, melted, lopsided, dips and ridges where the wax ran free. He couldn't feel anything on the surface of that arm, and so sometimes he had to look down at it to see if his shirt sleeve was rolled up or down. Sometimes he dug his fingernails in, hard, but all he felt was pressure on the bone.

"No, I mean that," the man said, taking hold of Alfred's good arm and holding it to the light. "What are you going to do about that?"

Alfred pulled his arm away and, quick as a gasp, had the other man's arm twisted behind his back. "Don't touch me," he growled. The man didn't speak to him again.

Hauling flour was exhausting work, and at night, he slept from the moment his head touched the pillow to the moment the sun reached his face. He heard of a clinic alongside Lake Harriet where the doctors understood about pain management, and gave out prescriptions for those who could pay for it. Alfred showed his injuries to a Dr. Karlson and explained his plan to go to the North Country after Christmas and work up there until spring. Dr. Karlson wrote a prescription for a winter's worth of tablets and four large bottles of tincture, plus additional morphine, two more needles, another syringe. Alfred paid for all of it, and noted that he was going north just in time. The drugs were cheap—a vial of morphine was cheaper than a bottle of whiskey—but still, his stack of money was growing lighter every day. The doctor told Alfred to try to limit his intake or he might have stomach trouble, difficulty getting going in the morning, problems sustaining energy throughout the day. Stay out of the dens, he warned Alfred. The smoking opium was mostly smuggled, and who knew what went into it. Stick to the prescription stuff, the stuff that had been checked out by the Board of Health. He took the tincture in the mornings and felt it travel his body as he ate his breakfast. The pills he kept in his pocket. The needles he saved for night. The itch that always began a few minutes after waking subsided by the time he began his walk to the riverfront, and everything seemed at arm's-length, as if he were looking at someone else's life. Before, in New York, he was so much a part of his own life that it nearly drowned him, but now, it was as if he floated alongside himself, and when something wasn't quite right, he could simply lean over and make an adjustment.

At the boardinghouse, Christmas was acknowledged with bread pudding, a round of carols, and mulled wine. A French Canadian named Luc, part Indian, sold him an overcoat from the Hudson Bay Company. From a consignment store he bought heavy blanket trousers and a shoe pack, and the patient clerk showed him how to ease them on over two pairs of socks. If he did it right, the man swore, his feet would stay warm and dry. He bought two pairs of thick wool socks, two shirts, two vests, a fur cap.

In mid-January, Luc told him about a pair of brothers who'd purchased several acres on the cheap, and needed a pair of good axmen. "Are you handy with an ax?"

"Sure," Alfred said.

"I'll bet you are," Luc said, but told him to meet him in a few days. When the day came, Alfred showed up wearing all the clothes he owned to find Luc had organized everything they would need onto two toboggans. When Alfred tugged his he guessed it weighed three hundred pounds. They had cornmeal, flour, lard, butter, a variety of smoked fish, ham, rice, molasses, axes, matches, picks, spades, hoes, sugar, guns, powder, and shot. Alfred had a season's worth of medicine buttoned into his interior pockets, and could hear the faint rattle of the tablets as he moved. Luc had arranged for a wagon to carry them to the crossroads nearest to the brothers' camp, and then they went the last twelve miles on foot, their toboggans sliding so easily along the crust of ice on the top layer of snow that they left no tracks.

They came upon the brothers after four hours of walking. Gustaf and Eric had made their camp on the edge of a pine grove, against a fallen tree trunk almost six feet thick. When they saw Luc and Alfred they stopped their work and walked over to pull the toboggans the rest of the way. The camp was as clever as Luc had described—poles cut neatly and laid sloping from the snow to the top of the tree trunk, topped with layers of spruce boughs and covered over by a rubber blanket. The brothers had banked the snow on the back and sides of this little structure, and built a fire in front. Each man had two blankets, and there was a pot slung over the fire.

It was a clean place, as sterile as white cotton, and Alfred felt his lungs growing stronger, his body becoming cleaner. Luc showed him how to wield the ax, how to bend the saw, and he got faster at it every day. Gustaf and Eric saw his burns and didn't question him when he administered his medicine at night, nor in the morning when he washed the pills down with black coffee. His body worked like a machine and there was peace in the sweating, the breathing, the aching at night that was so completely different from the ache of his hips after lying in a hospital bed for almost a year. He ate more in one sitting than he used to eat in New York over an entire day. The older of the brothers commented that Alfred was getting stronger, and Alfred knew it was true. He held one side of the saw and Luc or one of the Swedes held the other, and where it used to take fifty passes to cut through a trunk, now it took a dozen, sometimes less. Back and forth, back and forth, the teeth of the saw bit deeper into the pale interior of the trunk and he'd feel his heart throbbing when the Swede pulled for the last time, held up his hand to watch the tree fall. They dragged the timber to the river where, in the spring, they'd trade it for meat and fresh fruit.

The sun went down early, before four o'clock, but the moon was so big and the stars so bright that Alfred realized nighttime meant something else that far north. There was no wind, nothing to stir the trees, and everything was so still and silent inside the warm cocoon of his woolen knits and oilcloth that he forgot the temperature. Minnesota was something to experience, and Alfred thought of Mary, how she'd have liked to see the sky so clear. The tent was as warm as any house, and Alfred wondered at his old self, always searching the corners of his pockets for a coin to put in the gas meter, how every person in New York was a slave to what he earned. Out in the cold wilderness, he'd have no need of money until the spring. He wanted to tell Mary about it. He wanted her to see.

Then one morning after Luc headed off to the crossroads on an errand to trade timber for a stump extractor, and as the brothers were halfway through a trunk as thick as a man laid on his side, they could see that the tree was leaning in the wrong direction and beginning to tip. They shouted to each other in their own language and quickly, foolishly, Gustaf, the older brother,

threw his hands up and put his shoulder to the bark as it began
to fall. From across the cleared space, a distance of seventy-five
yards or so, Alfred watched in dumb silence. He saw Gustaf make
a sudden move, and then the tree was down, and Eric was shouting. Alfred stared for a second longer and then realized Eric was
shouting at him.

Gustaf was unconscious when they carried him into their
shelter, and when they opened his shirt they could see right away
that his shoulder was dislocated. "He's alive, thank God," Eric
said, and Alfred nodded. It was true, but what did that matter
now, when they were in the middle of nowhere with an injured
man. Luc was not due back for several days and neither Alfred
nor Eric had any idea what to do.

"Should we try to get it back into place?" Eric asked.

"I don't know," Alfred said.

Eric took hold of his older brother's arm, and after dipping
his head for a moment and drawing his breath, he placed a knee
on his older brother's chest to keep him still, and tried to shove
the arm back into the socket. He tried again, roaring as he did
so. Now Gustaf was awake and also roaring. Eric tried again.
Again. He tore off his brother's shirt to get a better grip. He gave
his brother a spoon to clamp between his teeth. As Alfred held
Gustaf's legs, it occurred to him that they'd want his medicine.
He'd told them it was for pain, and Gustaf's pain was clearly
worse than his own. He'd have to give it. If he didn't give it they'd
take it from him. They were peaceful men but they were brothers
and they'd sooner kill him than have one of themselves harmed.
He calculated how much was left from the clinic that overlooked
Lake Harriet. He'd been disciplined about his dosage, treating
himself to extra only a handful of times, and then only when the

air was so cold and the skin over his wounds grew so tight that he was afraid it would crack open again.

He offered before they could ask, and they took it gratefully. Days went by. A week. Luc had not yet returned, and Eric wondered out loud if he should go to the crossroads himself, or send Alfred. Alfred understood the dilemma: with just three of them at camp, and Gustaf too injured to move, the one left behind would have to put caring for Gustaf above all things, and only Eric would do that. On the other hand, electing Alfred to go to the crossroads meant trusting a virtual stranger to do what he'd been asked to do, to find help, send it back to the woods to the brothers. The brothers didn't trust him, Alfred saw now. Eric took and took Alfred's medicine for his brother, and when Alfred suggested that he'd given enough, that he had to save some for himself, Eric looked at him so coldly that Alfred knew his first instinct had been correct. Better to keep giving than be killed. His dreams grew terrifying and he found he couldn't sleep at all. His body hurt. He became nauseated. There were no odors in the North Country except pine and cold. The inside of his nose felt raw and he imagined a frozen path from his nostrils to his lungs.

He woke up one night to Eric shaking him awake. "What's wrong with you?" he asked and Alfred realized he'd been shouting, thrashing. There was no sympathy in the question, only accusation. It wasn't Alfred's fault that Gustaf had miscalculated the tree. The Swedes talked all day long and sang songs, and where before their red faces had seemed so merry now they seemed to Alfred to be part of their selfishness. They were monsters, the two of them. Who but a monster would choose to live so far from civilization, would dig a hole in the snow and call it a place to live? There were strange animals in the North Country, tracks he didn't recognize, and he knew they were all gathered somewhere deep in the shadows of the pines, waiting to see what he would do.

He would always be the odd man out, even if he handed over every single drop, every pill. Gustaf didn't seem to be getting worse, but he wasn't getting better, either, and now when Eric gave him more of Alfred's medicine, Alfred felt his blood rise. He doesn't need it, he said, and Eric looked at Alfred like he'd stepped out naked from behind a curtain. Alfred took bigger and bigger doses at night, and again in the morning so that he could get his share before the Swedes took everything. No more trees were cut. Where before the days had been full of the sounds of work—cutting, cracking, splintering, chopping—now the days were as still and silent as night except for the occasional sound of the skillet on the fire, the pop and crackle of bacon meeting the hot pan, Eric's boots crunching the top layer of snow outside their tent flap, and finally, ten days after the accident, the sound of cracking on the river, like a volley of gunshots every few minutes, a racket unlike any Alfred had heard in his life.

"You have to go to the crossroads," Eric told him one morning, two weeks after the accident. "Luc should have been back days ago. Send him back and bring help as well." He put his hand on his brother's head. "I think there's something broken inside. Not just the shoulder. A few bones maybe. I don't know."

"I'm not sure I remember the way. Did we pass one other clearing or two? Can I take the compass?"

Eric looked at him with disgust. "You are not an axman," he said bitterly as he shoved the compass to Alfred's chest. "Leave that medicine for my brother's pain." He put his hand on the barrel of one of the shotguns that was lying on its side by Gustaf's head. They kept it loaded in case of passing deer.

Alfred fished out one bottle of pills and gave it over easily, knowing he'd be back in the city soon.

"And the rest," Eric said, using the shotgun to tap Alfred's other pocket. Alfred closed his fingers around his last vial of morphine and the second bottle of bills. "I need it to get back. I can't walk all that way and pull my things without it. I need it for rest. I don't—"

Before Alfred could catch his breath he was on his back, and the Swede's knee on his neck. He reached down with his good arm, found the bottle and vial, and pushed both into Eric's face.

When he got to the crossroads he found Luc sitting between two men in the only public house for fifteen miles. All three glanced at Alfred as if they'd been expecting him. Alfred told Luc about the accident, told him about Gustaf's injuries, but Luc nodded off while he was speaking. So Alfred returned to the crossroads to look for something to carry him back to the city.

It was April, and spring had already arrived in Minneapolis. The stink of his body was strong now that he was back where women wore tailored spring coats and the men were neatly shaved. The smoking lounge was shut down. At the boardinghouse he asked about work so he could pay his way back to Chicago and then to New York, but no one knew of anything. He went to the clinic on Lake Harriet and bought more medicine with the last of his money. It was a mistake, this place, all its foreign cleanliness. The shops closed early. The food was bland. All anyone talked about was his next meal, the weather, going hunting on the weekend. He had to get home as soon as possible. Thank God he hadn't talked Mary into coming to this place.

He walked down to the stockyards, and then over to the train station, where several cargo cars were being coupled on the main track. When the railway man went inside the station house, Alfred walked along the track, peering into the dark cars. In one he sniffed corn. In another, buckwheat. In a third car he looked left and right and then noticed from within the darkness a pair of eyes. He felt a chill, and stepped back. "Get away," a disembodied voice growled. "Or get out of sight." Alfred climbed up and quickly moved to a shadowed corner. "Where is it going?" he whispered. "East?" As his eyes adjusted, he saw that the man was really a boy, fifteen or sixteen at most. Another voice said, "Boston."

"Hold on, buddy," the second voice said. "Are you sick?"

"No."

"If you're sick, we're not getting help. You understand? We'll bury you in this shit and leave you here."

"I'm not sick."

"You look kinda sick."

"If you get us caught, I'll kill you dead," the first voice assured him as Alfred leaned into his bed of yellow peas. After a while, he heard the lock thrown in place on the other side of the door and the train began to rock toward the Atlantic.

HIS BANNER OVER ME IS LOVE

TWENTY-THREE

As she walked from St. John the Apostle to Dr. Tropp's office, Mary clutched the torn-off corner of paper the nun had given her and prayed that Alfred had given the doctor his current address. She hadn't seen him in seventeen months. Who had visited him in all that time he spent in the hospital? Who had made sure the doctors were doing their best? Not Liza, she thought with relief. But not Mary, either. He'd been alone in this horror while she'd been oblivious, making pastry downtown.

She had never before walked the neighborhood above Columbia University, and noticed that all the hectic life and energy of Morningside Heights was muffled and then silenced in the space of half a dozen blocks. Around the university were brownstones as beautiful as those on Park Avenue, and residential buildings with elevators inside. The sidewalks were neat, the lawns trim. Clusters of rosebushes punctuated the green spaces of campus like so many bright and shining jewels. But just above that, outside Dr. Tropp's office on 129th Street, the sidewalks were silent, the trash bins unattended for weeks. The few automobiles scattered about the neighborhood were parked in every direction, some facing west, some east, some with their wheels up on the curb. There was a pigpen by the river, and the odor hung over the surrounding blocks.

No one answered her knock when she arrived at the doctor's office, so she let herself in and caught him dozing at his desk. "Excuse me, sir," she said, and when she was sure he was awake and paying attention, she told him that she was Alfred Briehof's wife, just returned from abroad, and needed Alfred's address. She looked around. There was no secretary. No patients. After hearing her business, the doctor's expression became one of doubt, but he turned and searched his desk for a file. "Briehof," he muttered as he moved papers back and forth. "I saw him only once since he came back from Minnesota. I can't remember if he gave me an address." Finally, he singled out a file from the mess and opened it. "Ah, yes," he said, and Mary's heart beat faster. "It's 545 West 125th Street."

Mary tried to check her anticipation, and reminded herself that she had not been kind to him the last time he tried to talk to her. Maybe he would turn her away now, just as she'd turned him away seventeen months earlier. Maybe the months he'd spent out west—doing what, Mary wanted to know—had taught him that the empty spaces in his life could easily be filled, and maybe he had no interest in Mary anymore. The satchel she'd been lugging around the city since leaving the boardinghouse felt much heavier than it had that morning. She thought of Mila and the boys, and wondered if Soper had gone looking for her there. She hoped Mila could convince him that she'd really left, and then Soper would leave them alone.

When she got to the building it seemed a little like a hotel, but one where the bellhop and the doorman had abandoned their posts years ago and left the lobby to be pulled down by cobwebs on the rafters, buried by mud tracked in from the street. She scanned the list of names beside the buzzers and there it was, halfway down. She pressed the button, and just as she began to worry that it didn't work, she heard the sound of a man's boots coming down the stairs. It didn't sound like the step of a sick man, an incapacitated man, a man hobbled with injury and pain. She knew he'd spotted her through the glass of the door when the boots stopped. He pushed open the door and stepped outside.

"Mary," he said, shoving his hands deep inside his pockets and leaning back on his heels. She noted the skin of his right hand, all the way up his arm to the place where his shirt was rolled to the elbow. His shirttail was hanging out over his pants, and he wore no socks in his shoes. There were dark rings under his eyes and his hair had more gray threaded through it than she remembered. But otherwise, he was himself, and within five seconds of seeing him again she knew that there was no Liza upstairs, no woman by any other name. She sniffed the air around him, out of habit, but smelled only aftershave, soap. His hair was damp, and he hadn't yet combed it. She tilted her head and looked closer. He had none of that wolfish quality he had when he was drinking, always moving and itching to get out, always fiddling with something in his hands. Nor did he have that look he had back in 1909, when she'd seen him at the hearing. He was not full in the face, nor was he gaunt. He was not jumpy, and yet he gave off a gentle hint of impatience. She couldn't quite read him.

"Can I come in?" she asked and watched his face as he noted her bag, the weight of it.

"Sure," he said, as if he'd seen her the week before. He walked ahead of her down the long hall, but waited by the bottom of the stairs for her to go up ahead of him. "Second floor," he said. He was quiet as he followed her up the stairs, his injured hand clutching the handrail. He moved slowly, carefully. When they got to the landing he nodded toward a door to her left and she pushed it open.

"I heard about your accident," she said once they were both inside. She held out her hand so that he would show his injured arm. The skin there was raw, melted and cooled, and she wanted to run her palm over the surface, learn the new topography. There was no hair on that arm, and his hand appeared swollen, lumpy, as if it needed to be drained. She pressed the swollen part with her fingertip.

"It's fine now," he said. "I was lucky."

"I just found out," she said, as if this would explain why she hadn't sought him out earlier. "Then Jimmy said you might have gone out west."

"Ah," he said, as if it didn't matter to him. "I was planning on sending you a letter, but then . . ." He trailed off, distracted by something she couldn't see or hear. He turned to the counter, began to open and close cabinet doors. His room was not neat, she noted, but it was not dirty. His bed was unmade but the sheets appeared clean. The counter was cluttered with mugs and bowls and spoons, but all seemed washed, left there to dry. Dirty laundry was piled in a corner instead of scattered everywhere underfoot. Once she understood that he was well enough to live in the world outside the hospital, she expected a scene, she expected to have to make her case to him right away, to roll up her sleeves and peel the years back and back and back until they were exhausted, and there was nothing further to say except what was new and now, and how they'd cope with tomorrow. She expected to have to draw a boundary and show it to him. She'd prepared herself for blame and had lined up a list of grievances she'd level at him if he implied for a second that their split was her fault. Instead, he seemed to barely register her presence.

"Coffee?" he asked without looking at her. He turned over the mug on the counter and found another from within a cupboard that held only a few mismatched plates.

"You all right, Alfred?" she asked. Maybe an accident like the one he'd had changes a person. Maybe she'd been too cruel, leaving him in the vestibule that time. Maybe he'd waited for her and waited for her, and when she didn't come back, and didn't search for him, he'd had to shake himself loose of her for good. Maybe he'd made his own vows to himself, and her showing up now had knocked him off balance. She cast her eye quickly around the kitchen and noted a single bottle of Powers Gold on the top shelf of the cabinet, two-thirds full. She noted an empty bottle of Baby Powers next to the sink. Maybe this was a new kind of discipline. She smelled the air again, and again came up with nothing. Maybe, like a doctor, he'd learned his dosage, finally, and had become strict in measuring it out.

He saw where she was looking and picked up the small bottle, dropped it in the trash can.

"I didn't say anything," Mary said. He leaned against the counter. Folded his arms.

"What is it, Mary? Has something happened?"

"I'm hungry, Alfred. Will we eat? Will I make you something?"

"I'll make it."

Slowly, and watching him carefully all the while, she explained everything to him over a supper of fried eggs and toast, cooked by

341

him and served to her on a dish so clean she wondered if Jimmy had warned him, somehow, that she was headed uptown to find him. He smirked for the first time when she pointed out that baking and cooking were two entirely different occupations, and looked at her over his shoulder as if to ask if she believed that, or if she hoped he would believe it, before turning back to the stove to flip the eggs, first one, then the other, and she paused her story to lift her chin and peer into the pan to see if he'd broken the yolks. When she saw the eggs had remained intact, she continued, telling him about the bakery, about Evelyn and Jacob, about throwing the plate of lemon squares when she saw Soper's face. She lifted her chin again and told him the eggs were ready, so he slid them onto two plates, put the toast alongside, and when she pushed into the soft center with the hard corner of bread it ran in a beautiful, pure, yellow river across her plate, exactly as it should. She told him about the Triangle fire, about how strange it was that she could remember every single detail of that day better than even the first day she left North Brother for the hearing, better than the day they set her free. She could remember what she was wearing down to the undergarment, the man with the ink-stained shirt, the shirt itself, pale pinstriped blue. She remembered the Lithuanians looking up at the rumbling ceiling with fear on their faces, and then the pandemonium outside, followed by the eerie calm of the days after.

"And you?" Mary asked. "The nun said you were released in November."

"I was," he said, running the tip of his finger across the plate and bringing it to his mouth. "I went to Minnesota for a while, but—"

"But?" Here it was. He appeared healthy, strong, sure-footed, and of steady hands, but here it was. Drinking on the job. Chronic lateness. What would it be?

"It wasn't for me."

He pushed back his plate. He got up to make more coffee. "What about you? Do you mean to stay here?" She felt him looking at her bag. She'd known him since she was seventeen. A lifetime ago, and still, she was nervous.

"Yes," Mary said. She turned in her seat to look at him. He was still for a moment, then he grabbed hold of the back of the chair where she was sitting.

"Good," he said. "That's very good."

That night, as she went to the small bedroom to change into her nightgown, he came in and sat on the edge of the bed. She'd gotten heavier since he'd seen her last. He'd gotten thinner. Her arms were soft. Her belly was soft. She'd never have children now, and that was a thing that took getting used to. Women said it so easily. When I get married. When I have a child. And then to find herself a forty-three-year-old woman who would not have a child, to know that that future had arrived already, was already part of her past.

When she had her clothes folded and stacked on top of the dresser, her cream and hairbrush placed alongside, he told her he was going out for milk and bread, and she felt for the first time that day that she'd made a mistake. He was on the wagon from the looks of it, but now here he was, not even a whole day with her and he was making excuses to go out. She had a vision of herself meeting the neighbors when he came home at two in the morning, howling. So she said nothing, only lay down on her side of the bed and closed her eyes. She was startled into sitting when, not fifteen minutes later, the locks slid in the door and he was back.

"You scared me," she said when he appeared at the bedroom door. He sat in the desk chair and brought to Mary's mind the image of a priest listening to confession, all those years ago, all the way across the Atlantic.

"How are we going to do this, Mary?"

"I don't know," she said.

He reached into the desk drawer and brought out a bottle of oil. He twisted off the cap, shook some into his palm, and rubbed it up and down his bad arm, briskly, like he was trying to rub that thick skin into what it used to be. When he returned the oil to the drawer, Mary noticed other small vials, a syringe, pills scattered like seed on a lawn. She got out of bed to look closer.

Alfred took out everything to show her. "For the pain."

"It still hurts?" Mary was surprised. The arm looked damaged, but closed over, like it had healed itself completely and had shut itself off from pain.

"Sometimes. They say I need it for maintenance."

"Is that unusual? So long after?" Mary noticed that his good arm was covered in gooseflesh.

Alfred shrugged. "The doctor keeps giving me the prescription." He put the vial back in the drawer and closed it. "Sometimes it's hard to sleep, so it's for that, too. It's been hard to sleep since getting back to New York." Mary knelt down beside him and took a closer look. It was like a tree trunk, thick with bark and impenetrable. Next to it, the pale white of his good arm looked vulnerable, like it would be easily broken, quick to burn.

"Is it just your arm?" she asked, and quietly, his movements sure, he opened his shirt, pulled open the right side where the fire had taken a swipe at his chest, from his collarbone to the bottom of his rib cage. It wasn't quite as bad as his arm, but it was there. She put her palm to it and felt his heart beating underneath.

"I started letters to you but I didn't know what to say. I was trying to think of the perfect thing so that you'd agree to see me again. And then you showed up. You just showed up."

Before he kissed her, he gripped her at the upper arms and put his forehead to hers. She closed her eyes, and the rough stubble of his chin and cheeks brushed up against the smooth skin of her neck as he breathed there for a moment, rested his head on her shoulder. She was tired, all of a sudden, and looking back over the twenty-six years since they met it seemed as if they never stopped, only worked and fought and went up and down stairs and opened and closed windows and counted their money at the table and fought again, and went out again, and once in a while they looked at each other, and talked, and laughed, and made love without rushing up to get somewhere after. Outside, a child shrieked, a woman shouted at him to hush. Alfred's room had grown dark, and what had seemed stark and bare to her before now seemed merely simple, spare. Notes of Alfred played around the room, his razor on the edge of the sink, his boots topsy-turvy by the door.

"I'm sorry, Mary," he said after a while.

"I'm sorry, too."

TWENTY-FOUR

They spent the rest of the spring catching up. Alfred was driving for the Teamsters and had been selected for training on a motor truck. When he went to work he packed his medicine with the careful attention of a doctor administering to distant patients, fearful of leaving something important behind. Gone was the man who used to send chairs flying back when he stood. When he came home from his shift he rarely went out again after, unless Mary coaxed him to the market or out for a walk. She wrote to Mila to tell her she was safe and that she was sorry if Soper had harassed her after Mary left. She wanted to know if Soper had come for her, if he'd brought police or not, but she didn't want to send Mila her new address, just in case Soper was monitoring the mail. "Is he allowed to do that?" Alfred asked, when Mary shared her worries.

"I don't know if he's allowed. But I know he would if he could."

She considered going to the Department of Health to explain what had happened, but she knew that no one at the DOH would buy her argument that cooking and baking were different, and now, looking back, Mary admitted she didn't buy it, either. But no one had gotten sick! Surely, they would have heard rumors at the bakery if Typhoid had broken out among their customers. But Soper would have warned every person at the DOH, and no one there would take her side. The testing would resume. She'd be taken back to North Brother. No, it was not worth the risk.

Their rooms were cheaper than the ones they'd shared on Thirty-Third Street, and Alfred's wages covered the rent, but Mary wanted to work. She didn't have the nerve to look into restaurants or bakeries in case Soper was looking for her everywhere, so she began taking in laundry. Their building was meant for single occupants only, and once in a while when she passed a group of neighbors at the mailboxes downstairs she heard them whisper about the couple that was flagrantly flouting the rules everyone else followed. He'd been injured, people heard. Had spent a year in the hospital. Where had she been, all that time? A man's loneliness is a thing all women understand. An injured man. A working man. What time did he have for himself? Poor thing. But her—where had she come from? What was she after? He was liked, Alfred Briehof. He kept to himself, went about his business. Her? She was standoffish, and she had ideas about herself. Now she was going around mentioning to people that she took in laundry even though she knew full well that there were two other women on the block who also took in laundry. She was never grateful, people decided. Never. A woman could bring her family's things to any one of the washwomen on the street, and so when she made a selection it was to be expected that the washwoman chosen might offer a cup of tea. A slice of cake. She might knock fifty cents off now and again. Not Mary.

She never seemed to care, and if you implied that a shirt collar had not been scrubbed as clean as one would expect, considering the price charged, she struck a wide-legged stance and her face became terrifying.

Autumn arrived, and a cool mist settled over the city. Hanging over the side of Mary's basket as she moved through the market were the moppy green heads of carrots, bunched and dirty. She selected potatoes—one for herself, one for Alfred—brushed dirt off their skins, guessed at the depth of the eyes and the black spots she'd carve out with the tip of her knife. Alfred was following her, looking blankly at the stalls, waiting for her to make selections. She cooked supper for herself and Alfred every night, and tried to make those meals as interesting as they could afford. When the Teamsters went on strike, Mary advertised her laundry services more widely, more urgently, and people responded. Her reputation grew. Women showed up with armloads of their husbands' shirts and Mary stopped bothering to put away the ironing board at night. Alfred was tired now, always tired. He slept in the mornings. He slept in the afternoons. He took his medicine when he woke, and at lunch, and before dinner, and when it was time for bed. The strike ended, and the Teamsters won lunchtime wages. They won Christmas Day. Alfred went back to work.

It was a different kind of life than any they'd had before. There were days when Alfred didn't feel well enough to drive, and had to take an extra dose of medicine, and they were together more than they were apart. Where before the small space inside their rooms might have pressed in on them, might have made them both as crazy as rabid dogs, now it calmed them. They each had their domains. Alfred stayed mostly in the bedroom, either sitting at the desk or lying on the bed, and Mary stayed mostly in the kitchen. When he came home from work he always went straight to the bedroom to rub his arm and chest with oil, administer the medicine that could be taken only by needle and syringe. When Mary looked in on him to tell him supper was ready, she usually found him curled on the bed, one hand balled under his chin, the other open, palm up, surrendered.

Sometimes he closed his eyes even while he was awake. The light bothered him, he said. Since the fire he had headaches. He had pain in his bowels. He had trouble staying warm. He felt dizzy. The medicine helped all that, but only temporarily.

One day in October 1912, he was driving a truck up to Riverdale when he fell asleep at the wheel and the truck went off the road. He was hauling brick for a stonemason, and though none of the brick was lost, and no one was injured, the company wanted to fire him. The Teamsters got him another job. It happened again—this time he was driving four thousand day-old chicks from Nyack, New York, to the Bronx—and they moved him again. Next time, they warned, he'd be getting a dispatch job. There was only so much they could do. He told them he was sure it would happen again, so they might as well find him the dispatch job, and after that, Mary noticed, he was even more distant, as if he'd lifted a hood over his head and stepped into a shadow.

On Christmas, they shared a roasted breast of goose and Mary read aloud from the newspaper. At the end of February 1913, Mary bought him a handsome gray wool overcoat to replace the ugly coat he'd bought for himself when he was in Minnesota. He wore the new one for the month and then she packed it away in mothballs for the following year. Spring came, and children appeared on the sidewalk like bulbs that had been planted in the fall and burst through the earth overnight. They shouted and shrieked and threw their balls in the street and dodged traffic and spooked horses while Alfred stood by the window and listened.

Summer came, and on a Sunday in late July Mary convinced him to go with her to the pink granite halls of Pennsylvania Station, where they purchased two tickets to Long Island and spent the day at the beach. She packed a clean sheet for sitting on the sand, a picnic lunch. They walked along the rocks, carrying their shoes, until Alfred got tired. They napped on the sheet before heading back to Manhattan. On the way back to the city, they said how amazing it was that they'd never done that before, that they would certainly do it again before the summer was over. But then the summer became rainy, and when the sun came out again Mary pointed out that train tickets were dear, and then Alfred wasn't feeling up to it, and next thing they knew it was autumn.

The leaves fell off the trees, and then came another winter, another new year. And then, in late February 1914, Alfred came back from Dr. Tropp's office looking ashen. He went straight to the bedroom and shut the door.

"What happened?" Mary knocked. He ignored her. When she turned the knob he was standing at the window, hands on his hips.

"Nothing," he said. "I can't get prescriptions from him anymore. A new law."

Mary frowned. "I don't understand."

"Me, neither. He just said there's a new law, and he can't write maintenance prescriptions anymore. He said the government is going to check every one he writes now, and if they don't like what they see they'll take his license. He said from now on I'm to go downtown to a maintenance clinic on Eighth Street."

"Well, that's not so bad."

"It's a reduction clinic."

"What does that mean? Will they give you something or won't they?"

"They will . . ." Alfred trailed off. He put his finger to the glass of the window and drew a circle. Next to it he drew a square. "It's for tapering off. For getting off the medicine entirely."

"But does it hurt, Alfred? When the medicine wears off?"

He rubbed his arm. "I'm not sure."

Toward the end of her life, when Mary had nothing to do except think about the things she'd done when she was still young, especially those months, when she was approaching the end of being young and beginning, finally, to be old, she wondered why she spent so much precious time trying to change things: trying to change herself and Alfred and the way they lived and what they thought and the things they had and the way they spoke to each other and the way they loved each other. Everything. Looking at the back of Alfred's neck, she wanted him to shake off this news, assure her it would all be fine. She wanted him to forget about his medicine, shave himself, go to work, earn his paycheck, come with her to the market, talk with her. And maybe, it came to her years later, all he'd wanted from her was for her to put her hands on his shoulders, kiss him on the neck, tell him that no matter what, it would all work out in the end.

The clinic had cut him down on his very first visit and wanted him weaned entirely in a matter of six weeks. Mary went with him. It had been nearly two years since Soper had discovered her at the bakery, since she'd fled from the back door. She thought of him less and less as time wore on, and looking back at those years of dreading her check-ins, straining into a pot while a fresh-faced nurse made conversation, she wondered if she'd been insane to comply with all of it. She'd been tired, confused, scared, angry. At the clinic, the young physician ignored Alfred when he told him that it was impossible, that he couldn't work without his medicine. The physician said that it wasn't medicine anymore, not since his wounds had healed, that what he was now was a drug addict, not a patient. Alfred's neck became mottled and angry, he balled his fists, but he didn't say a word. No, he hadn't been a patient in years. It wasn't his fault, the physician admitted, but now that they knew more about all those drugs it was up to Alfred to get himself free of this noose that had been cast around his neck. Mary expected him to argue, to explain that his wounds still hurt at night, that he was in a different category altogether, but Alfred just set his jaw and walked out. When Mary got to the sidewalk, he was gone.

Here is where you should have done better, the distant Mary thought as she looked back on the Mary of this moment. Here is where you should have helped him more, used all that strength inside you to shield him from whatever it was he feared. The price of the drugs had increased with the new law, and later, when Alfred told her that he wouldn't do it, he just couldn't do it, it was selfishness that kept her silent. She liked this Alfred. They hadn't fought in nearly two years. They sat at the table together for three meals a day and if he nodded off, occasionally, while she was talking to him, if he spent mornings staring out the window at the empty sidewalk across the street, it seemed a small price to pay for peace.

He told her that there were other places to buy the drugs. It would cost more, especially now, but it was the way things had to be. No way, Mary should have said. And to make her point, like she would have in the old days, she should have thrown what was left of his drugs in the fire and walked out. Instead she only nodded. "Where?"

The following morning, when he woke up before she did and pulled on a clean undershirt, she didn't ask where he was going, or what time he'd be home.

Staying silent didn't do her any good anyway. The peace of that time was ruined despite her decision not to stand up to him. Destroyed. Heroin was cheaper than morphine now, not as closely regulated, and he'd heard about a doctor on East Ninetieth Street who was quick to prescribe heroin for serious respiratory ailments. "Do you suffer from any respiratory ailments, Mr. Briehof?" the doctor asked when Alfred went to meet with him, his thumb fluttering the pages of his prescription pad. Alfred paid the man, and from the first instant he inhaled it he could tell it wasn't quite the same as what he'd gotten before. Morphine, too. Everything was being cut, mixed with milk sugar, baking soda. Even the laudanum was being diluted with alcohol, table syrup, juice. He measured his own dosages but it was no good. Sometimes he slept whole days away, but there was no peace in sleep anymore. He tossed and raked at his pillow, and when Mary went to him she often found he'd soaked their sheets even though she'd as likely find him shivering, clutching himself like a child. He shit himself and even when he was drinking he had the basic human sense to apologize for something so filthy. Now he shit himself and said nothing and just tried to move away from it. People who came with their arms full of laundry stopped at their threshold, drew in their breath, said they'd come back another time. The Teamsters wrote a letter to say that they could not reinstate his membership until he paid back dues.

Here is where she should have left. And here again. And if not there, then here. Here. He would have snapped out of it if she'd left, would have paid attention, but still, she stayed, and tried to make more money, and whatever she made she handed to him. The laws got stricter and the drugs got more expensive every month.

When a neighbor on the fourth floor came home from the hospital, Mary distracted herself by bringing up a quiche and a loaf of freshly baked raisin bread. When the woman was strong enough to make her way downstairs, she stopped at Mary's door to thank her, ask if she could make another one of those quiches for a friend. "I'll pay you, of course," she said, and something switched on in Mary. "Sure," she responded, and named her price, almost as much as half a day of taking in laundry. One quiche. And instead of balking, the woman seemed grateful, told Mary it was her quiche that had given her strength.

She no longer had any fear that Soper was hiding around every corner, spying on her through a crack in the door. She imagined baking out of their small oven, lining up what she made on the sill. She let it be known that she could cook and deliver dishes, and it went around that she had a talent for it. She stopped taking in laundry, and once, when Alfred was feeling well enough to keep her company in the kitchen, and cheerful enough to talk, he came up behind her and whispered that nowhere in the world was cozier than their tiny rooms when she had butter melting in a pan, when she tossed in a handful of chopped onion, diced carrots.

One evening he came home with a black eye and a busted lip, then was bad for days after that, retching into bowls and eventually knocking over the bowls when he thrashed. Mary put on her best dress and went to see Dr. Tropp, intent on making him write a prescription like he had so many times before, but when she got to the office his sign was gone, the door locked. She went to the druggist, and he said it was impossible. His license would be taken away. There was a register now, and men came around to check his orders. The only thing for it was to go to the maintenance clinic, and when Mary explained that he'd already been, the druggist shrugged.

"But there are places," she said to the man coolly. "There are places. You can't expect me to believe there aren't."

"There are places," the man said. "But you have to have money. And you have to have the stomach."

"I have the stomach."

The doctor on East Ninetieth Street had disappeared as suddenly and completely as Dr. Tropp, but they got the name of another doctor down on Spring Street. Alfred wanted to know the extent of every penny Mary had. She could tell by the way he was standing that he expected her to go wild, tell him it was none of his business. Instead, she went to the closet and together they counted everything. The pain in his stomach was too strong for him to make it downtown himself, so she put a little powder on her face and went on her own. She expected dark alleyways, locked doors, but instead she was shown a pleasant waiting room decorated with hanging plants and an oriental carpet, and after a while she was brought into a second bright, clean room, where a bearded man asked what exactly she needed. She told him what Alfred had been taking, he told her the price, and she counted out the money and slid it across the desk.

At home, her oven was always hot, and she bought more pans so that she could have things waiting while other things were cooking. She made pies, both savory and sweet. She made roasts, stews, casseroles. Word spread. She made more money, and once every two weeks—leaving out the price of their rent—she took everything she earned and went down to Spring Street to get more drugs for Alfred. When Alfred felt up to it, he sat at the table, out of her way, and watched her with the flat of his hand against the scars on his chest.

If anyone had gotten sick from what she cooked, she never heard about it, but she found herself asking, sometimes, when someone turned up whom she hadn't seen in a while. "I hope you haven't been feeling poorly," she'd say, but it was always something else that had kept them away, never her food, and she thought back on North Brother, and how silly it all seemed now. People got sick, and usually got better. When they didn't get better, it was sad, but how could they have blamed her, one woman, when the whole of New York City was teeming with disease, and doctors now said that even the hang straps on the IRT were under suspicion? Would they shut down the subways? Of course not.

A Mrs. Hughes stopped by one morning. She lived two blocks north and her son had just gotten engaged to be married. She'd heard about Mary and wanted something special to serve to her future daughter-in-law, something she could pass off as having made herself. "A custard, like they make in the old coun-try," the woman suggested. "I could serve it warm over sliced fruit. I'll bring you my dishes and you could arrange it all in them and I'll have it all home in a wink."

Mary stopped trimming the roast she was working on and felt her stomach drop.

"I'll make the custard," she said. "You have the fruit ready at your place."

"Well, if I'm paying you . . ."

"No," Mary said. "Only the custard." She had never refused anyone and it surprised her now to be refusing Mrs. Hughes.

"But why?" the woman sputtered.

"You want the custard or not?"

"No, not unless you do the fruit, too."

"No," Mary said, and crossed her arms. It wasn't because what they'd told her on North Brother was true, it was just because they'd spooked her so much that her thoughts had gotten jum-bled. That was all. It was criminal, what they did to her, and who could blame her if some of it had rattled her. She wanted to wash her hands and splash water on her face.

Mrs. Hughes put her hands on her hips. "I don't understand. I was told you do all sorts of cooking. That you're very good."

"Look, why don't I do a lovely baked fruit pie. That would be nicer anyway, this time of year. You bring me your pie plate and I'll do it lovely for you and walk it over there warm before they get there."

"But don't you have to slice fruit anyway for a pie?"

"Yes, but—" Mary sighed. "Fine. Bring me the fruit."

And then one morning, Mrs. Waverly, from the third floor of their building, came down and asked if she could speak to Mary about something serious. Mary swallowed, tried to think back on every single thing she'd cooked in the previous month. She hadn't worried so much when she was working at the bakery, but it was different there, the large kitchen, the line of customers out the door, Evelyn quietly kneading and slicing in her corner. They'd cleaned everything at night, and the equipment was always pristine when they unlocked the back door in the morning. There was ventilation at the bakery, sunlight, room to move, racks laid out specially for things to cool. Now that she was working out of her own kitchen, everything seemed cramped and every surface she touched felt sticky no matter how often she plunged a rag into hot water and wiped down the counters, the table, the cabinets, the floor. She braced herself for whatever Mrs. Waverly had come to tell her. But instead of talking about an outbreak of fever in the neighborhood, Mrs. Waverly asked Mary if she ever considered cooking in a more professional capacity.

"If you can turn meals out of this"—she took in the tiny kitchen, the small stove—"I can't imagine what you could do in a real kitchen." Mary kept her mouth shut and listened. "I'm head nurse at the Sloane Maternity Hospital and the cook there just quit. The wages are excellent and I can tell you that it's a nice place to work. Have you ever cooked on that scale? The beds are usually full, plus the doctors and nurses. Guests sometimes. I can put your name in." The woman laughed. "I'm in charge of finding the person so the deck would be stacked."

Mary swallowed.

"It sounds overwhelming, I know," Mrs. Waverly said, "but you'd have plenty of help."

"It's not that—" Mary said, placing her spoon on the counter and crossing her arms. She felt dizzy. She wanted to sit down except that she had shepherd's pies cooling on the seats of both chairs.

"Think about it," Mrs. Waverly said. "If you do a good job they'll raise you. It's steady work. The last cook was there for years."

Mary touched the edge of the counter. She imagined the size of the refrigerator they'd have in a hospital. The size of the oven, the compartments for roasting, for warming, the stacks and stacks of clean white plates, the copper-bottomed pots.

"Look, why don't you go down and talk to the administrator. You can ask any questions. Spell your full name for me and I'll let him know to expect you."

"Yes, that would be fine. Okay."

"Do you have paper? Mary what?"

"Oh, it's easy enough. Mary Brown. Like the color."

The interview would have made Mary laugh if she hadn't been so nervous. She washed the night before and again that morning, and cut her nails, and scrubbed her cuffs with baking soda and a toothbrush, and used some of Alfred's hair tonic to smooth every strand of hair away from her face. The administrator was no cook, Mary could tell right away, and asked only whether she could turn out on that scale, not a single question on how she'd stretch ingredients, keep things simple, how she'd make it so everything would be served hot and at once. He asked for a reference, and Mary swallowed, wanted to kick herself for not expecting it. "Yes," she said coolly. "There was Mrs. Emilia Borriello. I can write down her address. Also Mrs. Harriet . . . Mrs. Harriet Sloane."

"Sloane like our Sloane? Same name?"

"Same name," Mary said, realizing, and her heart sunk.

"Seems like a good sign," the man said, and wrote down her address. He printed her name on top. "You said Browne, yes?" he tilted the paper to show her.

"No *e* at the end," she said. "Brown."

He struck a line through the *e*. "Good," he said, and shook her hand. She expected him to say that she'd hear from him once he checked out her references, but since Mrs. Waverly had recommended her, he told her she could start the following week unless she heard from them to do otherwise. On her way out she passed a room where six women in six beds were recuperating, their babies next to them in bassinets.

TWENTY-FIVE

Once Mary got used to being addressed as Mrs. Brown, she decided that the hospital was, without question, the best situation she'd ever had. She'd seen childbirth before—she was charged with holding a leg when a neighbor of Aunt Kate's went into unexpected labor, and many times she'd waited downstairs with other staff while the mistress of a house moaned and roared until the doctor arrived with chloroform. She expected Sloane to be a chaotic place, and that she would have to weave through a dozen exhausted women as they walked the halls just as laboring women used to walk the halls of the tenements, trying to help the baby come, their fingertips brushing the wallpaper for balance. Instead, Sloane was organized. It was a clean, bright, shining place with strange contraptions in every room to help the doctors know more about the baby that was to come. The nurses made reference to Twilight Sleep and it took Mary a week to realize that they were referring to labor, which was mostly silent, and often the babies were born silent, too, which struck Mary as worrisome but didn't seem to faze the nurses, who swaddled their limp bodies into tight little packages and propped them up on pillows for their mothers to admire. Only later, hours, sometimes days later, would the babies come out of it, and begin to whimper and cry. Those babies who were particularly cranky got a soothing syrup of codeine to quiet them.

The doctors didn't care what she did as long as there were hot meals coming out of her kitchen. Unlike in a private home where the staff wasn't permitted to have an opinion about anything political, at Sloane they passed the time talking about President Wilson, the income tax, the war brewing in Europe. The administrator occasionally checked in with her, but only to ask if she had what she needed in the way of equipment and help. The staff was honest, and when she sent them out to shop they came back with what she asked for—what did she care if they snuck a few things home to their own pantries? She'd done it often enough herself.

She arrived at the hospital at five in the morning, and left at five in the evening, once she was sure the staff knew how to complete the supper she'd started, and that there would be enough to go around. Always, as her final chore, she left the oats soaking in water so they'd cook up quickly in the morning.

Then, one evening, about six weeks after she started at Sloane, and with two sliced-turkey sandwiches wrapped carefully in her handbag, Mary arrived at their rooms to find Alfred on the floor next to her side of the bed, his face gray and his skin like a cold piece of cod. She shouted his name sharply as she took his hands and tried to pull him up. She dropped his hands and slapped his face. "Alfred!" she said again. She slapped him again. And then, just as she was about to run out into the hall for help, he blinked, and tried to sit up. "Get Jimmy," he told her. "Or Mr. Hallenan. Someone strong."

"What are you talking about?" she demanded. "We're not on Thirty-Third Street anymore. Come on, Alfred. Stop it."

He was quiet for a long time, and she thought he might have fallen asleep with his eyes open.

"I'm okay now, Mary. I just got confused."

Mary let out a long sigh of relief. "You scared me."

The next day, she didn't want to leave him for twelve hours, and thought to ask someone from the building to look in on him while she was at work, but as she walked down the stairs she realized that although she knew her neighbors well enough to exchange pleasantries, and had done laundry or cooked a dish for many of them, she didn't know any of them well enough to ask for a favor like that, not when they'd have a thousand questions about it, and maybe tell everyone else. No, better to leave him sleeping. There were times when he slept all day long, and she predicted this would be one of those days. He'd stay curled under the covers until she came home again, and then, if she had luck, she'd get him to eat something. She'd left bread and butter on a plate beside the bed, and next to it, a tall glass of water.

She was distracted all day at the hospital. A new mother had died in the middle of the night. Sepsis, they determined, and the mood everywhere, including the kitchen, was somber. The nurses cried over the little baby girl left behind, and cried harder when the husband came and didn't seem to know how to hold her. They took Mary's silence as part of that sadness, and she was glad to not have any questions. It was terrible about the mother, terrible when any young person dies, but she couldn't stop her-self from thinking that they were rich, these women. The price of giving birth at Sloane was more than Mary would earn in six months, and if they had that kind of money then they also had a full staff, families to help. There were poor women all over the city dying every minute of the day, leaving two, three, four babies behind.

She wondered if Alfred had woken. She wondered if he'd seen the bread. Sometimes he felt a world better after he washed himself, and she meant to leave a bar of soap and a washcloth on the ledge to remind him. She could pretend a headache, leave early, go home to check on him. A walk would do him good, if he could manage it. Maybe they'd go out to eat that night. There was a new restaurant by the university and it might do him good to be in a busy place. The energy of the city would sweep him past the day's trouble.

She diced and sautéed and lifted the wooden spoon to her mouth for a lick, returned it to the pan, turned the food 'round and 'round. She shook salt, pepper, chopped fresh oregano, parsley, swept it from the blade of her knife with her finger, all while thinking about Alfred. She measured cream, checked for spots on glasses, bowls, forks, spoons. She asked one of the new girls to wash everything again.

When she got home, Alfred was better but didn't want to go anywhere, and so Mary sat in the dim kitchen by herself, her feet up on Alfred's chair. She felt tired, and realized only when she sat down how worried she'd been. She tried to read but she caught herself going over the same sentence again and again.

The next morning, the nurses were sharp with one another. Two were out sick, one of them Mrs. Waverly, and without her calm authority the rest of them were like children left behind in a room without an adult. Mary thought of Alfred, hoped he hadn't caught anything. Perhaps whatever was bothering him now had nothing to do with the medicine at all. Maybe he had the flu. Maybe he'd be up and better in a day or two.

That evening, he was bad again, and she could see he'd been up and around while she was at the hospital. The cutlery drawer was left hanging open. There was a glass in the sink. He was fully dressed but sleeping on their bed, and she had to say his name three times, and shake him, before he cracked his eyes to look at her. "Mary," he said, and put his hand on her lap before falling asleep again.

More were absent the next day at the hospital, and a mother who'd been released a month before was readmitted, with her child, both of them slack with fever. More sepsis, the kitchen assistant guessed. The administrator put the sick woman in a room to herself, and then came down the hall to ask Mary if she'd mind pitching in if she had a moment. There was so much to do, and it would only be for a few days, until everyone recovered from whatever was going around and they were back to full staff again. The doctors rushed through the hallways looking stern, tired, worried. The ones who normally left when Mary did now stayed on, some stayed all night. As she was rolling supper down the hall on the dining cart, she observed three of them talking in hushed tones in a quiet corner of the passageway. One took off his glasses to rub his eyes.

She was in a patient's room, lifting the top off a plate of braised beef, when the thought came through her like a tremor. A nurse breezed in, brushed by Mary, checked the patient's pulse, peeked into the bassinet to check on the baby, and noticed Mary. "Oh God, not you, too," she said, helping Mary to a chair. She held Mary's wrist for a few moments. "Your pulse is fast." She put the back of her hand to Mary's head. "But you've no fever."

"I'm all right," Mary whispered. "Just tired."

"You sure?"

"Is it sepsis?" Mary asked, trying to keep her voice steady. "Or something else?"

The young nurse sighed. "They thought sepsis at first, until so many came down with it, and now they're thinking Typhoid."

Mary felt her insides erupt into chaos. The nurse guided her back farther in the chair. "You should go home, Mary,"

"No, no," she said. "I'll be fine in a minute."

The nurse flagged down a doctor and pointed to Mary.

"Go home, Mrs. Brown," he told her. "If you feel well in the morning, then by all means come in, but otherwise stay home. We'll cope without you."

"I said I'm fine," Mary said.

"Doctor's orders."

Too tired to argue, Mary gathered her things, left instructions for the woman helping out in the kitchen, and was out on the sidewalk before noon.

She should have gone straight uptown to Alfred, but she walked instead, and when she actually paid attention she noticed that she was covering dozens of blocks without noticing. She turned with the traffic, and felt herself slip into a kind of trance as she took in the storefronts, as she stepped around patches of ice, piles of horse shit that had been frozen, petrified, and would stay that way until the warm days of late March. It was February 1915, and she walked with her coat hanging open, her pale, white throat exposed to the cutting wind. She wanted to lie down and sleep but instead she kept walking, and walking, and finally, she was home.

She opened the door to their rooms at almost the same time as she did most evenings, and decided if he asked what was wrong with her, she wouldn't tell him, wouldn't worry him; he had enough to deal with at the moment. But when she pushed open the door and saw him in the same heap as she'd left him that morning, she almost laughed. No need to have worried. He hadn't asked about her in weeks, not how the new situation was going, how she liked it, only when she'd get paid, when she'd get a chance to go downtown to visit that man again. She felt anger bubbling up in her belly and made no effort to quiet her movements as she filled the kettle with water, slammed it on the range to set it boiling for tea. Let him rot in there, she thought. I'm here working and worrying, and now this. Typhoid. Again. Jesus.

"Alfred," she called sharply toward the open door of the bedroom. "Did you eat? Did you go out today?"

It felt like the old days, asking questions she already knew the answers to. She knew she was only setting herself up to pick a fight, and yet she couldn't stop herself. What would they do now? How would he help? He had to snap out of it and get back with the Teamsters. He had to forget about his medicine entirely.

"Alfred!" she said again, slamming closed the window onto the airshaft. It was freezing in their rooms. She went into the bedroom and closed that window as well. She pulled open the curtains to let the last of the day's dim light into the room.

"Get up," she said, one hand on her hip, the other hand reaching down for the corner of the quilt. She had every intention of whipping it off him, yanking him to his feet, marching him around the neighborhood until he protested and gave her a little of the fight she needed if they were to keep going.

"Alfred?" she said, noticing, finally, that his face was gray, his lips tinged with blue. She dropped the edge of the quilt and touched his cheek, cold but not clammy. She dropped her face to his and felt for his breath. Run for help, she ordered herself and felt every small muscle in her body prepare to spring forward, propel her down to the sidewalk to hail a policeman, find a telephone. But all she could do was stare, and where a moment earlier her body had felt full of turmoil, now it felt perfectly still, like everything within her had paused, like a dancer who leaps and is suspended over the stage for one single second, halfway between one place and another but knowing she is on her way and will have arrived there as soon as she opens her eyes. Mary lifted the edge of the quilt and moved next to him, put her arm around his chest. As long as she stayed there, like that, as if they were sleeping, it hadn't happened yet. As long as no one knew, and no one else came into their rooms, and they didn't take him away. His pills were a mess, all over the desk as well as the drawer, and the needles he'd kept so clean and organized were separated, thrown here and there, mixed up with his dirty clothes, one propped inside an empty coffee mug. I should clean it all up, she thought, and realized she didn't care.

"There's Typhoid at the hospital," she said, looking at the ceiling, worried that she was already forgetting what it felt like to hug him when he was warm, and feeling her heart throb when she thought she felt pressure back. But he didn't say anything, and there was no pressure back, and after a few minutes, she walked to the grocer's to call for help.

TWENTY-SIX

The doctor on the telephone told Mary that he'd come directly after supper, and true to his word, he buzzed around eight o'clock. After checking Alfred and confirming what Mary had told him when they spoke, he glanced around the room. "Is that his layout?" he asked, looking over at the open drawer, the pills and vials. Mary nodded and then pulled the covers up to Alfred's chest, tucked them tightly all around. She still half-expected him to open his eyes. She kept thinking she saw him flinch. She stared at his blank face. She thought of the babies swaddled at the hospital, how contented they were when their blankets were wrapped tight.

"And you?" the doctor asked. He was younger than she by a decade, and reminded her of Mr. O'Neill, a young man dressed up in his father's work clothes.

"What about me?"

"Do you take any of that stuff?" he walked over to the desk, pushed some of the pills around.

"Get away from that," Mary said. She pushed the drawer shut.

The doctor shrugged. "The coroner will be by shortly," he said just before he left.

She should be more upset, she decided, but discovered she was too tired to muster up the energy. It was difficult to understand that they would take him away, and that would be the last she'd see of him. Typhoid at the hospital. One was connected to the other—she felt as sure of that as she'd been sure that wearing a hat identical to Mrs. Bowen's was what had sent her to North Brother. If she'd brought Typhoid to the hospital, to those new mothers, to those babies, then it was as they said, she'd brought it to the other places, too. She'd killed Tobias Kirkenbauer. A cold breeze rattled the panes of the window, and she looked down at Alfred again. She ran through their years together to think of who should be notified. Back and forth she went, and could come up with only half a dozen names. Among them, Liza Meaney. Her son. Fran. Joan. Jimmy Tiernan. Better not say anything at all, she decided, than have a funeral and face so few people, all impatient to get back to their lives. She opened the desk drawer again and rooted around for a pen and paper so she could list the things she had to do, and then as soon as the tip of the pen touched the paper she thought about how strange she was being, and how she'd better look at him again because it would be the last time. She turned to study him and realized that she didn't know what she was looking for. More than his coloring, which made him seem more unfamiliar to her with every passing quarter hour, it was the fact that he hadn't moved at all that upset her. Not a single finger, not a hair, not a cough or gasp or growl.

What had Mr. Kirkenbauer done when his wife died? He'd embraced her—lifted her from the bed and held her close to his broad chest. He'd cried big, hot tears and didn't care who saw. He'd kissed the top of her head and told her he loved her. In the total silence of their rooms Mary put the tip of her finger to Alfred's hand, the familiar row of knuckles. She examined the jagged fingernails. She studied his blank face. Where did a person go? She wished she knew. She said her good-bye in silence. I don't think I understand what's happened yet, but when I do, I will miss you. And I'm sorry.

The coroner came at eleven o'clock, with his teenage son to assist him. She signed the paper he placed on the table. "Right here, Mrs. Briehof," he said. "And here." She didn't bother correcting him, and signed "Mary Briehof" because it was easy, and then they would go away. They got Alfred onto a stretcher, and as they moved into the hall, the boy walking backward, the father forward, she heard the man say quietly to his son that this is what happened to druggies, he saw it all the time. The son said something Mary couldn't make out, and she tried to ignore the sound of them struggling on the stairs, tried to turn away from the image of his body shifting, sliding. The coroner had given her a contact name and address for the next morning, where she'd have to go to make arrangements, and she folded it over and over until it was as small as a pebble. Then she shoved it deep in her pocket.

It was impossible to sleep that night, and a little before dawn, still wearing the clothes she'd worn the day before, Mary went down to the sidewalk to clear her head. She walked west, to the Hudson, and crouched on the river's sloped bank to watch a small barge approach from the north. She wondered how long until it didn't feel as if he were at home, waiting for her. How long until the space he'd made began to narrow and close and until she wondered what it had been like ever to have known him, and to be known by him. Even in those months when they lost track of each other she knew he was out there somewhere, a dot on a map, and she could pass the time wondering if he was thinking of her, and if the dot that was him and the dot that was her were moving closer together without either of them realizing. A woman and child walked by and nodded to her. They can't tell by looking at me, she thought, staring after them as they ambled up the embankment and back up to the street. Seems like something they should be able to tell by looking at me.

She hadn't considered going to the hospital that day, but when the sun had fully risen it seemed better that she work, at least for a few hours, and besides, it already seemed like such a long, long time had passed. In the light of morning she remembered that it might not be Typhoid that was going around the hospital. Not every fever was Typhoid Fever, and the nurse hadn't been sure. And even if it was Typhoid, it mightn't have anything to do with her. She was only one person, and there were so many in and out of the hospital every day, from deliverymen to proud grandmothers. Who knew what invisible infestations they swept in with them when they came? She thought of the Borriello boys, and how they'd eaten anything she made for them and never got sick. She'd never made Alfred sick. Fran. Aunt Kate. She thought back on all the families she'd worked for. It was a coincidence. A strange coincidence, but still. What could she have done differently? What would they have done differently if they were in her shoes? She thought of the dairyman up in Camden and imagined him skimming the cream from his milk, walking his property with his grandchildren.

Staring across the broad Hudson at New Jersey, she also

372

wondered whether it was possible for a person to know something and not know something at the same time. She wondered whether it was possible to know a truth, and then quickly unknow it, bricking up that portal of knowledge until every pinpoint of light was covered over. When she thought back on the hot blur of days that marked her hearing, way back in 1909, and all the things they'd said about her—that she had no friends, that she didn't keep a clean kitchen—she felt that animal fight rise up in her again. They blamed her because she was opinionated, and Irish, and unmarried, and didn't bow to them. She walked quickly to the water to kick stones. The wind on her face felt cleansing, and she closed her eyes to it. And yet, and yet, and yet. As if crouched behind a small door that didn't draw attention to itself, a different truth sat. And now, as she considered how cold the river water was at that moment, how quickly it would numb the limbs of a swimmer, she closed her eyes and looked at that door, nondescript as it was, unadorned, just sitting, waiting to be opened.

She'd tell the administrator about Alfred so he'd be prepared when she asked for time off for the funeral. She might tell a few among the kitchen staff. Maybe she'd go over to the old building and tell Jimmy in person, stop in for a talk with Fran or Mila. It had been too long.

And anyway, if she didn't go to the hospital they might find it strange, and start looking into Mary Brown's history as a cook.

When she got to the hospital, she nodded to the doorman as usual but found herself studying his face for signs of exhaustion, signs that the fever was on its way. When she got to her floor, she opened the door to disconcerting silence, and continued down the hall passing empty rooms, not a single nurse. The recovery rooms were similarly empty, not only of patients, but also of beds. Only when she approached the kitchen did she hear the ebb and flow of voices in conversation. As she passed the doctors' lounge, Dr. Henshaw was standing in the frame of the door, watching her pass. She said good morning, but he didn't reply.

Fly away, she told herself as she took another step, and then another, toward the voices in the kitchen. Do it now. Moving down the hall was like walking through water, and she felt both light and heavy at the same time. Fly out now into the brittle winter air and don't look back. She glanced over her shoulder at the stair door. To her right was the bank of elevators, but it was as if they had her on a tether and now they were shortening the chain, wrapping it around the broadest part of their hands to draw her closer, and closer, until they had her where they wanted her.

Finally, she arrived at the kitchen. She was lifting her bag from her shoulder and toward the usual hook when, at the same moment, she noticed Soper standing not five feet away. Next to him was the head doctor and behind them were two men Mary didn't recognize. The mood in the room was one of calm patience, as if they'd been waiting for her all night and now that she'd arrived they could check off that final item on their long list of things to do. One of the unfamiliar men moved to the doorway through which Mary had just entered.

"Mary Mallon," Dr. Soper said without moving. He looked so pleased to see her that Mary wondered for a second if he could be there on other business. But no, she saw when he exchanged glances with one of the unfamiliar men; Mary had confirmed something that he'd suspected, that he'd suggested to the other men standing around, also waiting, and he was pleased to have his suspicion proven true. They spread out, almost imperceptibly, to fill the corners of the room. She went ahead and hung her coat alongside her bag as she did every morning, and then without looking at any of them she walked over to the stove and checked on the oats. She opened the icebox and made note of the fresh eggs and cream. Then she sat on the single stool, the one they used for peeling, put her hands over her face, and cried.

TWENTY-SEVEN

She gave them no trouble. She listened and nodded and only once remembered her bag, still hanging on the hook at the hospital. When Dr. Soper gave her his hand to step down into the boat that would ferry them across Hell Gate, she placed her hand in his and then took her seat. In the series of questions there were one or two about Alfred, and Mary said only that he was deceased, not that he'd died the day before, or that there was a burial to arrange, or that it was still so new that she didn't know what to make of it except that now that she was back on North Brother, at an actual, physical distance away from him, from their rooms, from their life, she seemed to be able to see it better—like backing away from a picture to take in the whole scene and not just the image at the center.

Her bungalow had not been occupied in the five years since she last saw it, and they were kind enough to air it for half a morning while she answered the doctors' questions in the main hospital. It wasn't like the first time around, where she fought and argued, and the tenor of their questions changed accordingly. Now she gave them the answers they sought right away, and they seemed grateful to her. She'd been asked to check in, and she hadn't. She'd been asked not to cook, and she did. She knew the terms of her release and she violated them with full knowledge. She nodded. She wondered if her egret was still living on the island somewhere, if John Cane was still commuting daily. "You put lives at risk," one of the doctors informed her, and she saw that they worried about getting through to her, that she mightn't understand why they'd taken her again. "Before, it was careless-ness. This time, it's criminal."

"I know that," she said, and when she said it she realized she wasn't just being agreeable; she did know. And that it had been a risk worth taking was something they would never be able to understand.

"And using a false name is an admission of guilt. Do you agree?" Mary nodded that she did, but again, there were so many things that were difficult to explain, things she didn't even understand herself. It was possible to live in such a way as to keep one's back to the things that were not convenient. People got Typhoid Fever when she cooked for them, and in some cases, those people died. But more often than not they did not get sick, and she was a remarkable cook, and wasn't it possible that those people were going to die anyway? If our lives are determined before we are born, then what could she have done about it? And if every person who is born will die, and if every person will rise again, and come together again, and if our time on earth is only a handful of seconds compared to the infinity of life after, then wasn't her crime very small? No greater than the crime of the East River that drowned Alberto Borriello? She'd taken a risk, but living was itself a risk, and most people agreed it was a risk worth taking.

And then she thought of the Kirkenbauer boy, his limp arm cast around her neck, his hot cheek against hers, and she felt a dead weight on her chest. She would not argue for herself. She would not fight them. If they decided to put chains on her ankles and drop her into the river, she would not object.

But they didn't want to throw her into the river. They simply wanted her to stay on North Brother, and as soon as she opened the door of her bungalow and leaned against the range to look about the room, she realized that finding herself back on North Brother was surprising only in that it wasn't entirely unpleasant. The ten-foot-by-twelve-foot room was so familiar to her, every fold in the dusty curtain, every creak in the floor, that within a few seconds she was astonished to think that just a short time ago she'd never expected to see it again. Every part of life feels strange, and every part of life feels inevitable. The mattress on her cot was rotted through, so they brought her another. She slept peacefully the first night, and in the morning John Cane left a sweet bun and a cup of coffee outside her door. When she saw him later, she'd ask him to let the coroner know that something had come up, but to use the little money she'd put aside for rent to buy Alfred a new shirt and tie, and to put him in a decent casket. "Tell him to take Alfred to St. Raymond's in the Bronx," she'd tell John Cane, and if the coroner didn't do any of this, if the coroner just took her money and buried Alfred in his undershirt in one of the city plots, she supposed she'd never know. She took one further step back: and if John Cane never went to the coroner, if he felt too tired to spend time tracking down a stranger about a man he'd never liked as a favor for a friend who hadn't reached out to him in five years, she supposed she'd never know that, either.

She was not as special as she'd been the first time around. In five years they'd discovered more healthy carriers, though the rest of them were allowed to live out their lives with family, at home. The papers that had taken up her cause in 1909 got word of her story again, but now cast her as villain. Jealous of young women who could still have children, and driven insane by an abusive and drug-addicted companion, she'd purposely gotten work at the hospital to infect those new mothers and kill their babies, was how one newspaper put it. Twenty-five people had contracted Typhoid Fever at Sloane Maternity Hospital. Two people had died. Mary read the article, and then she read it again, and both times had to catch her breath. She read it for a third time and then she folded it, left it on her front step, and decided she wouldn't read the paper again until her capture was no longer in the news.

John Cane came for a visit on her third day back, and though she felt him glancing sideways at her while she was looking away, he wouldn't meet her eye. So she talked a while but then drifted into silence, and as they sat, shivering, on the front step of her hut she saw the old retired horse in the distance, wearing a tartan blanket and looking across the water. "I thought he'd be dead by now," Mary said after a bit, and John Cane stood, clapped his hands, yelled at the horse to get on.

"Dead!" John Cane said as he clapped his hands a few more times to warm them, as he reached for his toes and the sky and back again. "He wouldn't leave North Brother for all the fresh hay in the kingdom." He looked at her, finally. "And I don't blame him. Life can be good here."

"Okay, John." Mary said. "Okay." And across the dark blue

water, a whistle sounded and a dozen or so strangers took a step back on the platform as the train they waited for pulled in. Mary stayed on the step just long enough to watch John Cane walk up the path and through the main door of the hospital. And then she went inside.

EPILOGUE

October 1938

The doctors have asked me to write something about my life and my time here, but they didn't say to address it to anyone, just to write it in the manner of a diary. A diary is something the writer keeps private, but I get the idea they plan on reading this one day, maybe after I die. Just write it any way you like, they say. They mustn't expect me to be around much longer or else they wouldn't have asked. I am almost sixty-nine years old and had a stroke in April. Walking is difficult but I can hold a pen and write, which is a blessing though it's slow going. Sometimes the tea dribbles from the left side of my mouth and that's embarrassing. It's a funny thing but when I had the stroke I recovered up in the hospital for a while and they took care of me and I thought this is what it's like to truly be ill and not just treated like an ill person when I am healthy. All that care and attention is far more welcome when it is needed and not pushed on me.

I've been what they call a special guest of New York City for twenty-three years now, and if you include my first time on North Brother that makes it twenty-six. They are good to me now and there are nurses here who weren't even born the first time I was on this island and who know nothing about me or my case, except that I am not sick in the traditional sense or at least not like those dying in the hospital.

My body is heavy and there are times when I am so ashamed to be the way I am that I don't like to come out of my bungalow for a few days. Sometimes I pass an hour thinking about how I used to be young and slim and strong but there's no point in thinking of differences like that, especially ones that can't be helped. I was beautiful no matter what anyone says, and smart, and I was a gifted cook. The only times I feel the unfairness of this is when one of the young nurses looks at me and I know she must think me ugly and awful. I feel it's important for her to know that I didn't used to be like this. Then to be fair I think of how much I brought upon myself by what I said and did and how I fought. Also I know I'd no longer be beautiful even if I had never set foot on North Brother—it's a problem of age, not geography.

Father Silva visits me more often lately and I think he means to bring peace now that I'm not very well but priests still annoy me. I suppose my faith is intact, or as intact as it ever was, but it's these idiotic priests I find so trying. The priest who used to visit me during the Great War used to pray for peace and an end to starvation in Russia and after all that praying he'd want a cup of tea and would be annoyed if the hospital had sent over plain scones instead of raisin or blueberry.

They let me work in the lab at the hospital for many years and that was good work. It was not so unlike cooking in that everything must be just so—the liquids and solids and the weighing and spinning—except in the end, of course, there's nothing wonderful to eat, just a report on a piece of paper. I would write down all the numbers and the researchers said I was helpful. One time I gave Dr. Sherman an apple I had taken from the cafeteria for myself but then decided it was such a nice-looking apple and my stomach was so full that I'd give it to Dr. Sherman instead, but she left it by the centrifuge that contained urine and had to throw it out. She apologized to me for that but I know she left it where she did on purpose so she'd have an excuse to throw it out. When that happened I understood that the old things they said about me would never be forgotten.

John Cane died in 1929, and as far as I know George Soper is still alive, though retired. John Cane was my friend and I've missed him. Sometimes when I'm tired I make a mistake and expect to see him and then I remember. Soper writes about me from time to time. I'm not sure whether he ever married or had children and I suppose I should confess that I hope he did not have those things since I did not. Sometimes I still think that all of this is his fault. Even Alfred's death seems to be Soper's fault, in a way. This is what Father Silva says I have to work on. It's not just Soper's fault. It's also my fault, and the city's fault, and no one's fault. It just is.

I keep up with the news, but even the most serious things seem at a great distance from me. None of the world events I read about applies to North Brother, where everything stays the same. Most days I pass a little time knitting with a group in the recovery ward of the hospital, and when it's sunny the nurses help us set up chairs in a circle outside in the sun. Sometimes on a Saturday they'll show a talkie in the cafeteria—just before my stroke they showed *All Quiet on the Western Front,* and I thought it was brilliant. Then someone told me that it came out several years ago and that threw me because I wondered what else has happened that I've missed and won't get to know for several more years. Once in a while a writer or reporter comes out here to see me, but that's rare, these days. Earlier this year they told me that I could leave the island if I want to, if there's anyone I want to visit, or perhaps just to visit the city itself. At first I thought they were kicking me out, but then I realized they were suggesting a day trip. Two things surprised me when this happened. The first, that I didn't want to be asked to leave North Brother for good, and the second, that I have no one to visit anymore.

Lately, I've been thinking more and more about the Kirkenbauer boy, and the Bowen girl, and the others they said died because of me. None bothers me as much as Tobias Kirkenbauer, and I mention him now knowing he'll be news to the person who reads this. I know the records on me go back only as far as 1901. He died in 1899. I don't really know what to put down on this paper about him except that I remember him, and I loved him, and if I ever believed for one second that I was bringing harm to him, I never would have stayed. If any of you were able to look into my mind, you would not be able to call my actions a crime, just an accident, a misunderstanding. Soper said to me way back in 1915 that I can make myself out to be the victim one time, but not the second time. He meant the maternity hospital, and the bakery, too, I suppose, and how I could go and put all those lives at risk. All I can say is that I thought I was doing the right thing, but I was doing the wrong thing, and it was a theme that repeated itself often. What I want to say about that sweet baby now is that if there is a heaven, and I see him there, I hope he remembers me, and runs to me, and forgives me.

ACKNOWLEDGMENTS

I am deeply grateful to my agent and friend, Chris Calhoun, for his confidence in this novel and for a perfect New York City day I will never forget. Many, many thanks to my incomparable editor, Nan Graham, for seeing the strengths in the early manuscript, and for pushing me to make it better; to Kelsey Smith, for reading with such a keen eye and helping me find solutions when I floundered; to my foreign rights agent, Jenny Meyer, for bringing Mary Mallon to places she's never been; to my UK editor, Jessica Leeke, for her enthusiasm and support.

From the pile of books and newspapers I consulted while writing this novel, I must single out Judith Walzer Leavitt's fascinating book, *Typhoid Mary: Captive to the Public's Health*. It served as my starting point and my touchstone for four years. For insight on the point of view of the late-nineteenth- and early-twentieth-century servant class, I am most indebted to a series of short autobiographies that originally appeared in *The Independent*, and were collected by Hamilton Holt in 1906: *The Everyday Lives of Undistinguished Americans as Told by Themselves.*

I owe much to the Ucross Foundation of Ucross, Wyoming, for granting me twenty thousand acres of silence for two critical weeks in 2010. Thanks also to the Free Library of Philadelphia, the Butler Library of Columbia University, and the English Department of Barnard College, where I did most of my research, and where I wrote large sections of this novel.

Of course, none of the research matters without time to write the book, and for that I thank my mother, Evelyn Keane, for taking such good care of my boys when I went off in search of a quiet place for a few hours, and my aunt Mae O'Toole for being there at a moment's notice when I needed her most.

Thanks to my dear friends Eleanor Henderson and Callie Wright, for taking time out of their own work to read and provide feedback on mine. Whenever I found I'd written myself into a corner I could always depend on one of them to help me find the way out.

My deepest gratitude to Julie Glass for thinking of me in the fall of 2011. I will never forget how a few generous words helped propel this novel forward.

Above all, thanks to Marty, for his patience and encouragement, and to our boys, Owen and Emmett, for being such dependable sleepers and such fun, thoughtful little men when awake. When you are old enough to read this novel, try to imagine yourselves all around it: chugging your trains around my feet as I type, coloring on the pages of the early drafts, searching for Mama worm and Papa worm outside with Bobo while I try to finish and hurry back to you. I love you.

Reading Group Discussion Questions for

FEVER

1. *Fever* is closely based on the true story of a woman known as 'Typhoid Mary'. Had you heard of Typhoid Mary before you came across *Fever*? If so, does this fictional account alter your previously held impression of Mary Mallon?

2. At the beginning of the novel, Mary is constant in her assertion that she is an innocent victim. Do you believe her?

3. When Mary is first arrested, what do you think of the doctors' treatment of her? Why do you think she resists them so fiercely? How does Dr Soper's dogged pursuit of his nemesis play its part in Mary's fate, and how is she singled out, compared with carriers discovered later in the novel?

4. If you were in Mary's position, facing the accusations she did at that time, what would you do? How far do you think she is to blame for her actions? Is she simply an ill-informed woman struggling to grasp new scientific theories, or is she wholly responsible for those lost lives?

5. Alfred and Mary's relationship runs through the entire narrative. What is your opinion of Alfred? Why do you think Mary is so drawn to him, despite their many differences?

6. Mary possesses character traits that occasionally make it difficult to sympathise with her. What are these traits? How do they contribute to the story as a whole?

7. Mary's culpability increases as the novel progresses – she continues to bake for friends and neighbours after being banned from cooking, and takes a job at a bakery, and even a maternity hospital. However, she continues to justify her actions. Do you think this is down to her innocence, her ignorance, or something darker?

8. Towards the end of the novel, we see part of Alfred's story from his perspective. How does this alter your opinion of him? What do you think of his actions while apart from Mary?

9. When Mary is finally arrested again and sent back to North Brother, what do you make of her reaction? Why does she seem almost glad to have been caught?

10. *Fever* presents in rich and vivid detail a story of immigrant experience. Mary Mallon is a survivor, a woman who has always had to battle for her place in the world. How does Mary's place in society contribute to the decisions she makes and the way she is treated?

11. Mary's story is set against a backdrop that includes the sinking of the Titanic, the Triangle Shirtwaist Factory Fire and the General Slocum Ferry disaster. How effectively does Mary Beth Keane conjure her historical setting and what does it bring to the novel?

12. To what extent is the press responsible for both the fame and legacy of 'Typhoid Mary'?

Meet the Author Q&A: Mary Beth Keane

In the range of fevers that could strike people down, where did typhoid sit in people's minds compared to cholera or TB in the early twentieth century?

Typhoid Fever was one of the 19th century's worst killers. Though it had abated somewhat by the early 20th century thanks to urban sanitation measures, those advances were threatened by population growth in the major cities, and by 1910 typhoid was still endemic in New York's most overcrowded neighborhoods. Though more people died of influenza, TB, and enteritis, typhoid was still highly feared, and New York City (and most other major cities) did not yet have any water filtration systems in place by 1910. Between 1900 and 1907 (the year of Mary's capture) there were between 3000 and 4500 new cases of typhoid reported in New York City, with a fatality rate of around 10%.

How did you first discover the story of Mary Mallon?

Though I'd long been familiar with the epithet "Typhoid Mary", I didn't know anything about the real woman until I happened to see part of a television documentary about her case. I was interested enough to seek out more information about her and about New York in this period.

What was it about Mary Mallon's story that compelled you to write it? What did you need to tell us, the reader?

I think I responded to her so quickly because she emigrated to NYC from Ireland, and as a cook she was part of the "servant class" (as they referred to it back then). My own parents came to New York City from Ireland in the late 1960s and were (are) members of what we call the "working class" – my father was a New York City tunnel-worker for more than 30 years. I imagined Mary a survivor, as immigrants have to be, and for some reason I felt sure I would have liked her, no matter her faults. Everything I read about her was written by people who couldn't have possibly identified with her experience – the doctors, the health officials, lawyers – and the more I read the more I felt it was important to give her a point of view.

In the story there are letters between Mary and her partner Alfred. What sort of source material did you find in Mary's own hand and what did that reveal about her?

Part of the appeal of writing Mary's story was how little there is in her voice, so I had plenty of space to move and invent while keeping the main events intact. She is quoted here and there in the major newspapers of the period but these quotes are likely paraphrased and often contradict one another. When she made the papers it was always because other people were talking about her, but she had little chance to speak up for herself.

There is exactly one letter in her hand as part of the habeas corpus file – intended at first for the editor of *The New York American* (a newspaper that had taken up her cause) but instead sent to her lawyer. Any person, after reading that letter, can get a sense of her frustration, her bewilderment. She made points about being treated unfairly but the only response the letter seemed to elicit was admiration for her excellent handwriting and spelling, which clearly came as a surprise to those holding her captive. A cook with excellent penmanship! And really, her intelligence was held against her. So at some points it seemed she was put away because she was ignorant, and at other points because she was too smart.

As the story unfolds, it becomes clear that the authorities discover other healthy carriers of typhoid. For instance, there is a dairy farmer in Camden who is believed to have infected hundreds of people compared to Mary's count of 49 deaths. Why do you think Mary was singled out?

Actually, only 3 deaths are officially attributed to Mary Mallon. She is accused of infecting between 47–50 people, with 3 of those dying of the illness. There were several cases of other healthy carriers discovered soon after Mary who disobeyed health department orders and continued working in food service. One man owned and operated an icecream shop on Bleecker Street in Manhattan, another a bakery and restaurant in Brooklyn. Both men were linked to more cases than Mary Mallon ever was, but neither man was ever held for longer than a few weeks. In newspaper coverage of their cases there is no reference to either man's personal appearance, ethnicity, or education-level (penmanship!) – like there is for Mary. She alone seemed to evoke deep-seated social prejudices. I believe she was singled out because she was a woman who didn't fit the mold of what society expected of women in that period. She flouted social mores and that made those in power uncomfortable.

Was there a point in deciding on the narrative that you felt you could have gone either way with Mary? Did she beg to be portrayed benignly?

I didn't set out to portray her as either a villain or a victim, and I still believe I haven't. History had already made Mary a character – a one-dimensional character – by the time she came into my life. My main goal was to release her from that one-dimensional status. I don't think I erased her flaws, and I don't think I would have been as interested in her if I thought she was entirely blameless. My point was that we are all, at times, at fault in something. We cloud the truth. We live in denial of things that we cannot accept. This is human nature. I think we're all just trying to survive and in the meantime make something of the lives we're given, and that was true for Mary.

"Dr." Soper appears to become fixated on Mary's case. Why do you think this was so?

As I understand it, he was obsessed with her case because it made his career. As long as she was in the headlines, so was he. And reading between the lines I think he found her so personally offensive that he became even more fixated on keeping her quarantined for life. One of my favorite research moments was reading that Dr. Soper approached Mary when she was still being held at Willard Parker and asked her if she would collaborate with him on a book about her life. He offered to give her the proceeds if she would simply sit for several interviews. Her response was to ignore him entirely and he was offended by her rudeness. I just thought: Bingo. These are two people who simply do not speak the same language. This man has just organized her capture, has taken her – literally – kicking and screaming to undergo medical tests that even most doctors at the time didn't understand, and here he thinks he's being a great guy by offering her the proceeds, impressed with his own generosity, and completely bewildered by her complete indifference to the prospect of income when she didn't have any. She was a cook! A servant! How could she decline? But she did decline, and it was in moments like that that I knew I liked her.

Tell us more about the very unusual love story of Mary Mallon and Alfred Briehof.
The love story between Mary and Alfred is semi-invented. I took a few tiny clues and elaborated on them. He was a real figure in her life – his name kept popping up here and there, always described as her "friend." What little is on record is damning. He is described as a man "with low moral character," and Dr. Soper claims to have given him a few dollars to be shown the rooms he shared with Mary. I ended up cutting that from the novel because it was just too terrible. Mary often stayed with Alfred when she was not staying with an employer, and after her release in 1910, after checking in the Dept of Health as required for two years, it seems that she went back to cooking around 1912 – around the time Alfred died. Her connection to him made her more interesting to me – why would a woman who was so tough in so many ways be brought down by a man like Alfred? Love. It makes people insane. But I think she needed love, and I was happy to give her a love relationship, even if it was not ideal. I do think, no matter what people will say about my Alfred, that he loved her very much.

You leave the story in Mary's own words, which suggests that she never really came to terms with being a carrier. Was she Typhoid Mary, the Germ Woman as the media portrayed her or, by our modern understanding of disease and the way it is spread was she wrongly accused?

To me – and, as I imagine it, to Mary – Typhoid Mary is a character, a cartoon of the real Mary Mallon. She wasn't wrongly accused in the sense that she really did carry typhoid fever and pass it through her cooking; she really did infect the people Dr. Soper accused her of infecting, and likely more. But the thing to remember is that she couldn't help being a carrier, and those who held her should have tried a myriad of other solutions before they opted to remove her from her life and force her to stay on North Brother Island. By the 1920s, when everyone had a better understanding of the concept of being a "carrier," the government helped those carriers who were found by giving them a stipend (if they were in food service) and training them for other employment. With Mary they just told her that the entire way she was living her life was wrong, and that was it. My Mary Mallon had started to accept the idea of being a carrier by the end of her life, but was still defensive, even at the very end. Put simply, she was a good, hard-working person who was accused of doing great harm to other people without realizing. I think that would be difficult for any of us to accept.

I imagine that coming to grips with this story and finding the way through it must have been an exhausting process. What subject are you going to tackle for your next project? Perhaps something lighter?

I had two babies while I was working on *Fever* – so finding balance was the most difficult part. Barring any surprises I hope this next novel is less physically exhausting! I'm in the early days but I can tell you it's contemporary – no Edwardian details to keep track of. As for whether it's lighter – I'm not sure. It will be less sad than Mary's story, but I suppose no less serious. I want to write something hopeful, with a happy ending. Maybe this next one will be it.